NOV 2 0 2002

TIME ENOUGH
to *Die*

A Novel of Mystery and Romance

YO-CAS-279

Other books by Lillian Stewart Carl:

Sabazel
The Winter King
Shadow Dancers
Wings of Power
Ashes to Ashes
Dust to Dust
Garden of Thorns
Along the Rim of Time: Stories
Memory and Desire
Shadows in Scarlet

TIME ENOUGH
to Die

A Novel of Mystery and Romance

LILLIAN STEWART CARL

WITHDRAWN

BLOOMINGDALE PUBLIC LIBRARY
101 FAIRFIELD WAY
BLOOMINGDALE, IL 60108
630 - 529 - 3120

WILDSIDE PRESS
Berkeley Heights, New Jersey

This Wildside edition
copyright © 2002 by Lillian Stewart Carl.
All rights reserved.

First Wildside Press edition: October 2002

Time Enough to Die
A publication of
WILDSIDE PRESS
P.O. Box 45
Gillette, NJ 07933-0045
www.wildsidepress.com

FIRST EDITION

For David and Shirley Smallwood.
Thank you for all the good times!

Chapter One

*T*he hand was delicately molded, the nails smooth, the flesh stained brown. It lay palm upward, fingers gently curved as though in supplication. Severed at the wrist, the hand rested on the block of peat that was one of a hundred ranged along a black, oozing gash in the earth.

Gareth March raised his eyes and looked across the moss and bog myrtle of the marsh to the higher ground at Durslow Edge. A misty rain moistened his face. But it was too late to weep for this victim, whoever she had been.

"I reckon it's one o' them bog bodies, Sir," P.C. Watkins said. "Every now and then the cutters will turn up a bit o' one. Like empty leather bags they are, after all those years in the peat. Maybe two thousand years, Dr. Sweeney says." The constable turned to the workmen who stood nearby, the peat-digging machine looming behind them. "Right, lads, bog body or no we'll have to have the boffins. Can you cut the peats somewhere else?"

With grumbles, good-natured and otherwise, the men moved away to plot a new strategy.

"Thank you for having us in," Gareth called after them. Watkins was right. The hand had to be investigated scientifically.

Gareth looked back at it. It was so well preserved he half-expected it to move.

"I reckon the rest o' the body were chewed up by the machine." Watkins squatted down and extended his own hand over the one almost camouflaged by the peat. His hand was large and pale, like an anemone. It completely covered the smaller one. "A woman, right, Inspector March?"

"The forensics chaps can tell, I think."

"I reckon she were a pretty one. Dainty, like a princess."

"Princess Diana was six feet tall." Gareth saw no reason to let a muddy relic of dead time seduce him into sentimentality. "We'll hand that block of peat in at the lab. No need to call out a scene-of-crime team. There's no crime scene."

"Yes, Sir," Watkins said.

The mist thickened into rain. A breeze ruffled the dark surface of the nearby lake. The air smelled of damp vegetation and age, not of human death. What did the locals call this place? Shadow Moss. To Gareth it sounded like a name out of a fairy tale.

It'd been donkey's years since he'd visited his grandmother's cottage in Aberffraw, since he'd listened to her stories of heroes and demons, of gleaming swords and magic cauldrons. His grandmother had claimed to have "the power" — second sight. But Gareth was thirty now. He no longer needed to believe in rubbish like ESP.

His transfer to Scotland Yard had just gone through. London had bright lights and loud music. London was a long way from the Welsh borders, Shadow Moss, and such petty concerns as bog bodies.

Hunching his shoulders against the November chill, Gareth turned and strode away. When the mud sucked at his boots, he wrenched them free.

*T*he taxi dived out of the parking lot onto the main road. Another car didn't crash headlong into it but passed harmlessly by to the right. Ashley Walraven exhaled, hoping the driver hadn't noticed her gasp of fear. They drove on the left here. She knew that.

She knew a lot. She'd studied hard, worked long evening hours in a supermarket, and stood her ground stubbornly to achieve this moment. "I've been accepted, Mom. Dr. Bates even wrote me a letter of recommendation to Dr. Sweeney. I'll pay my own way. It'd be just too cool to study in England. It'd help my career chances."

"Career?" her mother had replied. "Did you know that half of all divorces happen when the wife makes more money than the husband?"

"Mom. . . ."

Mrs. Walraven had turned away with a dull shake of her head. Only now, as she blundered toward adulthood, was Ashley beginning to understand her mother's despair — damned if you did, damned if you didn't.

This trip was going to make a difference in her life, Ashley assured herself. She looked out the window, hoping to see half-timbered houses, castle battlements, Morris dancers, any-thing. What she saw was modern Manchester with its ware-houses and concrete interchanges, cold, gray, and featureless beneath a cold, gray, and featureless February sky.

"Your first trip to the U.K.?" the driver asked.

Ashley considered his face in the rear view mirror. He was about her own age, with longish brown hair and a suggestion of a beard. His slight build was reassuring. The intensity of his gaze in the mirror was not. She shouldn't expect British men to react to her any differently than American men did. Yeah, she thought, you work and work to look nice, and then you get attention you don't want.

She sat up straighter and fixed her eyes on the window. "I'm spending a semester at the University of Manchester studying British history, art, and archaeology."

"Ooh, a scholar, now." His thin shoulders made a la-di-dah shrug.

Ashley set her jaw. So much for a polite answer.

"Mind your step. They found a blond lass like you out at Corcester yesterday, by Durslow Edge. Her throat was cut." The driver's long, bony forefinger made an evocative swipe across his Adam's apple.

Corcester. The old Roman fort where the dig was going to be. Great — the last thing she needed was for any of her mother's dire predictions to come true. The taxi swooped down from the freeway onto a street lined with shops that didn't look at all like those back home in St. Louis.

"She wasn't a student, though," the driver went on. "Shop assistant. Went missing last week. The police think she was shagging her boyfriend in a layby. They've charged him with murder. Says he didn't do it, though. Says he hadn't seen her for several weeks, that she'd given him the push. She'd been having it off with someone though. The boffins must've had a giggle finding that out. You have a boyfriend?"

Ashley didn't answer. Neither did she ask him to define his slang. She took a handful of change out of her purse and started sorting pounds from pence.

She'd worked a long time to earn this trip. It was going to make a difference. It was.

*T*he sky had leaked rain every day this week. With a grimace at the unrelenting overcast, Matilda Gray ducked from the traffic of Gloucester Road into the tube station. An assortment of Londoners trudged through the turnstiles beside her, heads tucked, collars turned up. Footsteps echoed from the high ceiling.

Oh to be in England now that April's here, Matilda thought sarcastically. Not that she'd expected sunny skies and balmy temperatures — she'd been here often enough over the years. But a lark or a daffodil or two could have had the decency to appear this time, to mark her first summons from Scotland Yard.

The stairs were crowded, as they usually were this time of the morning. Matilda played human pinball to the edge of the platform and stood there hemmed in by damp umbrellas and soggy carrier bags. In the people around her she sensed only an undercurrent of business and domestic worries, tamped by dull resignation.

Except for one hard, hot bolt of purpose. . . . She glanced to her right and intercepted the direct look of a young man.

Even as their eyes met he melted into the throng behind her. He'd hardly been flirting with her — Matilda was old enough to be his mother. Not that he reminded her of her own college-age son. Patrick had his moments of defensive tautness, when he yet to accept his own burgeoning persona. This youth seemed resentful and belligerent. It was an occupational hazard, Matilda told herself, to occasionally intersect some private trajectory of emotion.

A hot breath of exhaust stirred along the tracks, and the hem of Matilda's raincoat twitched. A rumbling roar and a bright headlight heralded the approach of the train. The crowd shifted expectantly. A sudden shove in Matilda's back thrust her forward.

For one long, breathless moment she hung in the air beyond the edge of the platform, suspended more by disbelief than by any law of physics. The wind of the onrushing train whipped her hair back from her face. Its roar filled her head to bursting.

A hand seized her arm and jerked her back onto the platform. She caromed off several bodies and came to rest gazing at a black-clad adolescent whose haircut made him look like a punk poodle. "Eh, luv," he said, "you mustn't stand so close to the edge."

Her mind gasped, coughed, and squeezed out thought. She'd sensed purpose, but not malice. Any number of people had been standing behind her, on a crowded subway platform during morning rush hour. Her near-fall — her near-death — had been an accident.

The train stopped, thrumming, and its doors slid open. Poodle-haircut guided Matilda across the gap and placed her in the only empty seat. She craned past the bodies cramming themselves into the car, but couldn't see the youth with the chip on his shoulder.

The doors closed, sealing her inside. The train jerked and sped away. Odd, how cold she was. She could hardly feel her own fingers clutching the strap of her shoulder bag. The stale air lay heavy in her lungs.

"Thank you," Matilda said to Poodle-haircut, who swayed above her grasping a ceiling knob.

"Yeh," he said diffidently, and turned away.

She looked at the Underground map above the windows. She had to leave the tube at St. James Park. She had an appointment at Scotland Yard.

That push in the back hadn't been an accident. She must be getting a great reputation — no one had ever tried to kill her before. The pusher might have wanted revenge for some old, successfully-completed, job, like the Mound Builder scam in Arkansas or the affair of the Greek vase and the

California museum. Or he might have intended to keep her from arriving at Scotland Yard and accepting a new job. Hardly fair, to attack her before she even knew what that job was.

Already she was a threat to someone, someone who knew her plans before she did. This promised to be an intriguing case. She'd have to raise her fee.

Matilda's mouth and chin set themselves in a thin line that her enemies would have called mulishness, but which she preferred to call tenacity. She sank back into her seat, closing her senses around her like a nautilus retreating into its shell. Still she felt cold.

Chapter Two

Gareth turned away from the window and its vista of gray buildings, gray pavements, and gray sky. The air of London scoured his throat like steel wool. His tea tasted metallic. In the back of his mind he saw the rain-softened greens of Anglesey and a brilliant blue sky arching over Holyhead and the South Stack Lighthouse.

"Inspector March," the sergeant called from the doorway. "Superintendent Forrest would like you to step into his office, please."

Very good! This might mean a new case, or even a new level of responsibility. He'd acquitted himself rather well, he thought, with the bombing at Christmas and the Ladbroke Grove murder in February. Gareth set his mug on his desk, adjusted his tie, and headed upstairs to the Super's office, a cluttered den overlooking Victoria Street.

Forrest was a bear of a man, jowls, shoulders, and paunch pulled earthward by the certainty of injustice and mortality. "Come in, come in," he said to Gareth, and nodded toward the woman seated in front of his desk. "This is Matilda Gray, from America. Dr. Gray, Detective Inspector Gareth March."

Gareth extended his hand. Matilda shook it in a cold but firm grasp. Her eyes looking up at him were a vivid blue, clear and bright, like the sky he'd just been imagining.

"Good morning," she said.

"Good morning," Gareth returned.

Forrest gestured him into the chair beside Matilda's, then glanced through the contents of a file lying open on his desk.

Matilda sat with her hands folded in her lap, her brows

oscillating slowly as she looked round the room. Gareth looked at her and wondered whether she was witness or plaintiff.

Matilda's chin-length hair was either dark blond or light brown, except for a silver wave like a cavalier's plume that dipped over her forehead. A well-cut dress camouflaged her waist and hips. Discreetly applied cosmetics mitigated the fine lines and gentle sags of early middle age. The sharp edge of her profile made Gareth suspect that even in her youth Matilda had traded less on appearance than personality.

She murmured, "Do I pass inspection, Inspector?"

"I beg your pardon," Gareth said.

"No problem. I distrust incurious people. They tend to be gullible."

Clearing his throat noncommittally, Gareth settled back in his chair and looked to the Superintendent for enlightenment.

Forrest closed the file and turned a thin smile on Matilda. "The British Museum recommends you as highly as Interpol and the International Foundation for Art Research do."

"My most important cases have been for various governments, USIA, UNESCO, Interpol, and IFAR. Rather under the table, you understand. The higher my profile, the less effective I can be. . . ." She frowned. "Someone tried to push me under a tube train on my way here this morning."

"Oh?" Forrest leaned forward, his face sagging even further.

"Ironic, isn't it?" Matilda continued. "A good reputation can be a double-edged blade."

She was remarkably composed, thought Gareth. Any other woman would have blurted out her suspicions and demanded protection before she'd so much as sat down. For just that reason he was tempted to discount her story as nothing more than an attempt to inflate her importance.

"The underground platforms can be very crowded in the morning," he said. "It might have been an accident."

"It might have been," Matilda agreed. "Coincidences happen, more frequently than we're comfortable with."

"Do you have a description of your assailant?" He reached into his pocket for his notebook.

"Not really. I noticed a young man about twenty, large,

unshaven. He was wearing one of those little Lenin caps and a blue jacket. He wasn't feeling any malice toward me, just resolve. But then, if someone had sent him to get rid of me, or even just to scare me, he wouldn't necessarily have felt any malice. It would have been a business deal, nothing personal."

"I'm afraid we can't . . ." Forrest began.

"Of course not." Matilda made a brief, dismissive gesture. "No evidence. I'll simply have to watch my own back, won't I?"

Gareth shut his notebook. So she'd known what the youth on the platform had been feeling, eh? *Pull the other one,* he thought sarcastically.

Forrest's seamed face shifted and settled into an expression that more closely resembled a concerned frown than an incredulous smile. "Not necessarily, Dr. Gray. Inspector March will be with you at Corcester. He'll guard your back."

With her? Corcester? Back to Cheshire? He thought he'd been doing so well here. . . . Gareth felt Matilda's quick, speculative glance, but didn't respond. He turned a part questioning, part truculent look on Forrest.

Forrest continued, "Your mishap at the tube station this morning might somehow be connected with the murder at Corcester. Inspector? You're familiar with the case?"

"It happened after I left the Manchester force," replied Gareth, "but I took some notice of it. The girl was a shop assistant. They questioned the boyfriend. He had an alibi. I've heard nothing else about it."

"There's nothing else to hear. The case is still open, but they're no forwarder now than they were in February."

"So they've asked the Yard for assistance," Gareth said, somewhat mollified. "You're sending me because I'm familiar with the area. Although I've never visited Corcester itself, mind."

Again Matilda glanced at him, with that same brow wave of perception she'd applied to Forrest's office. "Corcester," she said. "Celtic Eponemeton, Roman Cornovium. Later it became a Saxon town, and hasn't grown much since then."

"You're a history professor, then?" Gareth asked, a more polite question than, *and just what business do you have with all of this?*

"I've worn several hats over the years. Now I'm a freelance parapsychologist specializing in art, archaeological, and architectural problems — and in stopping the theft of cultural property worldwide."

"A para-what?"

"Parapsychologist. I identify fake artifacts, for example. I pinpoint where artifacts of dubious provenance came from, I track artifacts that have been stolen, I tell excavators and restorers what's below the surface soil or behind a wall, to help them allocate their resources. I'm like the police sketch artist who makes an educated guess as to a suspect's appearance, except I go out in the field myself. Most of the time I use my academic knowledge as much as my psychic abilities."

Right, Gareth said to himself, and averted his eyes.

The traffic noise from Victoria Street filled the room. Somewhere in the building a telephone rang and a door slammed. Forrest tapped the file folder, his eyes fixed unblinkingly on Matilda's face. "It says here you work on a contingency basis."

"That's right. If what I sense can't be proved — if there's no ground truth, as they say in archaeology — then I don't get paid. And I assure you I make a very comfortable living."

It wasn't like matter-of-fact Forrest to be done over by a charlatan, Gareth told himself. Maybe her references were forged. Maybe she was some sort of cabaret magician, and had fooled all the acronyms and the British Museum by sleight-of-hand. No matter what you called it, parapsychology or second sight, it didn't exist.

"I can't read minds," Matilda said to Gareth with what in another mood — or another woman — he might have found an attractive smile. "I can sense someone's emotions, but many people can do that. My skills are of no use in gambling, probably because I have no patience with gambling. Every now and then someone asks me to do a bit of ghost-hunting. That's very subjective, though, not like tracking stolen cultural property."

Gareth gritted his teeth. "And you think you can find out who murdered the girl in Corcester through — through ESP?"

"Perhaps I could help. What do you think, Superintendent?"

"Ah, well now . . ." the Super grimaced, his features collid-
ing awkwardly. "Actually, Dr. Gray, I was planning for you
to use your — ah — expertise in a different matter. Are you
familiar with the English law of treasure trove?"

Matilda seemed to be suppressing a smile at Forrest's
discomfort. "Yes. Anyone who discovers artifacts made of
precious metals is required to turn them over to the coroner.
He holds an inquest to decide whether the objects were buried
with intention of recovery, and whether they're now ownerless. If they're ownerless, then they're declared to be treasure
trove. They become property of the Crown and the finder is
compensated. If not, the artifacts belong to the finder. Theo-
retically, coins thrown down a sacred well wouldn't be treasure trove while coins a farmer hides from an approaching
army would be, but that's probably too fine an interpretation
of common law."

"And to most yobbos with their metal detectors," Gareth
said, "it doesn't matter the one way or the other. They simply
don't report their findings."

"Like the Thetford Treasure," said Matilda, "a fantastic
hoard of Roman artifacts. By the time the authorities heard
about them the site had been built over. And the Romano-
British bronzes from Icklingham, spirited away from a protected site only to surface in an antiquity dealer's shop in
New York."

"There was a case in Corcester," Gareth added. "A chap
named Reynolds claimed some Roman artifacts had been
nicked from the site of the fort, which is on his land. It's a
protected ancient monument, but the protection's only a
piece of paper, not land mines. The police couldn't help.
Neither could a solicitor. He would've had to file suit in
Canada, where the objects were on offer, and he hadn't the
brass for that. It all comes down to the brass, doesn't it?

"Adrian Reynolds," Forrest stated. "Owner of Fortuna
Stud, a horse farm."

"Yes, that's the man. My contact in Corcester says he's a
proper little git."

Matilda said, "Reynolds couldn't say where at the site the
artifacts were found, could he? He had no proof they were
stolen from him. Or from anyone, for that matter — they

obviously left the country with forged papers."

"Finding proof that antiquities have been stolen is almost impossible," Forrest stated. "Can you, Dr. Gray, find proof?"

"Perhaps, depending on the circumstances. I take it my job is a little more complex than that." Matilda's voice was a steady alto, her vowels flatly American but her diction crisp as a BBC news reader's. Her manner was grave without being stern. Gareth had seen surgeons without such professional dignity. Odd, how it never seemed to occur to her that anyone would not take her seriously.

"Quite," said Forrest. "When Reynolds was frustrated in his attempt to salvage his artifacts — what he perceived to be his artifacts, without any ruling to that effect — he went to Howard Sweeney at the University of Manchester. Do you know him?"

"We've met several times," Matilda replied. "I'd hardly call him a friend, though. More of a business associate. He's one of the top experts on the Roman invasion of Britain."

"When peat cutters found a severed hand at Shadow Moss last November," Gareth offered, "they had Sweeney in and he sorted it. Just a bit of a bog body, probably from Roman times."

"The torso turned up last month," said Matilda. "I've only seen pictures. What did you think of the hand?"

It didn't matter what he thought of it. It had been cold that day at the Moss. The hand had been both attractive and repellent. . . . "I suppose it's interesting enough to a scientist," he replied.

This time Matilda's level look made him stiffen.

"Reynolds went to Sweeney for help," Forrest continued. "Sweeney went to the British Museum, who went in turn to the Home Office. The looting of our historical sites has become an epidemic."

"It's a worldwide problem," said Matilda. "The international illegal antiquities trade knows no boundaries. Governments can hardly feed and house their citizens, let alone protect their cultural heritage."

"And like the drug trade, the antiquities trade can lead to violence," Forrest said.

"It's all a matter of the brass, as you say, Inspector March."

"Either we scientifically excavate every site in the country," Forrest went on, "which would be impossible, or we catch antiquity thieves in the act. That's what we're hoping to do in Corcester. Sweeney is setting up an excavation of the Roman ruins as part of a class he's teaching. He's asked for you to be his second, Dr. Gray."

Matilda's brows went lopsided with what Gareth interpreted as bemused surprise. So she could be surprised. That was good to know.

"Inspector March, you'll need some sort of cover for yourself. Reynolds only knows that Sweeney is excavating, he doesn't know we're setting a trap for the thieves."

"Won't all the people at the site scare them away?" Gareth asked.

"I'm afraid not," Matilda replied. "By excavating we'll be uncovering objects for them, saving them the effort. We can look at it as baiting the hook, I suppose."

"Make sure the local plod — what's his name?" Forrest asked Gareth.

"Watkins."

"Watkins sets a watch at night. You'll have to take him into your confidence, of course. Manchester can lend him a couple of men for the duration."

Matilda tilted her head at Forrest. "I assume, Superintendent, that you have a reason for singling out Corcester as your target?"

"The murder," said Gareth.

"Exactly." Forrest leaned back in his chair, his huge paws of hands crossed comfortably on his belly.

Parapsychology was irrelevant to a policeman, Gareth told himself. Crimes of history were peripheral at best. But murder now, murder was important. He leaned forward, turning the angle of his shoulder toward Matilda.

"The murdered girl was named Linda Burkett," Forrest said. "She worked for a small shop in Manchester's Borley Arcade that sells better-quality souvenirs — what the trade calls 'collectibles' — as well as the odd antiquity. Legal antiquities, Roman coins and the like, all properly certified. She was found with her throat cut so deeply she was almost decapitated."

"Where?" asked Gareth.

"Durslow Edge, three miles from Corcester. Beside an old well. Do you know the place?"

"I stopped by there once. It's a high sandstone ledge covered with trees. One can see it from miles away. The well is a spring, actually, but the locals call it Bride's well. Something to do with primitive marriage ceremonies, maybe."

"More likely it's named for St. Brigit," said Matilda quietly. "She was the goddess Brighid to the Celts. Who made offerings of severed heads to sacred wells."

It was a severed hand, Gareth almost corrected, before he realized she was making some wild extrapolation from the murder victim's injury. If Matilda wanted to show off her superior knowledge, let her. He was the detective. He was in charge of the important part of the case.

"Watkins will give you the details," Forrest continued. "What concerns us is that two days before she died, Linda Burkett sent a letter to the Greater Manchester Police saying that she knew the whereabouts of several pieces of Romano-British statuary that had been illegally excavated, and asking if she would get a reward for the name of the guilty party."

"Ah," Matilda said with a sigh.

"So the guilty party killed her to keep her from grassing," said Gareth. "The shop owner was interviewed, of course."

"Oh yes. She says she knows nothing about it, and we can't prove otherwise. It might be worth your while to talk to her again. Remembering that you're undercover, of course."

"Of course."

The telephone at Forrest's elbow went. He picked up the receiver. "Yes? Oh, yes. Half a minute." He said to Gareth, "The excavation begins next Monday, April 19. Get on to Corcester a day early and have a look round. Dr. Gray, mind your step. Your misadventure at the tube station might have been an accident. . . ."

"Or it might have been someone trying to settle an old score with me. Yes, I'm suitably warned, thank you." Matilda stood up and put on her raincoat, an expensive Burberry.

"Quite. You'll keep me updated, then." Forrest made a parting gesture and turned to the phone. "Yes, Commander, the security arrangements are well in hand."

Gareth opened the door of the office for Matilda. He half expected her to flounce away muttering something about liberated females, as though opening a door was a political act. She merely said, "Thank you."

They stood in the corridor, looking at each other. Matilda's slightly amused blue gaze made Gareth feel as though his clothes were transparent and he had holes in his y-fronts. But when she laughed, lightly and wryly, it wasn't at him. "So I get to work with Howard Sweeney, for my sins."

"He doesn't believe in parapsychology?" Gareth asked hopefully.

"Oh no, he's a good scientist, he'll accept what he can see proven. It's just that you need a whip and a chair to deal with his ego."

Gareth had no comment on that. "Would you like a coffee?" he asked halfheartedly. He didn't want a coffee. He didn't want to work with Matilda, for that matter. What he wanted was to keep her as minor an annoyance as possible whilst he solved the case. Another successful case and he might be up for a promotion.

"No thank you," she replied. "I need to go check some references at the British Museum. I'll be seeing you at the site in Corcester on — Sunday afternoon about two, shall we say? You can show me the area."

"And mind your back," Gareth pointed out.

"If necessary." Smiling ruefully, Matilda reached into her handbag. "Here's my card, with my cell phone number. Good morning, Inspector."

He thrust the card into his pocket without looking at it. "Good morning."

She walked off down the hall, stepping out briskly, back straight, chin up, not arrogant, he thought, but irritatingly self-confident. If she was a charlatan, she was also a superb actress. But acting ability was not something Gareth respected. It involved too much illusion.

He pushed open the doors of the incident room and sat down at his desk. The scene beyond the windows appeared unremittingly gray.

Chapter Three

*A*fter three months in England, Ashley Walraven knew she'd better appreciate the clear afternoon while she had the chance. She stood in the town square and turned her face like a flower to the sun. Around her the citizens of Corcester slowed and dropped onto benches and steps as if they were melting in the unusual warmth.

The brick pedestrians-only area was more accurately a town polygon. At one side two ancient black-and-white magpie houses leaned together, erect more out of habit than out of structural integrity. Even though the ground floors were filled by an appliance store and Corcester's Job Centre, Ashley was charmed.

Opposite the houses stood St. Michael's church, its red stone buttresses mortared by lichen. A yew tree drooped over weathered headstones. Bells pealed from a crow-haunted tower. This was what a church should look like, Ashley told herself. The one her mother attended was disguised as a civic auditorium. The cross, tucked away in foliage at the rear of the stage, looked like an afterthought. When she'd commented about "MacChurch," her mother had muttered darkly of disrespect verging on blasphemy.

Her mother. Ashley turned toward the building next to the two half-timbered relics. Mr. Clapper at the hotel had said — yes, there was a red mailbox pillar. She thrust her letter through the slot. Another Sunday, another letter home. She never thought she'd be grateful she hardly ever got a chance to check her e-mail and had had to leave her cell phone at home, but being reduced to snail mail had turned out to be a blessing in disguise.

It might take her mother's letters a few days to catch up to her, now that the students had moved from a dormitory in Manchester to the hotel in Corcester. Maybe for a few days she could get down off the co-dependency trip. Even though her mother did seem to be getting along all right without her — surprise, surprise. Still, her letters were full of the usual complaints, warnings, and commentary about Ashley's father's new wife — "almost as young as you are, Punkin, although you'd never know beneath all the make-up, calls herself a legal aide as though everyone didn't know she's a cheap little gold-digger. . . ."

Her mother's voice was so clear Ashley tensed and looked around. The only people nearby were two young men scanning the notices in the window of the Job Centre. They wore shapeless jackets and heavy boots, and jostled each other as though sharing a joke. The more supple and slender of the two turned toward Ashley and smiled.

His black hair was too shaggy to be fashionable, and his jaw was darkened by more than a five-o'clock shadow, something like a ten-o'clock eclipse. But he wore an earring, and his smile was the devil-may-care grin of a romantic hero, alluring, challenging, dangerous. Ashley felt the heat rush to her cheeks.

"Eh," he called, and jerked his head in a summons.

Oh yeah, right, Ashley thought.

A policeman materialized from a side street. "Here," he said to the men. "I suppose you're looking for employment, are you now?"

"Oh yes, Constable, that we are," replied the one with the smile, while his friend stood in a sullen lump.

"And I'm the Archbishop of Canterbury," said the bobby. "Push off, the both of you, get back to your caravans."

The young men strolled away, just slowly enough to be insolent.

The policeman turned, muttering something about travelers and caravans, and almost walked into Ashley. "Sorry, Miss," he said. His round face was puckered around something sour, and she knew he didn't really see her. The dashing black-haired man had seen her.

Making an about-face, Ashley thrust her hands into the pockets of her jacket and headed toward the narrow steps between the churchyard fence and some nondescript stone buildings. She plunged suddenly into shadow. Her steps echoed from the surrounding walls, faster and faster, until she popped back out into the sunlight at the foot of the hill. Beyond a battered wall built of brick-sized Roman stones stood the Green Dragon hotel. Its nucleus was an old black-and-white building only marginally more perpendicular than the ones opposite the church. Around that were cobbled together structures from various eras, Jacobean brick, Georgian stone, even a hideous modern annex that Ashley could only describe as bastard Swiss chalet.

A signboard above the door showed a kelly-green lizard gazing quizzically at a knight in armor, as though trying to decide whether to eat him or ask him to tea. Below the board gathered Ashley's classmates, all American students except for three Germans, a Swede, and an Italian.

"Where were you?" asked a tall boy with the brush cut and predatory white teeth of an American jock.

"Mailing a letter."

"The weekly chronicle to Mom? I bet you were asking for money."

"Like I'm going to ask for money when she's on a strict. . . ."

Jason turned back to Caterina Rossi's overstuffed sweater.

Sorry mine aren't big enough for you, Ashley told him silently. Not that she wanted to get anything going with Jason. If she'd ever met a use-her-and-lose-her sort of guy, it was him.

The heavy glass and brass doors of the hotel groaned open, emitting Howard Sweeney, his cell phone pressed to his ear. "Later," he said into it, turned it off, and tucked it into his pocket. "Very good then, shall we be off?" Without waiting for a reply, he led the group of twenty or so students across the street almost under the grille of a delivery van.

They passed a recreation center where shirt-sleeved men were lawn-bowling, and skirted a couple of houses whose gardens were sprinkled with daffodils and early tulips. Once across another road and through a gate in a stone fence, Sweeney stopped and gesticulated. "Behold, ancient Cornovium. Mind your step. Cows."

To Ashley, ancient Cornovium looked like a lumpy pasture that sloped down to the trees edging the river Thane. She squinted, trying to see the settlement she'd studied.

The thick grass of the pasture lay like a quilt over the banks and ditches defining the military fort. The four gateways, north, south, east, west, were gaps in the embankment. The occasional masonry angle jutting from the sod looked promising, but the rubbish dump beside the road didn't. And yet the civilian settlement outside the fort had extended beyond the road, toward the hillside where an amphitheater had once nestled and that was now crowned by the church.

Ashley turned to look back at the town, imagining the ancient equivalent of fish and chips shops thronged with legionaries. . . . Jason was feeling up Caterina. She was simpering up at him.

Sweeney marched off through the knee-high grass. Rolling her eyes — really, she'd thought Caterina had better taste — Ashley hurried after him. She liked Dr. Sweeney. He was in his fifties, probably, with gray crisp-crinkled hair, horn-rimmed glasses, and the hunched shoulders of the scholar. An impudent grin revealed a gap between his front teeth. He wore ascot ties tucked in the necks of his shirts and sweaters. She'd never known anyone who actually wore ascot ties. Her father, when he'd been around, had worn giveaway T-shirts and watched "Hogan's Heroes" reruns.

"Supposedly this was once the site of a Celtic temple, Eponemeton," Sweeney proclaimed. "Epona being the goddess of horses. T.J. Miller found a tessellated pavement, a double row of post holes, and some stone heads back in the 1930s, beneath the Roman layers. That, however, was only a quick and dirty test dig." He indicated a ditch clogged with weeds and mud that cut across one quadrant of the fort.

"This area, Cheshire and points south and east, was the home of the Cornovii tribe. Their capital was at Viroconium, modern Wroxeter. *Corn* means *horn* in Latin — hence 'unicorn.' Probably the tribe owed allegiance to the stag god Cernunnos, although the Celts also had bull gods. Miller found a subterranean chamber he thought might be a Roman Mithraeum. The sun-god Mithras was originally from Persia.

His influence spread because he was adopted by the legionaries. They liked the bit about slaying the bull, I daresay. Shocking what people will believe. True believers can be easily manipulated, can't they?"

Since that was a rhetorical question, no one answered. The group clambered up the crest of the eastern embankment. Several black and white cows regarded them incuriously. A chilly breeze rippled the grass, and the Thane glinted beyond its curtain of trees. A subtle scent of diesel and cooking grease was all that remained of modern Corcester.

Sweeney waved at a cluster of buildings and fences at the far end of the pasture, where a brown horse and rider paced sedately back and forth. "The land the fort is on belongs to the farm there. A horse farm, appropriately enough. Fortuna Stud. A lovely continuation of tradition, wouldn't you say? And when you consider that the Romans stationed here included a troop of Syrian cavalry, well then!" He spread his hands like a stage magician who'd just produced two doves and a rabbit. Ashley nodded appreciatively.

"Cornovium was an auxiliary fort. The primary fortress in this area was Deva, which is now the tourist haven of Chester. It was originally headquarters of the Legio II Adiutrix of which this was a cohort. Later Legio II Valeria Victrix moved north from Viroconium to Chester, and, we assume, here."

Two casually-dressed people came climbing up the northern bank behind Sweeney's back. The woman stooped, burrowed into a pothole at the base of a wall, and produced something that she showed to her male companion. He shrugged. She put the object in her pocket.

"Cornovium was established in 70 Anno Domini," Sweeney went on, "only ten years after Boudicca's rebellion, and was a going concern by 80. Whether Boudicca was a traitor or a freedom fighter rather depends on your perception of the situation. Suffice it to say, our Romans here kept quite the weather eye upon the local Celts. In 83 Agricola led Legio II Adiutrix north. He duly conquered the Brigantes and then carried on into Scotland. At what point Cornovium ceased being a Roman fortress and commenced being a Romano-British town we're not sure. Perhaps about 300 or so. That's one of the questions we're after answering here."

Sweeney paced toward the center of the camp.

The students moved in a gaggle behind him, Ashley at point, Jason and Caterina self-absorbed at the rear. Manfred, one of the Germans, turned a cold blue gaze on the slackers. Two American girls, Jennifer and Courtney, nudged each other and giggled. "Throw a bucket of water on them," muttered Bryan, his all-American freckles flaring indignantly. Ashley shot him a grateful glance.

"The headquarters building would have been about here," said Sweeney, "at the intersections of the via principalis and the via praetoria, with the commander's house just opposite. The early houses were only wood and wattle and daub, mind you, but were quite substantial even so, with all mod cons. The first commander of the garrison might even have brought his wife out from Rome. What she thought of being summoned to a howling wilderness such as Britain, is, perhaps fortunately, unrecorded!" He laughed.

Ashley smiled. The imaginary Roman woman and her "mod cons" — modern conveniences — would've found Britain a green paradise. Of course, the neighbors had been rowdy types given to head-hunting.

"Right. Here's our datum point, this masonry corner. We'll plot a grid and dig test areas there, there and there — hope you've swotted a bit on your maths, this must be surveyed properly before we begin. Manfred, you're in charge of the first team, Bryan the second, Jason the third."

Jason looked up. "Huh?"

Ashley looked down at her boots. She had the highest average in the class, but Sweeney didn't think she was leader material.

"So then . . ." Sweeney made a sweeping gesture that took in the two newcomers. "Well, well, well, what have we here? Matilda Gray, is it?"

"Hello, Howard," said the woman.

"Gareth March," the man said, and exchanged a brisk handshake with Sweeney.

"Ah!" Sweeney's brows coasted up his forehead. "You're our reporter. Going to write up the dig, eh?"

"The *Times* Sunday magazine. Our Roman Heritage."

"And Mrs. — er — Ms. Gray. . . ." Sweeney began.

"Dr. Gray," she corrected.

"Dr. Gray will be my second-in-command," he announced to the class, "being a scholar of some note on the opposite side of the Atlantic."

Gray smiled indulgently at Sweeney, and in greeting at the students. "Hi."

The students murmured hellos warily, as though trying to decide whether Gray gave pop quizzes. She seemed like a nice lady, Ashley thought, about her mother's age. But Laura Walraven looked as though she'd spent the last twenty years having electroshock treatments. Gray might have spent the same time sitting in the lotus position.

With a hand in the small of her back, Sweeney turned Gray toward the masonry corner. "I was just telling the students, my dear. . . ."

"My name is Matilda, Howard."

"Matilda," he enunciated. "I was telling the students about the excavation plans. If you'd care to back me up. . . ."

"That's why I'm here, to back you up." She stepped away from his controlling hand. "Please go on."

He did, launching into a dissertation on the trench and grid method of excavation versus the open field method, and adding footnotes on stratigraphy, soil sampling, and the importance of record-keeping.

Like a moon whose orbit is disturbed by a passing asteroid, Ashley found her attention wandering from Sweeney's plummy accent — he wasn't telling her anything she hadn't already studied, after all — toward Gareth March.

He was very handsome, more mature than her fellow students, not as shady-looking — if not as exciting — as the man at the Job Centre. He stood aloof and poised, inspecting the site and its surroundings. His mouth might have been generous if it hadn't been set in such a stern line. His eyes were a dark opaque brown. When they spotted the horse and rider at Fortuna Stud Ashley was obscurely surprised they didn't snap like camera lenses. He came across like an android, except an android wouldn't have such springy red hair, cut short as though to curb its enthusiasm.

He was watching two men walk along the fence — the same two men, Ashley realized, she'd seen at the Job Centre. One of them stopped and scraped the mud from his boots on the bottom rung. The rider pulled the horse's head around and trotted up to them. Ashley sidled closer to March, curiosity overcoming shyness. "Excuse me, are those men gypsies?"

He glanced around. "Gypsies?"

"I saw them in town a little while ago. A policeman told them to go away, and said something about caravans."

"I expect they're travelers," March replied. "New Age travelers, leftover hippies of a sort, unemployed young people living on the dole. They roam the countryside in clapped-out caravans — what you'd call travel trailers. There's a traveler encampment in a layby toward Macclesfield."

"Are they criminals or something?"

"Supposedly they harbor petty criminals such as thieves, drug peddlers, and tax dodgers. They fight mostly amongst themselves, though. The local people don't like them, don't trust them, and most certainly don't want them. They settle in large numbers and leave the land very untidy. Real gypsies, the original travelers, say the New Age travelers give them a bad reputation. Those two are probably offering to muck out the stables. Better than begging, at the least."

The horse trotted away, at this distance the sound of its hoofbeats not corresponding with the fall of its hooves. The men climbed over the fence and trudged toward the white-painted buildings.

So they *were* looking for jobs, Ashley told herself. The policeman shouldn't have been so rude to them. "Are they the people who used to have festivals at Stonehenge at the summer solstice?"

"Some of them. Proper rave-ups, they had. They left the grounds well and truly mucked about. The authorities can chase them away from Stonehenge, it's a protected ancient monument, but they can do sod-all about the camps in the country. No demonstrated reason to move them on."

Ashley imagined a rude, dirty mob trashing out her back yard. She imagined not being able to find a job or a place to live, having only fellowship and attitude between herself and despair. She imagined being a smart, sophisticated reporter pestered by a foreign girl's dumb questions. "Well, thank you for the report," she said.

"You're welcome," March returned, with a polite nod and a half-smile.

". . . Romano-British statuary," Sweeney was saying. Ashley jerked around. Oh no, she'd missed something. "From a first or second century Roman temple, Miller thought. He didn't have the resources to dig further. You can see them in the British Museum. Some new ones have appeared since then, and are the objects of great controversy. The University have a few small Celtic gold votives on display as well. Miller also uncovered the usual detritus of a military camp — tent pegs, straps, bootlaces, bits of armor, dice, combs, spoons, and potsherds, including some lovely Samian ware. There might be some very nice things beneath the ground still, although I'm not hoping for treasure." Sweeney grinned cheerfully.

Gray tilted her head and gave Sweeney the once-over. March edged along the outside of the group, his hands clasped behind his back. Jason murmured to Caterina, "You know, there was a girl murdered out here. We'll have to stick close together. Buddy system."

"What is a buddy?" Caterina asked, her eyes wide, her cheeks pink.

"I'll show you." Jason insinuated his arm around her waist. He was far from pale himself.

March regarded them both with what Ashley interpreted as a jaundiced eye. Men did eventually grow out of testosterone dependence. Or so she'd heard.

"All right then," said Sweeney. "We'll prepare our equipment tonight. I want to see the team leaders after dinner, which will be at slap seven-thirty, attendance required. I'll speak to Mr. Clapper about hot dogs and nachos, shall I?"

The Americans laughed. The Germans and the Swede looked puzzled. Caterina was busy.

Sweeney made shooing motions. "Cut along, then."

The students strolled in clumps back down the embankments. High clouds thinned the afternoon light, dulling the luster of the damp grass. Ashley started down a particularly steep spot and slipped. For a second she flailed backward, then was caught from behind by two sets of hands. Embarrassed, she looked around. "Whoa, am I ever clumsy, thanks. . . ."

"No problem." Bryan released her and ambled after the others.

Her other rescuer was Matilda Gray. "I never slip when I'm alone," she said with a warm smile. "I always do it when I have an audience."

"Oh yeah," Ashley agreed, and decided Gray was very nice indeed. They fell into step side by side.

"Are you enjoying your studies?" Gray asked.

"Yes. It's good to be away from home . . ." She caught herself.

But all Gray said was, "Everyone needs to try her wings."

Ashley held the gate in the fence open for her and for March, who was strolling silently behind her. "You've come here together?"

March quirked an eyebrow. Gray laughed. "We have a mutual friend."

At the hotel door Sweeney grabbed her arm. "Come along, Matilda, the computers need setting up. Mr. Clapper has generously set aside a cloakroom for us. Ta-ta," he added to Ashley, and headed down one of the corridors that opened off the lobby. March glanced at his watch and hurried up the staircase, taking the steps two at a time.

Ashley looked through a nearby doorway — oh, the bar. Down a short hallway two other doors opened onto a sitting room and the dining room. Another corridor led past the cloak and computer room to a closed door labeled, "Private." The lobby itself was only an open space holding a couple of chairs, a potted palm, and the students' suitcases and backpacks piled in front of the reception desk. Mr. Clapper, who seemed like a friendly sort of guy, was handing out their keys. "Five? Right. Twenty? Righty-ho."

Ashley was sharing number forty-two with Jennifer and Courtney. The three girls lugged their bags up the stairs and with some casting around among the convoluted corridors found their room. It was small and tidy, with three twin beds and a sink in the corner. They distributed their stuff among a wardrobe, a dresser, and a single glass shelf above the sink.

Jennifer slammed her suitcase and shook her head. "Wait until I write home about this place. Nothing wrong with a nice Holiday Inn, but no, they put us in ye olde quainte inne where you need a ball of string to find your way back from the bathroom."

"I think it's great," Ashley said. "Much more character than a Holiday Inn. All the blocked-off doorways, funny little flights of steps, unexpected niches in the halls, like hiccups — it's like walking around inside an archaeological mound."

"It's not like home," said Courtney.

Ashley was about to tell her, "That's the point," when a soft rhythmic thumping emanated from the wall. The faded prints of nineteenth-century shepherds slid askew. "Ghosts?" Jennifer asked skeptically.

"That's Jason's room next door," said Courtney. "Guess he and Caterina couldn't wait until tonight."

"He was really itching to get Caterina out of that dorm." Jennifer imitated a bloodhound on the scent, tongue lolling, breath panting.

Courtney giggled. "Wonder what he did with Bryan? Locked him in the closet?"

From beyond the wall came a banshee-like moaning. Courtney and Jennifer responded with whoops of laughter and catcalls.

"Get a life," Ashley told them. She slammed out of the room, down the corridor, and past the door marked W.C., to what might once have been a staircase landing but that now contained a red fire bucket. Through a bay window she saw Bryan leaning on the fence beside the bowling green. His baseball cap hid his face. From his body language Ashley figured he was as disgusted as she was. Jason and Caterina could do whatever they wanted to, they just didn't have to get in everyone's face with it, like sex was something special. . . .

Ashley had uttered a few banshee moans of her own, back when she and Chris were going at it. Since then she had wondered whether she'd really felt that good, or whether she'd been so desperate for him to like her she'd put on an act that had fooled even herself. It was because she'd been so needy, he said, that he'd left her. He'd told her to "get over it."

"Sour grapes?" she asked Bryan's slouching back. "Yeah, me too."

Turning away from the window she took a deep breath,

tasting the uninspiring flavors of mildew and bathroom cleanser. In the distance dishes clashed. The sitting room downstairs was stocked with books and a television set, wasn't it? Ashley set off toward the main staircase.

She was just about to push through a second set of fire doors when she saw a movement through the safety glass window. The police constable she'd seen earlier emerged from a room. "Well then, Sir, that's the lot. Enough to be going on with, I reckon."

Gareth March stepped out into the hallway and shook the bobby's hand. "Thank you, Watkins."

The constable walked off down the hall, his helmet tucked beneath his arm, and disappeared around a corner. March ducked back into his room and shut the door. Ashley waited a moment, then shoved the fire door open and tiptoed through.

March was sure efficient, she thought, interviewing the local policeman before the dig had even started. Although why the bobby would be much of a source for archaeological information, she couldn't say. Probably he had to keep vandals and looters out of the grounds or something.

There were the stairs. She creaked down them, found the sitting room, and switched on the television. A game show, an old movie, a soccer match, and some talking heads. Great.

She plopped down on the couch, tried to follow the game show, and wondered just who she thought she was fooling now.

Chapter Four

*T*he bar of the Green Dragon was decorated with dark polished wood, beer advertisements, and framed posters of old cricket matches. A speaker in the corner emitted a lushly-orchestrated version of "Some Enchanted Evening." Matilda would have preferred something with an edge to it, either Beethoven or the Beatles. She hadn't been consulted, though.

The students occupied the bar's settees and stools like a happy-go-lucky barbarian horde. Sweeney had amputated Jason from Caterina, and was now holding forth to him, Manfred, and Bryan. The young men nodded like metronomes in time to Sweeney's baton-like finger, while the Italian girl pouted prettily over a glass of Campari. *Jason's earning points by being a team leader,* Matilda thought at her. *Don't interfere, or you'll threaten his manhood.* But she couldn't transmit, she could only receive.

She couldn't make prophecies, either, no matter how she tried to read the amber swirls in her glass of single malt Scotch. She could only *feel,* and in the random waves of emotion that washed over her she felt awkward and unfocussed.

It was early days yet, she reassured herself. She'd barely begun this case. Focus would come, in time.

Gareth was standing at the bar checking his cell phone for messages. Apparently he had none — he holstered the phone, accepted his glass of ale from Clapper, and wended his way to Matilda's table, where he sat down with his back to the wall. "I'm neither fish nor fowl. I'm not a student, but I'm not in charge of anything, either."

"Being a reporter is a good cover story," Matilda returned. "You have a perfect excuse to ask questions."

"Yes." He drank deeply. The ale was the same deep brown with subtle sparklings as his eyes.

Matilda sipped at her whisky. The flavor of peat smoke french-kissed her senses. She smiled. "What did Watkins say?"

"He gave me copies of the crime scene reports, photographs, interviews, the lot. Precious little, as Forrest said. Linda Burkett's body was found by a local lad who lives just below Durslow Edge. He ran home, his parents rang Watkins, and he in turn rang Manchester. She'd been dead for two days. The shop owner, Celia Dunning, had just filed a missing persons report."

"There was a boyfriend."

"They had him in straightaway. Lorry driver. He said she'd given him the push at Christmas, over a month before the murder. That might have made a motive, save he could prove he'd been in Glasgow when she died. They couldn't run a genetic fingerprint on him, though."

"They had some physical matter from the killer to run a genetic fingerprint on?" Matilda asked.

Gareth looked down into his glass. "She'd had sexual relations soon before her death. No signs of a struggle — her clothes weren't disarranged — so it wasn't rape."

"Amazing how a knife or a gun will quell a struggle," murmured Matilda.

"Unfortunately," Gareth continued, "the victim was just finishing — well, that time of the month, you know — so the sample was contaminated with her own blood. Useless for DNA testing."

Matilda looked past Gareth's shoulder to see the pretty girl who'd slipped on the grass this afternoon walking stiffly to the bar, self-absorbed by her own — what? Uncertainty? Loneliness? Clapper drifted amiably toward her.

Focusing on Gareth again, Matilda said, "Not to mention that the man Linda was with might not have been the man — or woman — who killed her. I'd like to see all the information, please. Including the photos. And we need to find an excuse to look at the place Linda's body was found."

Gareth opened his mouth, probably to protest either that

the photos weren't especially attractive or that he was a detective, not a tour guide. He might even be thinking that the murder investigation was his territory, and that she should stick to her missing artifacts. Whatever, he thought better of speaking. He'd done that frequently the last few hours. She knew she — or her unusual skills, at least — rubbed him the wrong way. His slightly defensive, slightly suspicious gaze made her feel as though she'd dribbled her dinner on her blouse.

"What does local rumor say about the murder?" Matilda asked.

"That the New Age travelers did it."

"What do you think?"

"They had the opportunity — they were camped near Shadow End in February, not far from Durslow Edge. I looked over the files at the Yard, and no traveler has ever been charged with murder. They knock each other about fairly frequently, though — the victim could've been in their way for some reason."

"Linda," Matilda said. "Her name was Linda."

"Watkins," said Gareth, just a fraction more loudly, "showed the vic — Linda's photo round Corcester. Clapper recognized her, said she'd taken a drink or two here. I'll talk to him tomorrow, like a proper snoop of a reporter, eh?"

"Why don't you see if he knows anything about the missing statuary while you're at it?"

Gareth looked at her pityingly.

"Sorry," Matilda said with a grimace. "Are there any other rumors about the murder?"

"Just the sort of rot you hear in small country towns. That Linda was sacrificed. By witches or Druids or men from Mars, no one can say. I think that's right out."

Matilda sat back in her chair and chewed on her lip. "There was that case in the forties, the old man accused of witchcraft found murdered. Presumably by his fellow villagers, but the Yard could never prove it."

"And there's always rubbish about UFOs and crop circles," added Gareth. "I'd rather deal in facts, thank you."

"The fact is that this area was one of the last strongholds of the Druids. Howard thinks that your bog body was a sacrifice, dating to the early days of the Roman era. The modern neo-Druids base their beliefs on nineteenth-century romanticism. Completely harmless."

"Like the Eisteddfod in Wales. All the literary types playing at bards and Druids. It's harmless unless you're a poet with a whacking great ego."

"Whoever killed Linda wasn't playing. He or she was probably protecting an illegal artifact scam. Whether Linda's lover had anything to do with that remains to be seen." Matilda chuckled. "The clue of the stolen artifacts. Sounds like a Nancy Drew mystery."

"Here," Gareth said, "could you pick the murderer out of an identity parade?"

"Anyone who's able to justify his actions to himself, no matter how despicable they may be, can very likely pass a lie detector test and can undoubtedly get by me. I could only pick the murderer from a line-up if he had a very guilty conscience. You could do as much yourself."

Gareth discarded that flight of fancy with a flick of his brows. "What did Sweeney say?"

"We agreed I should use my skills as subtly as possible," Matilda answered. "No reason to deal any wild cards to the students, they're innocent bystanders, after all."

"The girls might be in some danger."

"They're the same age as Linda Burkett, true, but they don't know anything about stolen artifacts. Howard did notice those traces of unauthorized digging at the fort, by the way."

Gareth glanced over at Sweeney, who was sitting side-saddle on the edge of the table making gestures describing either gladiatorial combat or gardening. "He knows his business, then? Seems a bit of a prat."

"Oh, he's a prat, all right. He knows his business very well indeed, and he likes to make sure the peasantry realizes it. We need to have an expert in charge, though. This is a genuine dig, even if it does have ulterior motives."

The girl, Matilda saw, had ordered a glass of lemonade. She opened the ice bucket sitting on the bar and apparently found it empty. Instead of asking Clapper for more, she replaced the lid and turned away. There were no empty seats among the other students.

Matilda smiled and beckoned. The girl stared — *who me?* — then slipped into the chair next to Matilda, across from Gareth. "Thank you, Dr. Gray."

"I don't believe I caught your name," said Matilda, feeling certain it wasn't Nancy Drew.

"Ashley Walraven." Her eyes skewed from Matilda's face to Gareth's and collided with his level gaze. She looked abruptly down at the table top. Wings of blond hair fell like curtains around her face.

Hardly surprising, Matilda thought, that Ashley would find Gareth attractive. He was not only good-looking, he was also intelligent and polite. But he found Ashley no more significant than a kitten. Matilda didn't kick him beneath the table. Matchmaking wasn't in her job description. "What do you think of England?" she asked the girl.

"It's awesome, if kind of dark and wet. We've made plenty of cool field trips, Little Moreton Hall, Gawsthorpe, the Wirral. Even Shadow Moss. We saw them digging out the rest of the bog body." She waved toward the south instead of the north. Matilda didn't correct her.

"Did you get a good look at it?"

Ashley's chocolate brown eyes widened. "Not really. It just looked like a muddy sack in the ground. I got a good look at the hand in Dr. Sweeney's lab. That was enough. I had nightmares about it. It's the same size as mine." Ashley laid her right hand on the table, perfectly imitating the gentle curve of the severed hand.

Gareth flinched. Someone just walked over his grave, Matilda told herself. *How interesting.* "Nightmares?"

"Oh," Ashley replied with a shrug, "just dumb things about Druid rituals and stuff. I mean, we don't really know what the Druids actually did, most of our evidence is from Roman sources. Since they were trying to break the political power of the Druids maybe they made up lies about the sacrifices. They were pretty good at sacrificing people themselves, after all."

"The Romans did see for themselves the carnage from Boudicca's campaign. Her troops massacred an appalling number of people before they were massacred in turn."

"After what the Romans did to her and her daughters. . . ."

Ashley stopped in mid-sentence.

". . . .maybe they deserved to be massacred?" finished Matilda.

"Does anyone ever get what he deserves?" Ashley said into her glass.

The girl may not have understood where her flash of anger had come from, but Matilda did. Ashley's intelligence and emotions had been dismissed as unimportant so many times she no longer believed them to be valid. A shame — she was a sensitive girl, just the sort to be disturbed by the implications of the severed hand.

Gareth, whose profession should have accustomed him to such testimonies of mortality, stared into the middle distance. He wasn't nearly as easy to read as Ashley was — he was older, and a man, and his defenses were as carefully constructed as those of Carnarvon Castle. Matilda suspected that he himself didn't know what was lurking in his dungeons.

She drank the last of her whisky and tested the locks on the doors of her own dungeons. More than a few times she'd wished she were as blind, deaf, and mute as everyone else. As a child she'd been ridiculed for her skills. As a young woman Ashley's age she'd hidden them, not trusting them, not trusting herself to deal with them. As an adult of Gareth's age she'd at last accepted them and taught herself some measure of control. Now, in early middle age, she'd come to recognize that her skills could mend only the occasional injustice, not the world's pain.

"Well, well," said Sweeney over Matilda's shoulder. "Talking about me behind my back? And here I've ordered another round of drinks."

Ashley jumped. Gareth looked up. Matilda smiled politely. The man's round teddy-bear stomach was a tempting target, although poking it wouldn't make him deflate. "She was telling us about the bog body, Howard."

"Ah yes, fascinating item, that. A girl about twenty, give or take a year or two. We have the trunk and most of the legs, even though the head is still missing. I thought at first the hand had been cut off by the peat cutter. Now we know that the head was taken off on purpose — ritual decapitation, I'd say — so maybe the hand was as well. Our old Celtic friends coveted their neighbor's heads, no doubt about it, but I've heard damn-all about their taking hands." Making a peremptory taxi-calling gesture at Clapper, Sweeney sat down.

"If thy right hand offends thee, cut it off," Matilda said quietly, and amended, "Another mythology, although it seems apt."

"To this day," said Gareth, "in some of the Arab countries, the authorities will cut off the right hand of a thief."

"And the Celts would sometimes sacrifice condemned criminals?" Sweeney asked.

"I'm not sure it follows," admitted Gareth.

Sweeney said, "Dr. Gray is fond of saying that historians and archaeologists don't take myth and magic seriously enough. They're parts of our heritage, even though we've outgrown the need for them."

"Speak for yourself," said Matilda.

"Magic?" Ashley hadn't so much as blinked since Sweeney appeared. He could tell her the sky had pink polka dots, Matilda thought, and she'd accept it as truth.

"A people's beliefs affect their art, their architecture, their artifacts," Matilda explained. "We'll never fully understand paleolithic cave paintings, for example, because we don't know what the painters intended. Simply to depict the animals? Or to ensure a good hunt through a ritual?"

"Don't do that sort of thing any more," said Clapper. From a tray he doled out fresh glasses of beer, lemonade, and whiskey — "Scotch for you, Mrs. Gray, and bourbon for Dr. Sweeney."

"Thank you," Matilda told him. "Yes, we do still do that type of thing. Look at Nazi Germany and the swastika. It used to be a symbol of good luck but now it sends shudders down our spines. Would it mean anything to an Amazonian tribesman, though?"

Ashley nodded. "Churches are full of symbols."

"Definitely. Take St. Michael's, just up the street. It's laid out in the shape of a cross, like many older churches. The carvings of the capitals depict Bible stories. The holy water font and the altar are symbolic memories. And yet none of this would made sense to someone unfamiliar with Christianity."

"Just why is it St. Michael's?" pontificated Sweeney. "Because, like St. George, St. Michael allegedly killed a dragon. All across Britain churches built on hilltops are attributed to St. Michael. Hilltops were often pagan sanctuaries. Since a dragon could be a symbol of pagan power, you have a neat little allegory of triumphant Christianity. Of course, it's all academic now, the stuff of dusty tomes and crabbed scholars, eh, Matilda?"

They'd had this argument before. Matilda declined a rematch with a smile.

"There's Roman stones in the church, the vicar showed me," said Clapper, and walked away.

Sweeney said under his breath, "Occupational hazard, the unenlightened lower classes."

Gareth reached into his pocket and pulled out a notebook. "Is all this for public consumption, Dr. Sweeney?"

"Of course, of course, be sure to spell my name right, there's a good chap."

Gareth's pen made dark slashes on the page. Ashley's eyes moved speculatively from Sweeney's grin to Gareth's frown.

The hair twitched on the back of Matilda's neck. She looked toward the door of the bar. The man who stood there, his head thrust forward and his shoulders rounded, bore an unfortunate resemblance to a parrot. His dark, almost black, eyes ranged over the room. They paused appreciatively at the sight of Caterina nestling onto Jason's lap, and at Courtney's and Jennifer's denim-clad behinds presented to his view as they leaned on the bar. He strolled to their sides, ordered a lager, and made some remark to which both girls responded politely.

"Speaking of occupational hazards." said Sweeney with a sigh. "I say, Reynolds!"

Matilda had to agree with Gareth's description of Adrian Reynolds as "a proper little git." Even though his suit was well-cut and immaculately clean, he wore it as though he'd found it in a garbage can. His natty little moustache seemed painted on. She knew he'd reek of expensive cologne before she could smell it.

Reynolds walked up to the table and thrust his hand toward Sweeney. "Well then, Doctor, I see we're at the starter's gate, eh?"

"How very pleasant to see you again," Sweeney returned. "May I present Dr. Matilda Gray, my second, Gareth March from the *Times*, and one of my students, Ashley Walraven."

The fierce handshake left Matilda's fingers tingling. Gareth gritted his teeth and held his own. Reynolds bent over Ashley's hand, contemplated it, looked soulfully into her eyes, and said, "Charmed, I'm sure."

"Hello," said Ashley. As soon he relinquished her hand she wiped it off. Being young and pretty, Matilda thought, had its hazards.

"I was just speaking with Watkins," Reynolds announced, forcing a chair between Ashley's and Matilda's. "He says he has no cause to turf out those yobbos camped on the way to Macclesfield. No cause! Why, they're destroying property values! There's too much cosseting the criminals today, if you ask me, and not enough attention paid to the rights of the landowners who support this country." He paused to drink.

Gareth asked casually, "I suppose you get cheap labor off the travelers — mucking out the stables, that sort of thing?"

"Good God no," said Reynolds. "Wouldn't have them about the place!"

Then who had invited them in this afternoon? Matilda wondered.

"I suppose you hire local people to exercise your horses?" persisted Gareth.

"Silly little chits who hardly know a muzzle from a hock. I don't suppose you ride, Dr. Gray?"

"I've ridden. Mostly I hang onto the saddle and hope the horse is gentle."

"Any time you'd like to go riding," Reynolds said expansively, "just call round. I have several older mares, calm as a rocking chair. Even my wife can manage them. You too, March. And Miss Walraven."

Ashley made a face, maybe agreeing with Matilda that a horse was a very big creature.

But Gareth smiled. "Thank you. I like to ride, used to do a bit of steeplechasing in my younger days."

"Super!" Reynolds launched into a discussion with Gareth in which various equine terms figured prominently.

With an expression indicating he wouldn't notice a horse if it fell dead at his feet, Sweeney began to talk to Matilda about Romano-British artwork in general and the missing items from Corcester in particular.

Reynolds rounded on them. "Those statues are mine. I saw the photos in the Sotheby's catalog — there's a leopard inlaid with silver spots, and the heads of a man and a woman, and some little — votive figurines, that's what they're called. Disgraceful, when a man's property is stolen and even the police can't retrieve it!"

"Steady on," said Sweeney. "You can't prove it's yours, can you? Or even that it came from Cornovium."

"They're spitting images of objects Miller found in the thirties!" Reynolds sputtered.

"And what would you do with the statues if you had them back?" asked Matilda. "Donate them to a museum?"

"Not a bit of it," Reynolds replied. "There are collectors who'd pay a packet for that sort of artifact."

"I see," Matilda continued, unsurprised. "So looting is all right, then, just as long as the loot isn't stolen from you."

"What?" Reynolds demanded.

"It's poetic justice, I suppose, that the market for forgeries is booming right alongside that for antiquities. Half a collector's collection might be fakes. But he wouldn't know, would he, because he bought the items out of context."

"I know the laws of treasure trove," Reynolds huffed. "If temple offerings are discovered on my land then I'm either due fair compensation from the Crown, or they're mine to do with as I please. Good luck getting fair compensation through the British Museum. I can make a lot more selling my artifacts on the open market."

"Through dealers such as Celia Dunning in Manchester?" Gareth asked.

"She's one dealer I use, yes. Quite honest and aboveboard. Anyone who buys from her gets a certificate."

Sweeney's usual smile tightened into a toothy grimace. Had it taken him this long to realize, Matilda thought, that Reynolds was using him to find more art objects? The stable-owner wanted to have his cake and eat it too — legal antiquities as well as cash.

She offered him a crisp smile of her own. "It's like prostitution, isn't it? If men didn't want cheap, mindless sex, there wouldn't be any prostitutes. If collectors didn't stroke their egos by buying artifacts, there wouldn't be any looters and forgers supplying them. In each case, it's the customer, not the supplier, who's ultimately responsible for the trade."

Both Reynolds and Sweeney looked at Matilda with varying degrees of annoyance. "Go for it," Ashley muttered beneath her breath. Gareth smothered either a laugh or a coughing fit.

It was Reynolds who abandoned the field first. He gulped down the rest of his drink, flushed crimson, and stood up. "I'll try to remember that I'm a gentleman, Dr. Gray. Good night to you, Sweeney. I'll be doing what I can to assist with the excavation. Miss Walraven, another time. . . ."

He walked off with a deliberate saunter that was meant as a slap in the face. Matilda remembered she was a lady and didn't laugh out loud.

Sweeney's expression struggled between approval and censure, and finally divided the sides academically rather than sexually. "Good show, Matilda. That'll teach the man to keep a civil tongue in his head."

I doubt it, Matilda told herself. She stood up. "I'm going to go outside for a quick breath of air and then turn in. Tomorrow's going to be busy."

Sweeney didn't bother to rise. "Good night."

"I'd better go to bed," said Ashley, standing up. "Are you sure you want to go out in the dark, Dr. Gray? There was a murder here a couple of months ago."

Matilda didn't point out that the body had been found two miles away. "I'll get Gareth to come with me, if that'll make you feel any better."

"It's not a matter of *me* feeling better." Ashley yawned. "Thank you for taking me in. See you tomorrow."

"Good night," Matilda told her.

"Good night." Gareth looked around the room. A student or two glanced incuriously back. The undercurrents of emotion had calmed somewhat, Matilda noted, to a steady purr of anticipation with an occasional spike of casual lust. Jason and Caterina had vanished. So had a few of the others, but

Matilda wasn't going to make any assumptions without evidence. No one was projecting irritation at Ashley — Matilda hadn't inadvertently made her into a teacher's pet.

"Good show," Matilda said under her breath as she and Gareth walked into the lobby, "to get some answers out of Reynolds without him knowing he was being questioned."

"I try to earn my pay," Gareth returned.

They followed Reynolds out into the night. All they saw of him were taillights disappearing around the corner.

"I don't suppose you could read his mind," Gareth asked.

"I don't read minds," replied Matilda patiently. "I can tell that he thinks he's putting something over on us, but he's already betrayed that hand."

"And Sweeney?"

"The usual. Looking forward to the dig, not only for its own sake but as a chance to strut his stuff. I keep hoping the man will choke on his ego, but he never does."

The windows of the cottages glowed with the icy blue light of television screens. The bowling green looked like dark velvet. A car whizzed past, its headlights flaring and then winking out. Beneath the smeared indigo sky the fort was a study in shape and shadow. Gareth opened the gate and Matilda stepped through. The night was so quiet that she could hear the babble of the river and the wind rustling the trees. From the top of the turf-covered walls the lights of Fortuna Stud seemed suspended in nothingness.

"Like will-'o-the wisps," said Matilda.

"*Canhywallan cyrth,*" Gareth said. "Corpse candles."

"Like you see in bogs?"

He didn't answer.

Matilda took a few steps away from him. From her pocket she pulled the spindle she'd found in the disturbed ground this afternoon. It had called to her, and she wanted to know why.

When she heard the footsteps she thought at first they were Gareth's. Then her perceptions went hollow, and in the cavity that held a sense beyond the first five senses she heard a woman's low, cultured voice: "Marcus, I don't know. Do you think you should accept her?"

"I would insult the local chief if I didn't," answered the

quiet, authoritative voice of a man. "My orders are to keep the peace, Claudia."

Matilda turned slowly around. Gareth was a dark shape several paces away. He was gazing toward Corcester, showing no sign he'd heard anything.

Behind his back stood three shapes illuminated dimly from some unseen source, like actors picked out by a filtered spotlight. The man was in his thirties, with a chiseled face that expected, but did not coerce, obedience. He wore the armor and insignia of a legion commander. The woman who stood beside him was dressed in a gown of saffron-colored linen that complemented her dark hair. Her brows were drawn in a frown of concern.

Together they looked at a second woman, a younger one, whose red hair hung in long plaits over her rough-woven gown. She didn't stand in a servile pose, but with her shoulders back, inspecting the Roman couple as closely as they inspected her. Although for a Celt she was slender and delicately-built, she was almost as tall as Marcus. Around the trio, caught with them in a bubble of time and pale light, Matilda could see the painted walls and low furniture of a first-century Roman home.

Sweeney had spoken today of the first commander of the fort, who might have brought his wife out from Rome. Matilda was standing on the site of their quarters. She was looking at them now. She was hearing their voices. They were facing some dilemma of protocol, it seemed, as they had apparently faced many dilemmas together.

"What is your name?" Claudia asked the younger woman.

"Branwen."

"Of the Cornovii? Were you captured in battle?"

Branwen's lips smiled, even though her eyes remained cool and distant. "I am of the Iceni. And you might say I was captured in battle, if it pleases you."

"It would please the king of the Brigantes if I were to make you a servant in my household," said Marcus. He shifted his stance, as though he was tired. His armor clanked.

"I can cook," said Branwen. "I can spin and weave. I can mind your children."

"We have no children." Claudia spoke just a little too

quickly.

Marcus made a gesture of dismissal. "I shall tell the envoy we accept the king's gift, with gratitude. Claudia, find something for her to do."

"Certainly." But Claudia didn't turn toward Branwen. She gazed evenly at her husband, watching as his eyes moved from the smooth crown of the slave-servant's hair over the lines of her body.

Somewhere, several miles away, a familiar voice said, "Matilda?"

The lighted room, the three people, thinned and dissipated. Matilda blinked, momentarily blinded by the night.

"Matilda?" asked Gareth's voice. "What were you looking at?"

"You would call it a vision, I suppose. An echo of the past. A psychological sound-and-light show. A replaying of a scene that's already happened."

His face and form materialized from the darkness. "Ghosts?"

"Yes, depending on your definition of ghosts."

"Of the old Romans?"

"Yes."

"Ah, so you speak colloquial Latin, then, and can understand them."

She smiled. "That's a valid point. It's not like eavesdropping on the neighbors, though. I sense what they're saying is all."

"I hope they're saying something about the artifacts," he muttered, his skepticism overshadowed by annoyance.

"That I don't know. Yet." The night air was cool. In the distance an owl hooted. Shivering, Matilda turned back toward the lighted windows of the hotel. "Let's go in. Tomorrow will be here before we know it."

Silently Gareth walked beside her back to the land of the living.

Chapter Five

Gareth paused outside the door of Clapper's office to put on his reporter's face. Now that he thought about it, that face wasn't all that different from his police inspector's face, not when it came to questioning a witness.

The hotelkeeper was seated at his desk. Tidy piles of receipts and lists were ranged in front of him, and an open file cabinet gaped at his right. To his left a window overlooked the street and the mound of Cornovium. The windcheaters and billed caps of the students made a colorful accent in the drab morning light.

"I hope everything is all right?" Clapper asked Gareth.

"Oh yes, lovely. I just wanted to ask you a few questions, get some background material for my story."

"Well then. . . ." Clapper waved Gareth toward a chair and leaned back in his own, which creaked beneath his weight. His face was as soft and guileless as a baby's bare bottom.

Gareth sat down, set aside his camera, and produced his notebook. "I expect you entertain quite a few people who come to see the Roman fort."

"Some, yes. But there's not much to see, is there? Just lumps in the ground and a few stones. I'll be right pleased when the Doc digs up some buildings. Town council hopes to build a visitor's center, with a grant from English Heritage or some such group."

"Any plans for a museum? I believe any artifacts found in the fort now go to Manchester. . . ."

"Well now, that's what they say, isn't it?" Clapper tapped his nose and winked.

"Eh?" Gareth returned innocently.

"What's a Roman coin or two to the university? They won't miss the odd denarius turned up in the ruins by the local lads, will they?"

"So the local lads like poking about in the ruins?"

"I was born and raised here in Corcester. Many's the garden wall built of the old stone, and many's the drainage ditch lined with the old tile. There's no harm in a bit of recycling. The legions are gone. We live here now."

So he called it recycling. "There's a ruined chapel on Anglesey that dates back to the Age of Saints," suggested Gareth. "When archaeologists excavated it in the nineteenth century, the local people thought they were looking for treasure. After the scientists left they kept on looking and demolished the chapel."

"Yes, well, that's the Welsh for you," Clapper said.

Through his teeth, Gareth asked, "The fort's on Reynolds's land, isn't it? I suppose he doesn't miss the odd coin any more than the University would do."

"Him?" Clapper guffawed. "He makes you scrape the horse shit off your shoes before you leave his yard — it's his, mind you, every last bit of it."

"No wonder he's going on about the missing statuary, then."

Clapper leaned forward and lowered his voice. "If you ask me, he's narked he didn't find them statues first, so he could do a deal himself."

"And not report them?"

The hotelkeeper looked at the papers on his desk, picked up a pen, and signed a form of some kind.

Gareth told himself he was straying into forbidden territory. Clapper could probably see his friendly gossip printed as fact on the front page of the *Times*. It wasn't on to offend any local landowners armed with stable muck. "I suppose antiquities dealers come here frequently, just to see what turns up."

"Yes," Clapper replied. He put the pen down.

"The girl found dead out at Durslow Edge was a dealer in antiquities, was she?"

"She said she wanted to buy, right enough. Never showed

us any brass, though."

"So you knew her."

"She came round the bar for a drink."

"Alone?"

"She met Reynolds here. Seemed to me she already knew he owned the fort and was waiting for him to call in. They left together to look at his 'collection'." Clapper's sarcastic tone put quotation marks round the word, implying more than an academic discussion of Romano-British artifacts.

Gareth stifled his "aha!" response. Watkins had no doubt had all this from Clapper long ago. "I thought Reynolds was married."

"Mr. March, no one knows better than a hotelkeeper what little difference that makes when a bloke finds a bird he fancies."

No one knows better than a policeman. Gareth studied his notebook for a moment. He had veered away from his assigned topic of "Our Roman Heritage," but Clapper seemed perfectly happy to follow. "Who do you think killed the girl, then? Off the record, of course, just your opinion."

"It was one of them layabouts they call New Age travelers," Clapper replied. "They're after some odd jiggery-pokery in that camp."

"Illegal drugs, for example?"

"And devil-worship."

Gareth reminded himself not to show impatience. A real reporter would be sucking down that sort of rubbish. "You've seen them at it?"

"No. Some of the lads have done, though. And Emma Price what lives down the lane, there was a filthy row about her a couple of months ago."

"In February? What happened to her?"

"Silly little chit got herself in the pudding club. Said the baby's father was Nick, the bloke who's more or less the boss of the traveler's camp. Said he'd worked some sort of magic on her and the next thing she knew, poof, up the spout." Clapper shook his head over the foolishness of women. "Nick denied it, though. Her family organized an appointment at a clinic in Macclesfield, and that was the end of it."

Gareth doubted that. "Where's Emma now?"

"She's working in some posh shop in Manchester. Hear tell she goes back to the camp every now and then, although Nick will have sod-all to do with her any more. A good thing too — he's a bad lot."

"Do you know Nick's last name?" Gareth asked.

"Velotis, or something like that."

Gareth wrote "Nick Velotis (?)" and "Emma Price" on his page and told himself not to push his luck. "Would you say, Mr. Clapper, that living in a town built on Roman ruins gives you a sense of history and heritage?"

"Sorry?"

"You've learned quite a bit about Romano-British antiquities simply by living in the neighborhood."

Clapper re-arranged his receipts. "Not as much as maybe. I'm no scholar, not like the Doc. I could tell you some good ghost stories, if you like."

"Oh?"

"Distant trumpets, marching feet, shapes in the mist. Mostly seen by people leaving my bar or the pub down the lane, mind you. Still, ghost stories bring in the tourists. . . ."

P.C. Watkins strolled by the window. Gareth decided he needed to check with the local plod more than he needed to sit here talking supernatural rot. "Well, thank you, Mr. Clapper. All this has been very helpful."

"You'll mention The Green Dragon in your article, will you?" Clapper reached to the back of his desk and picked up several advertising brochures. "Here, have some of these for your mates. We serve breakfast, lunch, tea, and dinner, with bar meals any time."

"Thank you. Very much obliged." Gareth pocketed his notebook and the brochures, draped his camera over his shoulder, dodged the reception desk, and went out the door.

Watkins was standing at the curb looking over at the dig. Which, Gareth saw, was rapidly developing beneath the spades of twenty students. Already they had peeled back the turf and were cutting trenches into the dark soil. Sweeney, in a leather jacket and scarf, looked like a World War I air ace separated from his Sopwith Camel.

Matilda was walking back and forth, hale and hearty — not that her London assailant was likely to have another go at her whilst she was with the students. She'd survived the five days between Forrest's office and Corcester without Gareth hovering protectively over her. Her mishap in the tube station had probably been an accident. Still Gareth had walked her to the door of her room last night and made sure no one was inside. She'd thanked him politely. If she was frightened she was hiding it well.

"Morning, S . . ." said Watkins, the truncated "sir" making a sibilant.

"Good morning, Constable." And under his breath, "Clapper was telling me that Linda Burkett was seen with Reynolds."

"Several days before she died, that was," Watkins replied. "Reynolds was at home with his wife at the time of the murder, near as we could estimate."

"What about a local girl named Emma Price?"

Watkins frowned slightly. "What about her?

"She was having it off with a fellow named Nick, at the traveler's camp. She said he'd bewitched her or some sort of rot."

"That weren't witchery, that were biology, if you take my meaning, Ins . . . Mr. March. Some of the lads were nattering about devil-worship, true, but I reckon Nick and his mates were having them on. Finding Linda's body up on Durslow Edge in February gave everyone a turn, like. That's all."

Gareth was perfectly willing to believe that was all. . . . His shoulders prickled and he glanced round. Clapper was standing in his window, his massive frame wavering like a manta ray in the old glass. He smiled and nodded. Gareth smiled and nodded back again, then pulled out his notebook and scrawled a few random words in it. "Thank you, Constable. It must be very interesting to walk a beat in a town with a Roman heritage."

"Oh — er — that it is," said Watkins, and with a roll of his eyes toward the window ambled away up the sidewalk.

Mind your step, Gareth admonished himself. One person seeing him with Watkins was all right, but he didn't want anyone else to.

He crossed the street and skirted the cottages and the bowling green. As he crossed the second street a few raindrops plopped softly on his head. Some of the students glanced up in annoyance. Sweeney produced a furled umbrella and flourished it at the sky. Gareth felt no more raindrops.

The three trenches, dark gashes in the damp green grass, were already revealing muddy shapes. Except for the occasional "Ewww" when someone encountered a not-very-ancient relic of cow, the students were working quietly and efficiently.

Manfred stood over his group with transit and plumb bob, making sure the trench was exactly six feet wide and its sides were a proper ninety degrees. Jason was in the trench with his group, taking the shovels from their hands and doing the tricky bits himself. Caterina hunkered down, troweling a large flat stone. At least, Gareth told himself, she and her lover had the decency not to bring their extra-curricular activities to work with them. Lads that age tended to be frivolous and girls foolish, silly little Emma Price being a case in point.

Gareth could hardly blame these lads for moments of inattention, though, when the charms of the girls were displayed a treat by snug blue jeans. Ashley, the girl with the typical American unisex name, was using a small pick to clear a stone wall a few paces away from the others. Yesterday she'd reminded Gareth of a kitten. He'd felt like offering her a saucer of milk.

Bryan eyed Ashley's progress and said something encouraging, then walked on, checking that each member of his group was doing his or her assigned task. Jennifer put a camera back in its case, set it down with the other equipment, and picked up a sketch pad. Sweeney tucked his umbrella beneath his arm like a swagger stick and moved from group to group. "Objects are all to the good, children, but we need surfaces — surfaces, now, a light touch. . . ."

Speaking of jiggery-pokery, there was Matilda. No, that wasn't fair. Gareth had no proof that Matilda was a charlatan. Or that she wasn't. He ranged up beside her and saw that she was comparing what looked like old photographs of the area with its current appearance.

"Miller's expedition in the thirties," she explained. "The remains of some medieval buildings were still here then. I imagine they've gone to build the walls of chip shops and garages. Along here." Her forefinger sketched lines and angles over the turf.

Gareth didn't know whether she was extrapolating from the photos or whether she was "seeing" the after-image of a building. He didn't ask, any more than he'd asked her last night about her vision, or hallucination, or whatever it had been. He hadn't seen or heard anything. The air had been still and cold, the night so quiet it had rung in his ears. Matilda had stood looking intently at nothing.

"That trench over there, the deep one's overgrown," he said. "That's from the Miller expedition?"

"Yes, although those scars along its edge are much more recent, like the potholes I was pointing out yesterday. In fact. . . ." Matilda climbed down into the weedy ravine that cut through the northern embankment of the fort, Gareth at her heels. "I wouldn't be at all surprised if those statues came from that hole there. It's fairly recent — smaller weeds, and the bank has collapsed into it. A pretty good tunnel was driven in here, into the foundations of what used to be a substantial building, judging by the stone and pottery debris." She poked the dirt with the toe of her rubber wellie boot, turning up a few scraps of stone.

"Someone digging here would have been hidden from the farm and from the town," Gareth said. "Do you suppose they knew what they were after?"

"Whoever stole the statuary dug several pits in the area of the temple, the legion headquarters, and the commander's home, places where he could reasonably expect to find valuable items. Corcester town council offers a very nice map of the fort, the Miller excavation reports are available at the library, and metal detectors work just as well for the dishonest."

"So we're not necessarily looking for someone with specialized knowledge?"

"No, just someone with a bit of luck and no conscience. The statuary must have been buried just outside the temple, perhaps by a third or fourth century thief who never returned for his loot. According to the catalog listing it was found bundled into a cooking pot."

"This is the temple, then?" Gareth nodded toward the stone

scraps. They might just as well have been Tahitian seashells to him.

"Yes. This is where Miller found the tessellated floor of what was probably the Celtic temenos. The Romans might have built their own temple — to Mars, or Augustus, or some other deity — on top of its ruins, backed up to the perimeter wall. That would be one way of keeping the local people from returning to Epona's shrine."

Gareth thought of the Catholic pilgrims continuing to come to St. Winifred's shrine at Holywell despite the Reformation. He eyed the scraped and scrambled burrow in the slope of the embankment. Matilda had decided on the point of origin of the statuary by scientific deduction. He could have done that himself if he'd had the proper background. "And if the statuary came from the temple then it was deliberately abandoned and not treasure trove, if I take Reynolds's point correctly."

"Reynolds is straining at a gnat, trying to avoid having to sell his finds to the Crown. The statuary might just as well have come from the legion commander's home, but a much later home than the one I saw last night. That was from the earliest period, about 80 Anno Domini — not that they were measuring time Anno Domini, of course. . . ." She cut herself off. "Well now, I can't prove anything more than Reynolds can."

Gareth didn't reply. Matilda smiled, privately, and turned just as Sweeney scrambled down the slope. "Howard, I was telling Gareth that this is probably where the statuary came from."

"Wouldn't be the least surprised," Sweeney responded. "The beggar — Reynolds — has no documentation, though. No case."

"Perhaps every valuable artifact has already been removed from the site," suggested Gareth, and added, "valuable to collectors, that is."

"Not necessarily," Sweeney answered. "Remember Snettisham?"

Gareth didn't. Matilda moved in before he could say so. "A cache of gold torcs, Celtic necklaces, was turned up by a plow in 1948. Everyone said, how nice, but since it's a plowed field there won't be anything else there. More torcs kept turning up, though, and in 1990 the British Museum did a formal area excavation. They found an incredible hoard of gold still hidden. The ancient gold traders must have used the field as a safety deposit box."

"Ah." Gareth pulled out his notebook.

"Of course, with Matilda here," said Sweeney, "I suppose we could try and sniff out the valuables." He laughed — only joking.

If Matilda really could sniff out gold, Gareth thought, a thief would be more likely to use her than to kill her.

"Snettisham is in Norfolk," Sweeney went on. "So is Icklingham, whose owners lost some statuary much the same way as Reynolds. And Thetford. The Romano-British hoard at Hoxne is in Suffolk. Iceni country, all of it. The Iceni sat astride the ancient gold route, and as a result were one of the richest of the Celtic tribes. When their king, Prasutagus, died in 60 A.D., he willed half his wealth to the Romans, hoping they'd leave his family alone. Greedy beggars the Romans were, though, wanted it all. So they took it. Their mistake was to insult Prasutagus's queen, Boudicca."

Ashley had said something about Boudicca last night. Gareth scribbled gamely in his notebook. "What does a tribe in Norfolk have to do with Cornovium? We're in far western England here."

"The gold route ran clear across the country," answered Matilda. "Celtic gold came from Ireland. The only known Roman gold mines in Britain are in Wales. Are you familiar with them, Gareth?"

"The mines at Pumpsaint? No, I'm not." He shouldn't have mentioned the corpse-candles last night. That's when she'd caught him out. He'd worked hard to erase the Welsh lilt from his voice, the upward inflection at the ends of sentences and the softness in the vowels. His mates in Manchester might have called him "Taffy," but he'd earned his transfer, and his mates in London called him "Inspector."

"The ships landed in Anglesey," Matilda said, "and pack trains brought the gold through Wales and across what is now England to the country of the Iceni, from where it was shipped to the continent. Along the way it was worked into objects, beautiful objects, not only torcs but other works of art."

"Worth a packet, I suppose," said Gareth.

"To us, yes," Sweeney said. "However, the Celts saw gold as divine and the artifacts made from it as religious votives. To them, the Romans' lust for gold as wealth was sacrilegious. There's an outdated concept — sacrilege."

"What we had here," said Matilda, "was a serious failure to communicate."

Gareth shut his notebook. "Just what did the Romans do to Boudicca and her daughters?"

"Flogged the mother, raped the girls," Sweeney replied. "Mortal insult to the royal house, as you can imagine."

"Mortal insult to the women." Matilda looked toward the spot where she'd been standing last night. "I am of the Iceni. . . ."

She murmured so softly Gareth almost didn't hear her. With a shrug, he left Matilda and Sweeney discussing horizons, praetorians, and someone named Cartimandua, and walked about taking notes. After he'd filled several pages with comments less on the dig than on the various students — as though one of them would turn out to be the murderer — he took pictures of the emerging stones. By noon he'd slap run out of things to do. He'd always hated stake-outs, and this one promised to be even more boring than most.

The students and their mentors trooped to the hotel, ate sandwiches, fish and chips, and curry, and trooped back again. Gareth brought up the rear, feeling like the whipper-in of hounds at a fox hunt, whilst Sweeney led the charge, scarf flying in the wind.

Just in front of Gareth walked Ashley and Matilda. "I've seen the class records," Matilda was saying to the girl. "You should've been one of the team leaders, not Jason."

"Yeah, well, he's a jock," Ashley replied, as though that explained anything.

"You'd be embarrassed if I talked to Howard for you, wouldn't you?"

"Harassed is more like it."

"Maybe Howard could designate a fourth team. . . ."

Ashley looked sharply over at Matilda. "No, please. I

appreciate it, but — well, okay, maybe I could use some assertiveness training, but I'd rather do without than attract the wrong sort of attention. Jason's so immature, he's on my case already because I'm kind of shy and I write home every week. So far I've just shrugged it off. I'd like to keep it that way."

"Never let them smell blood," agreed Gareth.

Ashley glanced over her shoulder, her ponytail bobbing. Gareth deflected her look with a cramped smile. Smiling a lopsided smile of her own, she opened the gate.

Matilda, too, looked round at Gareth, then back at Ashley. "You've assessed the situation very well, I think. Don't worry, I won't interfere."

"Thanks."

Through the gate they went, and scattered across the fort, Ashley back to her wall, Matilda to make a circuit of the field. She paused at the far embankment, silhouetted against the cloudy sky. Her own jeans fit a treat, Gareth thought, loose enough to camouflage that she wasn't a willowy young girl, snug enough to show that she was a woman.

He was about to set down his camera and volunteer to shovel when he heard a nasal voice calling, "March! Hallo, hallo!" Adrian Reynolds sauntered down the near embankment. He wore riding pants and tall boots, and his tweed jacket flapped open round his puffed-out chest.

"Good afternoon," Gareth replied. "Have you been out riding, then?"

"Oh yes, nothing like a gray day for a good canter. How are you getting on?"

Sweeney was bending over the flat stone Caterina had been cleaning. "Very nice memorial stone," he said. "Probably set up outside the headquarters building. Let's see — *praefectus cohortus — equitatae* — yes, we knew there was cavalry here. . . ."

". . . *Domitianus,*" said Caterina. "The emperor Domitian. The stone is very early, yes? 'In memory of Marcus Cornelius Felix', yes?"

Sweeney stared at her.

"*Uxor,*" she went on. "That is *sposa.* Wife? The stone was set by his wife Claudia Sabina, yes?"

"You read Latin?" Sweeney demanded.

Caterina drew herself up, dark eyes flashing. "Signor Doctor, I am not only a student in Roman studies, I am myself a citizen of Rome!"

"Yes," said Sweeney, "of course you are. Well done, my dear. Good show."

Reynolds eyed the Italian girl up and down and whistled between his teeth. "Pretty little spitfire, eh? Those Mediterranean girls, they know a thing or two." He nudged Gareth in the ribs.

Gareth was tempted to sort the man out. He restrained himself. "Is your offer of a horse still good, Reynolds?"

"Oh yes, by all means. Would you like a ride?"

"Yes I would, rather. And Dr. Gray as well." No reason for him to ride out to Durslow Edge alone. He might as well take Matilda and get the tour over with.

"Go down to the farm and tell Jimmy I sent you," said Reynolds. "Ask him for Bodie for the lady, and Gremlin for yourself. They're two of my best."

"Thank you. Very kind."

Matilda walked back through the dig. She stopped at the gouge in the root of the embankment, considered it, then turned to Ashley. "May I borrow your pick, please?"

"Sure." The girl handed over the tool and watched curiously.

Matilda knelt, scraped at the weeds matted into the mud, and held up a coin. "A Roman denarius," she said. "That's interesting. It wasn't here before lunch."

"Are there any more?" Reynolds asked.

"No. Just the one," answered Matilda, without digging any further.

"Very good!" Sweeney took the coin from Matilda's hand, pulled out a handkerchief, and cleaned off the mud. "Reign of Tiberius. Fell from some legionary's pay packet, I daresay. Into someone's collection. This has hardly been buried for two thousand years."

"I just said that," Matilda told him. She gave the pick back to Ashley. Ashley's large brown eyes gazed at her in something between bewilderment and admiration.

Matilda knew someone had been at the hole, Gareth told himself, because the weeds had been tamped down. No ESP in that.

Reynolds scuffed at the muddy spot but turned nothing up. Sweeney glared at him and popped the denarius into his pocket. Matilda watched them both, her hands fixed on her hips, her expression inscrutable.

"I allow the local lads to go coin-hunting here," Reynolds said. "What's a denarius between friends, eh? Looks as though one of them was up here during your lunch break. I'll tell them to bugger off, if you like."

"It's your property," said Sweeney, and turned back to the memorial stone.

Gareth didn't like working undercover. Too many subtleties. "I'm having a recce," he said to Matilda. "Background material. Reynolds is kind enough to lend us horses, if you'd care to join me."

"Certainly. Howard, Mr. March and I are going to look around the area — he needs background pictures for his story."

"I'll need to fetch some more film from the hotel," Gareth added.

"Carry on," called Sweeney, with a glistening smile. "We want you to do a ripping good story, don't we?"

With a wave at Gareth and Matilda, Ashley settled back down at her wall. No, Gareth thought, Matilda shouldn't speak for the girl. The girl should speak up for herself. But he well and truly understood the importance of fitting in with one's mates. So they took the mickey out of her. It happened to everyone. She was dealing with it in her own way.

Reynolds strolled across the working area and inspected each trench. "How are you getting on, Doctor? Find anything of interest? Other than the coin, of course."

"Just this memorial stele, so far." Sweeney replied.

"What's it worth?"

Matilda and Gareth went through the gate in the fence and crossed the road. Beside the bowling green, Gareth asked, "What was all that in aid of?"

"Someone planted a coin to test my skills. It was Reynolds, probably, although he managed to project proper surprise when I turned it up. If I'd been paying attention I'd have let it lie. An occupational hazard — I distract easily. I'm sorry to throw a spanner into the works."

Gareth didn't see any spanners flying about. "He isn't supposed to know you have any skills. So how could he test you?"

"Howard Sweeney would confide in a fence post, if he thought it would be impressed with his knowledge."

"Sweeney didn't put the coin there. He wasn't out of my sight during lunch, not even in the loo."

Matilda shook her head. "No, Howard didn't know that coin was there. Reynolds took him by surprise. And Howard doesn't like being taken by surprise. We'll have to be sure we're not caught between the Scylla and Charybdis of their egos."

Gareth tightened his jaw. Until he and Matilda started speaking the same language, he'd reserve judgment on the entire episode. He held the door of the hotel open for her, and they went inside.

Chapter Six

Matilda exchanged pleasantries with Clapper while Gareth ran upstairs. "Fresh film," he announced on his return, and flourished a well-worn nylon camera bag. He probably had picked up some fresh film, Matilda told herself as they went out the door. The camera bag was also the right size for a folder of crime scene reports.

Gareth threw the bag over his shoulder and they headed toward Fortuna Stud, where horses moved slowly about pastures that glowed green despite the gray skies. Gareth paused by the stone fence that lined the road. "Do you see that big chestnut with the white blaze?"

"The brownish-red one with the streak of white on his nose?"

"That's Great Caesar's Ghost, ran at the Grand National last year."

Matilda looked at the sleek, long-limbed horse. He stood masticating a mouthful of grass, eyes glazed, like an elder statesman enjoying his gin and tonic in the library of the Reform Club. "So Reynolds is well-known on the racing circuit?"

"In an insignificant sort of way. Caesar is a one-off, probably worth more than all the other horses put together."

"How'd he do in the race?"

"He came in dead last. But there was a snap in Country Life, the Queen with Reynolds several paces behind her, looking like he'd been invited specially to share a Pimm's Cup with the royals."

"He entered the Grand National for the social contacts,"

said Matilda, "not for the race itself."

"Spot on."

The gate was adorned with several horseshoes. "To keep the boggarts away," Gareth explained. "A local superstition."

"Can't have any boggarts," Matilda agreed with a smile. She was glad Sweeney wasn't along to sneer at yet another testimony of faith, misdirected or otherwise.

They strolled down a long drive, passed a posh-looking brick house, and approached the stable buildings. The place appeared very tidy, whitewashed, mortared, and swept. A faint musky odor was the only evidence that large animals inhabited the premises. Across the cobbled yard came an old man with the apple cheeks and bulbous nose of a connoisseur of the local ales. Gareth called to him. "Excuse me, we're looking for Jimmy."

"You've found him, lad."

Gareth introduced himself and Matilda, and passed on Reynolds's directions, adding, "If it's no trouble. I suppose you're still putting away Reynolds's tack and rubbing down his horse. . . ."

"No, no horses been out today." Jimmy considered them, then turned and looked at the mound of the fort. "Well, it's trouble, right enough, but I can organize something." He ambled through the wide stable door, which, Matilda saw with some surprise, was festooned with cobwebs.

She glanced at Gareth. He was gazing into the middle distance, expression unreadable. He might be checking up on whether Reynolds had been riding this morning. He was also checking up on her theory of the hidden coin. Working with him would be valuable experience, but she'd have to keep on her toes a little better than she had so far.

The door of the house opened. A woman dressed in a beige skirt and sweater stepped out and stopped dead. For a moment Matilda thought she was going to pop back inside like a cuckoo into its clock, but no, she squared her shoulders and came forward. "How do you do," she said in a thin, breathless voice. "I'm Della Reynolds. Have you come about the note?"

A promissory note? Matilda asked herself, sensing a wave of anxiety from the woman. She and Gareth hardly looked like accountants in their pants and windbreakers. Hurriedly Matilda introduced herself and her colleague and explained about the horses.

Della's pale, almost colorless, blue eyes flicked to the fort and back again. Anxiety wilted into dull resignation. "Oh, well, yes. . . . Jimmy?"

The old man glanced out the door. "I'm working fast as I can, Missus."

"Oh, well, yes. . . ." Della looked down at her beige leather pumps. Even her hair was beige, held back by little-girl barrettes. Her features seemed to be only tentative sketches on her pale face. Cosmetics wouldn't help, Matilda told herself. The living woman was less substantial than the ghost of long-dead Claudia.

The silence stretched longer and longer. Finally Gareth shifted the camera bag from one shoulder to the other and asked, "Do you hire lads from the town to muck out the stables, Mrs. Reynolds?"

"Sometimes lads" she told her feet. "Sometimes girls."

"I suppose it's convenient to have the traveler's camp just up the way. They're always willing to do the odd job."

Della didn't look up. Her flash of terror was so quick Matilda barely caught it. Still it left an after-image in her mind, like the blank spot on her retina after a flashbulb went off in her face. "Oh no," Della said, "Adrian won't allow them about the place, not at all, no."

Jimmy emerged from the stable door leading two horses, a medium-sized brown one and a tall one of light gray. "This 'ere's Gremlin," he announced, nodding at the gray. "And this 'ere's Bodie." He extended the reins of the smaller one toward Matilda.

Both animals were huge moving masses of muscle and bone. Not that either was making any aggressive moves. Bodie exhaled through rubbery nostrils, somewhat bored, while Gremlin eyed Gareth up and down and shrugged away a fly. Matilda took the proffered reins, let Bodie snuffle at her hand, and then hauled herself into the saddle. At least she knew which side to mount from, she told herself, sensing a critical dart from Jimmy and Gareth both.

"You'll look after her, won't you?" Della asked.

"Bodie's yours, isn't she?" returned Matilda. "I'll take very good care of her — I'll check her air and water and change her oil. . . ." Della stared upward, her hands clasped. "Thank you very much for letting me ride her," Matilda finished.

"You're welcome, I'm sure." Della turned and scuffed toward the house, but not without one more glance toward the fort.

Gareth levitated effortlessly onto Gremlin's broad back. The horse pranced sideways for a moment. Gareth didn't even blink, let alone grab for the saddle. "Thank you," he called toward Della's retreating figure. "Much obliged," he said to Jimmy, who tilted his cap back on his head and spat thoughtfully onto the cobbles.

Matilda decided she could live with the hornless English saddle, even though it gave her less to hold onto in an emergency. She and Bodie had to make a couple of experimental circles before they reached a compromise about the use of the reins. "It's like steering a buggy," Matilda griped good-naturedly as she turned the horse's head to follow Gareth out of the yard.

He glanced back. "You're accustomed to Western-style?"

"Understandably so," she retorted. He grinned, but said nothing.

Let him feel superior when appropriate, Matilda told herself. It would make working together easier. Although she wasn't going to play dumb just to butter him up. She tapped Bodie's flank with her toes and the horse picked up her pace, drawing even with Gremlin. Side by side they turned down a lane that ran behind the farm.

Human figures bobbed up and down along the skyline of the fort. Beyond it the rooftops of Corcester gathered like skirts around the steeple of the church. St. Michael's was more impressive from a distance than when it was hemmed in by the other buildings. In its time the Roman fort of Cornovium would have been equally impressive, masonry and tile squares stamped indelibly on the green Celtic interlace of Britain.

Ahead the rolling Cheshire farmland faded into a mistily indistinct distance. Even so Matilda could detect a darker line where earth and sky met. On a clear day Durslow Edge would look like storm clouds massing on the horizon.

"I bet," Matilda said, "Reynolds was eager to lend us the horses so he could play Lord Bountiful."

"He's right chuffed about his possessions," answered Gareth. "Probably started out poor."

"Did you catch what Della said about a note?"

"Oh yes. They're not half in debt, I reckon. Perhaps for improvements to the farm — that's a tidy bit of property and no mistake."

"Except for the cobwebs hanging in the stable."

Gareth grinned again. "Spiders eat the flies that torment the horses."

"Oh." Matilda liked Gareth's grin. It slipped the tempered personality an inch or so from its police inspector's scabbard. If they'd been out riding for pleasure he might have eventually mellowed out. But they were on a mission. "Fortuna Stud," she went on. "Fortuna was the Roman goddess of Fate. Reynolds seems to think it means 'luck'."

"I wouldn't be surprised if he gambles on his own horses. He might owe a fair amount to his turf accountant."

"He's certainly eager to turn a pound."

The lane meandered across a couple of fields and then turned to follow the river. Willows lined the banks, their branches studded with green buds. Water gurgled around the stone piers of a ruined Roman bridge. Matilda's saddle creaked, chafing gently between her thighs. She felt the spikes of her mind flatten into slow undulations. "What part of Wales are you from?" she asked Gareth.

His chin went up. "Anglesey."

"How interesting! I bet you have red-headed Druids in your ancestry."

"My father's grandparents came from Anglesey, but beyond them I don't know. My mother's from London."

"Quite a culture shock for her, I suppose."

"I suppose," he said, much too casually.

That conflict was never resolved, Matilda told herself, and did him the courtesy of diverting the subject. "I've always enjoyed Tacitus's account of the battle between the Romans and the Druids on Anglesey. Suetonius thought he had pacified Britain. Then the messengers came galloping with news of Boudicca's rebellion. He had his greatest battle still before him."

"My grandmother used to say that when the RAF built an air base at Llyn Cerrig Bach during the War, they dug up huge chains, so well-made they used them to haul heavy equipment. Until an archaeologist realized it was pre-Roman work, two thousand years old. But they had no time to do a proper excavation."

"And the Celtic port disappeared beneath the air base, sacrificed to a troubled time." Matilda ducked an overhanging branch. "You must enjoy history."

Gareth shrugged. "They made some attempt to teach it me in school. I was never keen on it."

"What a shame," Matilda murmured. He didn't react. "My son is always interested enough when we do the old sites, even though he's majoring in computer science. I'd like to see him writing archaeological programs someday, but he's more likely to be one of the first settlers on Mars."

"You have a son?"

"One about the same age as the kids back at Corcester, and about as flighty, given half the chance. Patrick Kiloran Gray. Patrick after his father, and Kiloran for me, that's my maiden name." She sensed Gareth's puzzled query. He wasn't about to ask out loud, though. "I'm a widow."

"I'm sorry," Gareth said.

Matilda replied, "So am I."

The horses' hooves plopped along the muddy path, Bodie stepping solidly, Gremlin showing a tendency to shy at the odd blowing leaf. But Gareth remained firmly in control. Reynolds had probably given him Gremlin to test his claims of horsemanship.

The river looped away to the left. The path sloped upward among rocks that pierced the grass of the fields. The red sandstone escarpment of Durslow Edge loomed ahead, veiled with the black and pale green of trees. The higher they went, the fresher grew the breeze.

"I interviewed Clapper this morning," said Gareth. "Linda left the bar with Reynolds at least once, to see his artifact collection. According to both his and Della's statements, though, he was at home the night she was killed."

Matilda nodded. "Linda told the police she knew the

whereabouts of illegal artifacts. Maybe she and Reynolds were up to something together. I wonder if he really was at home that night, or whether he intimidated Della into saying so."

"I wonder if Della has enough sense even to be intimidated."

"Dullness is often a defense — if you don't let yourself feel anything, then you won't get hurt." Gareth glanced over at her. Matilda met his look blandly. If he wanted to put that boot on himself and shout that it fitted, let him.

A sprawl of travel trailers and old trucks filled an angle of road below them, crowded on the third side by the dark, dense bristles of a mature fir plantation. Smoke shredded down the wind. A motorcycle roared away toward Macclesfield and a dog barked furiously.

"The New Age travelers?" Matilda asked.

"Yes. They were camped on the other side of the river when Linda was killed, beyond Corcester, but about the same distance from Durslow. That's where she was last seen, in their camp."

"Was she killed for her money?"

"No. She was found with twenty quid in her handbag." Gareth urged Gremlin on up the hillside, and Bodie dutifully followed.

"Della was frightened when you mentioned the travelers."

"Was she then? Someone riding a brown horse welcomed two traveler lads to the farm yesterday. She said herself Bodie is her horse, didn't she?"

"Inviting them in behind her husband's back would frighten her, I imagine. That's pretty bold. Maybe it's an attempt at rebellion. Unfortunately, that kind of desperate rebellion is so undirected it can turn dangerous."

"You're thinking she's in danger from Reynolds? He looks the sort to knock his wife about," Gareth said indignantly. "I'll call round the traveler's camp and talk to Nick, the leader, see if he knows anything. Or if he'll tell me anything."

"It might be better if you waited a few days to do that. You're supposed to be here writing about the dig."

"It's early days yet." Gareth's tone carried little conviction.

The horses scuffed up a trail between russet sandstone boulders. Aged oak trees clung to the top of the embankment.

Interspersed among them were sweet chestnut trees just starting to bloom with pink and white flowers. "Those are Mediterranean trees," Matilda offered. "Brought here by the Romans. The oaks, of course, are the Druid trees."

Gareth didn't reply. Crows spun overhead, calling harshly, and somewhere pigeons cooed. A heave and a scramble and the horses stood snorting atop Durslow Edge.

Gareth pulled a map from his bag, consulted it, and led the way across the rough and tumbled top of the Edge. The scarred mouths of old mine workings gaped in barren patches of ground. On a low promontory a few cut stones among the trees showed where a fortress had once risen. One or two vestigial roads ended in car parks littered with aluminum cans, cardboard, and plastic.

At last they came to a rocky ledge in a cliff, wide enough the horses could walk along it comfortably, and so high that Matilda felt she had only to reach out and touch the writhing limbs of the oaks below.

Beyond the trees lay the countryside. Black and white houses and black and white cows dotted the fields. Corcester was a distant jumble of squares and angles. The Jodrell Bank satellite dish made a metallic accent on the far horizon. A smudge to the northeast hinted at Manchester's factories and traffic jams. The wind whipped Matilda's hair back from her face. She thought, *there is no black and white, only shades of gray.*

Gareth dismounted gracefully and held Bodie's bridle. Matilda levered herself out of the saddle. Nerve endings in her seat and thighs woke from their stupor and protested. She walked gingerly back and forth while Gareth secured the horses to a nearby log.

A few steps along the ledge a fissure opened in the face of the cliff. From it water poured into a rough-hewn basin. Cold water, Matilda discovered when she washed her hands in it. The stone before her face was marked with myriad scratches — old writings and drawings. She could almost make out faces looking at her, noses and eyes defined from bumps in the rock. Sacrificial heads? Bride's well. Brighid's well, whether it was technically a spring or not. Coins glittered at the bottom of the basin, and the neighboring tree branches were tied with bits of cloth. Someone still believed.

Gareth knelt, cupped his hands, and drank. If he was willing to brave any microbes, so was she. Matilda drank, too. The water filled her mouth with implications of stone and dirt and green. It wasn't its chill that made her shoulders pucker. She turned around.

Ghostly leaves swayed among the branches of the oaks, thick bunches of leaves casting dense shadows that fled before the guttering light of torches. . . . The torchlight thinned and dissipated into the dim sunlight. Matilda blinked. This was a ceremonial place. The rock beneath her feet hummed with an ancient power that if not malicious, was not particularly friendly.

Gareth was looking at her. "All right then, you tell me where Linda's body was found."

Matilda extended her senses, dissolving them into space and time. Her nostrils caught a whiff of smoke. She heard voices, perhaps a man's and a woman's, too distant to make out words. The sound of the crushing blow echoed from the cliff face. The woman's short cry of surprise did not.

"There." Matilda pointed to a leaf-and-dirt covered space about thirty yards from the basin, not far from the charred remains of a bonfire.

Gareth pulled several photographs from his bag and looked at them. One of his brows arched upward. "Spot on."

Together they cleared away the debris, revealing a leveled and smoothed stone floor. Matilda crouched and laid her hand flat on the rock. It droned beneath her fingertips like a long plucked string. "I wonder why the body was left here. . . ." The thought flicked away from her grasp and she shook her head. "You didn't tell me she was hit from behind first."

"You'll have read the reports already," Gareth replied.

"No, I haven't. Watkins gave them to you, remember? When are you going to start trusting me?"

"I don't think it's a matter of trust."

"Faith, maybe? Or credulity?" She stood up, brushing off her knees, and considered the detective's closed and almost belligerent face. "I want to read the reports and look at the photos, but not here. Too much rock for footprints, I suppose. Nothing conveniently left behind by the killer, no driver's license or anything like that."

"Nothing was here save the woman's body. She was wearing denim trousers and a coat — ordinary clothing. Her handbag was lying beside her."

"She came here with someone she trusted. A man, I suppose, although surely it was too chilly that night for much sexual activity."

Gareth jerked his head back the way they had come. "Car park's just there. It's filled with tire tracks."

"But who's to say whether she had sex here?" Matilda closed her eyes. The wind keened past her ears. It had been windy that night, too. Even if Linda had had time to scream, no one would have heard her. But she hadn't been frightened soon enough to scream. Thank God for that mercy, at least.

Matilda opened her eyes and looked around the area, not at the rocks and the leaves, but through them. There, something glinted. Not like the coin at the dig — gold had a distinctive shimmer to the eye, a deep note to the ear. This was something else.

She walked to a pile of brush not far from the ashes of the fire and pulled out a small piece of paper. It was damp and dirty but still legible. "A sales slip from a store called 'The Antiquary's Corner', proprietress Celia Dunning."

"That's the shop where Linda worked." Gareth plucked the paper from her hand. "Someone bought a vase there for eight quid on March 2. Well after the murder, more's the pity. This was dropped by someone gawping at the murder scene."

"Still, isn't it interesting that it's the same shop?"

"Yes." Gareth put the paper carefully into his bag.

"Were the ashes of that bonfire there in February?" Matilda asked.

Again Gareth consulted his pictures. "Yes. You think they'd have washed away in the rains since then."

"Perhaps there's been another fire lit here since then. The goddess Brighid had a sacred fire even after she was reincarnated as St. Brigit." Gareth blinked at her. "All right, what else did Clapper tell you this morning?"

"Some local lads have put it about that the travelers are devil-worshippers."

Matilda frowned. "Some people experiment with the occult

the same way they experiment with drugs, sex, music, and anarchy. It's not a good idea to invite something into your mind, though, if you can't control it."

"You don't believe that rubbish?" Gareth demanded.

"I don't know whether I do or not. Quite a few of what we call both devils and saints today were once gods. Some of them were the gods of the same Celts who either made this ledge a place of power or who discovered the power that was already here. Whether the gods exist as independent entities or live in the depths of our own minds I can't say. They're just as powerful either way. They can be just as inspiring, and just as deadly."

Gareth turned abruptly and walked back to the horses. "It's getting on for four. We'd better be getting back."

Matilda strolled up behind him, so that when he looked back at her they were standing a handsbreadth apart. "If nothing happens at the dig, why don't you go to the traveler's encampment next week?" she suggested. "They'd tell a reporter more than they would a police officer. I'll pay a visit to Ms. Dunning in Manchester."

"You mustn't go about alone!" he protested.

"We can't hang around together all the time, people will wonder why."

"Then get Sweeney to go with you."

"We can't both leave the dig. Besides," Matilda added, "you agreed that shove on the Underground platform was probably an accident."

Gareth exhaled in frustration, his warm breath blowing across Matilda's face. She could see herself reflected in his dark eyes. The tension in his body drew every fiber of hers erect.

"Go ahead," she said. "Remind me that the murder case is yours, not mine. Tell me that you're hoping to get a promotion out of it. Point out that I'm cramping your style. And I'll tell you that you're cramping mine."

"I don't believe in second sight, Matilda."

"I'm not asking you to. I'm simply asking you to work with me, not against me. Give me a chance to prove myself to you."

He looked right and left, up and down. Then, suddenly,

he laughed. The sound burst against the cliff face, shattering the tension so decisively that Matilda sagged backward a step. "I've never thought Superintendent Forrest had a sense of humor," Gareth told her. "He must have, though, to assign us together. All right then, make a believer out of me."

"That sounds like a dare."

"It is that."

"I accept." Formally they shook hands, and shared the same rueful smile.

Gareth led the horses to the well to drink. Matilda took one last look around the ledge and across the peaceful Cheshire countryside. *Shades of gray. . . .* Perhaps Linda's quick squeak of surprise hadn't gone unheard after all. Perhaps something had been listening. Whether it had accepted the sacrifice remained to be seen. And Linda had been a sacrifice, Matilda was sure of that. Not to some half-baked occult game, but to greed.

She avoided the ignominy of having Gareth boost her onto the horse. Still, she couldn't avoid wincing when she sat down. By the time they had gone several hundred yards, though, she'd gone numb.

Matilda kept Bodie just far enough behind Gremlin that she could contemplate Gareth's chiseled profile. He sat straight-backed, guiding his horse with barely perceptible movements, radiating determination. Of all the cases he could've been given, Matilda thought, this one, with its mysteries of belief and emotion, was the most difficult for his pride to handle.

They weren't heading back down the Edge at the same place they'd climbed up. "Where are we going?" she asked.

"Shadow Moss. Didn't you say you wanted to see the place the hand was found?"

"Sure."

They left Durslow looming behind them. Twisting in her saddle, Matilda could just see the ledge behind the intricate tracery of the oak branches. It was a lap in the huge body of the Edge. A frisson of awe and fear shivered down her spine. Firmly she turned herself around.

The silver sky was darkening to charcoal. More than once a spray of rain scudded down the wind. The horses put their heads down and plodded onward. Soon they left the dirt path and emerged onto the shoulder of a narrow asphalt road that led across open heath. A signpost read "Racecourse Road."

"More horses?" Matilda asked.

"I believe the locals used to race horses here in the eighteenth century or so."

"Are there any local legends about horses?"

"Always going on about rumors and legends, aren't you?" he asked, but his tone was light.

"Yes. They're important."

Gareth didn't commit himself to agreement. They crossed the heath and plunged through a thicket of swaying birch trees, then pulled their horses to a halt. A peat-cutter rose like some antediluvian beast above black gashes in the bog. Green mosses and spikes of yellow grass lined straggling dark pools. Bumps of red rock broke through the weeds. Clouds clustered overhead, closing the horizon. If Durslow Edge was a place of power, Shadow Moss was a sad place. *As strong as death,* Matilda thought. *As melancholy as the grave.*

"It looked like this two thousand years ago," she said. "Except for the peat cutter, of course. Where was the hand found?"

"Over there." Gareth made a gesture that might have included anything from the nearest pool to the Outer Hebrides.

"And they've found the body since then. While I'm in Manchester I'll have to go see the hand and the body both."

"Why?"

"They're important, too, I think. . . ." She stopped. She would eventually prove the truth of her visions to him, but only if she kept mere impulses to herself.

"Well then," he said, "whatever you think important." He pulled Gremlin's head around. Splashes of mud sketched dark patterns on the horse's pale flanks.

The taste of the well water lingered in Matilda's mouth, making her tongue feel mossy. The raw wind cut right through her jacket. She thought longingly of the fire in the bar, of whisky, of the heavy quilt on her bed. She urged Bodie to a faster pace.

Chapter Seven

*T*he rain scudded along horizontally, like a lawn sprinkler. Sweeney raised his umbrella. Two minutes later it blew inside out. "All right then," he called, "let's pack it in."

The more muscular boys spread plastic over the raw trenches. Tucking her pick beneath her arm, Ashley helped Jennifer gather up the camera equipment and sketch books. She glanced toward the farm. The gray horse and the brown one were nowhere in sight. She wondered where Gareth and Matilda had gone, and why.

Sweeney herded the students down from the mound, across the road, and into the hotel. They left their tools in a closet just off the entry and headed upstairs.

Jason walked behind Ashley up the staircase. "Whoa, your butt's so muddy it looks like Mom needs to change your diaper," he said.

"Hey," Ashley returned, "at least I'm not leaving it in piles for everyone to step in, like some people."

Jason made a sound that might have been a laugh. Beside him Caterina smiled blankly. Bryan stopped at the top of the steps and repeated, "Yeah, like some people, whose mother's called him half a dozen times already."

"I was only joking." Jason shrugged and grinned.

"No problem," Ashley told him sweetly. She winked her thanks at Bryan — he was nice, but so, well, ordinary — and ducked into her room. Gareth was right. Don't let them smell blood.

After dinner Ashley found Gareth sitting in the bar, meditating on a pint of ale. His hair glowed a burnished bronze in the dim light. Stopping by his table she asked, "How was your ride?"

He looked up sharply, then smiled his usual cramped smile. "Quite nice, thank you, if a bit wet towards the end."

"Where did you go?"

"To the viewpoint on Durslow Edge. I needed some photos of the area."

"I took riding lessons when I was little," Ashley said. "I kept hoping my dad would buy me a pony, but then he moved out."

Matilda slowly picked her way across the room and eased herself into a chair. "Someone needs to invent a saddle that sits like an easy chair. Would you like to join us, Ashley?"

"Thanks, but I was going to look at Jennifer's sketches. She's a real artist, she drew a great picture of that memorial stone."

"Memorial stone?" Matilda asked.

"The one Sweeney and Caterina were going on about?" inquired Gareth.

"That one, yes. It was set up in front of the headquarters building, and later on someone re-used it as a building stone, that's why it was so near the surface."

Matilda's head tilted to the side like a bird eyeing a worm. "And what were the names on the stone?"

"Marcus Cornelius Felix," Ashley replied, "and his wife Claudia Sabina. Makes you wonder what they looked like, doesn't it?"

"Oh my, how obliging of Howard and Caterina," said Matilda. "Marcus and Claudia. Ground truth."

Gareth repeated, "Ground truth, eh?"

Ashley, out of her depth, backpedaled. "Well, see you later."

"See you later," Matilda told her, and Gareth said, "Cheers."

He'd smiled at her twice now, Ashley thought. He was just being polite, though. She turned, and then stopped to let Clapper squeeze through the narrow lane between tables. Behind her Gareth said, "Now you'll be telling me it was this Marcus and Claudia you saw last night."

"Yes," Matilda answered, "that's what I'm telling you. Obviously I should have told you then for you to be convinced now, but I was trying not to annoy you. Not annoying you is turning out to be a task equal to telling the tide to turn, I'm afraid."

Gareth laughed. "Just give me the evidence, Matilda. I'll sort it out."

"That's the deal, isn't it?"

Clapper edged on by. Ashley plopped down beside Jennifer. Her attention, though, was still focused behind her.

Did Matilda mean she'd seen the ghosts of the old Romans? *Yeah, right,* Ashley thought, and yet something else in her mind said, *Cool.* Whatever, Gareth must be using Matilda's experience as an angle for his story, although it was odd he'd use the word "evidence."

Wait a minute, Ashley told herself. Durslow Edge. That was where the murdered woman's body had been found. And she'd seen Gareth talking to the local policeman, hadn't she? What if he wasn't writing an article just on "Our Roman Heritage" but also one on the murder, too? That kind of story was really popular. Bookstores carried dozens of true crime books, their covers lurid in red and black. Matilda must be co-authoring or researching or something. They had to keep a book deal a secret, of course. Journalists could be really competitive.

Ashley felt obscurely pleased with her deductive abilities and promised herself not to spill the beans.

Jennifer shoved the open sketch book beneath her nose and Ashley focused. The drawing of Matilda was rough and yet energetic, capturing her wise half-smile. "That's awesome," she said. "I wish I could draw."

"Pick up a pencil and try it," Jennifer told her.

"Oh, no, I wouldn't be any good."

Clapper plunked down a pile of cardboard coasters. "That's the lady doctor herself, isn't it? She's a canny one, she is."

"Yes." Ashley glanced over her shoulder at the bronze head and the fair one bent each over its own glass, like casual strangers thrown together on a subway platform.

*B*y early Tuesday afternoon Ashley had cleared the turf

from three feet of stone wall, uncovering several courses of masonry. She shouldn't probe any deeper without permission. She stood up, stretched, and looked around for Dr. Sweeney.

A cool breeze drove clouds like gray and white meringues across the sky. One moment the fort was in shadow, the next in dazzling sunlight. Squinting, Ashley spotted Sweeney by the east entrance, giving Adrian Reynolds his daily briefing. For every step the professor took backwards, Reynolds took one forwards, so that the two men danced an awkward waltz.

Reynolds looked like a sinister parrot. His beady black eyes darted hither and thither as he spoke, checking out Matilda and Jennifer poring over a drawing of the memorial stone, and Gareth shoveling busily in Manfred's trench. When he looked at Ashley she bent over her wall again, trying to shut him out. A gynecological exam didn't probe as intimately as Reynolds' eyes.

Caterina, the uninhibited one, stood up from her crouch at the edge of Bryan's trench and waved. "Signor Doctor, see what is here!"

Reynolds beat Sweeney to her side, but Sweeney elbowed him away. "What is it, my dear?"

"Look, little bits of rock with letters on. Broken writings, you would say?"

"Yes, I would say. Used for fill. Some idiot smashed up a lovely inscription to build a sheep pen or close in a doorway. I suppose he thought he was recycling."

"Idiot," Caterina agreed. "See here: *deo,* 'to the god' — it was an altar, yes?"

Matilda materialized on Caterina's other side. Stooping, she touched the jumbled rocks as though she were reading a message in Braille. "It might say *deo invicto mytrae.* 'To the invincible god Mithras.'"

"It might," Sweeney said.

"An altar to Mithras wouldn't be unusual in a military fort," said Reynolds. "Miller thought one of those underground temples was here. They went in for carvings and such, but not much in the way of votives, gold or otherwise."

"Inscriptions are just as important as gold," Matilda told him.

Sweeney took Caterina's trowel and scraped delicately at the jumbled stones. "You're becoming quite the expert, aren't you? I'd best mind my back, you might be planning a take-over."

"Oh no, Signor Doctor." Caterina giggled. "Here, here is another bit with the letter 'M' on it."

Reynolds turned over a couple of stones and Sweeney rapped his knuckles with the trowel. "Leave the artifacts *in situ*, there's a good chap. We'll put you in the picture when we have one."

Reynolds harrumphed and sauntered off. Bryan leaned curiously over Sweeney's back. Matilda pulled herself away. "This is a real treasure trove, Howard. In the beginning was the word, right? And here be words, lots of them."

"Yes, well, we shall see, won't we?" Sweeney returned.

Gareth, Ashley saw, was taking everything in with his usual quiet efficiency. Beyond him, Jason was leaning on his shovel and frowning, watching Caterina chatter away to Sweeney as the two of them knelt cozily side by side. Yeah, she'd expect Jason to be jealous.

Matilda followed Ashley's look, then leaned closer to her. "I bet Jason's more jealous of Caterina's competence than he is of Howard. He doesn't want her to look smarter than he is."

"He sure doesn't," Ashley agreed.

With a wry smile Matilda sent Jennifer to record the new find.

This wasn't a good time to talk to Sweeney about digging deeper along the wall, Ashley told herself. No matter how closely she looked, she couldn't find any inscriptions to offer him. So she puttered away cleaning out the crevices between the stones while shadows raced overhead and horses meandered across the fields below. A red MG turned out of the farm and zoomed away toward Manchester. A slightly-built figure astride the brown horse trotted away along the same northeasterly path Matilda and Gareth had taken.

Sweeney showed the students how to take two long metal poles, cross them, and then lean a ladder against them to form a tall tripod. Jason volunteered to climb up the swaying ladder and take photos of the dig from above. "Look, no hands!" he called. Caterina kept on troweling.

Manfred fussed at Gareth for not keeping the side of the trench perpendicular. Gareth presented him with the shovel and went to poke around in the Miller expedition gully. He must've liked working solo better. After a while Ashley heard him singing under his breath. The song was "Men of Harlech," maybe. He had a very nice speaking voice, but he couldn't carry a tune in a bucket. Ashley hid her smile.

Just as Sweeney called "Quitting time!" Gareth resurfaced with a bit of harness, which he showed Matilda on the way back to the hotel.

Several of the other students headed into town for dinner. Ashley hesitated in the lobby, then told herself to forget it. Even if Gareth showed up in the next couple of minutes he wouldn't want to come with them. Shrugging, she hurried after the others, up the street and through the shadowed alley beside the church. When she popped out into the pedestrian polygon she saw them going into a fish and chips shop on the far side.

A hand seized her forearm and spun her around. She was face to face with the dark-haired traveler. "I've heard that Americans are always in a hurry," he said.

"Hey!" Ashley wrenched her arm away.

"Sorry." His grin cut dashing creases in his clean-shaven cheeks. The wind ruffled his mane of hair. He stepped back, holding his hands open and empty. "We've not been formally introduced. Nick Veliotes, at your service."

"Ashley Walraven. Not that I need any service." She glanced over her shoulder, but the other students had disappeared. They probably never noticed her following them. Plenty of other people were walking back and forth, though, and Nick didn't seem particularly threatening.

"You're working at the old Roman fort, are you?" he asked.

"Yes. The dig is part of a history course I'm taking at the University of Manchester."

"You must be very clever, to have been accepted at university."

There wasn't the least trace of sarcasm in his voice. His golden-brown eyes were fixed on her face — only her face — as though he'd never encountered anyone so interesting. He had no preconceptions about her. She could be anything to him. Maybe he could be something to her.

"American universities are easier to get into than British ones," she said. "I've really had to study since I've been here, believe me."

"I do believe you. You're not studying now that you're digging?"

"The digging is kind of like the final exam."

"So you're sitting your exams, are you? I can be of service, then, as a tutor in history and legend."

"You know history?" Ashley asked.

He laughed. "Oh yes, that I do."

Nick didn't fit what Gareth had said about the travelers — he was as well-spoken as the reporter himself. And he didn't smell bad, either. His slender body clad in nondescript army-surplus pants and sweater was boyish, but his manner was self-assured. Several necklaces dangled on his chest, an even-armed cross, a horn, a crescent moon. Ashley quelled the little voice in the back of her mind that told her in so many words why he was paying attention to her, and smiled her best sophisticated smile. "Okay, tell me about history."

"Right." Nick gestured at the church. "St. Michael's. Four-teenth century, built on the foundations of an old Saxon church, built in turn on the foundations of a Celtic temple."

"I thought the Celtic temple was beneath the fort," Ashley said.

"There was more than one here. This entire area is knit together with dragon lines, lines of power running in straight tracks across the country. We've lost a good bit of that old knowledge, mind you, though it can be found if you know where to look."

"Really? Matilda was saying something the other night about St. Michael and the dragon."

"Matilda?"

"Dr. Sweeney's second-in-command at the dig. She's Ameri-can, too, but she knows an awful lot about British stuff."

"Ah," said Nick, with a thoughtful nod. "There's a green man carved into one of the pews in the south aisle of the church. I'll show you."

Ashley found herself escorted through the churchyard with

its ranks of weathered gravestones and into the musty interior
of the building. Nick guided her from nave to transept to
chancel, their steps ringing on the floor, pointing out paintings and carvings that, he said, had pagan subtexts. He spoke
of the old spirits of wood and stone and water. He drew
parallels between the mysteries of Greek Eleusis and Welsh
Annwn. He spoke movingly on the meanings of the bull, the
buck, and the horns of an altar until Ashley grew dizzy, with
information overload and physical attraction both.

"The white horse," he concluded as they turned from yet
another shadowed recess, "is the goddess Rhiannon. Rhiannon, Keridwen, and Brighid are the three aspects of the Celtic
mother goddess, expressed in fire and water. More recently
the white horse has been the symbol of the Saxons, and of
the House of Hanover. If you've read your Homer you
remember that the horse was sacred to Poseidon. Who was
Neptune to the Romans."

He might be pulling her leg, thought Ashley. She preferred
to think he was an amiable eccentric overdosed on Robert
Graves, James Frazer, and Joseph Campbell. A scholar, even,
like Matilda and Sweeney. "The Trojan Horse," she suggested,
"and the emperor Caligula's horse that he made a sena-
tor. . . ."

"Very good! I knew you were a clever girl." Nick seized her
hand and brushed it with his lips. A shock wave of sensation
ran up her arm, exploding in the pit of her stomach. She
retrieved her hand and ducked her head to hide her glowing
face. He was piling it on pretty heavily. But how exciting to
have a handsome, intelligent man pile on anything at all.

The stained-glass windows lightened and darkened as
clouds skimmed by outside. Nick led Ashley around a complete circuit of the church and returned to the porch, where
he pointed to a wickerwork contraption hung high on the
wall next to several impressive sets of antlers. "There's the
May Day Hobby Horse, and the horns for the dance. You'll
be here for May Day, won't you?"

"Oh yes. I saw a poster about the celebration somewhere
— in the hotel, probably."

"Clapper turns a few bob from the tourists. He lays in extra
beer and five kinds of film. Like most ceremonies, the May

Day rites have lost their original meaning and become an excuse to make money."

He pushed open the doors. Ashley blinked at the rush of sunlight and fresh air and almost tripped over the hollowed stone of the step. Two crows perched on the churchyard fence. Ashley waited for Nick to rhapsodize over them, too. All he said was, "I told you I knew my history."

"I'm impressed. What college did you go to?"

"University's for posh toffs with brass. I didn't even pass my O-levels. Doesn't mean I couldn't keep on reading, though."

"Reading's free," Ashley agreed. "Is there a good library here?"

Nick chuckled at some private joke. "Yes, but it's not the public one." He ushered her through the gate, took her hand and bowed over it. He didn't offer to read her palm. Instead he kissed it again, lightly. She felt as though she were holding a handful of his warm breath. Her fingertips tingled even after he released her.

"Thank you for the — er — mythology lesson," she managed to say.

"Would you like another one? This Sunday, perhaps? I'll meet you here, four o'clock."

"Oh, er, well. . . ." Why not? She shouldn't miss a valuable learning experience just because the New Age travelers weren't on the official curriculum. A learning experience of more than one kind. "Sure. I'll meet you here on Sunday."

"Super." Nick's grin was an in-your-face dare that defied both authority and convention. Ashley couldn't help but grin back.

With a backwards wave he strolled away. Beside the ancient magpie house he passed the police constable, who shot him a suspicious glare. Nick turned with a quick, controlled dance step and made an elaborate bow. The officer huffed and walked on by.

Ashley started back toward the Green Dragon. Image and sensation cascaded through her mind. She felt as though she were going over Niagara Falls without so much as a barrel to protect her. Her mother had always insisted that her main goal in life was to protect her daughter, as though Ashley couldn't be trusted with the truth. Her mother would have huffed just like the policeman and slammed the door in Nick's face. He was too brash, too vital. Even Chris, of late, lamentable memory, was blandly self-absorbed compared to Nick.

Compared to Gareth, for that matter, Ashley thought as she rounded the corner of the hotel and almost fell over him.

The reporter was standing by the curb, talking to the slight figure on the brown horse. The horse turned its large, liquid eyes toward Ashley and shifted its weight with a clack of hoof on pavement. The colorless woman on its back stopped abruptly in mid-phrase. Gareth looked around.

"Hello," he said. "Della Reynolds, this is Ashley Walraven, one of the students. Ashley, Mrs. Reynolds."

"How do you do," said Della.

"Hello," Ashley returned breathlessly.

"I'm off," said Della to Gareth. "Call in if you'd like to see them."

"Thank you. I'll do that." With a pat on the horse's flank Gareth stood back. Della and mount trotted away toward Fortuna Stud.

Matilda walked out of the hotel. "Hello there. Was that Mrs. R.?"

"Yes." Gareth told her. "She was offering to show me Adrian's antiquities collection."

"You do want to cover private collecting in your article," replied Matilda. To Ashley she said, "You look like the cat that swallowed the canary. What have you been up to?"

"I — er — I. . . ." She didn't want to admit she'd been hanging out with one of the travelers, since Gareth so obviously disapproved of them. He just didn't understand, no reflection on him, but. . . .

Matilda smiled. "I'm prying. Never mind."

"That's all right," Ashley replied gratefully. "Have you eaten? I'm going to get a sandwich or something in the bar."

"Yes, thank you," said Gareth. "Matilda, I need you to look over my notes, make sure I have the dates correct."

"Certainly."

All three of them walked together into the hotel. There was the poster by the reception desk, just as Ashley remembered it. "Corcester May Day Fair," it read. "Traditional Festivities. Song, Dance, and Real Ale." Below the words were sketches of costumed figures that were either dancing or fleeing for their lives.

Re-enactments for the tourists, Ashley thought. Nick thought the old traditions were still viable in spite of such debasement. And why shouldn't they be? Too many time-honored customs had been swept away by the pace of the modern world. Or so her mother often said, griping about the now ubiquitous "Ms." or the way no one bothered to answer an R.S.V.P. any more. As much as Ashley liked Dr. Sweeney, she couldn't bring herself to agree with his sophisticated cynicism any more than she could agree with her mother's blind belief. Just where Nick fell between those two poles she couldn't say.

Ashley waited in the lobby until Gareth and Matilda disappeared upstairs. Matilda was considerate, intelligent, and assertive without being aggressive, she thought. A good role model, even though she probably didn't have a sex life any more.

Then there was Gareth. In spite of his red hair, he was cooler than Nick — in terms of temperature, that is. His personality, like his body, was more compact. More adult. He didn't have to try to be sexy, did he? He just was, with that hint of hidden depths. So far, though, he'd looked at Ashley like a kid sister, if that much.

Nick was trying to be sexy. He might even be a version of Jason, more surface gloss than depth. But he wasn't Jason. He was polite, he was certainly exotic, and he was definitely making a play for her. A date with him wouldn't hurt anything.

Smoothing her hair, Ashley turned toward the bar. Her hand smelled sweet and smoky, like incense. Her hand smelled like Nick. A thrill tightened the back of her neck. She didn't analyze just what kind of thrill it was.

Chapter Eight

Gareth unlocked the door and ushered Matilda inside. She noted without surprise that his tiny single room was neat as the proverbial pin — although why a pin should be neat, she didn't know. On the back corner of the dresser sat a CD player and a stack of plastic CD boxes. She titled her head to read the titles. "A Celtic Journey." "Ton Gron," "Can Gwynt Y Gorllewin," and "Blas Y Pridd." Mozart and Puccini.

Matilda sat down in a chair and closed her eyes. Her deep breaths detected the odors of soap, starched laundry, and horse. She told herself that it didn't matter that Gareth had interesting tastes in music. It didn't matter which boy had been flirting with Ashley, or that Ashley was developing a crush on Gareth. Ashley wasn't the reason Matilda was in Corcester. She was here because of antiquities looting, and because of murder.

When she opened her eyes Gareth was looking at her doubtfully. "Telepathy?"

"Just trying to sift through all the impressions I've been getting. That's what they hired me to do."

Keeping a very straight face, Gareth pulled a briefcase from beneath the bed. "How are you getting on, then? Can you prove that the statuary was stolen from here?"

"No. The looters must have cleaned out the entire cache. If they'd left an artifact, or even a broken bit of an artifact, I could compare it with the ones in Canada."

"Surely there are a lot of artifacts still at the fort."

"Oh yes. Some very interesting ones, too. But that particular set of artifacts, the statuary, had not only been made at approximately the same time and place, it had been buried together for almost two millennia, so it would all feel the same. . . ."

The corner of Gareth's mouth tucked itself in skeptically.

"If I blindfolded you," Matilda tried to explain, "and handed you two handmade wool Aran sweaters and two factory-made acrylic sweaters, you'd be able to classify them by touch, wouldn't you?"

"I suppose so. Is that what it's like, then?"

"It's about as much like that as water is like Guinness Stout."

Laughing, Gareth opened the briefcase.

"As for catching the looters who took the statuary, and keeping any more looters from taking anything," Matilda went on, "I hope I'll be able to keep one jump ahead of them. I wouldn't be surprised if Reynolds is involved."

"Clapper implied as much. Perhaps Reynolds and Linda were working together to begin with, and she double-crossed him. Now Reynolds can't admit he knows for certain the statuary came from Cornovium, because he'd be admitting he took it himself."

"Many of our leads come from one looter turning in another."

Gareth spread several file folders across the bed, spilling papers and photos. "I told you what Clapper said about the travelers."

"Devil-worshipping druggies feeding at the public trough? Or was that Reynolds's line?"

"They agree, I expect. Here are the police reports and transcripts of the interviews, if you're sure you want to see them. A murder case is hardly an art fraud case." Gareth sat back against the headboard.

"It is when the victim is apparently involved in the illegal antiquities trade." Matilda fished her reading glasses out of her shoulder bag, moved to the bed, and began to sift through the pile.

The pictures made in the morgue at Manchester were well-lighted and clearly focused. On the stainless steel tray Linda's body seemed like a cool and clinical anatomical display, nothing human. It was the photos taken at Durslow that captured the horror of her murder. Her body had lain crumpled on the leaf-strewn stone, one hand outstretched, her head twisted back at an unthinkable angle, her face turned to the indifferent sky. Dead faces had no expression, but still Matilda thought that Linda had died surprised.

She glanced through the forensic reports. The right parietal of Linda's skull had been fractured in a blunt force trauma. Her esophagus, trachea, and associated tissue had been cut with several strokes of a small but very sharp knife. Only her cervical vertebrae still connected her head to her body. Blood had soaked the back of her clothing and pooled on the stone itself. A faint stain on the basin of the spring meant that the murderer had washed his hands there. He must have gotten blood on his clothing as well. His shoes had left no prints.

"No murder weapon," Matilda said.

"The murderer took it away with him," replied Gareth. "We can say 'him', if you like."

"Just to simplify the discussion, yes, let's."

"She was bashed from behind with a rock. There were certainly enough to hand, although the investigators couldn't find any that matched the injury. He had to bash her head in first, mind you. His knife was too small to have done much damage with the first thrust. She would have been able to fight back. But there were no parry cuts to her hands and arms. There were no bruises other than the natural lividity of the body."

Matilda put down the photos. Gareth was looking past the walls of the room, visualizing the murder scene. He'd been here three days and hadn't yet solved the crime. He hadn't even found any clues, other than the receipt from the antiquities shop in Manchester. If he could have produced a solution by sheer brain power, like calculating pi to the hundredth place, he would already have the criminal behind bars.

"And she lay there for two days until she was found," Matilda picked up another printed page. "Very cold weather, that was helpful from the forensics standpoint. . . ." She looked up. "Gareth, her body was found February third. She was killed on February first. February first is Imbolc, one of the old Celtic quarter days. Now February second is St.

Brigit's day, one of those saints who used to be a god."

He cocked his brows at her. "You think that's important?"

"It might be. So might the fact that she was killed at Durslow, an ancient sacred site."

"The murderer was familiar with the area, knew the ledge was an isolated place."

"Great stretches of countryside are isolated, especially in the Peak District east of here."

"Are we going back to the devil-worshipping nutters, then, with Linda as some sort of sacrifice?"

Matilda shook her head. "Rumors of evil conspiracies are no more than public paranoia. Satanists only prowl the streets looking for innocent victims in TV movies-of-the week, not in real life. One of the few genuine cases I've ever heard of was on the Mexican border several years ago. The leader of that cult was playing terrible games to impress his followers. You see the same thing happen in the odd Christian cult, unfortunately. It's a variety of mental pollution."

"Is there such a thing as authentic ritual?"

"Not to mention real magic? Yes, there is. In the world's great religions you can trace an unbroken ceremonial path back for thousands of years. For modern pagan ritual, though — the varieties are not at all synonymous — the best you can do is combine educated guesses with a lot of imagination. Which is why it probably doesn't matter that the ancient Celts would occasionally sacrifice a human being not on Imbolc but on Beltane, May first — the progenitor of Corcester's happy little festival."

"Would a group of nutters care about Imbolc or Beltane? They can make up the rules as they go along, just like the yobs in Mexico."

"Exactly. That's our variable in the case. If there's some kind of relationship between Linda's death and the rumors of devil-worship, there might be a relationship between the rumors and the stolen antiquities."

"That's a bit round the houses," protested Gareth.

Matilda sighed. "The Maypole and the horn dances and the hobby horses that look like children's games on the poster downstairs once had all the gravity, say, of Holy Communion to us."

"I'm an atheist," Gareth said.

"Even so, you're not likely to trash out a church, are you?"

"No. What's your point?"

"That just because you don't believe in something yourself doesn't mean that it doesn't matter. Whether something is real or not doesn't matter, as long as a person believes it's real and acts on his beliefs."

"That's as may be, but I'll carry on believing in fakes and phonies, myself."

"Fine," Matilda said with a smile.

Gareth shifted his weight. The bedsprings creaked and the piles of paper slipped sideways. Voices rose and fell in the hall outside. A phone rang. A door slammed. "The case might be a perfectly simple one," he said. "Linda was a confederate of Reynolds, he found out she was planning to grass on him, so he killed her. I'll have a go at Della, see if I can break his alibi."

"Be careful. She was very nervous talking to you tonight, and yet there was something — well — hungry there as well. She's a desperate woman."

"Super," he groaned.

Matilda leafed through the transcripts. The police had interviewed Adrian and Della Reynolds and the stable man Jimmy. They had talked to various travelers who identified themselves only as Bob, Sanjay, Shirl, Nick, Gordon and DeDe — none of whom had ever heard of Linda Burkett. The truck driver boyfriend had an alibi. Celia Dunning had been shocked at the entire distasteful business. Linda's relatives had been stunned into incoherence.

At last Matilda bundled everything into a pile. "Worse than a crossword puzzle, isn't it? You don't know what is a clue and what isn't. All you know is that you don't have all the clues."

"Well I won't say which one of us hasn't a clue," Gareth responded, but he grinned as he spoke.

Matilda whacked his thigh with a sheaf of papers. "I'll talk to Ms. Dunning in Manchester."

"That leaves me to the travelers and to Della. In the future one or the other of us should always be here, don't you think?"

"Yes." Matilda tucked her glasses away, stood and stretched. "Good night. Don't dream of gods, demons, and forensics."

"I rarely dream." Gareth got up and opened the door for her. "Be sure to ask Dunning about the stolen statuary as well."

Matilda looked at him pityingly.

He smiled. "Good night then," he said, and closed the door.

*B*y early Wednesday afternoon, Matilda realized she wasn't going to get away that day. The spades and trowels of the students were turning up enough bits of pottery, metal, and stone to keep both her and Howard busy. Jennifer enlisted Courtney and Ashley to make preliminary drawings. Courtney dashed off a pile of indecipherable sketches. Ashley labored with her tongue clamped between her lips and after an hour's work produced one smudged drawing of a six-sided die.

"I think that one's about ready for the Tate Gallery," Matilda told her.

Ashley laughed, easing the lines of concentration in her face.

Caterina was moving right along with the pieces of inscription. Her knowing some Latin helped, of course, as Sweeney told Reynolds during the owner's tour of inspection. "She's quite a bright little thing for a girl," he went on, "but at the limit of her competence, I'm afraid."

Matilda rolled her eyes upward, hoping Caterina's Latin was better than her English. "This is treasure, yes?" the girl asked. *"Il tresoro magnifico."*

"Better than gold," Matilda told her, and added with a glance at Reynolds, "Although some parties wouldn't think so."

By quitting time the assembled letters read *M Cornel Felix* and *deo invicto mytrae.* So Marcus had dedicated a Mithraeum, Matilda thought. That fit in with the bits of a tall votive lamp Gareth had unearthed yesterday. She climbed down the collapsed sides of the Miller trench, avoiding projecting rounds of column drum, to see what he'd found today.

Gareth stood, dirty hands on dirty hips, surveying his work. Foundations emerged from the damp soil at his feet, the apsidal end of an apparently narrow building not much larger than a camper-trailer.

Matilda touched the damp stone of the apse. Men's voices echoed in the rock. Torches flickered in her mind's eye. She heard the bellowing of a bull and smelled the sharp coppery odor of blood. A firm believer in coincidences, she nodded and said, "This is the Mithraeum. It was an underground chamber in the first century, that's why it's so deep now. Any fragments of a statue of a young man killing a bull?"

"Not yet." Gareth glanced over his shoulder. Ashley was the person closest to them, and she was several paces away at the top of the trench. Even so he lowered his voice. "Scientific inquiry is all to the good, and this is quite interesting and all, but I don't feel as though I'm doing my job mucking about here."

"Keep at it until you uncover something of value to use as bait for the looters."

"Treasure trove? Here?"

"Those column drums in the side of the trench suggest that this chamber was beside and below the main temple. The Romans always kept their payroll money in a cellar below the headquarters. Maybe they kept. . . ." She stopped, suddenly aware that her voice was speaking without the guidance of conscious thought. "Sorry. I just went into Delphic oracle mode. Suffice to say there's something here."

"And I'll know it when I find it, eh?" Gareth asked.

"Oh yes, you will."

Ashley leaned over the lip of the gully. "Everybody's going back to the hotel, and Dr. Sweeney says it's his shout for the drinks. Are you coming?"

Gareth scrambled wordlessly upward, returned Ashley's smile, and walked off. Matilda closed her mind to the long dead voices, and she, too, climbed back into the twentieth century.

*C*enturies of human touch had shaped the land with fields, hedgerows, and thickets of trees. Buildings nestled in folds of green. Roads stitched fences and streams into one multi-textured garment. Matilda stood beside her car and threw her senses onto the wind. She drifted with the clouds through a blue morning sky, flirted with daffodils and budding leaves, rode the wings of sea gulls that swooped down upon a tractor and plow. Her toes wiggled in the cool earth turned by the blade and her nostrils filled with its scent.

At last she reclaimed her perceptions. A chilly wind ruffled her hair. The tractor was so far away she could barely hear the noise of its engine. The gulls were wheeling white shapes behind it.

Matilda climbed back into the car, turned toward Manchester, and let herself think about the case.

There was only the one case, she was sure of that. It was like two skeins of yarn tangled together. When she pulled on a red thread of one, it tightened around a golden thread of the other. Dark strands ran through both, the ledge at Durslow and the severed hand from Shadow Moss, rumors of ancient gods and the passions of long-dead Romans. A knot in those threads had brought Linda Burkett to her death. A knot tied by Adrian Reynolds, perhaps, or by one or more travelers, or even by guileless townspeople such as Clapper, whose bar was information central.

All too soon the romantic country road fed into the maze of highway exchanges around Manchester, going from a man-molded landscape to a man-dominated one. Driving on the left made the interchanges mirror-images of the ones back home. Matilda concentrated on each turn until she arrived at the University, where she found and introduced herself to Ted Ionescu, one of Howard Sweeney's acolytes.

"Ah yes," he said, ejecting each word through prominent front teeth. "The American lady professor."

"Real professors being British and male?" Matilda inquired.

Ionescu's glasses glinted blankly. "Sorry?"

"I'd like to see the body and the hand from Shadow Moss, please."

"Oh-er. . . ." He opened and shut his mouth. "Very good. This way."

He was just the kind of assistant Howard would choose, Matilda thought, intelligent enough to make his boss look good, nervous enough to be easily intimidated, with too little personality to be competition. She followed Ionescu into a warren of offices and stopped dead beside a display case.

Gold votives gleamed next to carefully mended bowls and platters of Samian ware. An amphora leaned in the corner. Tiny black symbols crawled across crumpled and stained slivers of wood, rare examples of Latin cursive writing. "Are these the letters Howard wrote about in *Letters from Roman Britain?*" Matilda asked.

"Yes," Ionescu replied, "these are the originals. Or some of them, rather. He's saving the rest for another book. Of course he's very busy with other work just now."

"He has a finger in every pot, doesn't he?" Matilda allowed herself to be hurried along.

They emerged in a windowless room whose stainless steel ambiance reminded her of the morgue photos of Linda Burkett. But this room smelled more of disinfectant and formaldehyde than of raw mortality. Here death's sting was blunted, and the grave's victory made academic.

Ionescu brought two boxes from a refrigerated room, placed them on a bench, and removed the lids. He made the gesture of a maitre d' indicating the best table in the house. "There you are."

"Thank you." Matilda bent over the smaller box.

The hand was delicately molded, the nails smooth, the flesh stained brown. It rested palm upward, fingers gently curved. Matilda was reminded of Linda's hand, lying mute and suppliant on Durslow's vibrant rock. This hand, though, had come from the Moss. If Durslow was the Earth's bony brow, then the Moss was its throat.

Matilda barely kept herself from reaching across time and clasping the severed hand in her own. "What have you learned?" she asked.

"It's female," Ionescu replied. "First century A.D., probably. The calluses on thumb and forefinger indicate that she worked a spindle, making yarn. The hand fits the body perfectly."

A spindle? With a nod toward the infinite patterns of existence, Matilda touched the ancient spindle in her pocket and looked into the other box. The headless body did not have the compelling humanity of the hand. Its bones had dissolved over the centuries, and the flesh had become leather. Now it resembled a squashed brown satchel, with the arms and stumps of legs as straps. Its odor reminded Matilda of sad dark pools in an antediluvian bog.

"She was in her twenties," said Ionescu, "healthy if fine-boned for a Celt. Her stomach was empty except for a bit of baked and burned barley-cake. A ritual last meal, Dr. Sweeney thinks. We could tell by the smoothness of the cuts about the neck that she'd been deliberately decapitated, after having been bashed from behind. And there's a cord, a garrote, well up beneath her chin. . . ." He stopped dead. His pale skin went faintly green. "Oh bloody hell, I wasn't supposed to tell about that, Sweeney will have my own head, right enough."

"I won't tell him," Matilda said soothingly. "So her head turned up, too? When?"

"Three weeks ago, at the beginning of the month. Dr. Sweeney didn't have time to study it properly before he went off to the dig."

"May I see it, please?"

Ionescu looked around nervously, as though expecting Sweeney to leap out of a filing cabinet and crow, "Caught you!" Sucking on his teeth, he shuffled off to the storeroom and returned with another box.

The woman's head, too, was stained a deep brown. Her features had collapsed, making her grimace — although not in pain, Matilda thought, but in ecstasy. Long strands of hair colored red from the peat still clung to her scalp. As Ionescu had pointed out, her skull had been crushed from behind.

Squinting, Matilda could just make out the cord that was twisted around the severed neck. The furrow caused by the ligature didn't curve upward in the back, so it wasn't a noose. Someone had thrust a stick through the knot at the base of her skull and turned it, tightening the cord and choking the life from the hopefully unconscious woman.

"Howard's right," Matilda said. "She was a ritual sacrifice, killed three ways and given to the bog. Are there local legends about Shadow Moss?"

Ionescu blinked at her, thinking she'd changed subjects in mid-paragraph. "Legends? I'm a scientist."

Matilda desisted. She could get that type of reaction from Gareth. She spent another few moments looking from hand to body to head and back. The human shell, torn from its earthy womb, was drained of feeling. She sensed only that the woman had gone willingly to her death, surrendering her soul to the Otherworld without a backward look. The Druids had preached the immortality of the soul. The woman had believed in eternity. And here she lay, her hand not a relic of dead time but a message from a living past.

"Thank you," Matilda said. "I'll find my way out."

Musing on humankind's perverse taste for death, Matilda drove further into the city and left her car in the Burley Arcade car park. The Victorian wrought-iron and glass building brought a smile to her lips. There was not a straight line in all the polished exuberance of the place. The Antiquary's Corner occupied a space on the second floor, its windows presenting tasteful oddments of gold and porcelain as befit an exclusive shop in an exclusive neighborhood.

Matilda stepped inside. Baskets of soaps and potions exuded a rich floral scent that wiped away the odor of formaldehyde still clinging to her sinuses. A Chopin etude wafted from hidden speakers. Royal Doulton and Waterford lay temptingly to hand. She put her hands in her pockets.

The artifacts inside a row of glass-fronted cabinets seemed almost shabby. Matilda identified a bronze Saxon brooch, several Roman oil lamps, a glass vial, clay votive figures, an ivory crucifix, and a scattering of verdigris-encrusted coins that Dunning had been wise enough not to pretty up. Discreet white cards with prices stood before each item. Matilda winced.

A woman emerged from the rear of the shop. Her perfectly made-up face was crowned by a pouf of white hair. Her lavender suit was a designer model, tailored to her sylph-like figure. Her smile was gracious but cool. She'd already sized up Matilda, in her denim skirt and bulky sweater, as a lump of coal. "May I help you?"

"Mrs. Dunning? I'm Dr. Matilda Gray. I'm working with Howard Sweeney at the excavations at Corcester."

"I'm afraid I'm not acquainted with Dr. Sweeney."

"But you know he's a Ph.D."

Celia's smile stiffened. "As an antiquities dealer it behooves me to know who the experts are."

From the back of the shop stepped a girl no older than Ashley. In fact, she looked like a thin, brunette Ashley gone to seed. Her lipsticked mouth was turned down in a pout. She carried a stack of cardboard boxes and a roll of brown paper.

Celia turned toward her. "Make sure the receipt in the box matches the mailing label, Emma. If you send the wrong item to the wrong place again, I'll dock the return postage from your pay."

Emma bobbed up and down. "Yes, ma'am. Very good, ma'am." It didn't take psychic skills to catch the sarcasm in the girl's voice.

Celia turned back to Matilda. "What can I do for you, Dr. Gray?"

"I've been involved with a case or two of antiquities looting back in the States. I'm interviewing dealers here in Britain to see how they handle the situation. Which can sometimes lead to murder, I hear. Your own assistant. . . ." Matilda paused delicately.

"Dreadful business, that," Celia said. "Nothing to do with me, though. I don't deal in stolen antiquities. I buy only from the legal owner after he's completed the proper paperwork. I sell only those things for which I can obtain a proper expertise."

"And that's why your prices are so high?"

"Yes. Authenticity comes dear."

"Do you solicit the owners," Matilda went on, "or do they come to you?"

"I'm a well-known legitimate dealer. I don't have to — solicit."

And yet Linda, Celia's employee, had been soliciting Reynolds. Had Linda been working for herself? Matilda wondered. Or was Celia playing her cards very close to her fashionable lavender chest? A falling-out among thieves often led to murder. . . . The woman was impossible to read. Matilda felt as though she were facing the ice-wall of a glacier. The tip of her nose was growing cold.

"It's a shame you couldn't sell Adrian Reynolds' statuary for him," she essayed. "But the looters got there first. Fortunately the statuary turned up safe in Canada."

"Adrian Reynolds?" Celia asked.

"He owns the land in Corcester where the site of Cornovium is located. Surely you've heard of the stolen Romano-British statuary."

"Not at all," said Celia. She took two steps forward.

Matilda didn't retreat. "I imagine it was smuggled out of the country with forged papers. Pity, isn't it? If people refused to buy antiquities then the looters would have no market. A lot of sites would be saved. Antiquities belong in museums."

"No museum can afford to buy every antiquity that appears," said Celia. "Honest people who buy well-attested artifacts save them from destruction by the ignorant. Even artifacts that go to museums are likely to be bundled into a dusty corner. Private owners have the resources to properly appreciate our cultural heritage."

So that was her rationale, Matilda thought. And yet she had no reason to believe Celia guilty of anything underhanded, let alone murder. Matilda simply didn't trust people who had no emotions.

Emma rustled brown paper and gazed out at the two women from beneath penciled brows. A well-dressed couple strolled into the shop and starting inspecting the Waterford, exchanging comments in French. Celia's nostrils flared. "Please excuse me, Dr. Gray." She didn't wait for Matilda to respond. She advanced on the customers murmuring obsequious French.

And merde to you too, Matilda thought at the woman. She turned toward Emma and smiled.

Emma smiled tentatively back.

"Emma," snapped Celia. "Bring out the Edinburgh Thistle champagne flutes."

Shrugging, Matilda left the shop and, after a bit of window-browsing, Borley Arcade. She should turn Gareth loose on Emma — after separating her from the Snow Queen.

It was well past noon, and she was getting a headache. Matilda walked past a crowded pizza pub and a beef carvery and within a couple of blocks found a Greek restaurant tucked into the ground floor of an old brick office building. The posters of olive trees and ancient temples in the windows were curled and faded. The place had been there a while. Above the posters was painted the legend, "Acropolis Cafe. Constantine Veliotes, owner and manager."

She found a booth by the window and ordered a vegetable plate from the solitary waiter. From Mr. Veliotes himself, she corrected, when he rushed from the swinging door of the kitchen to the cash register and started making change for a departing customer.

Family photographs filled the wall behind the counter. Matilda traced the owner from a slender dark-haired youth with a fierce black moustache to his present incarnation, a man broadened by the inexorable pull of time and gravity, both head and facial hair dulled to gray. The woman who stood with him holding a baby in the oldest picture never reappeared, although the baby apparently grew into a handsome young man with a 200-watt movie-star smile. An even-armed Greek cross dangled from a photo of him standing before the shiny facade of Borley Arcade.

"Is that your son?" Matilda asked Veliotes when he set a bowl of lentil soup before her.

The man's burst of sorrow, anger, and fear almost gagged her. "I have no son," he said. "No son, no longer."

"I'm sorry." Matilda gulped and stared down into the soup bowl. That was interesting. Perhaps the wife had died. Perhaps the son had, too. Or was in prison. . . . Well, he was certainly estranged from his father. She sipped at the soup and told herself to mind her own business, which was already booming.

She hurried through her lunch, her appetite no longer quite so keen. While the dolmas, falafel, and tabouli were delectable they seemed to taste very faintly of ashes.

Soon she was out of the city and back on the country road. The afternoon darkened as black clouds crowded up the western sky. Gusts of wind bent the trees shuddering toward the east. The first raindrops splattered on the windshield as

Matilda passed the lay-by where she'd stopped that morning. A good thing she'd taken the opportunity to empty her mind. Now it was teeming. Her thoughts jostled each other like shoppers at a sale searching for items that fit.

Rain poured on the roof of the car, streamed down the windshield, swished around the tires. The countryside seemed to melt, its colors running. Matilda slowed. The road had no shoulders — she couldn't stop. She crawled around one bend and then another. To her left the land fell away into a silvery-green blur. A bus approached in the right, inside, lane.

Her windshield wipers sliced the scene into slivers of time. She saw the bow wave ahead of the bus's tires. She saw water spewing from its hood and roof. Only one wiper flopped back and forth on its streaming windshield. The bus's radiator loomed directly before her, sodden insects caught in its teeth.

She wrenched her steering wheel, turning the car toward the side of the road. A metal barrier stood where a shoulder should have been. Beyond that was nothing but flooded air.

Her tires skidded. The left side of her car screeched along the barrier. The bus grated along the other side.

And then, suddenly, the road before her was clear, a drenched strip of black tarmac lined with nettles. She braked, lightly, and looked in all her mirrors. The dark blur of the bus was gone. After the squeal of metal on metal the sound of the rain seemed soft and soothing.

It was at least a mile before Matilda started breathing again, two before she blinked, three before she loosened her white-knuckled grip of the steering wheel.

She drove on into Corcester by rote, thinking nothing, feeling nothing except the ebb of adrenalin from her body. The rain slowed and stopped, and a Jacob's ladder of sunshine broke through a rift in the clouds.

The clouds had burst in Corcester, too, she saw as she pulled into the parking lot beside the hotel. The gutters ran full and the flowers in the gardens across the way were drooping, beaten down by the rain. Sweeney had no doubt rushed all the students inside. The green mound of the fort gleamed pristinely. She hoped the trenches hadn't collapsed.

Matilda crawled from the car. She shut and locked the door and put the keys in her bag. Her knees were trembling. Slowly she walked across the street toward the dig.

Someone came out of the hotel behind her. Gareth. He had been waiting for her.

The fort was silent, its long grasses and the plastic sheets over the trenches rippling in the wind. Transparent human shapes moved among the ancient stones. Maybe Gareth would call them corpse candles.

Matilda passed the bowling green and skirted a puddle in the depression beneath the gate. The grass squeaked wetly beneath her feet. She felt as thin as the shapes before her, scraped like vellum, ready for a new message. Reaching into her pocket, she grasped the spindle.

The room that materialized in her mind's eye wasn't defined as clearly in the daylight as it had been at night. Still Matilda saw implications of furniture and window shutters. Marcus reclined on a couch, not comfortably but warily, as though expecting a centurion to call him to action at any moment. And yet he was dressed in a simple tunic and cloak. He wasn't on duty. He was watching Branwen spinning.

The thread spun between her thumb and forefinger and the spindle danced. Marcus rose from the couch. Slowly, his face set in a grimace of pain, he walked to Branwen's side. He raised his hand, palm up, fingers curved, and stroked her thick plait of red hair where it lay across her shoulder.

Her hand clasped the spindle, stopping it. She looked up.

He touched her cheek, and bent over her, and her lips parted for his. . . .

"Matilda!"

The image blinked out, snatched into another dimension.

"Matilda!" Gareth grasped her arms and shook her. "Are you all right? What happened to your car? Did you have a crash?"

"The hair on the severed head," Matilda said, "isn't red because of the peat. It was red in life. In her life. . . ." She started coughing as though she'd swallowed the wrong way, even though she had no memory of swallowing at all.

Gareth put his arm around her shoulders and guided her through the wet grass back into what he fondly believed, no doubt, to be reality.

Chapter Nine

*A*t first Gareth suspected that Matilda was leaning against him more to complete the scenario than because her knees had gone wonky. *She'd seen the ghosts again, eh? Pull the other one!*

She wasn't faking. Her face was stretched tight, so pale it seemed translucent in the thin evening light, and her blue eyes were dull as the overcast sky. Judging by the scraped sides of her car she'd had much too close an encounter with another vehicle on her way back from Manchester. He had the queasy feeling the encounter hadn't been an accident. He should never have let her go alone.

Ashley, Courtney, and Jennifer came bounding down the staircase as Gareth and Matilda plodded up. They gathered round, cooing like pigeons in St. James's park. "She's all right," Gareth insisted, "she had a bit of a scare on the road, a cup of tea and some sandwiches would be lovely, Ashley, if you'd see to it. . . ."

The girls swept on down the staircase and across the lobby, Ashley throwing a nervous glance back over her shoulder.

"A bit of a scare on the road." Matilda's shudder of self-possession made a seismic wave in Gareth's arm. He loosened his grip.

Her room was number 7, between 15 and 2. She fished her key out of her bag and after three tries got it into the lock. Gareth stepped inside and turned on all the lights. Her room was much nicer than his, with a four-poster bed and a bay window containing two chairs and a table. No one was hiding beneath the bed or in the wardrobe or adjoining bathroom.

Neat rows of personal items, a few lotions and a lot of books, emitted an aroma that reminded him of a summer's afternoon spent reading in a rose garden. Beside the bed sat a photograph of a fair-haired young man with his mother's Mona Lisa smile.

Matilda sat down, folded her hands in her lap, and closed her eyes. Through the window behind her Gareth saw the turf billows of the fort looming dimly through the dusk. Two people were walking about the excavation. Quite corporeal people, thank you, a man and a woman, probably Jason and Caterina. Gareth pulled the curtains shut.

"The incident in the London Underground might have been an accident," Matilda said. "So might the incident on the road this afternoon. But you can only stretch coincidence so far. Then it becomes deliberate action."

"The killer must want you out of the way, right enough, to have another go at you." Shaking his head, Gareth sat down and pulled out his notebook.

Matilda opened her eyes. Their blue was once again breaking through the clouds. "It was on that high, narrow stretch of road just before Wormsley. It was raining torrents. I had my lights on. There was a bus in the inside lane. It might have skidded, I suppose. Whatever, it almost forced me over the edge."

"There's a guard rail, is there?"

"A very sturdy one, thank goodness."

"Describe the bus."

"I only caught a glimpse of it. An older model, I think, with the engine forward of the body. A radiator full of bugs. Only one windshield wiper was working, the one. . . . No, it was the one on the driver's side. He could see out."

"Were the bus's headlamps switched on?"

"No. It seemed to spring out of the rain, coming straight at me."

"Did you sense anything?" Gareth couldn't believe he asked that. But whilst she might have copped a peek at the Burkett reports before their visit to Durslow Edge, she had yet to mess him about with crystal balls, tarot cards, and ectoplasm. Her *common* sense covered a multitude of sins.

"Yes, I sensed it was going to kill me. . . ." Matilda frowned.

"No, now that you mention it, I didn't sense anything beyond my own emotions. If it had been an accident you'd think the bus driver would have been surprised and scared as well."

Gareth duly noted that in his book, with a question mark. "Who knew you'd be on the road today?"

"Half the people at the dig, to begin with. I was talking to Clapper over breakfast. Reynolds saw me leaving. Ionescu at the University. Celia Dunning and her assistant. The man in the restaurant where I ate lunch. There wasn't any reason to keep my movements secret, even if I wasn't being entirely honest about my motives."

"Stick as close to the truth as possible," agreed Gareth. "It makes the — er — distortions easier to remember."

Matilda didn't manage a laugh, but her chuckle sounded almost human.

Gareth realized that the light tap-tap-tap he'd been half-hearing was someone knocking at the door. He hurried across the room. Ashley stood outside, both hands laden with a tray, tapping at the door with her foot. He wondered what, if anything, she'd overheard. They hadn't been talking loudly, though, and the clash and clatter of the dining room echoed up the stairwell.

Ashley set the tray on the table. "There's tea and everything, and Mr. Clapper made you some tomato and cheese sandwiches. He says he's sorry to hear, quote, you aren't quite the ticket, and he hopes the rozzers tear strips off the clot what did it. Unquote. Bryan says it looks like two diesel engines tried to make a sandwich out of your car. Are you all right?"

"Yes, thank you. It was just a fender-bender in the rain."

"Sometimes it can be scarier afterward than during." Ashley poured a cup of tea and handed it to Matilda.

"Thank you," Gareth said, and tried to urge Ashley on her way with his most charming smile.

Her return smile was oddly glazed. She sidled toward the door. "Oh — er — Mr. Clapper called P.C. Watkins and told him about the accident and he said he'd come by later on and make out a report. And Manfred went to tell Dr. Sweeney, but he and Caterina are checking the trenches for mud. We'll make sure he knows."

Gareth grimaced. He could hardly debrief Matilda in the

midst of a circus.

The tea was drawing the color back into her cheeks. Matilda settled back in her chair like a queen awaiting an audience. "I appreciate your help, Ashley. You're very efficient."

"I'll go wait for P.C. Watkins and show him the way up here." Ashley and her blond ponytail whisked away.

She was a pretty little thing, after all. Gareth shut the door and turned back to Matilda. "Tell me about the rest of your day."

"Not much to tell. First I went to the university. Sweeney's assistant Ionescu — my son would call him a geek — showed me the hand and the body. And the head, which just turned up, but we're not supposed to know about that."

The last things Gareth wanted to know about were body parts belonging to the uncanny hand. "Sweeney's keeping it under wraps, is he?"

"So he can present it with an academic dog and pony show after the dig, no doubt. He doesn't realize it has any significance for the dig itself."

"Is that what you were going on about tonight?"

"Yes. The hand belonged to a Celtic woman who was given to the commander of Cornovium in its early days. That he *was* the commander then is proved by the stele. What I don't know yet is why she died as she did." Matilda ate half a sandwich. The lines in her face began to ease.

Gareth nodded, committing himself to nothing. "And you talked to Celia Dunning?"

"If you can call it talking. She makes you look positively loquacious."

"Excuse me?"

This time Matilda managed a dry laugh. "I tried to start a conversation about collecting, looting, and dealing. I even said something about Linda's murder, which she shrugged away. Dunning claims she does everything legally, and that it's better to have artifacts appreciated by collectors than neglected or destroyed. Which is a debatable point, not that we actually debated it. You might make more headway with her by flashing your warrant card, but I doubt it. We should tackle the clerk. Dunning tyrannizes her and she resents it." Matilda ate the other sandwich half. "I can't see Dunning dirtying her shoes at Durslow, let alone being so careless as to drop a receipt. And logically it's the person who bought the vase who dropped the receipt. They got out of Dunning's shop for only eight pounds. That's quite a feat."

Gareth wrote "Dunning — assistant." "Did you catch the girl's name?"

"Emma."

"Emma. Now that's interesting. Clapper mentioned a local girl named Emma who was involved with the travelers. He said she was working in a posh shop in Manchester."

"Even if it is the same girl, it might be only coincidence. . . ."

"Deliberate action," Gareth reminded her. "We know that Linda Burkett knew the whereabouts of illegal antiquities. Were they in Dunning's collection? In Reynolds's? Is Reynolds using the travelers to help him dig or to smuggle artifacts? If we could make a connection between the travelers and Dunning. . . ."

"While conspiracy theories are entertaining, the simplest explanation is usually the right one. Besides," Matilda added with a grin, "Dunning would douse any travelers in sheep dip before letting them across her threshold."

Gareth shut his book. Not only was she right, her mild attitude didn't even give him the satisfaction of being annoyed with her rightness.

The new knock on the door was a firm one. Gareth admitted Ashley and Watkins, who tucked his hat beneath his arm and whipped out his notebook. "I had a look at your car, Mrs. Gray. What happened?"

Matilda told him. If Ashley hadn't been hovering solicitously over the tea tray she might have ventured into possibilities and motivations, but as it was she kept to a strictly factual version of events.

At last Watkins put his pen back in his pocket. "I'll have the lads on the lookout for a bunged-up bus — it had to have scraped a good bit of red paint from your car."

"It's probably miles from here by this time," said Gareth.

"That's as may be. But them travelers go about in clapped-out buses and vans. It was an older model vehicle, you said, Mrs. Gray? And them travelers, they're all nutters, probably driving drunk or worse."

Ashley fumbled the cup and saucer and they cracked together. Matilda's eyes snapped from Watkins to Ashley like headlamp switching from low to high beam. The girl was wearing a bland expression, and Gareth couldn't see any reason for Matilda's sudden interest. "I'll take these things downstairs now," the girl said, "unless you need something else?"

"No, thank you," said Matilda. "I appreciate your help."

When Watkins opened the door for Ashley and the tray, Howard Sweeney's plummy voice wafted down the corridor, ". . . women drivers . . ." He patted Ashley's shoulder as he swept into the room. "Matilda, my dear, I hear you had a close call. Are you all right?"

Ashley disappeared. Matilda sighed. "I'm developing a distinct streak of paranoia, but other than that I'm fine, thank you."

"I'm off," Watkins said. "Don't worry yourself none, the lads and I are watching over the dig." He tapped his nose significantly.

"Thank you, Constable," said Sweeney. And, as Watkins shut the door behind him, "Mr. March — Inspector — are you any farther in your inquiries?"

"I'm not at liberty to say," Gareth replied, hoping the standard refrain would conceal his lack of progress.

Matilda rested her head against the back of the chair and rubbed her eyes. "Do you know Celia Dunning in Manchester, Howard?"

"The trout with the souvenir shop in Borley Arcade? I don't believe we've met. She's very small beer when it comes to antiquities. Hardly a threat to us."

"Who is a threat to us? Reynolds?"

Sweeney laughed. "Half of his vaunted collection consists of forgeries. The other half reeks of clandestine digging and forged expertises. That's one reason I chose Corcester for our little venture. The man's had free rein with the place much too long."

That wasn't anything Gareth didn't already suspect. "Do you think Reynolds is capable of murder?"

"Hard to say, isn't it?" Sweeney replied. "That sort talks a good show, but often falls short when it comes time for action. Seems to me, though, he's doing his best to cast suspicion on the travelers."

"Very convenient," murmured Matilda, "to have the travelers to blame for everything from murder to tooth decay."

"Must dash," said Sweeney, "I'm meeting with my group leaders."

"Have you made Caterina a group leader yet?" Matilda asked.

"Whatever for?" Sweeney disappeared out the door.

Gareth remembered the first time a female Chief Inspector had been put in charge of a murder case. Some of the lads had acted as though she had them by the balls. In his opinion, she herself had the balls for the job, and that was that. Now it wasn't Caterina but Matilda who had. . . . Well, never mind.

Matilda shut her eyes and wilted even further into the chair. The best thing he could do for her was leave her alone. "Good night," he said quietly.

She pried open an eyelid and managed a wan smile. "Good night."

Gareth waited outside the door until he heard her turn the key in the lock. There wasn't much else he could do – he could hardly move into her room with her. He set off down the hall with his teeth gritted so tightly his jaw ached. She'd insisted on going off on her own, true, but he shouldn't have let down his guard. Maybe she'd learned her lesson.

He didn't slam the door of his own room. Being angry at himself or Matilda wouldn't help. He might as well be angry at Forrest for assigning them the case. Best be angry at the criminal. Who had tipped his hand today. He must be feeling threatened. That, at least, was encouraging.

Gareth lay for a long time in his narrow bed pondering whys and wherefores. He invented elaborate intrigues involving half the population of Cheshire. He imagined one super-criminal working everything personally. He remembered Matilda standing in the dusk, staring intently at nothing. He hadn't seen anything, or heard anything, or felt anything.

When he dozed off it was to dream of Aberffraw and Anglesey, of Gwydion ap Don and Keridwen's cauldron of rebirth, of spectral horses, oak-shadowed ledges, and a disembodied hand stroking his cheek in a lover's caress.

*Y*awning, Gareth pushed his way through the gate. The fog of his dreams still gathered in the hollows of his mind, just as mist clotted in the river valley and amongst the buildings of Fortuna Stud. The fort itself rose sleek and green toward the hazy sky. Matilda, he thought, acted as though the trenches in its sides were the open windows of a flat, and she was a Peeping Tom.

The focus of today's work was mud. Mud clung to the tools, to the diggers' boots, to the artifacts that appeared in the trenches. Gareth couldn't concentrate on the Mithraeum emerging at the bottom of the Miller ravine. He was too far away from the center of action. After a time his neck began to hurt as he strained giraffe-like toward the surface.

Just before lunch Matilda took the easy way into the ravine — from its mouth on the side of the hill — and checked over his work. She was still pale, but her alto voice was steady. "Looks good. If you ever decide to resign your police commission you could become an archaeologist."

"Chance would be a fine thing," Gareth responded skeptically.

Sweeney, with Reynolds on his heels, worked his way to their sides. ". . . the sun-god Mithras. Appealed to the legionaries, I suppose, because of the bit about the immortality of the soul. A shame the Druids and the Romans couldn't agree politically, the Druidic religion also believed in immortality. The Celts were fierce fighters, they thought if they died they'd move on to a better world — we've heard that one often enough ourselves, eh? Fools, the lot of them."

"Mankind's religious impulse is generally directed toward some concept of life after death," Matilda pointed out. "None of us want to believe that when the final curtain comes down, the play is over."

"Is that what ghosts are?" hazarded Gareth. "The actors lingering on for a few curtain calls?"

Matilda laughed. "That's as good an explanation as any."

"Ghosts?" repeated Reynolds, his voice edged with sarcasm.

"There are more things in heaven and earth, Horatio, than are dreamt of in your philosophy." Sweeney gestured toward the exposed column drums. "And these are the remains of the temple to Augustus or whoever — maybe that inscription Caterina is working on will tell us."

Reynolds's beady eyes glittered. "I reckon that's where my statuary came from."

"Could be, could be. . . ." Sweeney led Reynolds away.

Gareth looked at Matilda. Matilda shrugged. "I can only sense guilt in someone if he feels guilty. Reynolds might feel justified in stealing his own artifacts. He might feel justified in murdering someone who threatened to turn him in. That bluster of his is like white noise, it muffles a lot of what's going on beneath."

"Super."

"Cheer up. It's early days yet."

"No, it's not. Not when the beggar almost did you over yesterday."

Even Gareth's rudimentary senses picked up on Matilda's evasion tactic. "It's lunch time, isn't it? I think I'll have curry, it's a cold day."

They surfaced to find the students filing down the hillside, Ashley bringing up the rear. Reynolds had apparently invited himself to lunch. He walked along with Jennifer and Courtney, chatting them up. They laughed politely at his jokes.

Linda Burkett had stuck Reynolds's boorishness because she planned to do a deal with him, Gareth thought. He couldn't imagine why Della had married the man. Something to do with low self-esteem, probably. He opened the gate for Ashley and she skipped through, shooting him a smile. Distractedly he returned it.

Voices coasted down the wind. Matilda glanced back over her shoulder and Gareth followed her eye. Jason and Caterina still stood over the inscription. "Yeah, right," he said. "You were out here in the dark checking for mud. There's a word for girls like you, you know."

"I don't understand," protested Caterina. "It is treasure here. It is important. What is your problem?"

Jason responded with a four-letter directive Gareth hoped wasn't in Caterina's vocabulary. He drew back his foot as though to kick the scattered blocks of the inscription. Caterina defended them with a push so firm he staggered. Jason repeated his injunction and plunged down the hill, his face suffused with rage.

"That sucks," said Ashley. Matilda shook her head. Gareth closed the gate, muttering, "kids!" beneath his breath. But then, if everyone pursued their relationships in a calm and considerate fashion, he'd be out a job.

A white crane glided to a landing amongst the distant willows. Two crows glared balefully down from the eaves of the hotel as the students went inside.

Saturday dawned as cold and misty as Friday, but by the time Gareth emerged from the dining room satiated with eggs, bacon and sausage, the sun was breaking through the clouds. Most of the students had left early, taking the inter-city coach to brighter lights, although a few still lingered in Corcester. He glimpsed Ashley curled up with a book before the electric fire in the sitting room, the headphones of her CD player clamped to her ears. When she glanced up and saw him watching her, she made a face that was part grin, part grimace. He waved and went on his way.

Clapper stood behind the reception desk. "And what have you laid on for the weekend?" he asked.

"A little research, a lot of note-taking," Gareth replied.

He passed Caterina on the stairs. *"Buon giorno!"* she said cheerfully.

"Good morning." Jason had left with the other students — his and Caterina's affair was already over. Affairs, Gareth thought, are never bought on the cheap. More than one of his own had ended costing dearly in truth and trust. He collected his camera bag from his room and went back downstairs.

Matilda stood in front of the hotel contemplating the peekaboo sun. "I'm off for a ride," Gareth told her.

"To the traveler's camp?" she asked.

No point to flanneling with Matilda, was there? "It's time I had a look about the place, yes."

"Good luck. I'm going to check out the bookstore behind the bank. Don't worry, I'll stay out of trouble."

Gareth hoped so. With a half-salute he turned toward Fortuna Stud, where Great Caesar's Ghost was looking inquisitively over the fence. He offered the horse his hand and received a wet breath in return. He walked on wiping his palm on his jeans.

Reynolds's beak of a nose was already out and about, sniffing round the stables. "Chatting up Caesar, were you? Would you care to take him out? He needs the exercise."

"Oh yes, certainly," Gareth said, beaming. "I'm honored!"

Reynolds summoned Jimmy, who chased down the horse and had him saddled before Gareth could do more than inquire about Della's health.

"The old trouble-and-strife?" Reynolds answered. "She's a bit pulled down. Gone to see the doctor again. Can't stick the cold. Always at me to take her to Greece or Ibiza. Ought to send her alone, just to get shut of her."

Gareth forced a polite smile, wondered why Reynolds had married Della to begin with, and mounted Caesar.

What a magnificent animal! He paced out of the stable yard like his namesake entering Rome in triumph. No matter that he had hardly distinguished himself at the Grand National.

As soon as Caesar was warmed up, Gareth prodded him into a run. The horse moved effortlessly, his great muscles flexing, his hooves drumming the damp earth. Birds flew up from the trees along the river. Durslow loomed ahead. Exhilarated, Gareth turned Caesar toward the fence enclosing the rocky upward slope. The horse leaped the closed gate like a puff of thistledown.

Gareth glanced round, but no one had seen him taking liberties with such expensive horseflesh. He reined Caesar to a more sedate pace. Instead of taking the path upward to Durslow he took the one leading down to the road and the layby where the travelers were camped, pausing once or twice to take photos.

The encampment looked like a setting for a Mad Max movie. Battered caravans, cars, and buses were scattered haphazardly over what had once been an attractive little park. If any of the buses sported red scrapes Gareth couldn't tell. Their original colors had disintegrated into a patchwork of dents, paint, and rust.

Music blared from at least two caravans, the boom of the bass reverberating in Gareth's teeth. Heavy metal music wasn't evidence of devil-worship, though. Look as he might, Gareth didn't see a single bloody altar.

Dogs pawed through piles of rubbish. A woman carrying a child, a shovel, and a roll of loo paper picked her way over a broken-down fence into the shadows of the fir plantation. The cool breeze did little to dispel a stench of sausage, sewage, and smoke. Several scruffy men were nursing bottles of beer round a small fire. When they saw the approaching rider they stood and swaggered forward, their expressions far from welcoming. Gareth sat a little taller in the saddle. Caesar shook his head, making his bridle jingle.

"Who are you?" one of the men demanded.

"Gareth March. I'm from the *Times*. I'd like to interview you."

Another man suggested possible uses for the *Times*.

The door of a nearby caravan opened and a dark-haired man appeared, buckling his belt. Just as the door swung shut Gareth glimpsed a woman inside, wearing, so far as he could tell, nothing more than an unbuttoned shirt.

The others parted to let the man through. "Gareth-bleedin' toff-March," announced an anonymous voice.

"Nicholas Veliotes," said the man, with an unnecessarily familiar pat on Caesar's neck. "What're you on about, March?"

So this was Nick, eh? Gareth repeated his introduction, adding, "Wouldn't you like to have your side of the story represented in the *Times*?"

"That's rich," said Nick. "Who buys the *Times*, then, save sods of politicians who care more about their own arses than about making jobs and providing housing? They don't want to read about us. Out of sight, out of mind."

"Here's your chance to sort them out. Tell me your life story, where you've lived, how you get along. . . ."

Caesar leaped straight up, corkscrewed, and did a fair approximation of a jitterbug. Convulsively Gareth's knees tightened. He grabbed for the rim of the saddle and managed not only to quiet the horse but also to retain his camera bag. Scowling, he spun to face his audience.

The men were falling about laughing. Except for Nick, who took a bear-like man with a scraggly beard by the scruff of the neck and made him hand over a pen-knife. "Well done, boyo. Knock him about and the pigs knock us about, don't they?"

Gareth focused on the pen knife, swallowed, and said more calmly than he felt, "I'll overlook that, Nick, if you'll talk to me."

"Bugger off," said Nick. He tossed the knife in the air, catching and closing it as it came down, and grinned.

It wasn't on for a detective to murder his suspect, tempted as he might be. Gareth pulled Caesar round and touched his heels to his flanks. Tossing his head disdainfully, the horse leaped into a run, cleared the fence across the road, and thundered up the hillside.

Gareth didn't pull up until he was round the curve of the hill, out of sight of the camp. Muttering obscenities, he leaped down from the saddle and inspected Caesar's flank. A shallow cut about two inches long broke the smooth chestnut hair. It wasn't bleeding badly. Good show, he told himself. That interview had gone down a bomb, hadn't it, risking another man's horse, letting the sods make him look like an idiot — a good thing Matilda hadn't been along, even placid Bodie would've objected to a knife in the flank and thrown Matilda on her head.

Gareth apologized to Caesar, mounted again, and turned toward Corcester. At least, he thought, he'd spotted a possible murder weapon. In the hands of not only one, but two arrogant bastards with enough neck to make trouble, if not to kill.

Man and horse returned to Fortuna Stud very slowly, without any further incidents, although Gareth suspected his face was still red as a beet. Once in the stable yard he pointed out the cut to Jimmy, but before he could confess to its origins the old man said, "So you walked him into a thorn bush or a fence post, did you?" And with a hostile glare at Gareth, he led Caesar away. "We'll set you to rights, won't we, boy?" The horse whickered his grievances.

Gareth turned toward the house. He had to own up to exposing Caesar to danger. A task that might not be as awkward as he feared, he realized as he walked by the open door of the garage — Reynolds's red MG wasn't there.

Della answered his knock on the door. She really did look ill, flushed and feverish. Clasping her jersey tightly across the chest of her blouse, she waved away Gareth's apologies about the horse. "I'm sure it was an accident, the New Agers are really quite pleasant, simply down on their luck. . . . Please come in, surely you'd like to see Adrian's collection. He's not here, he's — well, he's gone away."

No time like the present. "If you're quite sure. . . ."

Della motioned him through the doorway.

Gareth stepped inside and left his boots in the entry. The house was stiflingly hot.

Della led him to a sitting room that was aggressively masculine, all dark leather and tweed, with a vague aroma of bay rum and cigars. A packed bookshelf stood against one wall. Against another stood a glass case containing polished stone, bronze, silver, and even a glint of gold.

"Would you care for tea?" Della asked.

What Gareth really wanted was beer, but he accepted the tea gratefully, and took advantage of her absence fetching it to look over the antiquities. Matilda would know what everything was, where it came from, and what its mother's maiden name had been. To Gareth the display might as well have been a museum jumble sale. Tiny faces looked up at him from various bowls, platters, and figurines. That was a lamp, he reckoned, and that was a strainer. Sweeney had said half Reynolds's things were fakes. Some of them looked bright and shiny enough to have been manufactured last week.

After the controversy over the Romano-British bronzes, Gareth had expected Reynolds to own large pieces of statuary. But everything here was small enough to fit into a rucksack. Easier to smuggle, he told himself.

Della returned carrying a tea-tray. Gareth cleared some magazines off a low table. He noted a Sotheby's catalog and a booklet of instructions for a metal detector, as well as two issues of *Treasure Trove*, one with a cover story on a sunken

Manila galleon and the headline, "Investment Opportunity!"

Perched on the edge of her chair, Della poured and served as punctiliously as the Queen at a garden party. Gareth sipped his tea and asked, "Are you also interested in antiquities, Mrs. Reynolds?"

"Della, please," she said with a shy smile. "In a way — I taught history once, before my marriage, at a public school. . . . I like to collect ceramic pieces."

"Dr. Gray was telling me about a shop in Borley Arcade that sells both ceramics and antiquities."

"Oh yes, I bought a lovely Portmeirion vase there, only eight pounds. Celia was a schoolmistress of mine. She gave me a discount."

Oh. All right then. Gareth ticked off one question answered, not that the answer wasn't going to create more questions. "The murdered girl worked there, didn't she? Did you know her?"

Della gaze fell so abruptly to her cup Gareth expected to hear a splash. "I met her, once, when she was here talking to Adrian about artifacts from Cornovium — the Roman fort. . . . Of course you know its name, you're working there."

"It must have been a terrible shock to you when she was found dead."

"I remember the night. It was filthy weather. Adrian had planned to go to a town-planning session but decided to stay in. Clapper rang up with the news."

"That would have been the night the victim was found, then, two days later."

The color drained from Della's face so quickly she went a sickly green. She fussed with the teapot. "Let me warm your cup for you, Mr. March. Gareth."

He extended his cup. The spout of the teapot clattered against its edge as she poured. Had the time lag between the murder and its discovery never occurred to her when she was giving her and her husband's alibi? He couldn't ask her point-blank, though. He didn't dare push her too hard.

Setting the teapot down, she clasped her hands in her lap, pressed her trousered knees together, and hunched as though avoiding a blow.

Gareth made a mental note to ask Watkins about the

weather on the first of February and changed the subject. "You taught history? You have a brilliant library." He nodded toward the shelf. Books leaned together across gaps. Many of the titles were about the Celts, others focused on the Romans. When he saw Antonia Fraser's *The Warrior Queens* he felt a leap of inspiration worthy of Matilda herself. "Your horse, Bodie. Is she named for Boudicca?"

Again a blush rose in Della's cheeks, and a furtive gleam touched her eyes. "Oh yes. How very clever of you. I've always admired Boudicca, she was quite the fighter, wasn't she? She paid the Romans back good and proper."

"And a lot of innocent people died for it," Gareth pointed out.

"Is anyone really innocent? I mean, really?"

That was a good one. Gareth didn't answer.

"Boudicca was a Druidess. The Celts didn't stifle women like the Romans did. Like we do now. . . ." She leaned forward. The top of her blouse gaped open. Gareth kept his eyes on her face, but even so she gasped and quickly buttoning the top button. Her enthusiasm, her color, drained away again. "I'm sorry. I was speaking out of turn."

"Not at all." Gareth was sweating. He could hardly breathe in the hothouse atmosphere. He put down his empty cup and stood. "Thank you. I'm terribly sorry about the horse, if there are any vet's bills. . . ."

"No, no," Della murmured into her chest. "Not to worry."

Gareth fled into the entryway, reclaimed his boots, and burst into the open air. He needed to talk to Watkins. The travelers had the means, Reynolds had the opportunity, and Della, perhaps, the motive. She seemed too timid to kill out of jealousy, though — assuming any woman in her right mind would be jealous of a git like Reynolds. The motive was greed — wasn't it?

He must tell Matilda that he'd traced the receipt. That he still had no connection between the travelers and Linda Burkett. That Della might be desperate, but she was also pitiful.

He strode back to the hotel, shaking the mud of Fortuna Stud from his feet.

Chapter Ten

*H*er mother would be proud of her for attending church. Ashley wasn't sure whether she felt virtuous or nauseated. She stifled a burp that tasted of her morning tomatoes and bacon and glanced at her watch. She was meeting Nick here at four. It was only eleven now. He wasn't in the congregation, no surprise there.

Light streamed in multi-colored beams across the rows of faces and into the shadowy corners of the ancient building. Matilda sat beside Ashley with her hands folded in her lap. Her serene face was lifted toward the pulpit, listening to the minister speak about loving one's neighbor as oneself. More than a few raised chins and tight lips in his audience — not least those of Watkins, Clapper, and Reynolds — suggested to Ashley that he was pleading for tolerance for the travelers.

Ashley tried to focus on the sacred rather than the profane. Not that Nick was profane. He was a scholar. If the local people only realized that, they wouldn't be so frightened of him and his friends.

Gareth wouldn't be so down on him. She'd hung around Gareth's table in the bar last night, but he hadn't asked her to sit down. He'd drunk three pints of ale and scribbled in his notebook, every now and then consulting with Matilda about something that'd happened while he'd been out riding. They were working on their book. Ashley didn't interrupt. She drank a lager and daydreamed about being carried off into the sunset by Gareth, or by Nick, or by anyone who split the difference between Prince Charming and a movie star.

The bar had been almost empty. Caterina sat with Dr.

Sweeney and Reynolds, ignoring Reynolds's double meanings and holding her own with Sweeney in a conversation about, as far as Ashley could make out, the column of Trajan in Rome. For several moments Ashley had wished she'd gone with Bryan, Manfred, and Courtney into the Peak District to go hang-gliding. She had a date, though, with someone cooler than her fellow students.

". . . and grant that this day we fall into no sin," intoned the minister, "neither run into any sort of danger . . ."

Matilda repeated the words beneath her breath. Ashley burped again. The church was growing warm with the sunlight and the bodies. It had been chilly when she'd been here on Tuesday with Nick.

The congregation rose. Ashley leaped to her feet a beat behind. ". . . and the fellowship of the Holy Ghost, be with us all evermore. Amen."

"Amen," everyone said. "Amen," whispered Ashley.

A moment of genuflection and the congregation began to file out. It'd been a very nice, old-fashioned service. You could see the altar and the minister much better without TV cameras in the way.

"Look. There's a green man." Matilda put her prayer book in her purse and pointed to the carving on the end of their pew.

Ashley eyed the rough-hewn face surrounded by leaves, pretending she'd never seen it before. "Does it mean the medieval villagers were still secret pagans?"

"No. It means the early church was tolerant of the old ways. It could gain more converts with open arms than it could with closed doors — and minds."

"You don't see that much any more. I mean, people being broad-minded of other people's beliefs."

"The tolerant ones don't make the headlines, unfortunately."

They walked out into the sunshine and past the whispering fronds of the yew tree. Matilda, Ashley thought, was a tolerant person. It might not hurt to tell her she'd seen the green man before, and with whom. And yet it was risky to expose your feelings to another person. That gave the other person ammunition to belittle you with.

"Fine, thank you," Matilda was saying to the Reynolds', man and wife. "And you?"

"You can tell your chap March," answered Adrian, "that if he wants to call on the travelers he can do it with his own property."

Mrs. R — Della — inspected her shoes. Matilda said, "He's not my chap," and walked away.

Ashley hurried after Matilda. "Do you like being an archaeologist? I have to declare a major soon, so far I'm just taking what I'm interested in, but my mother says I'd better buckle down and get a teacher's certificate so I can earn a living."

"Earning a living is important," said Matilda. "So is studying a variety of things. Making connections among different ideas and disciplines opens up a lot of opportunities. . . . Hello, Howard."

Dr. Sweeney stopped in front of the hotel and waited for them to catch up. "I'm having a recce at the fort. Rather a Sunday ritual. Would you ladies care to join me?"

Ashley said, "Sure."

"Certainly," said Matilda.

They wended their way past the cottages and the bowling green to the fort. The paths up the slopes were still muddy, and the grass was wet — the heels of Ashley's pumps sank into the ground. She found a bit of wall to stand on. Her cotton skirt billowed around her knees, sneaky little drafts teasing her thighs.

Matilda was wearing flats and a pleated wool skirt that wouldn't have dared billow. "Those walls must belong to the bath house," she said. "It's on the lower part of the slope. And that surface is part of a later Saxon building. It's looking good for a week's work."

"For a group of volunteers doing a quick and dirty survey," Sweeney replied. "Maybe next year I can do a proper open area excavation with proper excavators. I have too many other commitments at present, my kind of expertise is much in demand."

Ashley bit her lip. She'd thought she was doing all right, for an amateur. And Caterina was really strutting her stuff.

"The students are showing a lot of ability," said Matilda. "Your assistant in Manchester, Ionescu, also seems very capable."

"Within his limits, yes."

"You will send me the official report on the bog body."

"We academics will be arguing over that for years to come," Sweeney told her. "The post-mortem, for example, showed the presence of burnt barley-cake in her stomach. Does that imply famine? A Beltane ritual?"

"Or sloppy cooking?" concluded Matilda. "It'd be helpful if you had the head as well."

"Yes." Sweeney adjusted his ascot and surveyed the field. He looked like Nelson atop his column in Trafalgar Square.

Ashley peered narrowly around the mound. Interesting as it was to know someone who saw ghosts, she really wasn't up to seeing any herself. She crossed her arms and hugged herself, remembering the pitiful empty sack that had been a body like her own. Perhaps *she* had felt love, longing, and loneliness, too, but all you could dump on a laboratory table was the poor old slandered flesh.

Matilda almost seemed to be smothering a smile. "Howard, what are the old legends about Durslow and Shadow Moss?"

"Miller found the remains of an ancient timber causeway leading down into the bog," Sweeney answered. "That might have given rise to stories of a god — who has different names in different versions of the story — Cernnunos, Taranis, Teutates — riding a white horse from Durslow down to the Moss. This has been horse country forever, and there's that spring on Durslow — primitive people, mind you. Superstitious to a fault."

"Primitive people," said Matilda, "tended to be in much closer contact with the earth, the sky, the seasons."

"In early medieval times, Durslow was supposedly the abode of some saint. I forget which one — the early saints were thick upon the ground. Later on, in the seventeenth century, the local people supposedly wiped out a coven there. The victims were several old widows going about their business. Villagers tended to be paranoid about anyone out of the social mainstream. You had the same problem in America."

"At Salem? Yes, if I'd lived there then I'd have been in trouble, being both a widow and impatient with fools."

Sweeney shot her a sideways glance but Matilda was gazing

off toward the river, features bland.

Matilda's a widow, Ashley thought. What a shame. The photo in her room was probably of her son. It must be really depressing to be middle-aged and alone, much more than being twenty and alone. Not that Matilda seemed particularly depressed.

When they returned to the lobby of the hotel they found Watkins and Clapper conferring over a notebook. "Scheduling the May Day festivities," the innkeeper told Matilda and Sweeney. "We don't want to have the Hobby Horse and the Maypole at the same time, they're both big draws. Especially since May first is on a Saturday this year. We'll have people from as far away as Liverpool and Birmingham. This here's last year's Queen of the May." He showed Ashley a photo of a girl dressed in a snug bodice, flowing skirt, and gold-paper crown that owed more to Hollywood than to history. Her escort was a head taller than she was, a young man wearing the white shirt, knee breeches, and bells of a Morris dancer. "We've just chosen our new Queen. Has to be a local girl, you know."

"No offense, Miss Walraven," added Watkins.

"None taken," Ashley told him. Of course they wouldn't want a stranger to play the part. They didn't need to apologize.

Matilda was staring at the photo. "So these two are local kids?"

"Used to be," answered Clapper. "Emma there's moved away — bit of a local scandal, nothing you'd want to hear about. Clive's gone to live with relatives up north, no jobs here for a bright lad, more's the pity."

"Ah," Matilda said faintly. Frowning, she handed back the picture.

Matilda might be seeing something unusual in the photo, but it looked thoroughly ordinary to Ashley. She glanced at her watch, murmured, "Excuse me," and went to the room she had all to herself this weekend. There she changed into her good jeans and a sweater and picked up pencil and paper. Boy, was she going to be glad to get back to e-mail — not that her mother even had a computer.

She wrote about the dig, salting the letter with archaeological terms. What else would she write about — the murdered girl? Jason and Caterina? Gareth? Her mother probably wouldn't have approved of Gareth, him being a reporter and all. Nick? Nick would have given her a nervous breakdown.

Ashley ate a protein bar, brushed her teeth, tucked the envelope in her pocket, and set out for the mailbox across from the church. The day was still sunny, almost warm in the lee of the buildings. Several people wandered around the square, but none of them were travelers. It wasn't quite three o'clock. She could mail her letter and sit on a bench by the church. . . .

With a rush of adrenalin she recognized the red-haired man who was mailing a letter just ahead of her. Her feet tried to pull her two ways at once, with the result that she stood still. "Oh, hello," Gareth said as he turned from the pillar box.

"I write my mother every Sunday," Ashley blurted, and edged past him to thrust her letter into the slot.

"I was writing my mum as well," said Gareth.

"You're Welsh, aren't you? Is that where your mother lives?"

"We lived in Wales when I was young, yes. Now my mum lives in Brussels. Her husband's a bureaucrat with the EU."

So his parents had broken up, too. Ashley groped for something else to say. "It's almost May Day."

"Yes."

"I read a book once where people in Wales jump over fires on May Day."

"My grandmother did that as a child, but if you find anyone playing at it these days, it's simply a game, a bit of a lark. Like the Eisteddfod, clinging to the past for the sake of clinging to the past."

"Or because the future looks unsure?"

"Could be," Gareth conceded with a slight smile.

"So you don't believe in the old gods? You don't think they have any power any more?"

He glanced sharply at her, making her wonder if she'd gone too far. "No. The old gods are gone. If you'll excuse me. . . ." Gareth turned and walked off toward the hotel.

He was still treating her like a kid sister, wasn't he? He'd disapprove of her date, no doubt about it. If she had Caterina's self-confidence she'd throw Nick in Gareth's face and dare him to respond. . . . With her luck she'd alienate both men and be back to — well, no, not back to square one. If she'd learned nothing else over the last couple of years, it was that attracting a guy wasn't all that hard. It was keeping him that could be the problem.

Too restless to sit down, Ashley pretended to window shop, all the while glancing over her shoulder. She saw Jason trudging back from the bus station with his backpack over his shoulder and a preoccupied scowl on his face. She ignored him. He was turning out to have even more issues than she'd suspected. Fine, Caterina could deal with him.

"A penny for your thoughts," said Nick's voice in her ear, and she jumped. "Sorry, didn't mean to startle you."

She stammered something, but he already had his left arm firmly around her waist and was guiding her down a side street. "You'll be wanting to see the countryside. You can't stay in town all the time. Townspeople, they'll have your mind well and truly squeezed shut."

Ashley wasn't going to argue with that. She walked along beside him, not sure just where to put her right arm, and finally rested her hand on his shoulder. That same sweet, smoky odor clung to him. His hair rippled in the breeze. His grin flashed in the sunlight. The annoying little mutter in the back of Ashley's mind informed her that if something looked too good to be true, it probably was. She pushed the mutter down.

At the car park Nick threw open the door of a brown Ford Fiesta well past its prime, its bumper sporting a faded "Manchester United" sticker. He bundled up some old newspapers that, by their odor, had been used to wrap fish and chips, and threw them on the ground. *Whoa,* Ashley thought, *what a rebel, littering.* And the car didn't have seat belts, either. She climbed in, telling herself she was sure living dangerously now.

With a grinding of gears and a puff of exhaust, they set off. In minutes they were barreling along a country road, Corcester behind them. "Where are we going?" Ashley asked.

"Durslow Edge," Nick replied. "It's a place of power. You can't understand the landscape without taking its pulse."

That was where the dead girl had been found. Ashley's

smile stiffened. Nick dropped his hand onto her thigh with a quick, reassuring nod, as though they were co-conspirators of some kind. His hand, a starfish against the denim of her jeans, wasn't very large. His nails were clean. Its pressure on her leg sent little prickles of electricity into her stomach. *Okay* . . . she thought, and gazed out over the countryside that was whisking so quickly by her window.

The narrow road twisted toward what Ashley had always thought was a low cloud on the horizon, but which turned out to be an escarpment. Massive oaks thrust through red boulders the same color as the church. Pink and white blossoms clung to smaller trees. Nick pointed out weedy pockets in the woods that were old mine workings.

He stopped the car in a graveled area and ushered her along a rocky ledge beneath a cliff. Beyond the topmost branches of the trees lay mile after mile of countryside, a patchwork in shades of green. Ashley felt as though she could see all the way to Oz. Low in the west hung a creamy crescent moon.

"Thirsty?" Nick bent over a basin at the foot of the cliff, rinsed his hands in the water flowing from the rock, and drank.

Sending a silent prayer to Montezuma to spare her, Ashley sipped at the water. It was cold and musty.

"This is Brighid's well," Nick said. "From here, Rhiannon rides her white mare with the gold moon-crescent — the sacred sickle of the Druids . . ." he touched his crescent-shaped necklace, ". . . down to Shadow Moss. The Moss is a door into the Underworld."

Ashley nodded. She was getting a double dose of legend today.

"Or you could see the Moss as Keridwen's cauldron of death and rebirth," Nick went on. "The peat-cutters pull out bits of human bodies from time to time, sacrifices to the triple goddess."

"Yes, I saw part of one in Dr. Sweeney's lab."

"Did you? What did you sense in it?"

"Nothing. The body was sad, really. Just an empty sack. The hand, though. . . ."

A cold draft eddied down the cliff like water over a fall, and Ashley shivered. "I kept wondering if the hand was going to reach for me. Like when I was little and I'd jump into my bed from three feet away because I thought if I stood there something would reach out from beneath the dust ruffle and grab me and drag me under. Pretty stupid reaction, I guess."

"Not a bit of it. The hand was calling to you. A shame you had to see it in the lab — sterile surroundings mute the vibrations of the flesh." Nick slipped his arm around her waist again. "You wouldn't be frightened of your bed if you had a warm body in it, would you now?"

When she'd thought she wanted to be swept off her feet, she'd meant figuratively, not literally. But one moment she was standing next to Nick, the next he'd wrapped his other arm around her knees and laid her flat on the ground with a crunch of dried leaves. She had to hand it to him, he was smooth.

The heat of his kiss stopped her breath. With a little gasp through her nose she returned his kiss with her lips and tongue. Pinwheels spun behind her closed lids and the pit of her stomach melted into her groin. His hand probed beneath her sweater. His body was heavy, pressing her into the ground. Cold seeped from the stone into her back.

"Whoa," she mumbled against his mouth. Her voice caught in her throat. She hooked her forefinger through the gold hoop in his right ear and tugged gently, pulling his head away. "Nick! Time out!"

Instantly he released her. He shook the hair off his forehead and grinned. "It's not so comfortable here, is it? Sorry."

Wheezing, Ashley sat up. Well, it's not as though she hadn't known all along what he wanted. What she herself wanted, more or less.

"It's not time yet," he went on. "The power won't wake til the Friday. You'll come here with us then, to the ceremony, won't you?"

"What?"

"The townsfolk have their Festival, makes them a bit of brass, I reckon, but it's not a proper rite. The Druid only appears to the believers gathered here, not to the toffs in Clapper's bar. I'll collect you at four on the Friday and we'll come back here with the others. You can leap the fire with me. That would go down a treat."

Gareth had dismissed that as a game. In Nick's voice it sounded deadly serious, not to mention weird. Was he inviting her to an orgy? Or what? "Someone died here," was all she could say.

"I reckon a lot of people have died here over the years. But you mean Linda, I suppose."

Ashley supposed she did. She'd never heard the victim's name.

Nick's face clouded. He looked down the ledge, his lips that a moment before had been so agile now set in a tight line. "My car had a breakdown that night, or I'd have had Linda back to Corcester in time for the Manchester coach good and proper. It was a grand evening, cold but clear, so she said she'd walk, maybe hitch, if she could. The filthy berk who gave her a ride brought her here, didn't he? Bloody cheek."

Except for the sound of the wind and the leaves the stone shelf was utterly quiet. Gooseflesh rose on Ashley's arms, drawing the heat from her groin. He'd known Linda. He'd known someone who was murdered. He was on the rebound from a tragedy. Here she'd been casting Nick in some shallow romantic fantasy and he was dealing with the harshest of realities.

She set her hand on his arm. Below his sweater the muscle was as hard as the rock they were sitting on. "I'll try to come on Friday, to, to help out. Okay?"

With a noble little smile, Nick regained his composure. "Super."

He stood up and offered Ashley his hand. As they strolled away Ashley saw a couple of piles of horse droppings beside a log. Reynolds and his wife must ride up here. . . . No, it had been Gareth and Matilda, checking out the site of the murder.

She glanced back at the ledge. It might be a place of power, but the only power she'd sensed was Nick's libido and her own imagination. Maybe Friday, when the travelers staged their Druid rip-off ceremony, she'd pick up on the Force or something.

Nick seated her in the car. "You'll be needing a warm drink. It's a bit parky up here, isn't it?"

"Oh, well, yes, thank you."

It wasn't far to the traveler's encampment. Ashley gazed around, half-expecting to see what her mother would call hippies running around barking. The only people she saw seemed shabby and wan.

Compared to the scrubby busses and vans, Nick's car looked like a Rolls Royce. He parked it by a battered travel trailer. Ashley had time for only a quick look at the overshadowing fir trees before he whisked her inside.

She smelled sausage and incense. A miniature sink was piled with dishes. A bed with crumpled bedclothes was half-hidden behind a bead curtain. Books covered the table. Ashley sat down on the narrow bench to one side. The other bench was filled with cardboard boxes each labeled, *The Antiquary's Corner.*

She'd been expecting a cup of tea, but Nick produced a bottle of whiskey and poured a dollop into a thick glass. When in Britain, do as the Brits do, Ashley thought. Although even her father's 12 year old Scotch always tasted like battery acid, and this one was still in its infancy. She sipped and covered her wry expression by looking down at the books. Their titles ranged from *Chariots of the Gods* to academic tomes on archaeology and semiotics, the study of symbols. Two Sotheby's catalogs lay beneath a copy of *The Golden Bough.* Just as she'd thought, Nick was a scholar. And there sure weren't many jobs for scholars.

He scooted onto the bench beside her, captured her hand, and gazed into her eyes. He kissed her again, less insistently this time, without spilling either of their glasses.

Just as Ashley decided she liked the taste of the whiskey better on his tongue than on her own there was a knock on the door. Sighing in aggravation, Nick reached over and turned the knob. Two girls not much older than Ashley looked into the trailer. One had short, black, spiky hair, and a leather jacket. The other had long, lank, blond hair and a limp cotton dress with a shawl.

"Here," said the first, "didn't know you was entertaining, Nick."

"Ashley," Nick said, "Shirl and DeDe."

Ashley could feel her cheeks red-hot in the draft from the open door. Either the Scotch or the sex would've been enough

— both of them and she was glowing like a stop light. "Hello," she managed to say nonchalantly.

"Where you from, luv?" asked DeDe.

"St. Louis. United States."

"Oh, a Yank," Shirl said. "Developing exotic tastes, eh, Nick?"

He smiled. "Ashley's here studying British history. I'm helping her."

"Oh, so it's history she's studying." DeDe nudged Shirl and winked. "That's a new name for it."

They laughed. Their accents were so thick Ashley could hardly understand them.

But their scorn didn't need to be translated. The date sure wasn't turning out like she'd wanted, was it?

"Eh, Bob," called Shirl over her shoulder. "Come meet Nick's Yank."

"I need to be getting back to Corcester." Ashley put her glass down and shoved at Nick. For a moment she was afraid he wasn't going to move, keeping her trapped in the corner.

No. He pulled her to her feet and steered her through what seemed to be a crowd gathered at the door. "All right then, you stupid cows," he said with a laugh, "you've put the wind up her, thank you very much."

A hulking, smelly man Ashley assumed was Bob said, "Tough luck, boyo."

"They didn't mean anything," Nick told Ashley as she tumbled into the car.

No, they probably didn't. Still it was easier to blow off her own compadres than someone else's. She focused on her hands clasped in her lap and didn't look up until they were in open country, passing black and white houses and black and white cows muted to shades of gray by gathering cloud and evening both.

Nick didn't seem to be gnashing his teeth in frustration, but the pit of Ashley's stomach ached. Well, there was always next time, when maybe she could get something going with him in private, not in public. Assuming she wanted to get something going with him. Funny how things weren't working out according to her script.

"Tell me about the dig," he said.

She told him about the dig, sketched the personalities involved, and finished with an account of Matilda's close encounter with a bus.

"That was on the Thursday?" His dark eyes sparked.

"Watch the road!" Ashley yelped as another car whisked by them.

He turned back to the road. "The brakes on the bus packed up, I reckon. Simple as that."

They closed on a green car ahead of them, which was slowing for a traffic light at the outskirts of the town. Both cars stopped. Nick claimed Ashley's thigh again. Ashley suddenly realized that the car ahead of them was Gareth's. From the angle of his head she guessed the reporter was looking at the light, not into his rear view mirror. Even so, she ducked.

"Is that someone from the dig?" Nick asked.

"Yes. It's Gareth March, a reporter who's writing us up."

Nick sneered, "Yeh, March, the toffee-nosed git. Showed up at the camp yesterday on a horse, for God's sake, and handed us a right bit of flannel. Don't trust him, he's probably a pig in disguise."

"No, no, no," Ashley protested. "I've overheard him talking to Matilda."

The light changed. Gareth drove straight on ahead, unaware anyone was sneering at him. Nick turned left and dropped Ashley off in the car park by the town center. "Friday, then, for certain? If I can get away before then I'll — well, I can hardly walk into the hotel and ask Clapper for you, can I? I'll be in touch, eh?"

"Yes, of course." Ashley met his parting kiss hesitantly — there were people around — and waved goodbye to the Fiesta's dwindling taillights.

The breeze was chill, and again her skin broke out in gooseflesh. The greasy newspapers Nick had dumped earlier that day shifted back and forth across the pitted asphalt, in the twilight looking like the pale ghosts of dreams past. She gathered them up, thrust them into a rubbish bin, and walked briskly into the town square. She couldn't go back to the hotel, not yet. Matilda, Dr. Sweeney, Gareth — they'd notice Nick's fingerprints on her. Then she'd feel guilty. She didn't want to feel guilty. She sat down on a bench, looked up at the church steeple, and started shooting the rapids of her thoughts.

The remaining daylight leaked away behind the clouds. The lights of the town seemed feeble against the gloom. A siren sounded, not too far away. Several shadowy figures trooped through the square exchanging laughs and taunts. The familiar voices hauled Ashley out of her meditation. She stood up.

"Yo, Ashley," Bryan called. "What're you doing out here?"

"Watching the sunset." And starving to death, she realized. Food was sublimated sex, after all. She fell into step with the others. "How was the hang-gliding?"

"Great!" replied Courtney. "We found a youth hostel in Castleton. . . ."

They emerged from the alley beside the church. Below them lay the hotel, its windows glinting in the pulsing blue lights of several police cars. Flashlights swooped like demented fireflies over the dark mound of Cornovium. Clumps of human figures stood on the sidewalk and in the gardens of the cottages. Voices rose and fell in a staccato rhythm. Every nerve ending in Ashley's body blazed. What the. . . ?

"Mein Gott, was ist das?" exclaimed Manfred.

In one jostling mass the students raced down the hill and collided with the crowd before the door of the hotel.

The lights were so bright Ashley was blinded. It took her a moment to recognize the hands that grasped her arms and spun her around as Matilda's. "Ashley, where have you been?"

"Out — what's wrong?"

Matilda inhaled, nostrils flaring, then glanced from Ashley to Bryan and let her go. "Howard and Caterina were working on the inscription. They didn't come in when it started to get dark, so Gareth went to look for them. Someone hit Caterina over the head and pushed Howard down into the Miller ravine. She's unconscious, he's bruised and dazed."

The screech of an ambulance siren sliced the night. Matilda watched the vehicle turn onto the road and gather speed. Even after its lights winked out the sound of its siren lingered mournfully on the wind.

Ashley's mind stammered. The faces around her — Matilda, Courtney, Bryan, Manfred — smeared into leering masks of light and shadow. She turned toward the hotel. Gareth, Clap-

per, Watkins, and two more policemen stood in close conference right in front of the door. Jason stood between the two
cops, looking belligerently from side to side. "Yeah, I came
back early, I was tired, the hostel in Keswick was full — so I
had a fight with Caterina, so what?"

The policemen answered his question by hustling him over
to a patrol car and pushing him inside.

"I don't think so," Matilda said to Watkins. "Even though
the inscription Caterina was working on has been uprooted
and tossed around . . ."

Gareth interrupted. "We saw Jason kicking at it."

". . . and this piece of it was lying by the gate," Matilda
went on. She held up a bit of stone, the incised letters dark
with dirt.

"Good show," said Watkins, "to find that little bit in the
dark."

"I don't follow," Clapper said. "You think it was them
vandals and thieves again? I saw that Nick whatisit, the
traveler layabout, driving by just at dusk tonight — slowed
down, he did, and gave the professor and the Eyetie girl a
good hard look."

No, Ashley said to herself. He'd dropped her off, that's all.
Even though driving by here on his way back to the camp
would have taken him out of his way.

"What would thieves want with an old inscription?" asked
Watkins.

"It's what they thought was beneath the inscription," Matilda answered. "See, the inscribed word is 'spolia'. Spoils,
booty. Treasure. How many times has Caterina said something about treasure the last few days? She always meant it
figuratively, but not everyone would know that."

"Yesterday," said Ashley, and stopped, surprised at the
sound of her own voice.

The others turned toward her. "Yes?" Matilda said

"Caterina, Dr. Sweeney, and Mr. Reynolds were talking
about the column of Trajan in Rome. She said it's carved with
reliefs showing the Romans carrying home the booty, the
treasure, they picked up in Judaea."

"The bit you see reproduced most frequently," said Matilda, "shows a Roman soldier brandishing the menorah from

Solomon's temple, a treasure indeed. Very good, Ashley. That's helpful."

Gareth frowned. "You mean whoever coshed Sweeney and the girl thought there was treasure buried beneath the inscription?"

"There's some sort of Jewish temple in Manchester, right enough," Clapper offered. "I never heard of any of them candlesticks around here. We're mostly C. of E., those that go to church at all."

"I suppose," Watkins said firmly, "that the thieves thought there might be more of them Roman-British statues or what-not."

"Or some kind of booty, at any rate." Matilda brushed her hair back from her forehead. The harsh light, Ashley thought, made the older woman's face look pale and seamed. "We can speculate about this later on. Right now I need to follow that ambulance, make sure Howard and Caterina are all right. Constable, please make sure someone is keeping an eye on the fort the rest of the night. Mr. Clapper, please ask around here, I'm sure Jason's movements can be accounted for."

"Here, here, what's going on, my horses aren't half cut up. . . ." Reynolds came pushing his way through the crowd.

Gareth and Watkins exchanged a significant glance. "Mr. Reynolds," the constable said affably, "could we have a bit of a natter?"

"See you later," Matilda said to Gareth. And to Ashley, "Don't worry, they'll be all right."

Ashley murmured something appropriate, turned away from the lights that were ruthlessly exposing all her romantic fantasies, and followed the other students into the hotel.

Chapter Eleven

*B*y the time Matilda returned to the parking lot of the Green Dragon it was past midnight. Corcester had rolled up its sidewalks. The only human shape visible was the one leaning on the gate to the fort, spotlighted by the tiny spark of a cigarette. That the figure dared to light a cigarette reassured Matilda it was one of the constables from Manchester who'd been temporarily assigned to Watkins's beat.

She turned off her lights and her engine and exhaled through pursed lips. She could hardly fault the paramedics for taking Howard and Caterina to Manchester — head injuries could be tricky. But she had negotiated the route back to Corcester with her heart in her throat, expecting a bus to dive at her from the gloom. Here she was, though, safely back at the scene of the crime.

The front door of the hotel was locked. Matilda rang the bell, waited, rang it again. After several minutes Clapper came lumbering forth, swathed in a terry cloth robe. "How are they, Dr. Gray?"

"They'll be all right," she replied. "Caterina has a mild concussion, but she's awake and isn't too confused. Howard is scratched and bruised, with a bump on his head and a wrenched knee. Neither one of them has any idea who attacked them."

"Twere the travelers," Clapper muttered darkly, and locked the door.

Maybe so, Matilda thought as she toiled up the stairs. She opened the door of her room. Gareth lay on the bed, a book open on his chest and his head lolling to the side. Other books were scattered around him. Matilda shut the door behind her with an emphatic click.

Gareth sat up abruptly. "Oh, there you are. Sorry, I had Clapper let me in."

"So we can have yet another conference? Gareth, we have to stop meeting like this."

He wasn't amused. He was angry, she sensed, more at himself for not preventing the attack than at the person who'd actually done it. She understood that. If she'd so much as looked out the window she might have seen the assailant stalking his victims. But no, she'd been sitting with the dig computer, working her way through the dull but necessary details of the week's work.

"There're some sandwiches for you on the table," Gareth told her. "I knew tea would get cold and lemonade warm, so I laid in a bottle of beer."

"My hero!" She plopped down in the chair, untied her walking shoes, and peeled her socks from her aching feet. "There. I spent a couple of hours too many pacing the floor at the hospital."

The sandwiches were the usual tomato and cheese, and tasted like ambrosia. Between bites Matilda gave Gareth the medical report, concluding, "As far as I could make out between Caterina's accent and her addled condition, it was getting so dark she could hardly see the inscription when she heard Sweeney cry out. She looked for him. He was nowhere in sight. She called for him, took a few steps one way or the other, and then nothing. She doesn't remember hearing any footsteps or feeling the blow. She's still a bit shocky, not quite focused yet."

"Someone pushed Sweeney and then coshed Caterina," Gareth translated.

"Howard says he was standing there looking over the countryside, chewing his cud, I suppose, and he felt a tremendous shove from behind. I can sympathize with that." Matilda made a face. "He was dazed and didn't hear Caterina calling him. Or criminals stomping around, for that matter. He's not dazed now. He's reeking of offended dignity."

"It doesn't sound like the yobbo meant to kill, though either the fall or the blow could have done."

"I'm afraid so. Howard's sure it was Reynolds. He said the man was listening avidly while they were discussing the word 'spolia' Saturday night."

"He always has an ear in." Gareth nodded. "Sweeney's trap turned the trick, then?"

Matilda took a deep swig of the beer. Its astringent taste matched her mood. "No. He caught himself and an innocent student. There's no proof it was Reynolds who attacked them. The man isn't stupid. Why would he make a move under circumstances that would point directly to him? Why not let us uncover some kind of treasure and then steal it?"

"Reynolds has neck for two," Gareth asserted. "I reckon he intended Jason to take the blame — he heard the lad's row with Caterina."

"What did Jason tell Watkins?"

"He watched a football game on the telly in the sitting room and then chatted up one of the local girls in the bar. He'd put away several pints, no doubt of that, and the girl vouched for him."

"What about Reynolds's alibi?"

"He hasn't one. He said he was at home all evening. When Watkins sent a W.P.C. to interview Della, though, she couldn't knock her up."

"The policewoman knocked on the door of the house but Della didn't answer." Matilda translated.

"That's what I said. The W.P.C. fetched Watkins and Reynolds, who opened the door. Della was asleep. Out cold. When they finally woke her she said she'd gone to bed about five-thirty with a headache. There was a bottle of pain tablets by the bed, as well as a half-empty glass of gin."

Matilda frowned. "She shouldn't mix pain pills and alcohol. She could find herself taking a slow ferry across the Styx."

"Excuse me?" asked Gareth.

"She could die. Greek mythology. Sorry, I'll stick to Celtic." Matilda put down the empty bottle and the napkin and contorted her knees into the chair, trying to reach and rub her feet.

Gareth turned a wry smile toward the books lying on the bed next to him. "There's a good bit of Celtic mythology in these books of Dr. Sweeney's. *The Roman Conquest of Britain,*

Letters from Roman Britain, Everyday Life in Pagan Britain. The one with the letters mentions Corcester — Suetonius dedicated a temple here, to the victory over Boudicca, just before he went home to Rome."

"Which event may have prompted the infamous inscription. I'll have to re-read that book. Howard writes well, but he leaves the less glamorous parts to his students. He does the Druids, they do the plowshares." Matilda almost unhinged her jaw with a yawn.

Gareth pressed on. "Watkins and Clapper are still on about the travelers. Nick and Uncle Tom Cobleigh and all are perfectly capable of knocking Sweeney and Caterina about, but they have no motive. That we know, at the least. If they had a motive I could send Watkins to search the camp. As it is, I could only drive past several times this afternoon, and have another dekko at Durslow Edge."

"None of the travelers interviewed said they'd ever heard of Linda, but — well, I keep thinking there's some connection we haven't found yet."

"You should have seen Nick with that knife. It was like he knows who I am, and was slagging me off."

"I could have told you whether his confidence was real or sham. It would take confidence to murder someone with a pen knife, wouldn't it? So deliberate. . . ." Matilda shivered. Not only would it be easier to detect a criminal filled with remorse, it would make her less nervous about doing the detecting.

"Linda may have been seen with Reynolds," said Gareth, "but Della made a statement saying he was home with her the night of the murder. A night, Watkins told me when I asked, that was clear and cold. He never asked Della to describe the weather — why should he have done? The filthy storm she mentioned to me happened two days later, the night Linda's body was found. I think that's an important discrepancy. Watkins thinks it's a natural mistake for poor stupid Della."

"Della's not stupid. If she killed Linda, over illegal antiquities or over her husband — there's no accounting for tastes — she's keeping it well-hidden." Matilda tried another angle of knee and ankle. Gareth picked up her feet, propped them on his thigh, and started massaging them himself.

"Thank you," said Matilda, and went on, "Then there's the receipt from the antiquities shop, which could have gotten to Durslow in any number of innocent ways. Or it could have been planted there by someone else to throw suspicion on Celia or Della — Emma, for example. Didn't Clapper say she hung out with some occult group among the travelers, who might, I suppose, be building fires on Durslow.... Of course, we only have Clapper's word for that, don't we?"

"He has his ear in too, doesn't he? He as much as admitted to me he's nicked an antiquity or two."

"The question is, who's doing what with or for or in spite of whom? Who stole the statuary, and God only knows what else, and bashed two people over the head and committed murder? It is all the same person, isn't it?"

"God, I hope so," Gareth said.

Matilda didn't remind him of his avowed atheism. The room was so silent that the creaks and pops of the settling timbers of the building sounded as loud in her ears as her own heartbeat. "And I've got more for you. This afternoon Clapper was showing me a snapshot of last year's May Queen. I've already met her. Emma. What's very strange is that I've also met the young man, Clive, in the photo with her. He's the one from the underground platform in London. The one who may have tried to push me under a train."

Gareth's hands pressed so firmly into her feet she winced. His eyes darted upward. "Bugger! You're sure of that?"

"I'm sure. He might be one of the travelers now, his leaving town to look for a job being a convenient fiction." She yawned again. "All the pictures you took of the traveler's encampment, and I recognize a face in Clapper's publicity shot. Don't you love it when a plan comes together?"

"You're the expert on coincidence," Gareth said with a snort, and returned to his task.

Something in the back of Matilda's mind whispered, just when does happenstance become coincidence? You've built a career on coincidence, on the congruence of time and space, thought and feeling. And now it's not working, it's not falling into order, it's like a landscape after a tornado, straws driven through trees and clocks left ticking in the midst of ruin.

Gareth's right thumb pressed into the ball of her left foot. The pressure both hurt and drained away the tension. His hands were warm and strong. His downcast lashes cast shadows above his red-stubbled cheeks. "You should have a look at Reynolds's antiquities," he went on. "I reckon half of them are fakes, as Sweeney said. They're too pretty, all tarted up."

"Very good, you're learning." Matilda nodded approvingly. "And then there's Ashley."

"Ashley?"

"I smelled alcohol on her breath tonight. She was with Bryan — he seems a nice enough boy, and he does like her. Still, you know what Ogden Nash wrote, 'Candy's dandy, but liquor's quicker.'"

Gareth looked up, nonplussed.

"She's vulnerable," Matilda explained. "But then, who isn't, on some level?"

"Should I sort Bryan out?"

"No, no, don't interfere. Right now she's hugging that romance like a teddy bear. And it's not as though she had anything to do with the case."

"Caterina didn't have anything to do with the case, did she?"

"Thanks."

A car passed outside. Someone walked down the hall — one of the students going to the W.C., probably. Gareth massaged Matilda's feet. Frissons of delight played up her legs and she had to quell a sigh of pleasure. He was thinking of something else, something a long time ago and a long way away. His breaths were shallow but even.

"Which one of your relatives," Matilda asked gently, "has — what do they call it in Wales, second sight?"

He shot her a flash of exasperation from beneath his brows.

She returned a wry smile. "You weren't just skeptical about my skills, you were downright defensive. I suppose you still are, you're just covering it better. Unless the fact that I haven't demonstrated many skills. . . ." She cut off that line of reasoning. "I'm guessing there was some conflict about ESP in your youth."

"What if I told you my youth is none of your business?" Gareth said, but without resentment.

"You'd be right. It isn't."

He emitted a part sigh, part laugh. "My grandmother had second sight. Half the folk in Aberffraw would come to her for advice. She was a good Methodist, mind you, but she loved the old ways. My mother would take the mickey out of her for it. My father — well, he was a teacher. He had work to do."

"I see," Matilda said.

"Gran told me all the old tales. My middle name is Thomas, but she always pretended the 'T' stood for Taliesin."

"Taliesin, the bard? Aberffraw was the principal residence of the kings of Gwynedd, for whom he sang."

"Anglesey — Mon — is mentioned in one of his verses: 'There will come men to Mon to be initiated into the ways of wizards'. Or the ways of druids, if you like. I used to have whacking great stretches of the *Cad Goddeu,* the battle of the trees, off by heart. It's all gone now." Gareth stared down at Matilda's feet, as though suddenly surprised to see them in his hands. He placed them gently on the floor. "Gran didn't live to see me become a policeman."

Matilda felt as though she were eavesdropping. She'd told Gareth she couldn't read his mind, and yet, at that moment, she was doing just that. Her flesh tingled from the touch of his hands. His hands tingled from the touch of her flesh. Taken unaware, by subtlety rather than by force, he had lowered his drawbridge, opened his gates, and exposed the skeletons in his dungeons.

"I think," he said hoarsely, not meeting her eyes, "I'd better pack it in. I'm knackered. We're both knackered."

"And we have ditches to dig tomorrow, Sweeney or no Sweeney. Good night, Gareth."

"Good night, Matilda." Still not looking at her, he walked stiffly across the room and shut the door behind him.

Matilda contemplated the flutter of her pulse and the random fall of her thoughts. This wasn't the first time she'd been ambushed by libido and sentiment. It probably wouldn't be the last. *Not now,* she told herself. We're working.

Or Gareth was working. She hadn't exactly been making professional points. She'd prefer to think that indicated the coolness of her adversary, not some defect in herself. This was no time to lose her self-confidence.

Matilda rooted among the books and found her own copy of the *Cad Goddeu.* Closing her eyes, she opened it at random and set her finger on a page. She found herself pointing to the last verse of the poem. Holding the book at arm's length, she read:

> O druids, in your wisdom
> ask of Arthur who is more ancient
> than I, in the chants!
> Who is here
> thinking of the flood
> and Christ crucified
> and the judgment day ahead?
> Golden gem upon a golden jewel,
> I am splendid
> I am skilled in metal work.

Well, she thought. Druids and the passing of the old religion, the certainty of judgment and a hint of treasure. . . . The next few days would be very interesting indeed.

Clouds lidded the sky, seeming to compress the damp, still air against the earth. The excavation was a crazy quilt of green grass, black mud, and reddish-brown stone. Even though Watkins had reported that the malefactor hadn't left any booby-traps in the trenches, the students tiptoed up the sodden sides of the hill and huddled like sheep at the top.

"It's like getting back on a horse after you've fallen off," Matilda told them. "Start digging."

"How many times have you fallen off a horse?" Gareth asked from his post at her shoulder. "It's right painful."

"Don't step on my lines," she said. "Ashley, I want you to take Jason's place as group leader. The rest of you stay in your original groups. I'll take over the inscription. Gareth, you can go on working in the Miller trench, if you like."

He tipped her a salute that was every bit as wary as the steps of the students and clambered downwards.

Ashley stood stock still. "Me?"

"Yes, you," Matilda said.

"Oh well — sure — I can do it." Ashley shouldered her shovel. "Come on, gang, we need to uncover the rest of the bathhouse. If the caldarium was over there, the hypocaust must be about . . ." She led her group away. The other two groups exchanged shrugs and returned to their assigned spots.

Matilda looked back at the hotel. The students who'd decided not to stay with the dig were trudging up the street toward the bus station. Jason, not surprisingly, was in the lead. He'd sputtered all during breakfast about suing the Corcester constabulary for unlawful arrest. Even after Matilda had pointed out he hadn't been arrested, he'd been helping the police with their inquiries, he continued to fire random shots at everyone who crossed his bows. "Let him rant," Matilda had whispered to Ashley. "He's trying to repair his damaged manhood."

"Like he has much to repair," she'd returned. "You almost have to feel sorry for him."

Matilda had assured the defectors that she and Sweeney would arrange some sort of course credit for the work they'd completed. Not that she'd bothered to consult with Sweeney before telling them that. She was less irritated with him for setting up a situation where students could be in danger than with herself for going along with the idea.

She turned back to the dig to see Ashley putting Jennifer to work sketching several broken glass vials. Matilda was gratified the girl had decided to stay — most timid people hid a kernel of stubbornness. Bryan was staying too, just to give her a little extra motivation. Not that she was paying any attention to him. She was trying to act cool in front of Gareth, probably. Bryan stood holding a meter stick and eyeing the back of Ashley's head, frowning slightly.

A slight frown had been Gareth's expression this morning. Matilda couldn't speak for Bryan, but she knew what Gareth's problem was: He was waiting for her to take last night's moment of vulnerability and bludgeon him with it. With a grimace, Matilda picked her way into the Miller ravine.

Gareth stood, hands in pockets, glumly surveying the trampled mud and caved-in banks concealing his carefully-excavated apse of the Mithraeum. "Trust Sweeney to fall just here."

"It looks like a hippopotamus wallow," Matilda agreed. "But the paramedics had to do their job."

Pulling his trowel from his pocket, Gareth squatted down and began scraping at the mud-splattered stones. "I'll have at go at Dunning tomorrow, if Sweeney's back by then."

"He should be, unless he's developed complications overnight."

"Watkins tells me that Clive is a nephew of our Mr. Clapper — so we'd better start watching what we say in front of him. Although if the lad's in the area, he's keeping a low profile. You don't suppose it was him driving the bus that almost had you off the road, do you?"

"Elvis Presley could've been driving that bus," said Matilda.

"Right. Watkins agrees that it's time to bring Nick in for questioning — again."

"I doubt if they'll have a lot to say to each other. Maybe I should go out to the camp and look helpless or something, try to win his trust."

"Yes." Gareth's trowel grated across the rock.

That wasn't what I was doing with you, Matilda said silently, and added to herself, odd, how sometimes the best way to help a relationship along is to pretend it doesn't exist.

She turned away and inspected the trench. Between the rain and last night's stampede, its sides looked as though they'd been chewed and spat out. Column drums thrust themselves from the muck. Bits of mosaic tile lay among the weeds. Blocks of masonry in several different shapes lay scattered in no discernible pattern.

As the excavators peeled away the layers of dirt and time the ruins were opened not so much to the light of day as to the perceptions. It was like opening the doors of a concert hall, so that anyone who cared to stop and listen could hear the music inside. Matilda half-closed her eyes, conjuring the place as it had once looked.

Faintly, like an image on smoke, she saw the foursquare Roman temple before the perimeter wall. The stones of its foundations, skewed slightly from the wall, were larger and dressed more roughly than the Roman masonry. Those stones were relics of the temple to Epona, the Celtic temenos, razed by the conquerors as though tearing down a building would destroy the deity within. The entrance to the underground Mithras temple lay just outside the largest stone in the foundation. Inside was something else, a cellar room, perhaps, a crevice that rang hollowly like deep water. . . .

"Matilda?"

Matilda blinked away her vision and looked up. "Yes, Jennifer?"

"Manfred's found some armor. Do you want him to take the pictures?"

"I'll come, thank you."

Gareth was kneeling before the wall, focused on his task. She didn't speak to him when she left.

What with one thing and another, Matilda had very little time to work on the inscription, after all. She managed to fit the "spolia" fragment into place, and deduced that the message was, indeed, commemorating Suetonius's dedication of the temple. The Roman politicians must have rushed its completion, so that the old general would have ceremonial recognition of his victory before he was hustled away from the scene. Before he had a chance to be vindictive toward his former enemies.

And what of Boudicca? Matilda wondered. Supposedly she had taken poison after her defeat, and her grave now lay below platform ten at Kings Cross station in London. Whatever, her statue beside Westminster Bridge was a splendid bit of fantasy.

"Matilda," Bryan called, "we've found some cups and plates. . . ."

Howard Sweeney made his entrance right before quitting time, dapper as ever, needing only an ivory-handled cane to complete the image. In its absence he was leaning on Ted Ionescu's arm.

"Yes, yes," Sweeney announced, "I'm quite well, no thanks to the villain who pushed me down the trench. I was in more danger, I think, from Signor Alfredo Rossi, who came straight from the airport to the hospital and accused me of interfering with his daughter."

"No," muttered someone in the group of students, "that

was Jason."

"So is Caterina on her way home?" Matilda asked.

"Yes, the sweet young thing will soon be safe in the bosom of her family. I assured her that her services were no longer required here — she was only piecing together a bit of inscription, after all, anyone could do that."

His fall hadn't improved Sweeney's personality, thought Matilda. She backed away and let him introduce his assistant to the students. Ionescu smiled nervously, glasses and teeth shining. Serving as Sweeney's crutch probably wasn't anything new to him.

From the corner of her eye she saw Gareth emerge from the trench, splotched with mud from head to toe. His expression was less tense than it had been in the morning. He said something pleasant to Ashley, who grinned back. He still hadn't a clue that she had a crush on him, had he?

Gareth turned to Matilda with a brief but intense look that she felt in the pit of her stomach. So lust canceled out doubt yet again. That was one of nature's little tricks to keep life amusing and the human race viable.

"Let's tidy everything away," called Sweeney. "Jennifer, bring me your sketches. And I want to see the team leaders — Manfred, Bryan, Jason. . . ."

"Jason has gone," said Manfred. "Ashley is now the leader."

Sweeney swung around not to Ashley but to Matilda. "A little feminist conspiracy behind my back, is it?"

"It's called equal opportunity, Howard. Welcome to the new millennium."

Gobbling indistinctly, Sweeney gave Ashley a suspicious glare and then limped off toward the hotel, dragging Ionescu behind him.

"He's not going to be out to get me now, is he?" Ashley asked Matilda.

"Not at all," Matilda assured her. "He'll come around when he sees what good work you're doing."

"Let him take his lumps with the rest of us," Gareth added with a grin, and together they went in to dinner.

*I*t wasn't strictly necessary to go ghost-hunting at dusk. But there was no point in searching for echoes of personalities past when personalities present clogged the scene. And the lowering clouds added atmosphere, Matilda told herself. Not to mention darkness. She walked through the gate and up the side of the embankment.

A couple of cars passed on the road below. Distant music, or amplified noise optimistically called music, echoed from the town. The lights of Fortuna Stud glowed like Gareth's corpse candles in the gloom. Reynolds hadn't made his tour of inspection today. Whether he was sulking about being questioned by Watkins, or gloating at having pared a few witnesses away from his fort, Matilda wasn't about to guess.

A shadowy human figure slipped along the driveway and into the garden behind Reynolds's house. A traveler? Matilda wondered. There was no reason Reynolds, Linda, and Nick couldn't have been conspiring together. And why not Della and Clapper, too, just to make things even more interesting.

The gate by the road opened and shut behind her. Footsteps splashed and squelched. She knew without turning around that it was Gareth, come to protect her not from ghosties and ghoulies but from all-too-solid miscreants.

"Will I be in your way?" his voice asked.

"Not if you're quiet."

"Right."

Matilda picked her way through the excavated patches and along the edge of the Miller trench. A breath of cold air eddied upward, chilling her face. From her pocket she pulled the spindle she'd picked up her first day in Cornovium. *No coincidence,* she thought. *None at all.*

A shape resolved itself from the twilight like a sunlit image projected upon a dark screen. Columns of reddish-brown stone stood in parallel rows below a triangular architrave. Steps mounted upward, skewed just a bit at the side where the foundation stones were of a different shape. Just around the corner of the building a door opened into a low mound. The odor of incense tickled Matilda's nostrils, along with that of horses, bread, and sweat.

Claudia walked toward the temple carrying a basket of

daffodils. Her features were drawn tight, as though she was wracked by pain but was too proud to admit it. She climbed the steps and disappeared through the portico into the darkened interior of the temple.

Matilda followed. The stone steps felt like grass and mud beneath her feet. The columns dissolved around her. She found herself in a square chamber lit by high windows and lined with altars. An incense burner emitted a tendril of smoke. Opposite the door stood a heroic bronze statue on a plinth. "Dia Pater" read the inscription. God the Father, Matilda translated. It looked like Charlton Heston playing Moses with a better haircut.

At the god's feet were arrayed several small statues — a leopard, a bull, miniature warriors. Even now, at the beginning of the twenty-first century, those were magnificent pieces. New, unstained by time and larceny, they had been breathtaking. Matilda could hardly blame Reynolds for being bitter about their loss.

Claudia wasn't looking at either the votive statuary or the image of the god. Branwen sat on the top step of a short flight of stairs that led downward to a door closed by a grille. A solitary shaft of light illuminated the chamber within, filling it with the reddish-yellow glow of Celtic gold.

Matilda chanced one more step forward. She knew what Branwen was looking at. Near the door lay a careless pile of gold torcs, no doubt wrenched from the throats of defeated Celts. Some were thick coiled braids, some were chains, and some were fine strands of wire. Some had finials carved in intricate anthropomorphic patterns, others ended with simple knobs. All of them were symbols of the Celts' dedication to their gods, gods now disgraced by the display of gold as simple booty.

"Why are you sitting there?" Claudia asked quietly.

"I'm spoils of war just as surely as those torcs. Except I'm tainted, and the gold is not." Branwen extended her right hand and regarded it narrowly.

"Tainted? Not by Marcus, surely."

"No. He acts within right and custom, doesn't he? And he's a good man. . . ." Branwen's hand clenched. She turned swiftly around. "He doesn't know who I am."

"Of the Iceni, you said."

"My mother was Boudicca's daughter, violated by a Roman soldier. I'm not Iceni, I'm not Roman — I was conceived in degradation and born in shame. If my grandmother had won her war, perhaps I would know peace. But now, like this — I'll find peace only in the next life."

The tendril of smoke wavered in a draft. Claudia said, "I have heard that your priests, your Druids, preach the immortality of the soul. I too believe in a life after death."

"I thought Mithras was a man's god," said Branwen, nodding toward the underground temple on the other side of the wall from the treasury.

"Marcus follows Mithras. I don't." With a sigh Claudia sat down on the step beside Branwen, and did not protest when the girl inched away from her. "When I was a child I heard a man called Peter speak, not of a god, but of the son of God. He lived in Judaea, preached compassion and forgiveness, and died to bring us all to everlasting life."

Branwen tilted her head to the side skeptically.

"Like him, Peter was executed for treason, for saying that the emperor is no god. When I was last in Rome I visited his grave. It's become a shrine." Claudia reached into her basket and pulled out a short knife. With it she scratched a symbol in the stone, a "P" with an "x" and three horizontal lines superimposed on the stem.

A thrill ran down Matilda's back. Claudia had heard the apostle Peter. She had visited his grave. That grave was now deep beneath the Vatican's great basilica, enclosed by a stucco wall on which the symbol she had scratched was repeated over and over.

"And does this god demand sacrifice?" Branwen asked.

"The sacrifice of God is a troubled spirit." A spasm of pain crossed Claudia's face, quickly quelled and replaced by a thin smile. "And a few flowers." She spilled the daffodils from her basket across the stone she had scratched. Their cheerful yellow-gold made the gleam of the torcs seem tarnished.

"Pray to your god for me," said Branwen, and rose to her feet.

"Pray to yours for me, and for Marcus," Claudia returned.

"I pray to Brighid, Rhiannon, and Keridwen. I pray for an

end to this life, and glory in the next. I pray for the speedy arrival of the quarter-day. . . ." Branwen shook her head, as though she'd revealed too much, and fled the temple.

Claudia sat on the step, caught between the golden spoils and the golden flowers. "Marcus," she said softly, "I want you back. God forgive me, but I will have you back."

Matilda took a step toward the woman. Daffodils. Sacrifice. The spring quarter day. Beltane. Did Claudia realize what Branwen was telling her?

A hand grasped her arm. Matilda swam upward through currents of memory and desire and broke the surface of night. The air was ice-cold and still. Hard, crisp lights dotted the darkness. Gareth pulled her back from the rim of the Miller trench. "Sorry, you were almost over the edge."

Matilda returned the spindle to her pocket. She tried to speak, croaked, swallowed, and tried again. "Claudia's going to let Branwen go to her death, without telling Marcus, without trying to stop her. Against her faith, perhaps, but it's Branwen's faith that's compelling her."

"Excuse me?"

"Come on, I'll fill you in." Matilda slipped her arm through his, and leaning together with a subtle and yet unmistakable friction they walked down from the fort. She told him every detail, right down to the smell of the incense.

"Sounds like a proper soap," Gareth concluded, and added, ever practical, "It's all over and done with. Maybe the bog body is Branwen's, but you're a bit late to save her, aren't you?"

"Yes."

Gareth opened the gate for her and handed her through. "Is the gold still here?"

"Some of it is, I think. . . ." Matilda stopped dead, pulling Gareth around with her. Someone, a man, was crouching just past the corner of the bowling green wall. A student wouldn't have any reason to hide from them. Neither would one of the constables. Reynolds? Her hyper-extended senses picked up a low chuckle of amusement that didn't remind her of anyone she had met before. A receding chuckle, as the man slipped away into the night.

"What is it?" Gareth asked.

"Someone was hiding behind the wall — no, wait, he's already gone. . . ."

Gareth released her arm and sprinted around the corner. He covered thirty or forty yards down the road before he gave it up and came back. He was hardly breathing any faster. "No joy. I didn't see him."

"Thank you for believing that I did."

Gareth replied with a noncommittal sniff.

Now walking a demure two feet apart, they passed the cottages, crossed the street, and greeted the evening constable as he headed toward the fort. "Mind your back," Gareth told him. "Someone's messing about out there."

"That's why I'm standing about here instead having a pint in my local," the man answered, and walked on.

Ashley stood outside the door of the hotel, her blond hair glowing in the light streaming from the windows. Matilda had the distinct impression she was waiting for someone, or at least hoping for someone to appear.

"Aren't you a little nervous out there in the dark?" the girl asked them.

"You have to wonder what's in the dark with you," Matilda responded.

"Ghosts?"

Had some unguarded phrase tipped Ashley off, Matilda asked herself, or was the girl simply curious? "You know what Samuel Johnson said about the likelihood of ghosts? All argument is against it, but all belief is for it."

"Don't stay out long," Gareth said. "And don't leave the area just next the hotel."

Ashley nodded. "Don't worry."

The lights in the lobby were blindingly bright. Reynolds's nasal voice echoed from the bar, counterpointed by the saccharine strains of "If Ever I Would Leave You." Matilda saw Bryan sitting in the sitting room watching television. She wondered suddenly whether she'd been wrong about Ashley going drinking with him. If not him, though, who?

"So if you believe in ghosts they exist?" Gareth asked.

"Probably. But I know what I've seen here. Tomorrow I'll prove it to you."

"Right," he replied, not quite sarcastic, not quite affectionate.

Matilda offered him a conspiratorial smile, and went upstairs alone.

Chapter Twelve

*T*uesday morning dawned clear and bright. The students streamed up the side of the fort, chattering happily in the sunshine. Gareth reserved judgment — one sunny day doesn't make the summer, his grandmother had often said.

He settled his shovel on his shoulder and inspected the pavement beside the bowling green wall. He saw no footprints clear enough for a cast. Matilda might not have sensed anyone hiding there. She might not have sensed last night's episode of the Great Roman Soap. She wouldn't be the first intelligent, perceptive person who'd let her perceptions run away with her.

And yet, Gareth thought, she'd told him every detail of last night's vision, confident she could prove its truth. And she would prove it. It was no longer Matilda's intuition that was irritating, but his growing trust in it.

"Ah, March!" Howard Sweeney was seated in a lawn chair atop the fort, looking like a pharaoh overseeing his slaves. "Are we making any progress?"

At least six students and Ted Ionescu were well within earshot. Gareth answered, "That's for you to say. I'm merely writing up your results."

"And you'll do a smashing job of it, I'm sure. Matilda!"

Matilda emerged from the Miller trench. "Yes, Howard?"

"Are the group leaders doing their paperwork properly?"

"Ashley, Bryan, Manfred," called Matilda. "Are you doing your paperwork properly?"

"Yes — no problem — *jawohl*," they answered in chorus.

She gave Sweeney a look that would have withered a rhinoceros. "Anything else I can do for you?"

"No, no, carry on," he replied with a wave of his hand. "Ted. . . ."

Ionescu sprang to attention.

Matilda disappeared. Gareth followed her into the cool, damp shadows of the ravine. "A pity Sweeney's not the one got the concussion," he said.

"His offensiveness is a shield," she replied, "and a darn good one at that. I remember thinking when I first met him, at a conference in Boston six or seven years ago, how little of the real man I could sense through the bravado. I suspect he's protecting something rather small and raw inside. Many hard-working, ambitious people are."

"Right," Gareth told her, not about to touch that one. "Did you tell Sweeney about — about what you saw last night?"

"More or less. He'll take me seriously when he sees the evidence."

"That's good police procedure. Where shall we start?"

Matilda pointed to a column drum lying just free of the muddy side of the trench, about ten feet from the pit left by the thieves. She'd used string and stakes to mark off a small area behind it. "There. The cellar treasury is on the other side of the foundation wall from the Mithraeum. I'm sure the balk — the trench wall — was originally vertical. Miller was a good archaeologist for his time. But sixty years of erosion and inquisitive feet have broken off the soil at the top and let it accumulate at the bottom."

"In other words, the wall's at enough of a slant we can cut into its base without bringing its top down on our heads."

Matilda took a notebook and measuring tape from her pocket and began taking measurements of the Mithraeum. "You did a nice job cleaning this up."

"Thank you." Gareth dug carefully into the compacted dirt, keeping the sides straight and the slope above cleared. Every time he spotted so much as a chip of stone or a coin he beckoned Matilda, who rushed forward with her notebook, a collecting box, and a label.

He should be interviewing Dunning and Emma, Gareth told himself. He should be keeping an eye on the travelers. The dig was taking too much of his time and energy. And yet the dig was the focus of the case. . . . His shovel scraped against stone. "Matilda, here's a whacking great rock."

He stepped aside and took off his jacket. The sun peeked over the rim of the trench and struck silver in Matilda's hair. She scraped at the stone with her trowel and then stood back, brows knit with concentration. Her body moved with fluid precision. Her stance was straight and yet balanced. She made the Queen seem awkward.

Gareth had worried at first that his sudden physical attraction to her was a result of the celibate life he'd led recently. But half the girls on the dig were prettier than Matilda — and, he suspected, more readily available — and he felt only a distant appreciation for them. He valued self-possession in a woman, and Matilda was nothing if not self-possessed. . . . *Not now,* Gareth told himself.

Matilda glanced up, catching his eye, and he felt like a little boy caught out with his hand in a sack of sweets. Her smile humored his appetite even as her words modeled patience. "This is the foundation wall of the temple, all right. The smaller Roman stones above it have been robbed out — half the town is built from them. Let's break for lunch, and afterward we'll get several of the kids down here and go in over the top of the stone."

Over the top, Gareth repeated silently. That seemed appropriate.

Sweeney was in fine form during lunch, cleverly disparaging friends, Romans, and countrymen alike, his comments interspersed with no doubt important calls on his cell phone. After the meal, he sent Ionescu back with the students whilst he went to his room to have a nap.

By the time he re-appeared at the dig the entire student body was crowded round the trench. Three mud-spattered boys leaned on their shovels and Gareth perched precariously on a column drum taking pictures. Matilda herself knelt in the cool, oozing gash cut into the side of the trench, Ashley handing her trowels and dental picks like a nurse aiding a surgeon.

"What's all this in aid of?" Sweeney asked.

"Another inscription," replied Ionescu. "She went straight to it. Dead brilliant, if you ask me."

"I didn't ask you." Sweeney limped back and forth, trying to get a better view. "Matilda, come out of there and give me a report."

Gareth smothered his grin as Matilda looked upward, her expression sweet as an angel's. "Howard! How nice to have you back! Here's the monogram on the rock. Do you want to tell the students about it, or shall I?"

"Please, carry on." Sweeney plopped down in his lawn chair.

"This bit of masonry," said Matilda, "was once the coping stone of a stairway. See the steps, still in place?"

Everyone crowded forward.

"The stone was rolled over, its original face turned down, probably to hide the monogram scratched on it. This means, ironically, that the monogram is in perfect condition, its edges sharp and its surface not weathered."

"If it was inside the temple," Bryan said, "it'd be protected."

"Yes, you're right. The monogram might have sat face up for any number of years before the temple was abandoned. More likely, though, the stone was turned over while it was new. The Romans were tolerant of most religions, but not Christianity. Because the Christians refused to believe in the divinity of the emperor, and so were a political threat."

Gareth visualized the scene, Claudia and Branwen comparing gods as poor Marcus went about drilling the troops or inspecting bridle bits or mucking out latrines — well no, he was an officer, officers didn't muck.

"At first glance this is a chi-rho symbol," Matilda went on. "The Greek letter 'chi', which looks like an 'x', superimposed on a 'rho', which looks like a capital 'p', making 'Ch-r', the first letters in 'Christ'. This is why we shorthand 'Christmas' to 'X-mas', by the by. What is especially interesting about this particular symbol, though, is these three little lines to the right of the vertical stem. If you see the letter not as a Greek 'rho' but as a Latin 'p', the lines make an 'e', giving you 'Pe' for the apostle Peter. To whom Christ said, 'I will give you the keys of the kingdom of heaven'. Looks like a key, doesn't it?"

Everyone oohed and aahed understanding.

"It's a nice little bit of code for a time of persecution.

Historians have found this monogram on dishes, games, manuscripts, tombstones, all sorts of items. But only when it was found on the actual tomb of Peter beneath St. Peter's basilica in Rome did anyone realize its significance."

Sweeney cleared his throat loudly. "And there you are, class, today's lesson in semiotics. If you have time whilst you're in Britain you can view the Christian mosaics at Lullingstone and Hinton St. Mary."

"Semiotics?" Manfred asked. The English-speakers looked just as puzzled.

"The study of symbols," stated Ashley, with a peculiar little frown.

"Quite so. Let's get to it, there are other interesting bits to uncover, I'm sure." Sweeney turned to Ionescu. "Ted, work up a way to give partial credit to the students who buggered off. I don't want to get pathetic letters from their advisors pleading extenuating circumstances."

"I can use the same system we've used for the adult education students," Ionescu said. "They're always coming and going — lorry drivers, housewives, that lot."

"Yes, yes, that would be splendid." Sweeney's jacket trilled. He pulled out his mobile phone and began a long, rambling conversation about nothing in particular, so far as Gareth could tell.

The students filtered back to their groups. Gareth stepped down from the column and made a mental note never to take an adult education course from Howard Sweeney.

Ashley handed Matilda her tools. "That's really cool."

"Pretty cool of you to know about semiotics," Matilda returned.

"Oh, well — I just saw a textbook the other day. . . ." Ashley skipped upward and made shooing motions at her group.

Matilda sat down on what had once been the top step of the stairway, her hands folded in her lap. Gareth propped his foot on a handy rock and started to change the film in the camera. He hoped she wasn't expecting a formal apology from him. He was wrong, she was right, and nothing he could say about her skills could add anything to the sentiment he'd shown her Sunday night.

She wasn't paying any attention to him. Her face was

intense, as though listening to something a long way away. Her entire body tilted forward. Super — she was doing it again, leaning over a temporal garden fence to join Branwen and Claudia and their gossip of imaginary deities. . . .

"It's there," Matilda said.

Gareth jumped. "What?"

"Gold. The treasury was filled in. See the rubble at the foot of the staircase? Only one puny little bit of gold is still there, right at the edge. The rest was taken away a long time ago. This ground hasn't been disturbed in a long, long time. Unfortunately, we've now opened it up to thieves and vandals. Let's see if we can beat them at their own game without committing too much archaeological mayhem."

"Right." Gareth reassembled the camera, put the used roll of film in his pocket, and picked up his shovel. "Where?"

He used his shovel and she her trowel, opening a narrow shaft where the rubble fill met the foundation stone. They paused every so often to take pictures, draw sketches, and make measurements. The sun moved on and the ravine plunged into shadow. The students' voices drifted down from the surface, punctuated by a few brief, harsh caws as Reynolds had another shufti round his property. Gareth tensed, preparing to throw his body protectively over the new discoveries. But with a casual glance and wave down the trench the landowner left again, Sweeney's greasy courtesies easing him on his way.

Unlike Reynolds to show so little interest, Gareth thought. And he hadn't stopped by at all yesterday. He must know he was on the short list of suspects.

At last Matilda stretched out full length on the muddy stone and reached down into the hole with her trowel. Gareth craned this way and that, but her head was in the way and the hole was dark. . . . No it wasn't. Something glimmered in the shadow, in Matilda's hands.

She sat up, gently buffing a twisted bit of wire on her shirt. It was a torc, a small simple one, squashed out of shape. Beneath its coating of dirt it gleamed the red-gold of the setting sun. "That's magic," Gareth breathed. He reached out, wanting to feel its warm gleam on his fingertips.

"Wow!"

Gareth snapped his hand into a fist and spun round to see Ashley watching them.

"Dr. Sweeney called quitting time fifteen minutes ago," the girl explained. "Everyone's already gone back, but I thought maybe you didn't hear. That's gold, isn't it? Cool."

Matilda levered herself up on Gareth's shoulder and tucked the torc inside her shirt. "Don't tell anyone about this, Ashley. Nothing draws thieves and vandals faster than gold."

"Don't worry," Ashley returned. "I can keep a secret."

Gareth took a few more photos of the area, hoping there was enough light, and escorted the women across the street and into the hotel. With more than one curious backward look Ashley went into her own room. Matilda knocked at Sweeney's door.

The professor threw it open. "Ah, Dr. Gray, what a positively brilliant lecture you presented. So you succeed again. How very convenient to have an extra sense over and beyond the five allotted to mere mortals."

Matilda produced the torc.

With a gasp, Sweeney snatched it up. "Lovely. Absolutely lovely. Are there any more — Snettisham, you know. . . ."

"This seems to be the only one," Matilda told him. "You realize we have to keep this quiet."

"No, no, my dear — we want to draw the thieves out. You'll agree with me, Inspector March."

"We have to keep it quiet," Gareth said. "You and Caterina got off lightly the last time, when the thief was after only a rumor of treasure. Now that there's actually been treasure found, he'll be at the dig with a squad of navvies and a bulldozer."

"Yes, well, I suppose you're the expert on criminals." Sweeney rooted among the books and boxes piled on the bedroom furniture — his room was even nicer than Matilda's, Gareth noted — and found a cardboard box just big enough for the torc. He nestled it on a bed of cotton wool, wrote out a label, and taped down the lid. "Here, Inspector. If you'd be so kind as to hand this in at the police station. I've already sent Ted back to Manchester, more's the pity, or he could have carried it to the lab for cleaning. But all in good time, all in good time."

Gareth tucked the parcel beneath his arm. He and Matilda walked down the hall, round the corner, and through the fire doors to her room. She was frowning all the way. "Tuppence for your thoughts?" he asked once they were safely inside her door.

"No thoughts, really. I'm just aggravated at Howard. His ego is more inflated every day. He'll take all the credit when this case is over, mark my words."

"If there's any credit to be taken," Gareth said darkly.

"You don't think we'll catch the bad guys, do you?"

"I wonder if Sweeney wasn't right, if we shouldn't blow the gaff about the torc, let Reynolds have a go at the dig."

"That would be a difficult situation to control."

"We're not in control of the situation now, Matilda. All we're doing is lying doggo beside the waterhole, hoping a tiger will come to drink."

"And you'd rather go tiger-hunting, wouldn't you? But there's a lot of jungle out there, and a lot of dangerous animals other than tigers."

Gareth grimaced. "I'll give the torc to Watkins, and put a flea in his ear — he still hasn't had Nick in. Tomorrow I'm off to Manchester and the antiquities shop."

"Go for it," Matilda told him. "Just consider one thing. If we're going to be careful around Clapper, we should be careful around Watkins, too. Remember that Linda Burkett wrote her letter not to him but to the Greater Manchester police."

"Oh for the love of . . . I've known Watkins for. . . ." Gareth scowled, feeling a furtive sympathy for Sweeney's impatience with Matilda. "If the torc does a bunk from the police station we'll know who to blame, won't we?"

Matilda smiled at him. "Yes. See you later."

Gareth swung down the staircase and through the lobby. He was getting a headache. And it wasn't the sort of headache an aspirin would cure.

*B*orley Arcade had been rather too posh for Gareth's taste when he lived in Manchester. Now, as a day tripper, his opinion wasn't changed.

He stood outside The Antiquary's Corner and considered his tactics. Pretending to be a rich collector might work, although his informal shirt and canvas trousers gave that the lie. . . . No, wait, he could imitate Matilda's accent and pose as an American toff. Yank tourists tended to wear any old clothes. But no again, he had no ear for accents just as he had no ear for music, much to his father's despair.

Taking a deep breath, Gareth decided the direct approach was best. There was already too much misdirection in this case.

He opened the door and walked inside, feeling like the proverbial bull in the china shop. Everything was light, delicate, polished. Even the music that wafted through the air was insubstantial. The only thing heavy in the shop was the floral scent of the soaps.

Several well-dressed customers browsed among the break-ables, guided by a scrawny silver-haired woman wearing a pink twin-set and pearls. Gareth drifted toward the far wall and the glass-fronted cabinet filled with antiquities. Unlike Reynolds' collection — unlike everything else in the shop — the artifacts looked bruised with age. Gareth wondered how many of them really were old. The coins, probably, and perhaps that little green glass vial with the tarnished lid. . . . He stepped closer. Reynolds had a vial exactly like that one, except its lid glowed bronze.

"May I help you?"

He turned. Celia Dunning stood with one hand resting on her hip, shoulders back, chin up. The stance that seemed balanced in Matilda looked stiff and haughty on her. "Good morning," Gareth said. "I'm interested in this glass vial. Roman, is it?"

Her examination felt like an icy draft down his neck. "Yes, it is."

"Was it found in this area? Chester or Corcester, perhaps?"

"I'd have to check my records."

"May I see it, please?"

"I'd have to unlock the case. Are you interested in making a purchase? I'm asking one hundred pounds for it."

She was right about one thing. Gareth didn't have a hundred pounds to spend on a bit of glass, no matter how old.

"How often do you get new items for sale?"

"Every so often." Dunning looked back toward the other customers.

"Perhaps you could ring me when more Roman artifacts arrive."

"Give my assistant your name and telephone number." With a frosty smile not reflected in her eyes, Dunning dismissed Gareth as small game and returned to the trophy consumers who were fingering several twee ceramic figures.

On to Plan B, Gareth told himself, and turned toward the rear of the shop. A girl no older than Ashley stood behind the counter. Her dark-rimmed eyes looked at Gareth with considerably more warmth than Dunning's pale ones had done. She was dressed in a white blouse and black skirt, to which her slouch gave a raffish air. So this was Emma, then.

He picked his way through the ceramic and crystal mine field to the counter, where he explained his interest in Roman artifacts, left his name and the number of his mobile, and added that he was stopping at the Green Dragon in Corcester.

"Corcester?" she repeated. "I grew up there. It's a proper dump, isn't it?"

"Well, yes, compared to London. I'm only there for the dig at the Roman ruins. I'm writing it up for the *Times.*"

"London?" She smiled hungrily. "I'm right keen on the Romans and that lot."

"Super! When's your lunch break? Could we do an interview?"

"Twelve. Meet me on the lower level, by the staircase. Name's Emma."

Rewarding her with the most charming smile he could muster, Gareth left the shop and went downstairs to wait out the twenty minutes until noon. Once again Matilda had been right. Emma was the weak link on Dunning's side.

The girl arrived ten minutes late, her dark hair freshly sleeked back, her brows penciled, her lipstick painted. "We'd better go somewhere outside the Arcade," she announced. "There's a Greek caff up the street, as cheap as you're going to find in this neighborhood."

"Lovely," Gareth said, falling into step beside her. "Haven't I seen you somewhere before? In a photograph at the Green

Dragon?"

"Oh that, the May Queen and the Festival. Bit of a giggle for the tourists. Not the real thing, you know."

"The real thing?"

"Yeh, the rites of spring from the old days. You know, orgies in the woods." She elbowed him in the ribs and winked.

"The lad in the snap with you," Gareth persisted. "Is he someone special?"

Emma's smile displayed every tooth. "You're a sly one, asking if I have a boyfriend. No, luv, Clive's legged it right and proper, haven't seen him in donkey's years."

"A pretty girl like you must have lots of admirers."

"A few. No one actually in the saddle, though."

They hurried across the zebra crossing and gained the other side of the street. Gareth took advantage of the pause to change the topic. "Do you like working at The Antiquary's Corner?"

"It keeps me in tights and cosmetics, don't it? And it's real educational, too," she added hastily.

"You're lucky to have found a good job."

"Lucky for me. Not for the girl who had it before me. She was murdered."

Gareth hoped his expression looked properly horrified. "Not the woman found up on Durslow Edge! Did you know her?"

"Oh no, no, never clapped eyes on the woman."

No point, then, to asking Emma to speculate about Linda's relationship with Dunning. "So you simply lucked into the job?"

"Not quite. The Dunning and I have a mutual acquaintance, like. Old school chum of hers, put in a word for me."

"That wouldn't be Della Reynolds, by any chance? She's one of the people I interviewed."

"Yeh, Mrs. Adrian-bloody-Reynolds it was." Emma's grimace indicated distaste for one or the other of the Reynoldses. "Here we are."

It was a down at the heels restaurant on the ground floor of an old building. "Acropolis Cafe" read the letters on the window, "Constantine Veliotes, Proprietor."

Veliotes, Gareth repeated as he opened the door. Coincidence was Matilda's province. . . . He spotted the photograph of Nick behind the till before he was quite in the door.

They seated themselves cozily in a booth and scanned a flyspecked menu. The proprietor looked enough like a Nick devoured by time and circumstance that Gareth assumed he was the traveler's father. But Constantine looked at Emma with dull eyes, registering no acquaintance.

Gareth ordered lemon soup and a gyro sandwich. Emma requested the same, with an order of chips. When Constantine walked heavily into the kitchen, Gareth asked the girl, "Speaking of photographs, I've seen the bloke in that one hanging about Corcester. Do you know him?"

Emma turned and looked. Her face crumpled in what Gareth could have sworn was genuine puzzlement. "I might have done, at one of the festivals, maybe. Looks like a film star, don't he?"

Gareth made no comment on Nick's appearance. Clapper's testimony — or at least the gossip about Emma and Nick he'd repeated — was looking more and more suspect. Gareth decided he'd better ask something about the Romans or he'd look suspect as well. "Tell me about the artifacts you sell."

"I don't know why people want such tatty old things. The trout sold one of them glass bottles like you was looking at to Adrian Reynolds for five hundred quid! Nothing like a posh horse form to put you in the brass, eh?"

"Fortuna Stud?" Gareth asked. "Oh yes, that's a bit of all right. But you're not so keen on Reynolds himself, are you?"

"He's a right bastard. Can't see what Della wants with him."

"I'd wondered that myself," Gareth told her in perfect honesty.

Constantine appeared with their food. Gareth ate with good appetite, pleased he was finally making some progress on the case. So did Emma, darting predatory glances at him through her spiked lashes. He kept the conversation on an academic level, learning from her that Boudicca was one of them Roman queens and that Cornovium's walls were once cannon emplacements.

At last Emma eyed her watch, frowned, and applied more lipstick to her pouting lips. "The trout'll give me a proper wigging if I'm not back on time. She goes on at me if I don't leave on time, for that matter."

"She doesn't like for you to work late?"

"Oh, every now and again when I'm not finished with the packing. Most times she wants me gone as soon as the shop is closed. I think she has a boyfriend, if you can credit that."

"A boyfriend?"

"Yeh. She tarts herself up with some posh perfume and unlocks the back door, don't she? One morning I found a man's coat in her office. A dried-up old stick like that, a boyfriend!"

"You've not seen him, though?"

"No. Not so sure I'd want to."

Gareth slipped out of the booth, Emma so close behind him he almost elbowed her in the eye. No use in asking her if Dunning was dealing in illegal antiquities or even keeping two sets of books. Emma was only a pawn. Although pawns had their uses. . . . Reminding himself that Emma had already moved *him* to King Four, Gareth paid for the meal and tried to strike up a conversation with Constantine. The man gazed blankly at him, defeated.

Back at the Arcade, Emma paused at the foot of the staircase and leaned against Gareth's chest. "My mates and I are having a rave-up Friday night," she murmured. "The rites of spring, you know. Our party's not nearly as starchy as the Festival in Corcester. Would you like to come along?"

"Sounds right tempting," Gareth said with a smile. "I might have to spend the weekend in London, though. I'll ring you, shall I?"

She scribbled a number on a scrap of paper from her bag, pressed it into Gareth's hand, and raised her lips.

Gritting his teeth and thinking of Scotland Yard, he kissed her. Her tongue seemed rough, like a cat's, and he evaded any further intimacy. "Cheerio, Emma."

"Ta-ta," she returned, and hurried up the stairs.

Gareth scrubbed the lipstick off his mouth. Laying the murderer by the heels would justify the ugly red smudge, like blood, on his fingertips. Not to mention the parcel of lies he'd told over the last couple of weeks. . . . No, he thought sourly, his lies weren't for Scotland Yard, or even necessarily for Linda Burkett. They were for his own ambition.

Gareth went out to the car park, climbed into his car, and pulled his notebook and pen from his pocket.

Chapter Thirteen

*W*ithout Gareth's matter-of-fact presence the morning's work dragged. Matilda puttered about the Miller trench, helped Ashley measure and draw her hypocaust, and argued with Sweeney about whether Caterina's inscription should be left *in situ* or dug out, stabilized, and taken to Manchester.

"But my dear Matilda," he concluded, "until the good people of Corcester bestir themselves to make a proper museum of the site, we must take all the important finds to the laboratory where they'll be safe."

With an exasperated gesture she gave up. It was almost noon. High gauzy clouds smudged the sun and a damp breeze hinted of burgeoning plants and the not-so-distant sea. Gareth was right — it was time for action. When Sweeney and the students trooped into the hotel dining room for lunch, Matilda freshened up and set out for the town square, trolling for travelers.

For a time everyone she saw was moving purposefully and tidily about. Soon, though, she spotted two girls in their early twenties. One wore long, lank hair, a shapeless dress covered with a shawl, several earrings and a nose stud. The other sported crew-cut hair and battered fatigues, but her delicate features betrayed her sex. Both were pitifully thin. They ambled aimlessly across the square, checked out the interior of a trash container, and went into the tiny fish and chips shop behind the two magpie houses. Matilda followed.

Even though the atmosphere of the shop was heavy with suspended grease molecules, the frying food smelled delicious. Something in the human psyche, Matilda told herself, finds fat comforting. She ordered a plank of fish and some chips, which came across the counter liberally sprinkled with salt and malt vinegar. She sat down at a dirty chrome and vinyl table next to where the two girls had settled. They were sharing one paper plate of fried potatoes and exuding boredom.

A poster advertising the weekend Festival hung in the scummy window behind the girls. Matilda leaned across the aisle. "Excuse me. The Festival on that poster, is it the genuine article?"

"Eh?" asked the crew cut girl.

Matilda tried to look at the girl's eyes and not the bolt piercing her lower lip. "There's a picture of the green man carving from the church — the spring spirit, you know — and the hobby horse and the Maypole. But is it the real ancient ceremony, or just pretend for the tourists?"

"Oh," the long-haired girl said, "you're one of them, are you?"

"I'm studying the old religion, if that's what you mean," Matilda told her. "I'm Matilda Gray. I'm working on the dig at the Roman fort. Actually I came all the way to England hoping to find some kind of authentic May Day ceremony, but it's almost the end of April and all I've found is tourist trap stuff."

The two girls looked cautiously at each other. "Well," said crew-cut, "we don't know much about that lot, mind you. There's a bloke who does."

"You mean there really are practitioners in the area?" Matilda smiled her most engaging smile. "Could you tell me where to find your bloke?"

"The Druid," long-hair said sarcastically, and lowered her voice. "What do you think, Wendy?"

Wendy shrugged. "He likes a bit of skirt, don't he?"

"Younger than her," returned the other, quietly, but not quiet enough.

Matilda pretended not to hear. "I promised to do a piece for my coven's newsletter when I get back to the States. However, I've been very disappointed. And I just couldn't bring myself to tell my son in Philadelphia the bad news. He's squatting in an abandoned tenement, turned against the materialism of the world, he says. I thought he'd like to know there are still spiritual values. . . ." She ate a few bites, drooping picturesquely over the plate. Patrick's taste actually ran to studio apartments festooned with enough electronics to furnish NASA shuttle control, but he didn't need to know his mother was taking his image in vain. That she was lying through her teeth, to be accurate.

The two girls were no longer wary but amused. "She's a nutter, Shirl," whispered Wendy. "He gives us such aggro about history and all that bunk, let's set her on him."

Shirl. Matilda recognized the girl's name from the police reports — Watkins had interviewed her about Linda's murder. She'd claimed ignorance.

"Here," Shirl said to Matilda, "it's hard remembering dates and places when all we've had to eat is a few chips. We're skint."

Matilda opened her handbag and pulled out a five pound note. "I'm so sorry, I should have offered you something earlier. Get yourself some nourishing food — whole grains, vegetables. . . ."

"Yeh," said Wendy. She folded the money into her pocket. "Ta."

"You know where the traveler's encampment is?" Shirl asked Matilda.

"Is that the one the road to Macclesfield? Are you living there? My son would love being out in the country like that, close to nature."

"Close to nature, yeh." Shirl rolled her eyes. "Call round an hour before sunset on Friday. Someone can take you to the party. The rites of spring, he calls it. A right rave-up it was last time. Are you up for it?"

"I'll bring along my reading glasses, my cane, and my hearing aid," Matilda told her.

Shirl laughed. Wendy inhaled the last of the chips and stood up. "We'll tell him to look out for you. Ta-ta."

Matilda watched the girls walk out of the shop, across the square, and around the corner. *Him*, she repeated. Nick? He'd better be looking out for her, she had no idea what he looked like. But her hunch that there would be an alternative Beltane ceremony was right. Whether her hunch that the old Celtic holidays had something to do with the case was right, was another matter.

She ate a few bites. The food was congealing fast. Her lips and chin felt greasy. The penalty for speaking with forked tongue, she told herself, and started back toward the dig.

Halfway there she spotted Della Reynolds, astride Bodie, pacing up the road. "Mrs. Reynolds! Good afternoon!"

Della looked myopically down from beneath the tiny bill of her riding hat. "Oh, Dr. Gray. Hello."

"Let me tell you again how much I appreciate your letting me ride Bodie the other day, especially when I hardly know what a saddle is." She held her hand out to the horse, who snuffled amiably at it.

"Bodie's a good beast," Della said. "Not so temperamental as Caesar and Gremlin."

"Gremlin did seem a bit skittish," returned Matilda, "but then, I'm very much the amateur, not like you."

Della seemed to perk up a little, like a parched plant given water.

"My colleague, Mr. March," Matilda went on, "tells me you're a historian."

"No, not really, I just like to read."

"Many self-educated people know more than the experts. You must know a great deal to have put together such a fine antiquities collection."

"That's Adrian's. I go in for Waterford, that sort of thing."

"Collecting takes real skill. I wouldn't be able to tell a genuine Waterford vase from a jelly glass. Antiquities, now — well, even though that's my field, I can always learn more."

Della smiled. "Come for tea tomorrow afternoon, Dr. Gray. Adrian would love to show you his artifacts. And we can have a quick lesson in collectibles, if you like."

"How very kind of you! About four-thirty? I'm sure Gareth would love another look at the collection."

Della's cheeks grew pink. "See you tomorrow."

"Have a nice ride," Matilda told her, and patted Bodie's shoulder.

"Oh, I'm just out and about. . . ." The woman's voice trailed away as the horse clopped on up the street.

Shameless, Matilda chided herself. Utterly shameless. But

she didn't have time to beat around the bush with Della.

Beltane was two days away. She knew, with the same subliminal certainty she knew the shape of the Roman ruins beneath the sod, that time was running out.

Matilda picked a table in the corner of the bar and sat down, her back to the wall. The speakers were silent tonight, thank goodness. Perhaps Clapper's sugary tapes had congealed, like Jell-O.

Sweeney leaned against the bar telling Clapper some extended joke. The innkeeper nodded and laughed. Matilda rolled her eyes. Typical Sweeney, to fiddle while Cornovium burned.

Ashley, Bryan, and Jennifer occupied a table nearby. ". . . no way," Ashley was saying. "I'm sure not going to go home and tell my mom I got scared and couldn't stick it out. She kept telling me I was wasting my time coming here anyway."

"My dad kept griping about how much it was costing," said Jennifer. "I figure I have to stay, just to make his investment worthwhile."

Bryan said, "You know, there comes a point you have to tell the old parental units to buzz off. Of course, it helps if you have good grades and some independent income when you tell them."

Bryan was a nice boy, Matilda repeated. He and Ashley could have a positive relationship. But she looked at him the same way Gareth looked at her, polite and oblivious. The two students hadn't been together on Sunday. Matilda could only assume Ashley had been with some local lad, and hope that he, too, was a nice boy. As for Gareth. . . . Sorry, Ashley, she thought. He's not auditioning to play your Prince Charming.

Gareth threaded his way through the tables, sat down, handed Matilda her glass of single malt, and swallowed a deep draft of his ale. Then he pulled out his notebook and flipped through several pages of notes.

Matilda rolled the single-malt around her mouth and considered Gareth's profile, cut as clean as one on a Roman coin.

There was nothing quite as rejuvenating as sexual friction. By the time the threads of the case spun themselves out, she and Gareth might find that the friction was sufficient in and of itself. Or it might prove to have been a deliciously prolonged foreplay.

Matilda dropped her eyes as Gareth raised his, not wanting to distract him from the matter at hand.

"Dunning gave me the elbow, too," he said.

"Dunning knows her clientele, doesn't she? What about Emma?"

"I took her to lunch and chatted her up. She got the job at the shop through Della Reynolds, but she knows sod-all about history. She says Dunning has a secret boyfriend. Adrian Reynolds, I reckon, getting in a spot of slap-and-tickle along with his antiquities smuggling."

"Reynolds? He would find Dunning very useful, wouldn't he? Clapper told us he was exerting his dubious charms on Linda. . . ." Matilda chased some elusive tendril less of thought than of impression through her mind and lost its trailing end in ambiguity. "I still feel I'm missing something. There's some strand in this tangle that I'm just not seeing. I don't know why, and that bothers me."

Doubt glinted in Gareth's face. With a toss of his brows he discarded it. "Give over, Matilda. It's not that complicated. Everyone in Corcester can't be conspiring together."

"No, I suppose not. But I can't see Reynolds playing Moriarty, the sole mover in the case."

"He's using Dunning to sell the antiquities he looted from his own property," Gareth insisted. "He has expensive tastes. He needs the money. And Linda caught him out. Maybe she caught Dunning out as well. Linda was no fool, her records say she passed her A-levels but couldn't afford university. She threatened Reynolds with exposure. He lured her to Durslow Edge and eliminated her. Then Reynolds found Dunning a new shop assistant, one so thick she wouldn't recognize illegal statuary if she fell over it."

"That's logical," Matilda assured him. "It would also be logical if Linda and Reynolds were conspiring together and fell out over the statuary. Or Dunning and Linda ditto, although I must admit I can't see Dunning cutting a throat.

Too messy. Clapper could be part of the plot. Almost certainly Della knows something. Was the attack on Sweeney and Caterina a misguided attempt at treasure — pretty clumsy, if so — or a warning to us? We can theorize all we want, but finding enough solid evidence to bring someone — anyone — to trial. . . ."

". . . is another matter entirely. I know that." Gareth scowled, seeing either justice or his promotion slip through his fingers. "I did once wonder whether Della killed Linda out of jealousy, but she hardly seems capable of jealousy, let alone murder."

"Mice have a way of roaring." Matilda glanced again at Ashley.

". . . and then," Jennifer was saying, "my dad takes me into the den and says very seriously, don't get involved with any English men! As though English guys have two heads or something."

"Or something," Bryan said with a grin.

Jennifer laughed. Ashley smiled secretly into her lemonade. A local lad, definitely, Matilda thought.

The corners of Gareth's mouth turned in opposite directions. "A shame you can't see a re-enactment of the murder and give us some leads, instead of wasting your time on an ancient domestic row."

"I'm not wasting my time. It's much easier for me to read ancient events or inanimate objects than living people. The Romans' actions are carved in time — they're set pieces now. It's like going to see 'Hamlet' in theaters all over the world. No matter what the production is like, it's still the same play. Artifacts are finished, completed, things, no matter how resonant with the minds of their makers, while living people are dynamic processes. Simply watching a person often causes him to change direction."

"That's a common feature of a murder investigation," Gareth conceded.

"Of any investigation. Although I've never done one quite like this. This is like. . . . Well, my son will sit with the remote control and surf through one TV channel after another, watching each one for only a few seconds. You get a bit of dialogue, a quick image, a burst of music. Nothing in context.

It drives me crazy. That's what this case is like. Because of the murder, probably. The strong emotion."

"Does your son have the sight — ESP?"

"Not a hint of it."

"I rather doubted he did." Gareth rubbed his eyes, squeezed the bridge of his nose, and took another long drink of his ale.

Even Patrick would have sensed Gareth's annoyance and frustration. The only way Matilda could ease his mind was to solve the case. To help him solve the case, that is. Even if she had to sacrifice the personal attraction to do it. She sipped at her whiskey. The room was becoming warm and close.

"Emma might be acting dumb for your benefit. Not that she struck me as terribly bright in the glimpse I had of her. She's resentful, I think. Feeling life has done her wrong. You asked her about Clive, I assume? Now there's someone who could well be involved. Even Moriarty had his Colonel Moran, his muscle."

"Emma said she hadn't seen Clive in donkey's years," Gareth replied.

"Did you ask Emma about Nick?"

"Well now, that's interesting. Emma and I had our lunch in a Greek caff just outside the Arcade. . . ."

"Oh yes, I ate there, too."

"Did you now!" Gareth exclaimed, and then lowered his voice to a husky whisper. "Why didn't you tell me? That's Nick's father's place — it says 'Veliotes' plain as a pikestaff on the window. Didn't you see the snap of the man himself on the wall behind the till?"

"What?" Matilda leaned across the table. "Gareth, I've never laid eyes on Nick. And I had no idea what his last name is!"

They stared at each other, appalled. Here she'd been contemplating melding bodies, Matilda thought, when what they needed to do was meld minds. What else did Gareth know that she didn't, and vice versa? "The café is where Nick met Emma?" she hazarded.

"I doubt it — she didn't start working at Borley Arcade until February. Clapper says she and Nick were having it off last year and that she keeps throwing herself at him." Gareth glared at Clapper, who was pulling another pint of beer, his round face perspiring with virtue. "Emma looked at Nick's photo and said she might have seen him at one of the festivals, that's all. It's either a discrepancy in Clapper's story or in hers."

"Did you believe Emma's story?"

"Yes, I did. But then, I believed Clapper's, too. I don't have your ESP trick, do I?"

"It's no trick."

"No, I don't think it is," he said wearily.

Matilda swallowed the rest of her whiskey, assessing the play of light and shadow in Gareth's eyes. She had convinced him of her skills, yes, but it was his own skills he trusted to solve the case. When all the lies were at last scoured away, nothing would be left except belief, and faith, and trust. Ground truth.

"Linda might have met Nick at the caff," Gareth said. "I'd give a month's pay to find out if they knew each other."

"The break between Constantine and Nick could have been quite recent."

"He does have an eye for the ladies — Nick, that is, not his dad. I saw him with a woman myself, that day the yob cut Caesar."

"It wasn't Emma you saw him with?"

"I wasn't looking at her face." Gareth drained his glass of beer and looked truculently into its foam-flecked bottom. "I can't tie the travelers in with any of this."

"I imagine they've done some clandestine digging at the fort, with or without Reynolds. Beyond that, I don't know. Maybe they're just a school of red herrings." Matilda shook her head. "Tell me everything Emma said. Don't leave out a word. . . . Oh, hello Mr. Clapper. Business looks a bit off tonight."

"What do you expect, with them murdering travelers hanging about." The innkeeper eyed Matilda's and Gareth's glasses. "Another round? No? Righty-ho." He retired to the bar, poured another drink for Sweeney, and laughed perfunctorily at several more of the professor's jokes.

Gareth reconstructed his conversation with Emma. Matilda tried to draw out his impressions, but other than his admission that he believed what she'd told him, he steadfastly refused to concede he had any. "Then she invited me to a rave-up Friday. Not the loud music sort of rave, I gather. She called it 'the rites of spring'."

"Friday night is Beltane," said Matilda. "Both Clapper and Emma were right about one thing — there is a pseudo-neo-pagan group operating in the area. The group might not have anything to do with Linda's murder or with the thefts, either, but it's the only lead we've got and I can't help feeling that it's important."

"What?" Gareth asked.

She scooted her empty glass across the table so that it pinged lightly off his. "I went into town at lunchtime and followed two traveler girls, Wendy and Shirl, into that little chip shop. I got them to tell me about what I assume is the same party Emma invited you to — the rites of spring, they used the same words. But they're not confirmed members of the group — they kept giggling about it. I doubt if the group consists entirely of travelers."

"It's a convention of nutters like Nick?"

"The girls kept talking about *him.* I suppose they meant Nick — they said he liked 'a bit of skirt'. They called him 'the Druid'."

"But Emma didn't recognize Nick."

"If he appeared in costume she might not have gotten a very good look at him."

"Sounds like play-acting to me."

"It is. So is the Christian rite of communion, if you squint and look at it sideways."

"Emma said it was 'the real thing'."

"To her it is. Reality, like magic, is in the eye of the beholder. You don't have to actually summon the devil to do devilish things. You don't have to actually consort with angels to be virtuous."

"It was real enough to Linda Burkett," Gareth agreed. "You mustn't go to the party alone, it might be dangerous."

Matilda shook her head. "Some groups, the more manipulative ones, can be vile, but those also tend to be very secretive. That we're able to get into this one so easily is a good sign." Gareth didn't seem convinced. Matilda plunged on. "Shirl and Wendy didn't say where the party was, just that I should come to the camp an hour before sunset. I'm betting it's at Durslow Edge — a place local people are more likely to know."

"Nick is local, isn't he?" Gareth said with a sigh. He pulled a scrap of paper from his pocket and inspected both sides for nonexistent clues. "Emma gave me her telephone number, said to ring her if I wanted to come to the party. I can just about stick it, I reckon. Anything else?"

"Yes. On the way back from town, I ran into Della and Bodie. I got us an invitation for tea tomorrow afternoon."

Gareth's face went lopsided with rue. "I'm glad you decided to work for the law instead of against it. You'd make a brilliant confidence artist."

"No I wouldn't. I don't enjoy lying. My stomach was sick all afternoon, and not from the fish and chips."

"I became a policeman because I valued honesty, didn't I? We're for it now."

"We're in over our heads, no doubt about . . ." Matilda's thumbs pricked. She raised her hand to warn Gareth and looked toward the door. Adrian Reynolds stood there. His black pellets of eyes fell on their cozy corner table and he sauntered toward them.

He started talking while he was still twenty feet away. Every face in the room turned toward him. Ashley ducked. "Hullo, hullo! My wife tells me she invited you to tea tomorrow. I'll try to be there, she doesn't know the first thing about my antiquities, she collects these frightfully twee dishes and vases." He pulled out a chair and sat down.

"Do you have business interests other than Fortuna Stud?" Matilda asked.

"Just a bit of investing here and there," Reynolds replied. "I say, March, sorry about ticking you off Sunday. Caesar's a pet of mine, you know. He came close to winning the Grand National, but it just isn't on to pass the Queen's horse, is it now?"

"I suppose not," said Gareth politely.

Sweeney advanced toward the table. So did Clapper, since Reynolds hadn't ordered anything at the bar. Matilda felt as though her picnic was attracting ants. A trickle of sweat started between her shoulder blades and ran down her spine, making her wriggle uneasily.

"The usual," Reynolds told Clapper.

The publican turned and trudged away.

"And you," Reynolds said to Sweeney as the professor took the remaining chair. "Come to tea tomorrow. I've some new items in my collection — a Roman glass vial, for one, dreadfully expensive but a one-off, of course, positively unique."

Except for the one in Dunning's display case, Matilda told herself. The last thing she wanted was Sweeney absorbing all the air in Reynolds' sitting room tomorrow. She tried beaming words to him — *no, thank you, I can't come. . . .*

"Thank you, no," Sweeney told Reynolds. "I must run into Manchester after work tomorrow. I have to attend to some laboratory work — you can't imagine what a trial it is having an incompetent assistant."

"Quite difficult, isn't it?" Reynolds returned.

"As a matter of fact, I'm giving the students a holiday on Friday. Let them enjoy all the quaint local festivities, eh?"

This was news to Matilda. Obviously Sweeney included her in the incompetent-assistant category.

Clapper appeared at Reynolds's shoulder. He set a glass of beer on the table and said to Matilda, "P.C. Watkins is in reception. He says they've found the bus what almost ran you off the road, and he needs you to sign a complaint."

"Certainly." Matilda extricated herself from her corner seat. Gareth made some excuse about interesting sidelights to his story and followed.

Watkins was waiting in the thankfully cool lobby, his hat tucked beneath his arm. "The bus were found abandoned in a quarry beyond Macclesfield," he announced. "The fresh scrapings on its drivers' side wing and wheel arch match the ones we took from your car. It's a right mess inside, bedding, bits of food, the lot. Probably belonged to some travelers, but which ones, we don't know."

"No proof," muttered Gareth. "There's never any proof."

"I finally laid Nick Veliotes by the heels," Watkins went on. "He's a greasy one, ain't he? Says he didn't cosh Dr. Sweeney and Miss Rossi. He wouldn't even admit being in Corcester that evening until one of the lads at the bus station said he'd seen Nick snogging a lass in the car park. You're not going to like this, Dr. Gray — it was one of your American students."

Matilda's heart sank. "Blond hair, right?"

"Spot on. Pretty and blond."

Gareth's face flushed the color of his hair. *Great,* Matilda thought. *Now he gets protective.* "Not Ashley," he said. "There are other blond girls."

"She'd been drinking with someone that night," Matilda told him. "She came walking down the hill from town with the other students and I thought she'd been with Bryan. But her attitude toward Bryan is friendly, not romantic, and he feels she's way out of his league."

"Stupid little. . ." sputtered Gareth. "That's just what Emma Price did to herself, isn't it?"

"Hardly to herself," Matilda corrected.

Watkins's round face settled heavily into a square. "It was Emma's family put it about that Nick was the father. She never named names. I reckon it was Clive Adcox myself, before he went north. No matter now."

Matilda gave Gareth a significant look. Clapper's testimony about Emma and Nick had been simple transference, then, removing a misdemeanor from a family member and dumping on an annoying stranger.

The flush leached from Gareth's complexion. "What else did Nick tell you?"

"He says he never met Linda Burkett, he don't know anything about devil-worshippers, and if he was in Corcester the night Sweeney was coshed it's no business of mine. Since I couldn't charge him with anything, I let him go."

"Nothing for it," Gareth told Watkins, and stood silent while the constable left the hotel.

"Ashley hasn't gone overboard with Nick," Matilda told Gareth. "Not yet."

"How can you tell?"

"Because she's still cherishing her romantic illusions." Matilda left Gareth working that one out and walked back into the bar.

". . . drugged-out criminals moving about the countryside causing trouble for the law-abiding citizen," Reynolds was saying. "Like the berk — excuse me, Mrs. Gray — the bloke driving that bus. You could have been killed. There ought to be a law that these layabouts can only draw benefits in the town where they were born. Keep them away from us honest people, eh?"

"Like some of the travelers aren't local people?" muttered Ashley.

Matilda, slipping back into her seat, heard her. The girl was thinking of Nick. That everyone was speaking against him probably made him all the more attractive. It'd certainly kept her from revealing their acquaintance. And, Matilda supposed, it was only fair that someone took Nick's side.

There was the classic parental dilemma for you, whether to rush around with a safety net extended or to avert your eyes when the kid comes plummeting past.

Sweeney looked as though he smelled something bad. "If you'll excuse me, I'm turning in. I have a busy day tomorrow."

"Haven't we all?" Reynolds smiled liplessly, like a snake.

Gareth returned to the table just in time to catch that smile. He shot Matilda a told-you-so glance. She started sweating again. The currents of hostility swirling about the room seemed like hot desert winds.

Sweeney wafted away, but the room didn't grow any cooler.

Gareth glanced over at Ashley. "I'll sort her out," he muttered beneath his breath.

"Gareth, don't . . ." Matilda began, and then stopped. He would only convince Ashley she couldn't confide in them. But telling him that Ashley might be going with Nick because she couldn't go with the detective himself wouldn't help.

". . . not as much progress as I'd hoped on the dig," Reynolds was saying. "Dr. Sweeney has his methods, I suppose."

Matilda said something appropriate to Reynolds and beamed calming thoughts toward Gareth's scowl.

"As do you," Reynolds went on. "Fascinating, how you turned up that gold coin the first day you were here. Would you say there was a bit of — well, the old country people call it second sight, but I suppose educated people like you and I should say. . . ."

Ashley, Bryan, and Jennifer stood up and headed for the lobby. Gareth launched himself from his chair and followed.

Matilda turned to watch him stride, coiled with self-right-eousness, toward the door.

". . . does the gold cause an itch in your palms?" Reynolds asked.

I didn't come here, Matilda told herself, *to babysit either a twenty-year-old student or a thirty-year-old detective. . . .* "What did you say?" She spun back toward Reynolds so quickly she gave herself whiplash. He was looking at her, his black eyes glittering, like a cobra swaying gently before its prey.

He knew about the gold torc. And he was daring her to do something about it.

Chapter Fourteen

*J*ennifer yawned. Bryan waved Ashley through the doorway ahead of him. "End of another day. Who had the bright idea of our paying them to work our butts off?"

"Look at the bottom line, Bryan. The lines that are on your resume." He was a nice guy, Ashley added to herself. A shame he didn't have an exotic bone in his body.

Just beyond the door Ashley stopped, letting the others go ahead. She wondered if she dared go back in the bar and sit down with Matilda and Gareth. But Reynolds gave her the creeps. He was like a pterodactyl, eyes cold and shoulders sloped, watching for prey in the jungle below.

Sweeney, now, Sweeney was okay, even though he sure liked to play the lovable English eccentric. Well, not entirely lovable. Maybe geniuses — genii? — didn't haven't to follow rules or be politically correct or whatever.

Matilda was a genius, and that didn't keep her from being considerate of other people's space. She wouldn't make me feel guilty about Nick, Ashley thought. As though there was anything about Nick to feel guilty about. He was pretty darn bright, he just didn't have it together yet. Being with him was like being on a roller coaster, both scary and exciting.

Gareth wasn't scary. He was a strong, silent type who needed a woman to warm him up. Not that Ashley was likely to be that woman. It wasn't that she wanted to get anything going with him — he was way out of her league. She just wanted him to notice her. She turned back to the door of the bar, encouraging herself with expressions about birds in the bush and pushing the envelope.

Gareth was walking directly toward her. *All right!* She inhaled to say something, anything — letter-writing, the dig, his
newspaper article.

"Here," he said. "I need a word with you."

She exhaled. "Sure."

"One of Watkins's men saw you with Nick Veliotes Sunday
night. He's a bad lot, Ashley. You'd better leave him be."

What? Her heart went into free-fall, diving through shock,
embarrassment, and hurt into a loud splash of anger. How
could he? This wasn't what she wanted from him!

"There's no saying what sort of jiggery-pokery Nick's involved in, but it's nothing good, I promise you that. If I were
you I'd give him a miss."

"You're not me, are you?" she retorted.

Gareth leaned forward patronizingly. "Now, now, I'm only
trying to protect you."

"I don't want you to protect me. I want you to get off my
back!" Ashley turned on her heel, sprinted up the stairs to
her room, and slammed the door. A picture fell off the wall.
Shit, she thought. *Shitshitshit.*

Courtney had gone home. Jennifer's make-up case and robe
were missing. She must be in the bathroom. Ashley hung the
picture back up and braced herself on the window sill, scowling at her reflection in the glass. For a few moments she tried
desperately to shape Gareth's condescension into jealousy —
he wanted her for himself, that's why he was down on
Nick. . . . *Yeah, right.* All the time he'd been smiling at her
he'd thought she was just another stupid kid.

Through her own pale image in the glass she saw Reynolds
spurt from the door of the hotel and walk briskly toward the
car park. Of course he had to drive his precious red MG the
few hundred yards between his house and the hotel. She
watched the car's headlights cut an arc from the gloomy night
as they swung toward Fortuna Stud.

As quickly as a flashbulb, the lights picked out the shape
of a man standing by the bowling green wall. So she hadn't
imagined him standing there Monday night while Gareth and
Matilda walked down from the fort. She'd stood in the door
of the hotel, willing him to come to her, but she hadn't had
enough courage to plunge into the darkness after him. Now

she did. Gareth might see her as a child. To Nick she was a desirable woman.

Putting on her sweater, Ashley crept back to the head of the stairs. Below her, Clapper turned off the lights in the bar and lumbered into his office. In the distance a door shut.

She tiptoed down the stairs and out the door, waited while a car whizzed by, and hurried across the street. From one of the cottages came pompous soundtrack music. The other cottage was silent, only one window lit. Cornovium rose in front of her, a black ridge against the muted glow of an overcast sky.

Even though she knew he was there, when he spoke she jumped. "Eh, Ashley. You shouldn't be out on your own."

"So why are you here?" she demanded.

His grin was a flash of white in the shadows. "Oh, just fossicking about. How's my lass?"

"Mad. P.C. Watkins saw me with you on Sunday night and told Gareth, and he just had to tell me off." She almost added *I don't know what I ever saw in him.* But she did know, that was the problem.

"It's none of their business, is it?"

"No. It's not."

Nick draped his arm around her shoulders, rather distractedly, she thought, without the conviction he'd displayed on Sunday. He must be mad, too, at the busybodies who tried to run his life.

A couple of cars sped down the road. Maybe it was the rush of their headlights that made it look like something was moving in the deep shadows of the excavation. Ashley shrank closer to Nick, wrapping her arms around his waist. She could hardly feel his body beneath her double armful of jacket. His sweet smoky scent teased her nostrils, along with an elusive breath of mildew.

"Did you know," she said, "that someone hit one of the students over the head and pushed Dr. Sweeney down the trench Sunday night?"

"I was told," Nick replied. "Extensively, by our local bloody-minded plod. Who's after blaming me for it."

"Watkins ought to be going after Adrian Reynolds. Anybody that obnoxious must be up to something underhanded."

Nick laughed humorlessly. "That's the way of the world, lass, everyone getting and grabbing and trampling the other chap underfoot. Look at my dad. Has a little caff in Manchester. Not posh enough for the neighborhood, so the landlord's trying to turf him out. It's all he has. He's lived in the flat over the shop since he came to this country. I was born there. My mum died there. And the bloody landlord says either tart it up or get out."

"He can't afford to fix it up?"

"Business is worse every year. I thought if I left he'd have a few extra quid. No, the old fool ticked me off, said I was deserting my family." Nick's lips tightened. Ashley tried to hug him a little closer. His body was stiff, unresponsive. "Toffs like Reynolds can commit any sort of crime and the police look out for some poor sod like me to blame. You have to look out for yourself. No one else will do."

Ashley wasn't quite sure she agreed with that. "I always thought the world would be a better place if people just followed the golden rule."

"The toffs go to church on Sunday and rabbit on about the golden rule, don't they, and on Monday they screw you over. It was better in the old days, when gold belonged to the gods, not to man. . . ."

He straightened abruptly, his chin going up. His earring and the three necklaces on his chest winked in the light. Yes, there was someone or something moving on the embankment of the fort.

"Matilda says there're ghosts up there," Ashley whispered.

"Rubbish. They only told you that to keep you from treasure-hunting. I heard them talking the other night, didn't I?"

"It's not literal treasure, it's . . ."

"Hush." He drew her back behind the wall.

She peered into the gloom until her eyes burned, but could see only shadow upon shadow — no, there, a human form was etched briefly against the sky and then disappeared down the far slope.

A light shone out from the street, sharp and bright as Luke Skywalker's light saber. A flashlight, she realized, carried by a man with a steady step. Nick seized her hand and pulled her along the wall and around the far corner of the bowling green. They huddled in impenetrable blackness beneath the eaves of the recreation center roof. "Watkins?" she asked breathlessly.

"Or one of his goons," Nick replied.

The dim shape of the constable and his helmet was illuminated only by the backspatter of light from his flashlight. He crossed the road, stood at the gate, and shone the beam of light across the mound of the fort. But the lurking figure was gone, and the moving patch of light illuminated only grass, dirt, and ancient stone. The constable turned off the light. A moment later Ashley saw a tiny point of fire and smelled cigarette smoke.

"At least Watkins is keeping Reynolds from his usual nighttime scavenging," said Nick.

"If you know he's actually stealing things, why haven't you turned him in?"

"The police don't believe anything I say, do they?"

"It doesn't sound like it, no," she conceded.

"Well then," Nick said. "I'll collect you at half past three tomorrow afternoon. The ceremonies don't begin til sunset, but the fires need laying, and the Druid's altar draped with mistletoe."

"How many people will be there?"

"I don't know. Some come for the party. Others are searching for the gods. It's not just my lot, mind you. The celebrants come from all over the country."

"Is the, ah, ceremony at Durslow Edge?"

"Of course. The place of power. Brighid's well. Where else?"

Like they were going to do it in a school gym festooned with paper streamers, Ashley told herself. Still her skin crawled — Durslow was eerie enough in the daylight. She shrugged the qualm away. "What should I wear?"

"Anything you like. It's not like the toffs parading up to the church on Sunday, is it?"

She'd take his word for that.

"You'd better be getting back before Gareth-bleeding-March misses you." Nick steered her down the side of the wall away from the fort and behind the two cottages. He stopped across the street from the lighted doorway of the hotel.

"See you tomorrow." She turned her face up. His kiss was just as distracted as his embrace and his mouth was sour — it was just as well he wasn't any more enthusiastic. She trudged across the street wondering whether the problem was his or hers.

Nick could be a great source for Gareth's book about the murder case. Except the murder case was a little too close to home for poor Nick. No wonder he was down on the police, when they hadn't solved Linda's murder yet. No wonder he didn't want to talk about it. Ashley could just see getting Gareth and Nick together. It'd be like throwing a match onto a puddle of gasoline. Nick would think Gareth was trying to exploit his lover's death, but even now Ashley didn't think Gareth was that crass.

Wondering vaguely how many other lovers Nick had had, she tried to open the door of the hotel. It was locked. *Damn!* She'd either have to ring the bell to summon Clapper or stay outside all night. Alone — Nick was already gone, vanished like Dracula into the darkness. She rang the bell.

Matilda bustled out of the sitting room and unlocked the door. "There you are! I went to your room but Jennifer said she'd seen you going down the stairs with your sweater. I was worried about you."

"I was just across the street. There was a policeman standing at the gate to the fort. No problem."

"You weren't with the policeman, were you?"

Sometimes Ashley thought Matilda could read minds. "Well, no."

The door from the back hall opened. Like a jack-in-the-box Clapper peered out, said, "Oh, thank you, Mrs. Gray," and popped back in.

Matilda shooed Ashley into the sitting room, shut the door, and pointed toward an overstuffed chair. "Sit down, please. I want you to talk to me."

That was a different tack from her mother's, "I want to talk to you." Ashley sat down and clasped her arms across her chest. She was tired. She wished people would just leave her alone.

"I gather Gareth planted his foot square in his tonsils," Matilda began, sitting down opposite.

"He's not ready for the diplomatic corps, that's for sure."

"It's odd how men and women operate so differently. I once stitched a sampler for my son — I have one just about your age, that's his picture in my room. . . ."

"He's cute," Ashley told her.

"I think he is, too, but I'm biased. Anyway, I stitched him a sampler saying 'Come in, state your business, and leave. That way no one gets hurt.'"

In spite of herself, Ashley smiled.

"While for me," Matilda went on, "I'd have to stitch a sampler along the lines of, 'Come in, tell me about your family, express your ambitions, discuss the cut of your new dress, and exchange recipes. Oh, you have *business?*'"

"I know, I know. Gareth thought he was helping me."

"He doesn't know you have a crush on him. If he did he'd be embarrassed."

"How'd you . . ." Ashley looked down into her lap. She hadn't realized she was being that obvious. "Okay, yes. But he thinks I'm a kid."

"He's still struggling with his own maturity. Cut him some slack."

"Sure, when he cuts me some." She looked back up.

Matilda's smile was thin and wry. "What did he say, exactly?"

"That Watkins saw me with Nick — you know that, too, don't you?"

Matilda nodded. Instead of leaning forward she leaned back in the chintz-covered chair.

Ashley had expected another lecture, not silent listening. She went on, "He said Nick was a bad lot, that he was up to no good, that I shouldn't see him any more."

"Is Nick a bad lot?"

"No! He's really intelligent and well-read, he knows as much about history and mythology as you and Dr. Sweeney, but he can't afford college. His father's about to lose his restaurant, he can't help being poor. Sure he's got issues, who doesn't? Plus he's depressed and mad about his girlfriend. She's the girl who was murdered. Linda."

Matilda's eyes flashed. She didn't actually leap from the chair, but still Ashley got an impression of cartwheels and handstands. "Linda was Nick's girlfriend? Oh, Ashley, Gareth was just saying he'd give a month's pay to know that."

"For his book, yeah."

"Book?"

Ashley's own tonsils tickled. "Oh — well — sorry, I couldn't help overhearing you and Gareth talking about the murder case. I figured that since he's a reporter, he was writing a book about it. And you're helping him with the archaeology angle."

"How clever of you to come up with that explanation!" Matilda rested her head against the lace doily on the back of the chair and laughed. Finally she managed to say, "You're wrong though. Dead wrong, if you'll pardon the expression."

"Oh." Ashley looked around the room, at the blank face of the television screen, at the rows of dog-eared books, at the squashed but comfortable couch. Bryan's New York Yankees hat lay on the coffee table on top of copies of *Country Life, In Britain,* and the *Sunburn.*

"Ashley," Matilda said, "you told us you could keep a secret."

"I never told anyone about the gold torc, did I?"

"Reynolds knows about it, more's the pity, but I'm certainly not going to blame you."

"Maybe he has ESP."

"No, I'm the one with ESP. I'm a professional parapsychologist. That's one thing I'd like for you to keep quiet."

"You're a what?"

"Let's skip the explanations for now, okay? Suffice it to say that I'm here not only as an archaeologist — that much is perfectly genuine — but also to investigate the theft of some Romano-British statuary from Cornovium. In January Linda Burkett wrote a letter to the Manchester police saying she knew who stole it. The first of February, someone — the thief, I expect — killed her."

"Whoa." Ashley broke out in gooseflesh, as though a cold hand stroked her spine. "Why would she know who stole it?"

"She worked for an antiquities dealer in Manchester. She went around the countryside looking for antiquities to sell. She was here, talking to Adrian Reynolds, not long before she died."

"Do you think he killed her?"

"He's on our short list. There's not enough evidence to charge him, though. And he probably had at least one confederate, perhaps among the travelers."

"Not Nick," protested Ashley. "He hates Reynolds' guts, for one thing. And Nick's no criminal. His caravan has lots of history books and magazines and there are a bunch of cardboard boxes stamped with — what was the name — 'The Antiquary's Corner'. Sounds like an antique store."

"It's the shop where Linda worked," Matilda told her. "It's just up the street from Nick's father's cafe."

Ashley slumped down in the chair. Great, she'd just dug Nick a deeper hole than he was in already. Unless he really was working with Reynolds, and was just using her to get information on the dig. If he could get sex, too, then that was a bonus. . . . *Shit.* "Why are you telling me this?"

"Gareth and I realized tonight we hadn't been comparing notes thoroughly enough. Now it turns out that you know some important things we don't. Knowledge is power."

"Aren't you and Gareth writing a book about the case?"

"No, we're trying to solve the case. That's the other thing I need you to keep secret. No one except Howard and me knows that Gareth's not a reporter, he's a Detective Inspector from Scotland Yard."

"Scotland Yard?" Ashley repeated. "I just told a cop where to get off?"

"He won't hold it against you professionally. What Gareth needs to know is what Nick told you. So far Nick's never even admitted he knew Linda."

"Go figure. He thinks the police are out to get him anyway." Ashley sighed. "He probably thinks Reynolds killed Linda. I bet that's why he was waiting outside the hotel tonight, not to see me but because Reynolds was inside."

Floorboards creaked overhead and water gushed down the pipes that, thanks to architectural renovation, were on the outside of the hotel's walls. Matilda brushed her wave of hair away from her forehead. She had small hands and short unpolished nails. Capable hands, Ashley thought. She flexed her own hands into fists and loosened them again, wondering if they were big enough to hold everything that had been dumped into them.

"I'm also telling you all this," the older woman said, "because your knowledge might put you in danger."

"Danger from Reynolds? He doesn't know me from any of the others."

"No, danger from Nick. You understand, don't you, that he has to be on our suspect list, too?"

"I understand. But if he had some sort of antiquities scam going why would he live in a trashy travel trailer?"

"Camouflage? I don't know. It's all — complicated." Matilda shook her head wearily.

Ashley pulled her legs into the chair and wrapped her arms around them. She'd gotten over Chris by working and studying and anticipating her trip to England, hoping it'd be an adventure. Now that it was — well, who said, *be careful what you wish for, you might get it?*

"Are you still having nightmares about the severed hand?" Matilda asked.

Taken by surprise, Ashley answered honestly. "Yes, sometimes."

"Has Nick told you anything about the so-called 'party' Friday night?"

"Yes. It sounds like some kind of pagan rite re-enactment."

"A re-creation of the ancient Celtic festival of Beltane. Were you planning to go with him?"

"Yes — well, I mean — they're not actually going to sacrifice anyone, are they?"

"I sincerely hope not. I imagine some of the participants will be there to party, some will be there searching for God."

"That's what Nick said, except he said gods, plural. The old gods? Are they still around?"

"As long as someone believes in them," Matilda said, "they still exist."

Ashley felt like she was cramming for an exam, even though she didn't know what the test going to be and who was going to decide whether she passed or not.

"There's a terrible fascination to death, isn't there?" Matilda went on. "Dramatic death. Branwen sacrificed to expiate sins she'd never committed, rather like Christ, I suppose.

Linda murdered."

"Branwen?"

"One of the ghosts at the fort."

"You really can see ghosts? Nick said you were just saying that to discourage treasure-hunters."

"It would take more than that to discourage treasure-hunters. And yes, I really can see ghosts." Matilda stood up. Stretching, she walked over to the fireplace and stared down at the cold, silent electric fire. "The problem with a cult of the dead, like the Druid cult, is that it so often leads to a cult of Death. Such a tight a focus on the end of life sometimes makes living lose its relevance, and the final surrender becomes more important than the struggle."

"Yeah," Ashley said cautiously.

"Myself, I believe in patterns of time and fate. A time to sow and a time to reap, a time to love and a time to hate, a time to be born and a time to die. There's always time enough to die. There's no need to rush toward it like rushing into a lover's arms." Decisively Matilda shook herself, like a cat shaking off water. "Ashley, think very carefully before you go with Nick Friday night."

"You're not going to warn me not to go?"

"Would it make any difference if I did?"

Ashley shrugged. "When he asked me to go I figured he just, you know, wanted sex. But tonight he was talking about having to set up the Druid's altar, that sort of thing. He hardly seemed interested in me at all. So I guess he's got another agenda."

"The Druid," Matilda repeated. "Is Nick the Druid himself?"

"He didn't say."

"Of course not. Ashley, a lot of people around here have agendas — Gareth and me not excepted. Please, please, keep alert and be prepared to duck."

"I will." Ashley unfolded her limbs. This had gone on long enough. Her brain was going to explode and so was her bladder.

Matilda continued staring into the fireplace, unfocussed. It must be her ESP that made her so empathic. How could she bear risking so much in touching other people? "Can you read my mind?" Ashley asked.

"No," Matilda replied. "When there's very little distraction I can sense moods. Like how you're getting impatient right now."

"Sorry."

"Don't apologize. Go to bed."

"Yes, ma'am." Ashley got up. At the door she turned back into the room. "Thanks, Matilda, for being on my side."

"I'm not on anyone's side. I'm on the side of what's right. But you're very welcome."

Leaving Matilda meditating in the sitting room, Ashley scurried upstairs. The hotel was weirdly quiet, considering the number of people who were sleeping beneath its roof. She wondered if Matilda's dreams were disturbed by the dreams of others, flooded with images of flight, sex, and severed hands.

Ashley stopped in the W.C. and then slipped into her room. Jennifer was asleep. She hurried into her pajamas, burrowed into the bed, and lay shivering beneath the weight of the comforter.

She felt as though she'd been picked up by the heels and shaken. The people around her were lying, and worse. She no longer wanted to go to the rites, she no longer wanted to see Nick, she no longer wanted to see Gareth, she — no. She didn't want to go home. She couldn't, not and keep what self-respect she still had.

She just might forgive Gareth for his high-handedness, even though it hurt that he only looked at her as one of the kids. And yet she had, however inadvertently, achieved something Mr. Detective Inspector hadn't. By making friends with Nick instead of suspecting him she'd found out about his relationship with Linda. . . .

The idea didn't light up like a light bulb above her head. It came like a swelling chord of music, starting in some obscure neuron of her brain and rolling forward to absorb her entire mind. Ashley would have sat up in bed with the exhilaration of it, except the room was too cold.

She was the missing link. She could tie everything together for Gareth and Matilda and help them solve the case. She could prove herself — not just to Gareth, not even to Matilda, but to herself.

All she had to do was go to the rites with Nick and find out what he knew about Linda and what he knew about Reynolds. All she had to do was go out to Durslow Edge in the dark, with someone whose designs on her body might be the least of her worries.

Ashley lay wide-eyed, staring up at the shadowed ceiling, as the travel clock beside her bed ticked the time away.

Chapter Fifteen

"We'd better be quick," Gareth directed. "The students have already gone to the dig." He sat down on the edge of the bed.

Matilda yanked the sheets and comforter smooth, driving Gareth to the chair. If he'd been a woman she'd have described his motion as a flounce. He radiated irritation — with her, with Ashley, with the case. She wasn't exactly calm herself. "Not to mention," she said with more than a trace of sarcasm, "that evildoers come scurrying out of the woodwork like cockroaches as soon as you turn your back."

"Did you talk some sense into the girl?" Gareth asked.

"I talked with her, yes. I can't tell her what to do about Nick, though — that's up to her. And it's far too late to cut her out of the case."

"The case is none of her business."

"Yes, it is her business. She more or less tripped and fell into it, true, but she's up to her neck in it now."

"Stupid, silly . . ." Gareth muttered under his breath.

"Come off it," returned Matilda. "She's young, she's naive, she's desperate for affection. Don't tell me you weren't ever young and naive. And if you start giving me any kind of double standard crap so help me I'll throw this pillow at you."

Gareth stared at the carpet, his mouth set in a straight line. Even the curls in his hair were tight and stiff, like compressed springs.

"Ashley has done something neither of us has done," Matilda went on. "She's earned Nick's trust. Or enough of it, at least, that he told her he and Linda were — well, quite good friends, judging by the forensic evidence."

He looked up abruptly. "So the penny drops at last, does it? What else did she say? Is there enough evidence to charge him?"

Matilda re-arranged the notions and potions on her dresser. She pulled out her cell phone, checked it for messages, put it away again. She summarized her conversation with Ashley and concluded, "Nick sounds like a very interesting person. I'm looking forward to meeting him at the ceremony tomorrow. If you want more than that, I suggest you talk to Ashley yourself, starting with an apology for being rude to her last night."

"I wasn't rude to her."

"She interpreted your directness as rudeness. She thought you were trying to boss her around. She doesn't realize you're concerned about her. And she has a crush on you, which made it worse."

"She fancies me? Good God, does the girl think I'm after robbing cradles?"

"It doesn't have much to do with you at all, frankly. It has everything to do with her own romantic dreams, ones you and I have to respect. She'll forgive you, given the chance — she seemed quite dazzled when I told her that you're from Scotland Yard. . . ."

"You blew my cover?"

"If she knows we trust her then she'll trust us. Maybe she'll help us."

"You're not letting her go to the nutters' rave-up tomorrow!"

"It's her decision. I warned her as best I could."

"Jesus!" The muscle jumped in Gareth's jaw. His eyes flared. Matilda thought of Vesuvius quaking and rumbling and emitting little bursts of smoke while the citizens of Pompeii went innocently about their business.

She retrieved *Letters from Roman Britain* from the nightstand and added it to the stack of books on the table. On its back cover was a photograph of Howard Sweeney, striking a pose amid the wind-swept ruins of a fort on Hadrian's Wall. "Sweeney must've told Reynolds about the gold torc. At least Reynolds knows about it, and the only other person he could have heard it from is Watkins, but I just can't believe Watkins is on the take."

"You told me not to trust Watkins," Gareth said.

"I know, I know." She squared the stack of books.

"What did Reynolds say?"

"Nothing specific, just hints. Daring me to confront him, I think."

"What did you say to him?"

"It was nice talking to you, good night. Do you think I'd blurt the entire case to him?"

"You blurted the entire case to Ashley."

"At the risk of stating the obvious, D.I. March, Adrian Reynolds and Ashley Walraven are two different people in two different situations." Matilda told herself to lower her voice. She slammed into the bathroom and starting folding the laundry hanging from the shower rod. The silence in the room behind her grew ominous.

She carried her unmentionables back into the bedroom, half-expecting to see lava running from Gareth's ears and pooling steamily on his shoulders. He was sitting just as she'd left him, tight, tense, and controlled. His lashes curtained the fire in his eyes. "The char will clean your room for you," he said, very quietly.

"I'm just being nervous," Matilda replied.

"If you've quite finished lecturing me, I'm off to the dig."

"I'm sorry you think I was lecturing you. I've finished telling you what I know." She stood back while he rose, stalked across the room, and shut the door firmly behind him.

Well, she thought as his steps receded down the hall, maybe she wasn't after robbing cradles, either.

*T*he rain was too light to send the students back inside and too heavy to make working comfortable. It certainly did little to quench Matilda's own volcanic mood. She stood atop the mound and surveyed the surrounding countryside. The trees along the river shivered in the cool, fresh breeze that fanned her cheeks. The buildings of Corcester and Fortuna

Stud resembled a watercolor, all muted colors and smeared lines. On the horizon Durslow Edge was a purplish-gray smudge like a bruise.

Gareth was digging much too busily in the Miller trench. Ashley sat at the edge of the emerging bathhouse with her back to him, although she offered Matilda a cramped smile. Sweeney was wearing a tweed deerstalker and a fatuous grin. "Good morning, Mrs. Gray."

One of these days, Matilda told herself, she was going to take her Ph.D. diploma and stick it in his — teeth, she hastily amended. "Howard, why did you tell Reynolds about the gold torc, after we agreed not to?"

"Why my dear, what makes you think. . . ."

"I'm not your dear."

Sweeney had the grace to look shamefaced. "One can't sell you a dummy, can one? Yes, I plead guilty. I don't happen to like being chucked down holes, you see, whilst the rotter who did it falls about laughing."

"We have no proof Reynolds did anything to you. Or stole anything, or murdered anyone."

"That's just the point. We have to draw him out, make him and his confederates tip their hand, or whatever idiom you use in the States. It's time we had this charade well and truly finished."

"I agree with you there," Matilda admitted.

Bryan walked by with the sketchbook, delivered it to Ashley, stood around joking with her for a moment, and then returned to his own trench.

Sweeney dropped his voice to a whisper. "There were at least two blighters climbing about the dig last night. I saw them from my window. If I had your skills, I might have been able to send some telepathic warning to our well-meaning but unfortunately dense local constable."

Matilda considered making some remark about telephones working better than ESP when it came to calling the cops, but she saved her breath.

"I hope you twig something at the Reynolds's this afternoon," Sweeney went blithely on. "Please excuse my not coming. The last time I took tea with Adrian, Della served soggy scones, dry sandwiches, and bitter tea."

"Some of us will simply have to make the sacrifice," Matilda told him, and turned toward the Miller trench.

Gareth had uncovered quite an array of stones — building, inscribed, and rubble. Raindrops sparkled on his hair. His cheeks were pink from the chill. When Matilda slithered through the mud to his side he looked around in weary resignation rather than rage.

"I'm sorry," she told him. "I was making decisions about the case without consulting you."

One brow and the corner of his mouth lifted in a shrug. "Decisions have to be made, don't they? Do you think Ashley will talk to me?"

"Yes. Just be your usual charming self."

"I don't want to give her any ideas."

"Don't worry. She's pretty well disillusioned."

Groaning, Gareth hoisted himself up on a column drum. "Ashley, would you be so good as to bring the sketchbook?"

"Oh," said the girl's voice. "Oh, yeah, sure."

Matilda turned to the ancient stairway and the monogram of St. Peter. If for nothing else, she told herself, Corcester would be remembered by the history books for that. And remembered by the popular mind for the gold torc. A shame the other torcs had been stolen long since, carried away and melted down.

With a muddy squelch, Ashley arrived in the trench. She eyed Gareth with a mixture of caution and anticipation, as though expecting him to rip open his shirt and display a badge tattooed on his chest. "Do you really want the book," she asked in a stage whisper, "or do you want to see me?"

"You," Gareth told her. "I — ah — I'm sorry — last night — I meant well."

"I know," she returned, with a shrug that was more of a spasm. "It's okay."

"I need to know what Nick told you about Linda."

"Nothing much," Ashley said to her feet. "She'd been at the camp, and Nick was going to drive her back into Corcester, but his car broke down. It was a nice night, cold and clear, so she hitchhiked. That's all."

"He didn't see who she hitched with?"

"No. I mean, he couldn't have seen, or he'd know who

killed her."

"Not necessarily," said Matilda. "but we need to locate the driver of that car. I bet it was someone Linda knew."

"Unless Nick killed her himself," Gareth said. "He was the last person to see her alive. That doesn't look good."

Ashley's chin went up. Her eyes sparked. "That's exactly the reason Nick won't talk to the police. To you. Why even mention Linda to me if he was guilty? But you wouldn't believe him if he said today was Thursday. He says toffs — rich people — commit crimes and the police look for poor people to blame."

Gareth winced. *Whoa,* Matilda thought, suppressing a grin, *the kitten has claws.*

"Nick says Reynolds has been scavenging here at the fort," Ashley went on. "He's been watching him, trying to catch him."

"Or helping him," Gareth said, and added grudgingly, "How better to keep an eye on him?"

Rain ran down the back of Matilda's neck. She turned and looked at the stairway and the rubble-filled treasury. Gold. The gold of the gods. The gold of misers. Greedy gold. Sacred gold. No, the palms of her hands didn't itch, but something in the back of her mind did.

"The travelers were camping along the Manchester road beyond Shadow Moss when Linda died," Gareth was saying. "Somewhat closer to Durslow than they are now. What else did Nick tell you?"

"Nothing more about Linda," Ashley replied. "He talked about mythology and history and weird religious stuff."

Matilda eyed the stairway. In the rain the coping stone was the deep crimson of old blood. Very old blood, she thought. With her forefinger she traced the line of the monogram. It was rough to her skin and to her thoughts as well. Claudia had scratched the rock. Branwen had left the temple.

"Are you going with Nick to the — ah — ceremony tomorrow night?" Gareth asked Ashley.

"Yes," she answered, without adding, *so what?*

Gareth shot a troubled glance at Matilda. "We'll be there, too. Give us a shout if you — well, if there's anything we need to know. I'll make sure you have a mobile phone."

"If anything seems even the least bit wrong to you," Matilda added, "call. Or better yet, bail out. Don't worry about looking stupid."

"I won't." Ashley offered them the artless smile that Matilda had often seen on Patrick's face. It said, "No problem," "What me worry?" and "Get off my back," and was guaranteed to drive an adult bonkers. "Do you want the sketchbook?" she asked.

Matilda took the book. Ashley clambered out of the trench. Gareth looked after her as though he wanted to spank her.

"Well done," Matilda said. "You didn't spook her."

"Excuse me?"

"You didn't scare her away."

"She ought to be scared. Linda was murdered on some old Celtic holiday, another holiday's come round, Nick's keen on mythology, and yet she thinks *I'm* after doing *him* over? I don't like it."

"Neither do I. She's feeling some purpose that I didn't sense in her last night. Stubborn purpose, excitement, and anxiety. I'll bet half the reason she's going is because she wants to help us."

"Super."

Matilda sighed. "What I don't like the most is the feeling that I'm missing something. The one thread that's knotted into every other one."

"The Antiquary's Corner?" Gareth suggested.

"It could be. Isn't it time to enlist Emma?"

"I'll ring her this evening, after she gets off work."

Kneeling down by the stone, Matilda turned the pages in the book until she came to the sketch of the monogram. The scratches corresponded perfectly with the drawing. But did they correspond with her memory of the scene? No, she decided. The two horizontal marks, the ones that made an "E" from the stem of the "P," were cut deeply into the stone, too deeply to have been scratched by Claudia's little knife.

Matilda frowned. Again she touched the stone. It was gritty and damp. . . . That was it. Branwen had returned to the temple and had deepened the scratches. Enough construction work had been going on at the fort for her to have obtained a chisel. Why? Had she intended to emphasize her own religious vision at the expense of Claudia's?

"Ogham," Matilda said aloud. The ancient Celts, the Druids in particular, had used a system of writing in which each letter was indicated by parallel marks to one side or another of a line. Many stones with ogham inscriptions, trailing like tooth marks down the edge of the rock, were still extant, especially in Ireland.

Irish gold, she thought. Irish gold brought through Anglesey and northern Wales, through the country of the Cornovii to the Iceni. . . .

"Now what?" Gareth said in her ear, and she jumped.

"Something I'll have to look up," she replied, and tried to explain.

"But how do you. . . ." he began, and then shook his head. "Never mind. I don't want to know." He picked up his shovel and started scraping away at his pile of rocks.

The rain stopped. Sweeney led everyone across the street for lunch, where he announced tomorrow's holiday. "It will be one long Kodak moment," he concluded. The students emitted a cheer and went back to devouring all the hot potato and leek soup Clapper's kitchen could produce.

Matilda slipped upstairs and checked one of her reference books. Two short lines perpendicular to the long ground line indicated a "D." And, in the Celts' tree-symbol alphabet, "D" was also "Dur," or "oak." The name "Druid" supposedly came from the same root. Not to mention, Matilda thought, the name of Durslow Edge with its primeval trees.

She no longer doubted that Branwen had died at Durslow Edge. Willingly, as a very special sacrifice. And had the death of Boudicca's grand-daughter, with her Roman blood and her Roman lover, achieved its magical ends? Matilda thought that, on the whole, it had. Almost all of Britain had in the end been subdued by Rome, but Ireland had never fallen. At least, she thought with a smile, Ireland had never fallen to political Rome. Its conquest by Roman Catholicism was another story.

Thoughtfully Matilda returned to the dig, and puttered about in the trench beside Gareth but not really with him. He, too, kept his silence. By late afternoon the sky thickened again, and the rain fell. Sweeney called it quits just before four. He supervised the unrolling of the plastic ground sheets, said to Matilda, "Enjoy your Mad Hatter's tea," and headed toward Manchester behind the wheel of his white BMW.

Watkins and Clapper huddled beneath the eaves of the hotel, muttering about the rainy weather cutting down attendance and where the Morris dancers could go to practice. From the hall window Matilda saw a squad of workers struggling to erect the Maypole at the bottom of the slope behind the church. She smiled ruefully, acknowledging its ancient symbolism. The male member could be a finely-tuned instrument of pleasure. It was shame so many men used it as a bludgeon.

Quickly she tidied up, going so far as to put on a skirt and stockings. Gareth was heading toward the stairs when she emerged from her room, and they shared an umbrella across the parking lot. The workers had left the may-pole drooping disconsolately. Gareth's gaze touched it and moved on. He was either unaware of or stoically ignoring any anatomical references.

His Rover made fast work of the short distance to Fortuna Stud. Two or three horses stood in the pasture. Gremlin, his gray coat appearing silver-white in the rain, peered hopefully over the gate. Light streamed from the stable, and as Matilda shut the door of the car she heard the clop of hooves, the occasional snort, and Jimmy's cracked voice soothing his charges. Gareth looked in that direction, wanting to visit the horses more than he wanted to visit Della. But he squared his shoulders, unfurled the umbrella, and soldiered on.

Della opened the door. "Filthy weather."

"Isn't it just?" Gareth agreed.

"A holiday in Ibiza or Majorca would go down a treat," Della said. "Adrian now. . . ." She fluttered around relieving Matilda and Gareth of umbrella and coats, leaving her sentence dangling. After the cool rainswept outdoors, the house seemed as warm and still as a greenhouse. A couple of potted palms stood wilting in the entryway.

Although Della was wearing a pink satin dress that made her complexion resemble a porcelain doll's, her perfume was patchouli, the old hippie favorite that reminded Matilda of mosquito repellent. Gareth's coat and tie and Matilda's plaid skirt would have seemed clumsy next to Della's fancy dress if Della herself hadn't been moving as awkwardly as a marionette on strings. Her agitation made Matilda's teeth hurt.

"Adrian sends his apologies. He had business somewhere — Derby, Sheffield." Della ushered them into a wood-paneled and stuffed-leather sitting room that had obviously been furnished by her husband. That was no doubt his desk against the wall, its shelf displaying photographs of horses and jockeys but not one of Della. Books on a variety of historical and mythological topics lined one wall — in spite of the gaps opening here and there, several lay horizontally on top of the others. Some of the books were gone, Matilda told herself. Della had told Gareth the travelers were actually quite pleasant. Ashley had seen books piled up in Nick's caravan.

On the opposite side of the room gleamed a display case. "Is this your collection?" Matilda asked.

"Those are Adrian's things. He's done a nice job of tidying them up, hasn't he? Please have a look. I'll put the kettle on."

He'd done too nice a job, Matilda thought as she peered through the glass. He'd not only cleaned the artifacts, he'd touched up some of their cuts and bruises. No wonder Sweeney thought half of them were fakes. The strainer with its coy Victorian-era image of Bacchus probably was, and she had her doubts about the vaunted glass vial. But the rest of the plates, cups, lamps, necklaces, and assorted votives radiated authenticity. She would have to actually touch them to be positive, which would mean asking Della to open the case. There was, however, no point to touching them. The authenticity of these artifacts was not the issue.

Gareth stood shifting his weight from one foot to the other. "So Reynolds couldn't be here. He's probably with Celia Dunning."

"Or other collectors and horse people," Matilda replied. "He seems to spend most of his time schmoozing."

"Schmoozing?" asked Gareth.

"Chatting people up. Making deals. Earning social points with people he hopes can help him. Schmoozing is like gambling, you can hit it big or you can spend a fortune on nothing but glamour."

"If he put as much effort into working he wouldn't have

financial problems, would he?"

Della's voice came from behind them and they both jumped. "It was my inheritance that bought Fortuna Stud, Mr. March, as well as quite a few of the items in our collections. Adrian rather resents that, I'm afraid. He does work, very hard, to keep up appearances. It's not his fault he has very poor business judgment and has made some bad investments."

"I beg your pardon," Gareth said.

"That's quite all right. You're a reporter aren't you?" Della took a deep, shuddering breath, as though her assertive speech had exhausted her. "Please, come through, let me show you my collection."

Matilda signaled Gareth with a tilt of her head. *All right, you've been authorized to ask questions. Go for it.*

Della led them to an identical display case in the dining room. The Portmeirion vase occupied a place of honor amid several Caithness Glass paperweights. Hummell and Lladro figurines stood next to Limoges snuffboxes. Every facet of the Waterford crystal gleamed, as did the Lalique, but the antique Staffordshire displayed its cracks and discolorations proudly. The case looked like a miniature of Dunning's shop. "Very nice," said Matilda.

"Brilliant," Gareth added with an ingratiating smile.

"Thank you." Della trailed a hand affectionately down the side of the cabinet. From the next room came the whine of a boiling kettle. "I'll bring the tea to the sitting room," she said, and hurried away.

In her absence Gareth showed Matilda the magazines on the sitting room coffee table: several treasure-hunting rags and a Sotheby's catalog. "Reynolds sees himself as a real wheeler-dealer," she said.

"Above the law, perhaps?" Gareth returned.

Della pushed her way past the door carrying a huge tray, and laid out a meal that wouldn't have been out of place in Buckingham Palace. Sandwiches, scones, and petit-fours filled a three-tiered serving plate. Dishes of butter, jam, and clotted cream surrounded sugar bowl, cream pitcher, and steaming teapot. Each cup and saucer nestled on a linen napkin. "What lovely china," Matilda said. "Crown Derby, isn't it?"

"Yes, yes, quite. Please sit down."

Matilda could feel her cheeks glowing in the anxious warmth of the room. The hot tea didn't help. The food was delicious but heavy. Beside her on the couch Gareth inhaled cucumber sandwiches and talked. Part of his police training, perhaps, was how to dispense with chewing.

Led by Gareth's smooth voice through a discussion of the weather, the agricultural prospects, and the market for collectibles, Della blushed and stammered and rattled the crockery. If she's so frightened of us, Matilda asked herself, why ask us to tea? Perhaps something else frightened her more.

Gareth finally broached the subject of the murder. "I thought it would be an interesting addition to my article to mention the illegal antiquities trade, and how the girl murdered on Durslow Edge seems to have been involved in it."

Della's eyes glinted so sharply that Matilda's own eyes narrowed.

"The girl was killed on a stormy night?" Gareth went on.

"No," replied Della, "it was a stormy night when Adrian and I heard that her body had been found. She was killed two days earlier, wasn't she?"

"I believe so."

"That night was clear and cold. Adrian went out in his MG — to Liverpool, he said. He didn't get back here until very late. Or so I suppose. You remember the night Dr. Sweeney was attacked, I'd taken my sleeping tablets — migraine, you see. I had migraine that night, too."

"You knew Linda, the murdered girl. You must have done, she worked at The Antiquary's Corner."

"We met, yes. That's all, though. I had no idea she was — well, whatever she was doing illegally. Celia wouldn't dream of doing anything illegal, but, if you'll pardon my saying so, I'm not so sure about Adrian. He met Linda at the Green Dragon more than once, to talk antiquities."

"Weren't you — not to put too fine a point on it, Mrs. Reynolds — weren't you a bit jealous?"

"Oh no, no, they were talking business."

"Of course, you've seen the receipts."

"Oh no, there were no receipts, just amounts entered in

the checkbook."

Della hadn't blinked once during her testimony, Matilda noted. Her skin had gone so pale her modest application of lipstick and eye shadow seemed clownish. Her hands were knotted in her lap.

Gareth settled back on the couch, his cup balanced on his knee. If he'd been a cat, thought Matilda, he'd be licking his whiskers. "Celia Dunning is an old school friend of yours?" she asked.

"A teacher, actually. In British history, which I went on to teach in turn." Della's gaze fell to her lap. Deliberately she loosened her fingers and spread them on her knees.

"Your book collection is very impressive, too," Matilda said. "With the Romans ruins next door and Durslow on the horizon, the past must seem very close."

"There's the Festival tomorrow. I always enjoy that."

"Beltane. Aren't there other celebrations in the area, as well? A couple of traveler girls were talking about one in the chip shop the other day."

"Oh that," Della said faintly.

"It must be helpful," said Gareth, "to have the travelers nearby, always ready to do the mucking out on the cheap. Adrian doesn't like them, but I imagine Jimmy's only too ready to share the labor, isn't he?"

Della gulped, looking as though she'd suddenly swallowed a frog, and color flooded her face. "Jimmy's been with me for years. I'm loyal to him and him to me. The work gets done and Adrian's none the wiser. It doesn't hurt."

"Of course not," said Matilda. She could hardly breathe in the hot, airless room. No wonder she'd felt so hot last night, in anticipation.

"I'd like to interview the travelers," Gareth went on. "Perhaps you could arrange an introduction. They seem so completely divorced from the past. . . ."

"Not a bit of it," said Della. "They've returned to the past, to the ways of the ancient Celts, living off the land, rejecting the materialism of the modern world."

"Drinking," Matilda added, "listening to music, and fighting. It's very good of you to lend them your books. You might inspire some to continue with their educations."

"Ah." Della lifted her cup. Her hand was trembling and tea slopped into the saucer. Her face went a rosier pink than her dress.

Whatever Della's motive had been in inviting them to tea, she was now desperate for them to go away. Matilda took pity on her and glanced at Gareth. "My goodness, look at the time. We have to meet the students at six. Mrs. Reynolds, thank you so much, everything was lovely."

Gareth took the hint. Murmuring appreciation, he and Matilda edged toward the entry. "Thank you for coming," said Della by rote. "Please come again soon." She shut the door behind them.

Matilda lingered on the doorstep just long enough to hear the woman burst into sobs inside. "I'm sorry," she said over her shoulder.

Gareth stood on the gravel driveway, mopping his forehead and gazing upward into the clearing sky. "What was all that in aid of?"

"I was afraid if we stayed any longer she was going to faint. In the car, come on, I don't want to talk here."

They opened the windows and luxuriated in a cool breeze. The lights of the hotel made a cheery contrast to the dark, almost menacing bulk of the ruined fort. Gareth parked the car and stopped the engine. A strain of sappy music — violins playing "Tomorrow" — emanated from the back door of the bar.

Gareth propped his left elbow against his headrest and turned to Matilda. "I expected her to cover up for Reynolds. Instead she shopped him good and proper. Why? And why tell us?"

"To answer your last question first, she might be worried that with Reynolds such an influential landowner in Corcester Watkins wouldn't pursue the issue. So she tells a nosey reporter who would love to blow open the case. I bet it was when you pointed out that Linda was murdered two days before the stormy night that Della realized what she knew." Matilda licked her lips. They were still layered with cloying sweet cream and jam. "When we first arrived she was nervous, like an actor before the curtain goes up. But she went through with it. Damning Adrian is probably the bravest thing she's ever done."

"She's easy to read, is she?"

"I think she was telling the truth, if that's what you're asking."

"So then, why expose her husband?"

"We've been wondering all along why Della would protect him when he treats her with such contempt. And she told us tonight that he's even spent a lot of her money," Matilda replied. "Well, we were wrong. Remember what she said to you about Boudicca? How she has the travelers in behind Adrian's back? She hates him. It's payback time. You saw how cool she was as she turned him in — except for her hands knotted in her lap."

"She wasn't telling us everything she knows," Gareth said.

"She has another motive, yes. We were getting too close to it when we stopped talking about the murder and started talking about the travelers. She didn't deny she'd been hiring them and lending them books. But there's something else about them she doesn't want us to know." Matilda set her hand on Gareth's arm. "The woman you saw in Nick's caravan. Was it Della?"

In the shadows Gareth's face was a mask, eyes opened wide, brows arched. "I don't — I wasn't. . . . It could have been, couldn't it? She could have seen the yob cut Caesar, and knew I'd bring him round straightaway. So she rushed back here by car to meet me. I thought she seemed feverish that day, and Reynolds said she was ill."

"It's faster to go from Corcester to Durslow across country," said Matilda, visualizing a map, "but you can get to the traveler's camp faster by car. And you were nursing Caesar along. She had time."

"She wants to get shut of Adrian so she can have Nick," Gareth stated.

"This is looking more and more like a French bedroom farce, isn't it? Now I'm even more interested in meeting Nick. His androgen levels must be off the scale."

"Androgens?"

"Sex appeal, basically."

"I've never understood why women fancy berks like him."

Matilda shook her head. "The thrill of the forbidden, I

think, along with a female genetic attraction toward the self-confident, and, one assumes, strong man. Remember the old ballad, 'Blackjack Davy'? 'Late one night the squire came home, inquiring for his lady. Some denied and some replied, she's gone with Blackjack Davy'."

"Oh, that one. He catches up with her and she ticks him off."

"'What care I for your goose-feather bed, the sheets turned down so bravely, when I could sleep on the cold, hard ground along with Blackjack Davy.'" Matilda smiled impishly. "And then there's the male genetic attraction toward the bimbo, something *I've* never understood."

"No brains, no backtalk," Gareth told her with a grin. Sobering, he went on, "It's no farce. Della might not be jealous of Adrian, with Linda or with Celia Dunning, for that matter. I reckon she's right jealous of Nick, though. And if she's not telling us everything she knows, he's not telling us anything, is he?"

Several human shapes loomed out of the dusk, cat-calling to the couple in the parked car. Matilda turned around so that the light fell on her face. "Sorry," said Bryan. "We thought we had an X-rated movie here. Didn't realize it was just a study hall." Jennifer and Manfred grimaced in embarrassment, Ashley winked conspiratorially, and the students strolled on by.

Matilda turned back to Gareth. She heard her own voice saying, "I think I've been insulted."

For a long moment he looked at her, expression impenetrable. Then his lips parted and softened into a wry smile. "And me, as well." His fingertips stroked the angle of her jaw, his touch as light and curious as a butterfly's kiss.

Shivering with delight, she leaned toward him. For a long moment his warm breath bathed her face. Then, just as his parted lips were closing in on hers, she caught herself and turned aside. "No. Not now."

"No." His mouth closed and tightened. He glanced toward the hotel door, which was just swinging shut behind Ashley. "We have several things that need doing."

"Like phoning Emma," said Matilda.

"Right. I'll make the call from my room, less chance of

anyone overhearing." With a strobe-like flash of the ceiling light, they climbed out of the car. "Are you coming?" Gareth asked.

"In a few minutes."

"Stay nearby." He headed toward the hotel, his stride measured and purposeful, his body straight but far from stiff.

It's not, Matilda thought, as though she were robbing any cradles. Gareth was an adult, even if the inner child still wriggled through his defenses from time to time. Fewer years separated her from him than separated Marcus from Branwen. . . . That was another time, if not another place.

Matilda crossed the street in front of the hotel and stood on the sidewalk that ran beside the cottages and the bowling green. She put her hand in her pocket and closed her fingers around the spindle.

She saw the fort, its walls almost complete behind their scaffolding. In the setting sun of her vision, their shadow stretched far across the green turf. Beyond the shadow stood two tall men. Their long blond hair was stiffened by lime, so that it resembled the tail of the horse whose halter one of them held. Their cloaks fluttered in the breeze. Atop the walls several guards leaned on their spears and watched.

The gates of the fort opened a crack. Branwen stepped outside. She was pushing a small handcart, an ancestor of a wheelbarrow. Upon it sat a wicker basket apparently filled with soiled linen. But if the basket held laundry or cast-off garments, the cloth was oddly heavy. Branwen had to throw her entire weight against the handles of the cart to move it down the muddy path.

Without a backward look at the fort she joined the men. One of them relieved her of the cart. The other boosted her onto the horse's back. They led her away from the eye of the sun, toward the night. . . .

The countryside plunged into a darkness cut only by torchlight within the fort and starlight overhead. Voices came to Matilda's ears, at first faintly, then more strongly, until she felt as though the speakers stood next to her, invisible in the night.

"The sentries saw her leave," Marcus was saying.

"You told them to let her come and go as she pleased," said

Claudia. "She left of her own will. She's returned to her people."

"The lock on the temple treasury was broken open by a chisel. The torcs have been stolen."

"They've returned to their people, too."

Silence, strumming with tension. Then Marcus said in a strangled voice, "The Brigantian envoy tells me that tomorrow is a Celtic holy day. That tomorrow there will be a great sacrifice. That it is not for us to interfere."

"It isn't. The gold doesn't belong to Rome, any more than Branwen belongs to you. Let this savage land claim its own, Marcus."

"As you claim me?"

"If God wills it. If He will forgive us both."

Marcus sighed, the breath as long and agonized as the last breath of a dying man. Or as the first breath of one re-born.

The breath dwindled into time past. The night thinned into dusk. Matilda was standing on the sidewalk. The momentum of a passing truck tugged at her skirt and its roar deafened her. Watkins walked by and said, "Good evening, Dr. Gray."

Her throat was too clogged to speak. Her shoulders were bowed beneath the burden of sacrifice. A white horse, she thought, picking its path from Durslow Edge to Shadow Moss. A pale horse, with its pale rider named Death.

Stooping, she buried the spindle in the mud beside the gate. Even as she turned toward the welcoming lights of the Green Dragon, Matilda wondered if there would be space on Durslow tomorrow for not only the warm bodies of the living but for the wraiths of the immortal dead as well.

Chapter Sixteen

*T*he telephone went several times. Gareth was about to give it up when Emma's breathless voice answered. "Yeh?"

"Gareth March here. Good evening."

"Hello, luv!"

"My appointment in London tomorrow's been canceled. Is the ceremony still on?"

"Oh yes, that it is. Where shall I meet you — at the Green Dragon?"

Let's not set Emma down in Clapper's vicinity, Gareth told himself. "I need to photograph the church. I'll meet you there at half past four. Can you leave work early?"

"The Dunning's closing the shop at noon. I might even be able to hitch a ride with her, if she'll let me sit in that posh car of hers. Says she always goes to the festival, it's good for antique-hunting."

Better and better. Gareth softened his voice until it was the texture of Della's clotted cream. "Emma, I need your help. I'm afraid I wasn't quite honest with you Wednesday."

"You're married."

"No, no, no. It's when I told you about the article I've been assigned. I'm writing on 'Our Roman Heritage' for the *Times*, yes. I'm also writing an article for the *Sunburn* about the murder of Linda Burkett."

"Oooh! Dead thrilling!"

Gareth rolled his eyes heavenward, realized what he was doing, and quickly lowered them. "You gave me a lead when you told me about Dunning's boyfriend. He might be involved. My editors need to know who he is. There could be a packet of quid involved. If you could search Dunning's files for letters. . . ."

"No need, luv. I got curious, like, after we talked, so I hung about after closing tonight and actually saw the bloke. I reckon they're having it off at this very minute."

"Super! It's Adrian Reynolds, isn't it?"

"Yeh — looked like him, stoop-shouldered. . . . Well, it was just a glimpse, wasn't it, through the window. He slipped the trout a paper folder and a box. I'll watch for them when I do the filing tomorrow, shall I?"

"Brilliant! Emma, if you can bring them to me, I'll make sure you're rewarded."

"I know just the thing. There's posh hotel in Chester, the perfect place for a dirty weekend. . . ."

"Sorry," Gareth said. "Call waiting. See you tomorrow, Emma. And thank you again."

"Pleasure's mine. Ta-ta."

Gareth switched off his phone. He sat on the edge of his bed looking round the room but not quite focusing. Whether he was prepared to prostitute himself for Scotland Yard was a question that didn't yet need answering. With any luck, once Emma found out who he really was he'd lose his appeal.

Gently he burped cucumber and strawberry jam. A walk, that was it, he needed to have a walk. Maybe Matilda would like to go, too. She couldn't be eating supper with the students, not after that tea. Not that she starved herself like some women he'd known — Nicole, for example, he'd almost chipped a tooth on her rib cage. Or scraggy little Emma. It wasn't natural for a woman to have a body like a twelve-year-old boy smuggling balloons in his shirt. Matilda's body was well-proportioned, as a woman's should be. He wondered which posh hotel in Chester Emma had been thinking of. Matilda would prefer to see Wales. Holywell. Gwytherin. Carnarvon. Cozy little inns with canopied beds.

Gareth found Matilda in the sitting room. She'd cleared away the magazines and was spreading pieces of graph paper across the coffee table. "Did you talk to Emma?" she asked.

"Yes," he replied. "She actually saw Reynolds with Dunning tonight. He gave Dunning a folder and a box. Emma's going to nick them for me."

"All right! Well done!"

"It's still not a complete case," Gareth warned. "I hope the box and the folder turn out to be the final bit."

"The last straw, or the keystone — whatever. Oh yes." Matilda distributed photos of the dig round the table. "Emma's sure the man was Reynolds? Might it have been Nick?"

"No, she wasn't sure. But the man fits Reynolds's description. And she'd have smelled Nick's androgens from forty paces. Besides, how many women can a chap handle?"

"I've always wondered that." Matilda looked up at Gareth as though he were an Old Master painting and she an art critic. "As for Reynolds being the murderer — I don't know."

They'd already quarreled once today, Gareth told himself. There was no need to go at it again because she was still doubtful. He changed the subject. "Would you like to have a walk, see if the Maypole is up yet?"

"Thank you, I'd love to, but the students are coming in here after supper for a mini-course in plotting and stratigraphy. Give the Maypole my regards." Her blue eyes twinkled.

"I'll do that," he returned, and walked out into the night tempering his concerns with Emma and Reynolds, Della and Ashley and Nick, with musings on the ancient and honorable rites of spring.

It was barely light when Gareth awoke abruptly from a deep sleep. He heard a scratching and shuffling. Someone was in his room. . . . No. The noise came from his window.

He slipped from the bed, his heart thudding against his rib cage. Every object in the room was outlined with a thin translucent shimmer. The curtained window was a square of silver. He was on the second story, he reminded himself, with the ground and first floors between him and any evildoers. Only a monkey could climb the drainpipe or the ivy. He leaped forward and yanked the curtains aside.

A crow, the largest he'd ever seen, stood on the sill. It ruffled its feathers and looked at him with eyes like icy beads of jet.

With a convulsive shudder, Gareth shrank back. It was a *derwyn corph*, a corpse-bird. His grandmother had told him tale after tale of how the uncanny bird tapped on the window of someone who was about to die. . . . *Steady on,* he told himself. The festival preparations had disturbed one of the crows that lived in the tower of the church. There was nothing supernatural about this one. It wasn't even tapping on the glass.

He flung open the window. With a harsh cry the crow launched itself into the air and went winging away toward Fortuna Stud. Gareth leaned over the sill watching the bird until it disappeared, the only moving thing in the mist-shrouded silence of dawn. The chill of the air drew gooseflesh from his naked torso. He slammed the window, went back to bed, and pulled the covers to his chin. But still he felt cold.

*T*he tea was hot and milky sweet. Gareth downed his first cup and poured a second before he told Matilda about the crow. "There I was," he finished, "looking forward to a nice lie-in, and the damned bird knocks me up."

"A bird of ill-omen," she replied. "Did it give you nightmares?"

"No," he lied, and ducked her knowing look. They finished their late breakfasts and wandered out onto the street to discover that the mist had cleared, leaving the morning polished by sunshine.

Whistling, Clapper was setting up a sandwich board advertising his menu. One of the cottage-owners across the street hung a banner over his wall proclaiming, "Parking, £1". The lawn bowlers, kitted out in straw hats and white jackets, were setting up a souvenir stand. From atop the fort Gareth and Matilda watched Reynolds canter toward the river, Gremlin's coat gleaming in the sunshine.

"Hi ho Silver and away," Matilda said.

"When he gets back," said Gareth, "his head will be well and truly in the noose. Not literally, more's the pity. People who play dangerous games have to pay the price when they lose."

"Does that mean us, as well?" Matilda asked.

"We're not going to lose." Gareth turned to see several of the American students, along with some local youths, hiking up the side of the hill. They were carrying bits and pieces of silver-painted plastic armor and an assortment of bed sheets. "Looks to be another Roman invasion."

"Clapper's idea," said Matilda. "He was asking my advice last night. The kids are going to dress up as the ancient citizens of Cornovium and show tourists around the dig — in the process making sure no one steps on the edge of a trench or makes off with bits of inscription."

"Tell them to mind the ghosts." Gareth left her to run through the script with the impromptu guides and strolled toward the town. Gaily-colored streamers fluttered from the top of the Maypole. The vicar was supervising a squad of stained-glass-window washers.

Ashley stood looking at the book shop's display of volumes on history and folklore. "Good morning," she said. "Cool books, huh?"

"I don't think I've read a one of them," he replied.

"I've seen a few. Nick has most of them in his caravan...." She shot a glance at Gareth, half-defiant, half-pleading. "He's a real scholar, you know."

"Ah — yes." *We'll see*, he told himself, and went on, "Did Matilda give you the mobile phone?"

"Yes, she did, said she bought it for me specially. Thanks."

"Well, take care." It would've been easier to throw himself on a grenade to save Ashley's life than to send her to do his work for him. Gritting his teeth, he went on his way.

After roaming through the town and stopping into a cafe for a coffee he returned to the hotel feeling better. Emma would bring him the last piece, wouldn't she? Ashley would be all right, they were only harmless nutters. It would all be over soon, the crow be damned.

He found Matilda with Ashley just inside the door, their gestures indicating a serious discussion of clothing styles. "Thanks," the girl said, and bounded up the stairs.

"She wanted to know what she should wear tonight," Matilda told Gareth. "I hope she keeps focusing on such mundane details, then maybe she can keep her head if anything goes wrong."

"You're expecting something to go wrong, are you?" Gareth asked.

"Yes." The corners of Matilda's mouth tucked themselves in, producing a stiff upper lip.

Good show. "I'll fetch my camera," Gareth said. "A few snaps of the students in costume. . . ."

Watkins burst through the front door of the hotel looking less like the cavalry coming to the rescue than General Custer at his last stand. He seized Gareth's arm and in a husky whisper said, "The peat cutters found a body at Shadow Moss."

"That's Dr. Sweeney's department," Gareth began, but Matilda interrupted.

"Who is it?"

"From the description, it's Adrian Reynolds. His head's been bashed and his throat cut. It's another murder, right enough."

"Have you told Della yet?" Matilda asked.

"W.P.C. Innes went to collect her."

A house of cards collapsed in Gareth's mind, thoughts skittering to and fro and landing in a messy pile. Reynolds? But he was the murderer himself, wasn't he? *Bloody hell.*

Watkins coaxed Gareth toward the door. "I rang Manchester, you'll be wanting to have a look before they arrive."

The crow had flown toward Fortuna Stud. . . . *No, no, no,* Gareth told himself. He hurried out the door and into Watkins's orange-striped squad car. It wasn't until the constable sped away, siren blatting, that Gareth realized Matilda was sitting in the back seat. He turned round, mouth open to speak.

Her level gaze intercepted and blew away any protest he'd been intending to make. Closing his mouth, he faced front again. The countryside streamed by in a green blur. A bit of forest momentarily compressed the sound of the siren. The car sped down Racecourse Road and turned onto a muddy track that bumped and shivered across open heath dotted with birch scrub.

Even in the sunshine Shadow Moss seemed like an otherworldly place. The air was heavy with a musky, weedy smell.

Amidst their green mosses and reeds and white-tufted bog myrtle the dark pools reflected no light. The smudge that was Durslow Edge loomed like a thunderstorm on the horizon. Gareth's head spun. He was caught in a weird time conversion not of past centuries but of his own life. He had been here before, squelching with Watkins across the boggy ground. No matter that it had been chill and damp then, not warm and sunny. He and the constable had only to say the same words, in the same order, and it would all happen again, time repeating itself, Linda Burkett dying and Matilda sitting in Forrest's office. . . . *Steady on,* he ordered himself.

The peat-cutting machine was a mud-stained metal contraption on the opposite side of a black sheet of water. Two workmen lounged beside it — the rest, Gareth assumed, were spending the day dancing and drinking in Corcester.

Judging by his wilted suit and tie, it was the foreman who was waiting beside a patch of stone that shouldered through the tussocks of grass and shrub. The man twitched aside a tarpaulin, then fled upwind. What lay beneath the cloth was not a brown severed hand, both horrible and beautiful. There was no beauty in Adrian Reynolds's corpse.

Matilda sighed. Watkins swore quietly under his breath. Gareth knelt down and made a quick inspection of the remains.

Reynolds was lying face up. His open eyes were beads of jet. They didn't reflect any light either. His face was blank, wiped clean of expression. The back of his head was crushed. Dark crimson blood stained the rock on which it rested. A gaping wound sliced across his throat, exposing the severed ends of trachea and esophagus. Flecks of blood spattered Reynolds's white shirt. . . . No more than flecks. Gareth lifted and jiggled Reynold's limp arm. He replaced the tarpaulin, stood up, and caught Matilda's eye.

"It was violent and sudden," she said. "He was angry, and then he was dead. I can still feel his fury, thwarted now, unfocused. How sad, to die angry."

"It's better than dying scared." Gareth turned to Watkins. "It was the blow that killed him. Since there's very little blood on his clothing his throat was cut some time after his death. He's been dead about two hours, I'm estimating. The medical examiner can give you the details."

Watkins stopped looking dubiously at Matilda and started looking quizzically at Gareth. "Someone cut his throat after he were already dead? That's a bit of devilish jiggery-pokery, isn't it?"

"It looks that way." Matilda frowned. "What was used to hit him, Gareth?"

He scouted the area. The stone where the body lay was an outcropping of the same red sandstone that formed Durslow Edge. A few loose pebbles lay scattered about, but none were large enough to have made such a crushing wound. The flat of a shovel might have done, although its edge would have left a relatively well-defined furrow. "The killer must have taken the weapon away with him. I don't know what it was. Something large and slightly rounded."

The wind lifted Matilda's hair from her furrowed forehead. "Like the Earth?" she asked.

Gareth knew immediately what she meant. "Yes, that's it. We saw Reynolds ride out on Gremlin this morning. Gremlin can be as skittish as a colt. He threw Reynolds on his head."

"He were thrown off his horse," said Watkins, pulling out his notebook.

"Caesar almost had me on my head when the berk at the traveler's camp stabbed him," Gareth added. "If — someone — saw how effective a move that was . . ."

"One of the nutters stabbed the horse, causing it to throw Reynolds onto the rocks," Watkins stated, writing busily. "The fall killed him. Then the nutter cut his throat."

"So that his death would resemble Linda's?" Matilda asked. "It's no coincidence to find him here. One of the most persistent local legends is of the goddess riding a white horse down from Durslow Edge to Shadow Moss."

The nutters aren't supposed to be dangerous, Gareth shouted silently. If she heard, she didn't reply.

He inspected the rock beneath the body. Except for a few muddy scuff marks it held no footprints. There were no tire tracks closer than the road. The boggy ground was like a sponge — except for the clear print of a horseshoe on a patch of moss, it revealed nothing. "One of the travelers might have thought of this method of murder," he said. "Nick Veliotes.

Maybe he planned it with Della Reynolds."

"What about Celia Dunning?" asked Matilda. "She's probably too cold-blooded to fall for Reynolds's Lothario routine. I bet she's been using him just as much as he's been using her. Whether she's cold-blooded enough to kill someone who was attracting too much attention to the operation is another matter. You'll have to see if Emma can alibi her."

"Emma Price?" Watkins asked. "Who's this Lothario?"

Quickly Gareth put him in the picture, concluding, "At least that's what we decided after we talked to Della last night."

"Right," Watkins said faintly, and licked the point of his pencil.

"I'm afraid we might have inadvertently encouraged her to this," said Matilda. "Or at least into taking some action that led to this. It's more fate than coincidence that Reynolds died on Beltane, May Eve."

"Because Beltane was our deadline," said Gareth, "and that caused us to press Della. Yes, I follow that."

Watkins apparently didn't. He was still gamely writing, but his eyes were starting to cross. "Della might have caused Reynolds's horse to throw him. So then she cut his throat because Linda Burkett's throat. . . . Here!" The constable gestured with his pencil toward a track that skirted two pools.

Down the path came Della Reynolds, riding not Bodie but Great Caesar's Ghost, leading a lathered and mud-spattered Gremlin. She drooped over the saddle, her eyes red-rimmed and her face ashen. She didn't falter when she saw the police car and the tarpaulin on the ground.

The horses' hooves plopped through the mud, slower and slower. Gremlin snorted and shook his head, jingling his bridle. Caesar stopped, nostrils flaring. Della's dismount was a boneless slither. If Matilda hadn't stepped forward and caught her arm she would have crumpled like an empty sack to the ground.

Gareth took both sets of reins from Della's unresisting fingers, patted the blaze on Caesar's nose, and took cautious note of the white rims round Gremlin's dark eyes.

"Mrs. Reynolds," Watkins said. "You've not been at the farm, I take it."

The heavy breathing of the horses didn't quite conceal Della's quick, shallow gasps. She reeked of patchouli and sour sweat. "It was an accident," she murmured, her voice so thin Gareth had to lean forward to hear her. "He was shouting, slapping the reins against Gremlin's neck. Gremlin — just shrugged him away, like a fly. I touched him. There was nothing I could do for him. I couldn't — I couldn't bear to touch him any more. It was so quiet, just the wind in the reeds."

Gareth's skin crawled. Matilda closed her eyes and opened them again. Watkins turned to a new page in his notebook. "So it weren't murder after all, then."

"Gremlin ran away," Della said. "He's always been the nervy sort, but Adrian liked his spirit. . . ." She swayed. Matilda held her up. "I went after him, I was afraid he'd fall into a pool, break his leg, do himself damage. There was nothing I could do for Adrian, at least I could save the horse. When I caught him I just — I just sat there, for a long time."

"Why are you riding Caesar?" Gareth asked.

"Adrian wouldn't let me ride him. He said he was a man's horse. He let you ride him, not me. He said I wasn't good enough. But I did Adrian over yesterday, didn't I? This morning I felt, I felt. . . ." She licked her lips. Her eyes swam from side to side, as though the word were hiding in the peat. The wind rippled the tarpaulin.

"Strong?" Matilda suggested with a sharp look at Gareth.

"Yes," whispered Della. "Strong. So I took Caesar. Adrian had already left. But he'd forgotten something and he came back and saw that Caesar had gone missing. He threatened to sack Jimmy if he didn't tell him where I was. Where would the poor man go if Adrian sacked him? It's not his fault. He didn't know. . . ."

"Didn't know what?" Gareth asked. "What would happen? Or who you were meeting here at the Moss?"

The gray color drained from Della's face, leaving her skin almost green. She sank into a crouch. Matilda went down with her. "It's all right," she said quietly. "How you feel about Nick is your own business. We just need to know what happened to Adrian."

With an exasperated frown, Watkins turned to the next

page.

"Della, we haven't been quite honest with you." Gareth hunkered down beside her, so he wouldn't appear quite so threatening. "I'm only pretending to be a reporter. I'm Detective Inspector March from Scotland Yard. I'm trying to find out who killed Linda Burkett."

"I don't know anything about that," Della gasped, shaking her head convulsively. "It could have been Adrian. I told you that. I told you, didn't I?"

"Yes, you did," said Matilda. "Do you think Adrian killed her?"

"He's — was — a selfish man, a fearfully self-centered man, but. . . ."

"But?" Watkins prompted.

"But he's never been at all interested in religion, old, new, any kind. If he killed her — I wouldn't put it past him, mind you — if he killed her he'd simply bash her one and throw her in a ditch, wouldn't he?"

"He could have been trying to make it look as though someone else did it," offered Matilda. "He could have been trying to frame one of the travelers. So many people in Corcester were gossiping about ritual sacrifice and devil worship, he would have known what to do."

"Nick is interested in the old religion, isn't he?" Gareth asked, as softly as he could. "He knew Linda."

"They were lovers," whispered Della. "He'd talk to me about her. He didn't like her doing business with Adrian. When she died he cut up rough. I tried to help him."

You couldn't have picked a better method, Gareth thought acidly. Aloud, he asked, "Did Nick tell you he suspected Adrian was the murderer?"

"No. I hadn't thought about it. I hadn't wanted to think about it, not until you told me about the clear night, and the stormy one, and I realized. . . ." She stopped, biting her lip. The tears leaked slowly, painfully, from her eyes.

Matilda rocked Della's head against her shoulder. "Go on. Tell us. Share it, so it won't hurt you as badly."

"I was to meet Nick here, this morning," Della whispered. "He said this is a place of power. I suppose it is, isn't it? He wasn't here when I arrived, I swear it. He wasn't here whilst

Adrian was shouting at me. He wasn't here when Gremlin — when Gremlin ran away. I don't know where he is."

Watkins shouted toward the hovering workmen. "Any of you lot see a black-haired traveler here this morning?"

"Yeh. Driving an old banger that way, right smart-like." The foreman gestured toward Corcester. The horses moved restively, breathing steam down Gareth's collar. He stood up and made reassuring noises at them.

"Adrian was so still," moaned Della. "So still. There was nothing there any longer. One moment he was tearing strips off me and the next he was gone. All gone."

Whatever Matilda was hearing she kept to herself. Gareth could hear a distant siren. He took Della's hand, hardly less cold and limp than her husband's, and drew her to her feet. "We need an official identification, next of kin and all that. I know it's difficult. Just a quick look, please, and then P.C. Watkins and Matilda will take you back to town."

Della wobbled, as though the bog were hiccuping beneath her feet. Matilda took her arm and shot Gareth a resigned glance — *all right, we have to know.* Watkins folded his notebook, tucked it in his pocket, and lifted one corner of the tarpaulin.

Della went stiff. She stared. A shudder racked her body. She screamed.

Watkins dropped the tarpaulin. Della kept on screaming, even as Matilda tried to soothe her. The sirens grew louder and louder. The horses started tugging at their reins and prancing backward, dragging Gareth with them.

Thank God some level head amongst the Manchester lads thought to turn off the sirens once the cars turned onto Racecourse Road. With a gurgle and a wheeze Della stopped screaming. But she was trembling so violently it took Matilda several minutes to ease her into Watkins' car.

"Do you believe Della's story?" Watkins asked Gareth.

"Yes, I do. She didn't know his throat had been cut, did she? She'd already seen him dead, but not like that."

"It were Nick taking a bit of revenge, weren't it? A shame I can't charge him with murder. Interference with a dead body should do, though." He clapped Gareth on the shoulder. "You've solved the murder and a mysterious death as well.

Good show, Inspector."

Matilda closed the door on Della and looked back at the two men.

"I'll take Mrs. Reynolds to the station" Watkins went on, "so's she can make a statement. You as well, Mrs. Gray. No need to put it about the town what's happened. Might spoil the festival."

"Don't let Ashley out of your sight!" added Gareth to Matilda. "She mustn't go anywhere with Nick, not after this."

"You're right. He must be half out of his mind with fear and grief. I'll call her and tell her to cancel our plans." Matilda paused whilst Watkins walked round to the driver's side and opened the door. "Gareth, did Reynolds kill Linda?"

"I was afraid you were going to ask that," Gareth returned. "Nick thought he did do."

"Nick's attitude toward Reynolds was colored by — what? Resentment of the man's wealth and arrogance? Jealousy of his relationship, whatever that was, with Linda? Anger at his treatment of Della?"

"If Reynolds didn't kill Linda, who did? You thought she went to Durslow with a man."

"Yes, but. . . ." She shook her head. "Della's out of contention, I think. Dunning? Nick himself? Emma's boyfriend Clive? Clapper? Zondor from Planet X?"

"Matilda, we're at the end of the case, not the beginning. Reynolds must be the killer. All the evidence points that way."

"Does it? We're at the end of the case, all right. I just wish I felt more confident we'd solved it." She threw Gareth a rueful salute, climbed into the car beside Watkins, and pulled her mobile phone from her bag.

Here came the other cars, their blue lights repeating the blue of the sky. And of Matilda's eyes, Gareth thought irrelevantly.

Watkins's car backed and filled and, its wheels spinning in the mud, started back the way it had come. The cars and vans from Manchester skidded to a halt and deployed a dozen people of various races, genders, and uniforms.

Gareth felt numb inside. Not elated, not proud, just numb. Damn Adrian, for coming to such a banal end. Damn Della, for taking away the pleasure of arresting him. Damn Matilda for nobbling this moment of triumph. Well, he'd get the proof he needed from Emma. It was all academic now. *Wasn't it?*

"March?" called someone from the crowd gathered round Reynolds's body.

He went forward, made his own statement, and then turned the crime scene over to the experts. "I'll take the horses back to the farm."

"Ta," said one of his colleagues. The others were busy.

Gareth pulled himself onto Caesar's back. Della's saddle was a bit too small for him, but it wouldn't be a long ride.

He peered at the looming, lurking horizon. At Durslow Edge. What if Matilda was too late to stop Ashley? What then?

Gremlin jerked at the reins. Caesar tap-danced away from Adrian Reynolds' all-too-mortal remains. Turning toward Fortuna Stud, Gareth gave the horses their heads. The sooner he got back, the better.

Chapter Seventeen

A siren yowled suddenly in the street below her window. Ashley jumped. Her heart pounding, she looked out. A police car, lights ice-pale in the bright sunshine, took off up the street. Maybe there'd been a car accident, with all the people coming to the festival. *Jeez,* she told herself, *you'd think they were coming after you.*

The sound of the siren wobbled into the distance and died. Ashley turned back to the little mirror over the sink and inspected her own image. She was wearing her best jeans and a nice cable-knit sweater over a T-shirt, which would be easy for Nick to get off, if it came to that, not that she was sure she wanted it to come to that.

Whatever, it wasn't as though she was going to church or anything. And she sure wasn't going to wear her pumps, not tramping around outside. She laced up her boots and stuffed her ID and some money into her pocket. The cell phone, she saw, was set to vibrate, not ring. Good. She hooked it over her waistband, beneath her sweater. If Nick saw it, she could always tell him Matilda gave it to her in case she needed a ride back to town. That was close enough to the truth that it wasn't a lie.

She was working for Scotland Yard, Ashley assured herself. Chin up and back straight, she went down the stairs and threaded her way through the throng in the lobby. The sidewalk outside was hardly less crowded. Bryan, wearing plastic armor and helmet, jeans and basketball shoes, waved people toward the dig. "I stepped on Jennifer's sheet," he confided, "and it came off, so she sent me over here to shill."

"She was wearing a leotard underneath, wasn't she?"

"Yeah!" Bryan grinned.

Ashley laughed. "Keep up the good work," she told him in her best Matilda voice, and headed toward the center of town.

Spectators gathered around the polygon. Morris dancers, wearing white shirts, knee breeches, and bells, capered to a sprightly flute tune. Another group whacked staffs together as they danced, clicking and clacking as well as jingling. From the wooden torso and horse's head of the hobby horse stuck two human legs and a huge stomach. Clapper, Ashley realized. He cut a swathe through the crowd, bopping people over the head with a balloon tied to a stick and telling ribald jokes. Several robed figures wearing the ancient antler head-dresses emerged from the church and began chasing the hobby horse. The audience laughed, cheered, and took pictures. It was more like Disneyland, thought Ashley, than a religious event.

The hobby horse bore down on her. One of the antlered figures brushed against her, filling her nostrils with the scent of sweat and mildew. She liked the dancers better. She could see their faces.

There was Nick, leaning against the window of the Job Centre where she'd first seen him — when? Two weeks ago? Ten years ago? In his drab army-surplus clothes he looked like a crow in a drift of confetti. He was facing toward the dancers and the maskers but was looking right through them. Of all the faces in the crowd his was the only one empty of expression. He looked like those pictures of soldiers who'd been on the front lines too long, Ashley thought sympathetically. Stressed out.

She fought her way to his side. "Nick?"

His dark eyes stared at her, then, with a blink, cleared. "Eh, Ashley. Are you ready, then?"

"As ready as I'll ever be," she told him.

With a last glance over her shoulder toward the music and laughter and colors, she followed Nick down the street toward the car park. His mud-spattered car was parked at the edge of the crowded lot, in a no-parking zone. He climbed into the driver's seat. She clambered into the passenger side as he started the engine.

Ashley tried several questions about the dig, the festival, the ceremony. Nick answered with monosyllables. *Great,* she thought. How was she going to prove to Gareth that Nick was innocent if he didn't say anything? And part of her mind answered, *if he doesn't say anything, then you won't find out that he's not innocent.*

Ashley stopped talking and tried not to hold her breath.

The camp was silent. The dark fir trees repelled the sunlight. After the bright afternoon the interior of Nick's caravan seemed particularly dingy. Water dripped over the dishes in the sink. The air was stale.

"Wendy and Bob went on to Durslow, to gather brush for the bonfire. We need to bring along that lot." Nick gestured toward the boxes stacked on the bench, each with its neat *The Antiquary's Corner* label. Instead of picking any of them up, though, he dropped down on the opposite bench and stared at a saucer full of cigarette butts.

Ashley leaned uneasily against the cabinet. If she could only get Nick to see it was in his best interest to help Gareth and Watkins. But how? Reason didn't seem to be Nick's strong point.

He chose a misshapen cigarette butt, scrounged in his pocket for matches, and lit up. He inhaled deeply and leaned his head back against the wall. The smoke had a sweet pungency unlike the acrid stench of tobacco.

Ashley rolled her eyes. Like getting wasted was going to help? That was just the sort of thing that gave people like Reynolds — and Gareth and Watkins, for that matter — ammunition. Nick's attractions were fading right before her eyes. Today even his hands were dirty, flecked with reddish-brown dirt or paint.

At least pot left people mellow, not combative like her father after a few drinks. Nick sat with his eyes closed, his furrowed expression smoothing itself out, bestirring himself only to offer Ashley the burning stub. Emphatically she shook her head. If nothing else, she had to keep sober while she was with — well, he *was* a suspect. And who knew what his friends were capable of.

She forced open a small window above the sink and

breathed eagerly of the fresh air. *Come on,* she urged herself, *let's see some of that assertiveness.*

Ashley took the joint from Nick's fingers seconds before it burned them and squashed it on the saucer. Then she opened the door of the caravan. A gust of wind dissipated the pall of smoke. The metal fabric of the trailer creaked and popped.

Smiling lazily, Nick opened his eyes. "What're you on about?"

"If you're going to be on about your business, you don't need to knock yourself out with that stuff."

"My business? You mean the ceremony?"

"Yes, the ceremony. And solving Linda's murder."

"That's never going to be solved, not now," he said.

"Don't give up so easily. Clean yourself up and go to the police. They'll believe you if you act believable."

"No. . . ." His voice trailed away. He stared down at his hands. Slowly, laboriously, he stood up. He contemplated the dripping faucet for a long moment, and then rinsed his hands off.

For the first time Ashley began to understand how her mother felt when she herself started acting squirrelly. Except she doubted if her mother's frustration was ever edged with fear. "You don't have to go to Watkins. Go to the Manchester police, they're not prejudiced against you. Point out how your father is a local businessman."

Nick's expression said, *yeah, right.*

"Tell them Reynolds is stealing the artifacts, ruining the local heritage. Then tell them about Linda. I bet a formal investigation of Reynolds's affairs would gather enough evidence to convict him."

"I've already convicted him," Nick said, with a thin smile that made Ashley step back a step.

If it feels wrong. . . . Getting in his face wasn't working. Fine. She turned toward the table and picked up three boxes. "Here, let's get these loaded into your car. You don't want to be late for the ceremony."

"That might not matter any more, either," Nick returned. But he let her pile a few more boxes in his arms and cajole him out the door.

Small objects rolled back and forth in the boxes she held. She peeked, and saw several crystals, a candle or two, a wreath of withered green stuff that was probably mistletoe. Magical accessories.

"The Celts came from the east," said Nick. "So did my family. Now we're isolated along the fringe of the west. Now we're knocked about by materialistic society. Greedy sods like Reynolds, lying and looting and killing."

"Then you need to turn him in, Nick." Ashley opened the car door and piled her boxes in the back seat.

Nick gazed into the distance, to where the lowering bulk of Durslow Edge closed the horizon. "He's lied about so much, maybe he was lying about everything. Maybe he was using the true believers to his own ends."

"Excuse me?"

"The Druid sends messages through Bob. I've never seen his face. I don't know whether Bob has. But once I saw Bob mucking out the stables at Fortuna Stud — well, I've done that often enough myself, to turn a few bob. . . ." He looked vaguely puzzled at his unintended pun.

Now we're getting somewhere. Ashley took the boxes from his hands and loaded them in the car. "You think Bob's been working with Reynolds?"

"I've never liked him. He's a stroppy berk. Bob, I mean."

"Your point being?" asked Ashley.

"What if Reynolds was the Druid? What if it was all a lie — no, no, it's can't be a lie, the ceremonies. . . ." Nick's face crumpled and for a moment Ashley thought he was going to cry. She patted his arm. Poor Nick. He was just a kid, wasn't he? In some ways they were a lot alike. They were both in over their heads.

The wind stirred the needles of the fir trees. No human beings moved among the motley collection of vehicles, but Ashley wondered whether faces were watching her from the scummy windows. *If it feels wrong, bail out.* She assumed her Matilda voice. "It's what you believe that's important. If you believe it's true, it is. That's the way religion works. Your faith can give you strength, just as long as you don't use it to hurt people."

"Hurt people? No, I'm not the sod's been hurting people."

He shook his head. "Come back inside, luv. A bit more of the weed, or a drink, that'll do."

"No it won't," Ashley told him. "Tell you what, I'm going to head back into town. I — ah — I forgot something. I'll meet you at Durslow at sunset."

"You're going, are you?"

"I'll be back. You get yourself some coffee or something." She turned and strode toward the road, breaking free of the chill shadow of the trees. When she got around the corner she'd call Gareth and ask him to come pick her up. She'd tell him she was resigning her commission because she wasn't up to the work, it was too complicated and frightening and she didn't know who she could trust. . . . *Shit.* And she'd wanted to impress him, too. That little scrap of information about Bob and the Druid was hardly anything important.

She felt Nick's eyes on her as she walked away. Maybe he was hurt. Maybe he didn't care. All she knew was that he wasn't what she thought he was.

At the first bend in the road she glanced back. He was still standing there, a solitary human figure in the mechanical detritus of society, overshadowed by dark trees like a memory of nightmare. Then she was around the corner and he was gone.

She lifted her sweater and took the cell phone out of her waistband. Oh — she had two messages. What with Nick and everything she'd never felt the phone vibrate. Had they been checking up on her? She pressed the keys and listened as Matilda's voice said, "Ashley, don't leave town with Nick. Stay at the hotel. I'll be there to explain in just a few minutes." The second message was also Matilda, sounding even more breathless. "Ashley, are you with Nick? Get away from him, now. Call me, let me know where you are. Now."

What was that all about? No problem though — she'd already gotten away from Nick. . . . A white BMW came up the road behind her, slowed and stopped. The passenger window glided down and Howard Sweeney leaned across the seat. "Hullo, hullo! What are you doing here? Don't you know big bad wolves gobble up little girls like you?"

All right! It was someone she could trust, someone who knew the truth about Gareth and Matilda. She'd even forgive him his appalling sense of humor. "Can you give me a ride back into town, Dr. Sweeney?"

"By all means. Hop in."

Ashley climbed into the car, and sank into its leather-scented interior thinking that there was something to be said for materialism.

"Why are you carrying that mobile phone, my dear?" he asked.

She set it down in the bin between the seats. "I was supposed to be helping Gareth. Detective Inspector March. So much for that bright idea."

"Really? Tell me about it." He glanced over at her, his teeth gleaming in a smile.

The sun dropped further into the west, lengthening the shadows that reached toward Durslow Edge.

Gareth delivered the horses and gave Jimmy as reassuring an account as he could of a very unsettling matter. He left the old man murmuring calming words to the animals that were not reflected in his seamed face, and sprinted toward the hotel. A tiny pulse in the back of his mind beat, *hurry, hurry!* Why? he asked himself. Reynolds is dead.

Hurry! He ran up the road and into the Green Dragon. The first familiar face he saw in the throng was Bryan's. The lad was just raising a glass of lager to his lips. "Have you seen Ashley?" Gareth demanded.

The glass reflected the amber glow of the westering sun. "Yeah, maybe an hour ago. She went up to the town."

"Bloody hell!"

"Something wrong, Gareth?"

"If you see Matilda, tell her to wait here for me."

"Sure thing. . . ."

Gareth dived back onto the crowded pavement. In the marketplace he was engulfed by a group of Morris dancers and several nightmarish antlered figures that looked like Bambi re-interpreted by Picasso. He glanced down the street toward the police station. Yes, the police car was parked out front. Della was presumably inside. Matilda could be anywhere. So could Ashley.

Emma, dressed like a cheap tart in mini-skirt and high heels, was sidling along the churchyard fence, chased by the grotesque hobby horse. Gareth elbowed his way through the crowd, arriving at the gate in time to hear Clapper's voice — and smell a strong odor of beer — emanating from the roughly carved horse's head. "Now, now, sweetie, don't you be giving me the push — everyone knows you're none too dainty about your boyfriends."

"Get knotted, you old geezer," Emma retorted, "You think I give a toss what sodding everyone think they know?"

Snickering, Clapper cantered away.

"Hello, Emma," said Gareth. "Did you bring the papers and the box?"

"And a lovely afternoon it is to you, too," she replied acidly. "What've you been at? Digging peat?"

Hurry, hurry, ticked Gareth's mind. "Sorry. There's been a spot of bother. Where's Celia Dunning?"

"Looking for blood to suck. I said thank-you for the ride but I don't have to be seen in public with her, do I?"

"Have you been with her all day?"

"Yeh, what of it?"

"Did you bring the papers?"

"In me bag here. She put the box in the safe. Let's find a pub, a ploughman's and some plonk wouldn't come amiss."

"Later. I need to see the papers now."

Emma's red mouth made an inverted U in her white-powdered face, lower lip protruding. Her spiky black lashes looked like little spear points.

With a grimace, Gareth drew her through the gate and into the churchyard. A crow perched on a gravestone, head cocked to the side. The Morris dancers went click-clack-jingle. Gareth pulled his warrant card from his pocket. "I'm from Scotland Yard. I'm investigating the murder of Linda Burkett. I think Adrian Reynolds was the killer. But he himself was killed this morning in a fall from his horse. If those papers don't implicate Reynolds, then. . . ." *Then what?* Falling on his sword wasn't on.

"Oh, so that's the long and the short of it, is it?" Emma ripped open her handbag and thrust a handful of paper at

Gareth. "Thank you, Mr. March. Thank you very much."

"Sorry," he mumbled, even as he leafed through the sheaf of papers.

The letters were printed neatly on University of Manchester stationery. All of them began, "To whom it may concern." The next paragraph of one letter described a second century Romano-British silver salver. Another letter reported on a first century Celtic mirror. A third mentioned a gold torc, a relic of Boudicca's campaign, found in the treasure room of the temple of Deus Pater at Cornovium. . . . The torc?

Feverishly Gareth skipped ahead. The last paragraph of each letter was academic prose that he pared down to its essence: "The above artifact is genuine. It was obtained legally and is offered for sale in accordance with the antiquities laws of Britain." The signature in every case was that of Howard Sweeney.

Gareth's mind went blank, as though his brain had been knocked sprawling by a prizefighter's punch. Sweeney? He was working with the police. The killer had chucked him down the trench. Sweeney was a right arrogant bastard who enjoyed a joke at another chap's expense. . . .

"Good God!" exclaimed Gareth. He seized Emma's hand and dragged her down the alley beside the church and past the Maypole so quickly he almost pulled her right off her shoes. "Here!" she protested, but was too out of breath to say more. In the doorway of the hotel they rushed by Bryan, who called, "Matilda wants you to come up to her room."

Gareth dragged Emma up the stairs. He raised his hand to pound on Matilda's door. The late afternoon sun cast horizontal beams through the corridor windows.

*M*atilda shut the door of her room and braced herself against it. Still she could hear Della's defenseless weeping in the back room of the police station, still she could sense Adrian's helpless rage dissipating into the dank air of Shadow Moss. A tiny pulse in the back of her mind beat, *hurry, hurry!*

Bryan had given her Gareth's message and told her Ashley had already left. With Nick, presumably. So the girl hadn't gotten her message. Hell! She pulled out her phone and tried again. Still no answer. Matilda left another message, trying to keep her voice from shaking.

What Nick's mood was Matilda couldn't begin to guess. She hoped to heaven the boy had satisfied his taste for violence, and that Ashley was in no danger from him. But every instinct Matilda trusted told her the girl was in danger from someone. *Who?* Matilda demanded of herself.

Hurry! She pushed herself away from the door and gazed belligerently around the room. At more than a few moments of crisis over the years she'd tried to focus her sixth sense like a magnifying glass. She'd never succeeded — it was too elusive. Ever since her arrival in Corcester she'd felt as though she had a blank spot in the center of her senses, a perceptual rather than a visual cataract. She'd kept expecting the spot to clear as the case cleared. Even now, however, neither case nor cataract looked any less blurry.

Something wasn't right, something wasn't working — her senses were betraying her. *Hurry! Hurry!*

Matilda kicked the table. It tilted. Her pile of books shifted. *Letters from Roman Britain* slipped over the edge and fell onto her foot. She almost welcomed the pain. That she could understand.

She picked up the book. Her fingertips tingled. Ionescu had said something about it when she first met him in Manchester. . . . That was it. That Sweeney hadn't published all the letters in this book. There were other ones, some of them also dealing with Cornovium, which he was saving for a later volume. Trust Sweeney to parcel out his glory.

The sounds of revelry from downstairs and outside fluctuated like a police siren. Gold, Matilda thought. Celtic gold. What if one of the unpublished letters was an inventory of the temple treasure room?

She turned and flung open the door before Gareth could knock. A thin girl dressed in a fashionable hooker get-up leaned against the wall opposite, panting. Emma, Matilda realized. What a contrast from her fairy-princess festival photo.

Gareth seized Emma's wrist, pulled her into the room, and dumped her on the edge of the bed. He shoved a sheaf of papers at Matilda. "Dunning's boyfriend gave her these letters last night. It wasn't Reynolds, it was Sweeney. He's stolen the gold torc." His eye lighted on *Letters from Roman Britain.* He pulled the book from Matilda's hands and showed its back cover to Emma. "This is the man you saw last night, right?"

"Well, yeh. . . ."

Quickly Matilda flipped through the papers. Her heart melted into her stomach — no, not Howard. And yet that was his signature — she'd seen it a dozen times. "He's been signing expertises for Dunning. What a tidy little scam. It's his job to report the artifacts he uncovers. If he never reports them, no one will know they've been stolen. And with these papers they can be sold anywhere in the world."

"I don't know anything about it," Emma said from the bed. "Tell your rozzer friend here I'm just an innocent by-stander."

"Of course you are," Matilda said. "All we'll need from you is a statement."

Emma's red mouth turned up and then down again, the pout winning over the smile.

Matilda and Gareth stared at each other. She felt as though she had one end of a rope in her hands, and as soon as she tugged she'd haul in a net teeming with fish and worms and slimy bottom feeders. *It can't be Howard. Because if it is Howard, I'm an idiot.*

Gareth pulled out his cell phone and punched in a number. "P.C. Watkins, please. . . . March here. Did Howard Sweeney collect that gold torc from you last night? He did do? Damn and blast — sorry — meet us at the hotel straightaway." He switched off with another vicious punch. "There's your box, Emma."

Matilda picked up her own phone. "Hand me my address book. There, on the dresser. Thanks." Her fingers raced over the keys. "Come on, Ted, be a good little flunkey, be at work."

"Ionescu here."

"This is Matilda Gray. Did Howard bring you a gold torc last night?"

"I haven't seen Dr. Sweeney for several days, Dr. Gray."

"Do you know where he is now?"

Ionescu hemmed and hawed. "Oh, well — I don't suppose

he'd mind my telling. It's all a bit of a giggle, isn't it?"

"What?"

"He's involved in a re-creation society. They wear costumes and play at being ancient Celts — like that lot in the States who play at knights and ladies. Dr. Sweeney's the Druid. They're having a party tonight at Durslow Edge, a bonfire and some beer and sausages. All in good fun."

"I wouldn't be so sure of that." Matilda rolled her eyes toward Gareth. Twin flames burned in his eyes. Behind him Emma inspected a long red fingernail. "Ted, does the name Linda Burkett mean anything to you?"

"She's the girl who was murdered. Dreadful business. She was doing quite well in the adult education evening class."

"The class Sweeney teaches?"

"Oh yes. He said she was his brightest pupil. Linda and Clive Adcox. Clive's still with us, though, no trouble there."

Matilda's stomach was tying itself in a knot. Her heart seemed to have stopped beating. Howard. The unutterable gall of the man. Her own excruciating blindness. "Ted," she said, "stay there at the lab. There'll be a police officer by presently to take a statement."

"I beg your pardon, Dr. Gray?"

"Just do it, please, Ted. You'll hear much more than you want to know soon enough." She ended the call and turned to Gareth. *Hurry, hurry!*

"It was Sweeney Linda hitched with," he said, without her having to repeat Ted's testimony.

"Yes. Reynolds thought Sweeney was out to stop his antiquities trading — such as it was, he was pretty small beer compared to Sweeney himself. And Howard *was* out to stop Reynolds, but not for the obvious reason. Sweeney's been doing his, well, worst, to frame Reynolds for Linda's murder, even to the extent of stealing Della's receipt and leaving it at the murder scene. If Reynolds were in prison he could hardly be competition."

"Sweeney had us in," Gareth stated with a mixture of astonishment and exasperation.

"And there's more. to it than Reynolds." Matilda scowled fiercely. "I think he knew about the gold torcs in the temple and asked me here so I would find them for him. He was sure

I wouldn't catch on to his scheme. He was right, wasn't he? God help me if I'm not the world's biggest fool!"

Gareth took her arm in a grip every bit as fervent as her scowl. "You've known him for a long time, why should you suspect him? He had us all well and truly on a string."

"He hit Caterina himself and then jumped down the trench, didn't he?"

"Clever bit of work, that. But we have him now. Where is he?"

"On his way out to Durslow for the Beltane ceremony. He's been using the travelers and the other neo-pagans like he's been using us, damn it all."

"Here, what's this?" asked Emma. "Something rum with the ceremony?"

"Yes, something very rum with the ceremony," Matilda hissed. She pulled Gareth's hand from her arm and stood for a moment holding it. His grip was as firm with resolve as hers. She sensed the pulse beating in his mind just as it did in hers, *hurry, hurry!*

"It's not too late," he told her. "We won't let it be too late."

Emma regarded their pose skeptically. The long rays of the westering sun pooled gold in the middle of the room, and cast shadows dark as boggy pools in the corners.

*W*atkins's eyes bulged from his face in surprise. His mouth set itself in a straight line of rage. "I'll lay Dunning by the heels," he said. "If she don't talk to us now, she'll be in the dock with Sweeney, and no mistake."

"No mistake," Gareth repeated. He turned to Matilda and Emma. "Come along. We have to find Ashley and Nick."

"Ashley?" asked Emma. "One of your students, is she? And Nick? The dishy one in the photo?"

"I'll make a dish of him, right enough, if he doesn't give me some straight answers." Gareth started the engine of his Rover before the women had slammed their doors. The pulse in his mind ticked on, like a hammer tapping inside his skull, as disturbing a sensation as he'd ever felt. And he'd felt quite a few sensations.

Once beyond the town Gareth pressed the accelerator to the floor. The countryside smeared into a glimmering green and gold blur. Passing cars reflected explosive bursts of sunlight. Matilda sat biting her lip, her white-knuckled hands pushing the buttons on her mobile, over and over. But Ashley never answered.

It wasn't Matilda's fault, Gareth thought. She'd told him since the beginning her sense wasn't infallible. He was the one who'd made a proper cock-up of the investigation. He was the one whose list of suspects had been one name short.

Who could you trust? That's what it always came down to. Who could you trust?

Gareth braked and swung the car into the encampment. He remembered only too well which particular bit of rubbish was Nick's caravan. If the sod had Ashley inside. . . .

A fully dressed Nick opened the door to Gareth's battering ram of a knock. He stared with bloodshot eyes at the warrant card almost touching his nose. Gareth smelled the smoke gathered inside the caravan and snorted like a horse. "Detective Inspector Gareth March, Scotland Yard. Matilda Gray. Emma Price. We want to talk to you about Linda Burkett."

"I knew you were a pig," Nick muttered, but the insult lacked any force. "Please, step into my stately home."

Gareth handed Matilda up the step and shot a searching glance round the caravan's interior. Unless Nick had chucked Ashley's body into a cupboard, she wasn't there. But his relief was tempered quickly by the thought, *If she's not here, then where is she?*

From the step Emma made a quick inspection of Nick's haggard features. "I remember you, the bloke with the mistletoe," she said with a shrug. "I'll wait here, shall I?"

"Just there," Gareth told her. "Don't run off." He left the door swinging open, hoping to air the place out, and turned on Nick. "Where's Ashley Walraven?"

"Dunno," said Nick. "Went back to town."

"When?" Gareth demanded.

"Half an hour, maybe. Maybe more. Dunno."

Matilda's eyes glinted. When Nick sat heavily down on the bench beside the book-littered table and reached for the smoldering cigarette, she whisked the ashtray away and dumped it into the sink. "You've royally fouled things up for us by involving Ashley in your plots and plans," she told him. "And by not telling the authorities what you know about Linda's murder and the antiquities scam."

"Linda who?" said Nick. "What antiquities?"

Gareth grasped Nick's shirt front and half-lifted him from the seat. "Your lover, Linda Burkett. The antiquities that might have been packed in boxes like those on the opposite seat, there. We've talked to Della and to Ashley both. Stop wasting our time with the flannel."

Fear flashed in Nick's face, the fear of a child caught in an undertow of time and place and circumstance he doesn't understand. Nothing like fear to sober a man up. Gareth dropped Nick back on the seat.

"Dunning was nobbling the goods, wasn't she?" said Nick. "She and Adrian Reynolds. Linda said they were stealing from the past, stealing from the gods. . . ." He licked his lips and swallowed. "Linda pretended she was working with Reynolds to get evidence against him. He found out. He killed her."

"Did you see her with him with night she died?" Gareth asked

"My car had a breakdown. She said she'd hitch a ride into Corcester. Reynolds is always poncing about in that red MG, isn't he?"

"Yes, he is. But his wife was with him the night Linda died."

"Not a bit of it," said Nick. "She was wrong about which night it was. She was wrong about a lot, Della was. What do you expect from a sweet helpless child? Like Ashley, she was, asking for some sod to do her over."

Gareth's hand closed into a fist, but he kept it at his side. Della had been only too willing, it seemed, and Ashley was — well, if she wasn't intact, it wasn't Nick's doing. "Neither of them is as stupid as you think. And you're bloody well not as clever as you think."

"How old are you, Nick?" Matilda asked. "Twenty-three or four? You're not the first man to mistake sexual bravado for maturity. Della helped to ease the pain of Linda's death in the only way you'd accept. So did Ashley. It's a shame you couldn't bring yourself to trust either one of them. You would have found your answers a long time ago."

Nick stared up at Matilda, both resentful and grateful, Gareth estimated. He looked down at his own muddy shoes and for a moment felt sorry for Nick, pinned in the light of Matilda's uncompromising gaze.

Voices drifted in the open door. Gareth spared a quick glance outside. An even scraggier girl with long, lank hair was greeting Emma. Emma said, "Hello Shirl. Yeh, it's me, turned up again like a bad penny."

"Where is Ashley?" Matilda asked again.

"I told you," replied Nick. "She couldn't stick it. She went back to Corcester."

"How did she go back to Corcester?"

"Walked. I saw her off down the road. She's safe enough, Reynolds snuffed it good and proper, didn't he?" Nick leaned his head against the wall and shut his eyes.

"Is Reynolds dead, then?" Gareth asked quietly. "That's interesting. Tell me about it."

Nick's eyes flew open. "You're the clever bugger, aren't you?"

"Not clever enough by half." Gareth took an evidence bag from his pocket and held it open. "Give me the knife." With a grimace, Nick pulled a pen knife from his own pocket and dropped it in the bag. It was stained a dark umber brown. "You'll need to make a statement. Several statements. If you cooperate you might get off with a fine for molesting a dead body."

"Reynolds did worse."

"Did he?" Matilda asked. "Even if he had killed Linda, two wrongs wouldn't have made a right. And he didn't kill her."

"Eh?" Nick looked from face to face. "Now you're flanneling me. . . ."

"Here," said Emma, clambering into the caravan. She bumped into Gareth, who bumped into Matilda, who with a jangle stepped into the bead curtain defining a bedroom. "This Ashley, does she have long blond hair?"

"Yes," said Gareth.

"Shirl here is telling me she saw Nick's bird with the blond hair picked up by a posh white BMW."

Gareth felt the blood slowly drain from his face. Matilda's went stark white between one heartbeat and the next.

"Shirl's scared," Emma went on. "Said she was going home to Chelsea. Her Dad's an accountant in the City, can you credit her living like this when her Dad's an accountant in the City?"

Matilda took Gareth's arm in a crushing grip. "I asked Ashley to trust me. I asked her to trust you. I told her Howard knew who we were and by extension she could trust him. . . . Gareth, it's going to be Linda all over again, picked up by someone she trusts. And we're the ones who put her in harm's way!"

Her anguish scraped fingernails down his spine. The blood flooded back into his face. "Steady on," he said, even though he felt anything but steady. "She has the mobile phone — though he'll have that off her, won't he?"

Nick's body seemed to change from jelly to steel as the last molecules of the drug burned away. "What the hell are you talking about? Who's this bloke in the BMW?"

"Howard Sweeney," Matilda spat. "Sweeney's the professor from the University who's in charge of the dig at Corcester. He's the man who's been working with Celia Dunning to steal and sell antiquities. We have proof of that."

"Linda was in one of his night classes!" Nick said. "She called him a dotty old dear. She would have hitched with him, right enough. And asked his advice on how to catch Dunning. He killed her?"

"Seems so, doesn't it?" Gareth told him. "We have to find him before he kills Ashley, too."

"He's on his way to Durslow for the ceremony," added Matilda. "He calls himself the Druid."

"He's the Druid, is he? Of all the bleedin' cheek!" Nick leaped up, cracked his head on the overhanging ceiling, and sat back down. "We have to catch him out."

"We?" Gareth demanded. "You've fancied yourself a detective long enough, Sunshine, it's time to leave it to the professionals. . . ."

He couldn't tell whether it was own body or Matilda's that was quivering like a harp string. "I know what we need to do, Gareth," she said, "but we're going to need their help. Nick, Emma, tell us about the ceremony."

"Well then," Nick began, frowning in concentration.

Emma leaned against the door jamb, interjecting a phrase or two. Matilda nodded, drawing out their words, shaping them into images. Gareth saw what she was after and quelled the impulse to clap his hand over her mouth.

He could see what she was planning, what Nick was thinking, what Emma was feeling. The pulse in the back of his mind ticked as briskly as the clock on his grandmother's mantelpiece at Aberffraw. He wanted to crouch, his hands over his ears, until he couldn't hear it any more. And yet he had no choice but to listen.

The sun was a blood-red globe just above the western horizon.

Chapter Eighteen

The crimson light that flooded the western sky slowly drained away, drawing darkness across the Cheshire countryside. The scene, Ashley thought, was like one out of some old Celtic tale, blood and shadow mingled in the hands of the gods.

No wonder the place was getting to her, with Sweeney emptying the bottle of wine into her glass. She was just a little buzzed. So much for her resolution to stay sober. But it was such a relief to be with someone she could trust. "Thanks for the picnic," she said

He lounged against the hood of the BMW, looking at her with the same indulgent half-smile her mother smiled just before she said, "I told you so." What Sweeney said, though, was, "Do you know about the pagan re-enactment scheduled for tonight?"

"Oh yes," she said, "I heard about it."

"Would you like to attend? It's not an exclusive group, by any means, despite the misguided folk who take it all seriously."

Ashley remembered Nick's exhausted face. He took it seriously. How misguided he was she couldn't say. Whatever — with Sweeney she could see the ceremony after all, without having to watch her back. Then she'd have a really good report for Gareth and Matilda. It was like eating her cake and having it, too. "Yes, I would, thank you."

"Come along, then." Sweeney gathered up the bottle and the plastic sandwich wrappers. He seated her inside the car, shut her door, and drove them away from the viewpoint. She looked around for the cell phone but didn't see it. She'd find it later. No problem.

Sweeney had listened with flattering attention to her tale of antiquities theft, Adrian Reynolds, Linda and Nick. "I'm delighted our intrepid detectives are making such good progress," he'd said when she finished, and turned into a small grocery store on the outskirts of Corcester. "It's a grand evening. Let's indulge ourselves in the sunset. Do you prefer red or white wine?"

They'd watched the sun sink below the horizon and disappear, all the while chatting about the dig and the murder investigation, munching sandwiches and drinking a way too expensive chardonnay. Sweeney, too, voted for Reynolds as the murderer. "The sooner he's behind bars," he'd proclaimed, "the better for all us law-abiding folk."

Now, as the car purred over the rutted roads atop Durslow Edge, he said nothing. The deserted mines were bits of wasteland in the fading light, and the gnarled oak trees rustled mysteriously. Several other sets of head- and tail-lights winked through the dusk, converging on the ledge.

Sweeney pulled into a hollow among the trees. He opened Ashley's door and locked it behind her. In the shadows his car was ghostly pale, like Rhiannon's white horse, she thought. A faint strain of music filtered through the trees, a flute and harp playing a slow melody. For just a moment she thought, *if something seems too good to be true. . . .*

Sweeney opened the trunk of the car. "We must wear the proper attire, my dear. That's part of the game. I always carry a spare costume, one never knows when one will encounter a neophyte. There you are." He handed her a garment that resembled Jennifer's bed sheet toga and a shapeless white headdress. "And a garland of flowers — flower children and all that, eh?"

Well, if he could dress up she could, too. Although he could lose the patronizing "my dear." Ashley pulled on the gown and settled the headdress on her head — yeah, like the early Celts had had elastic. Sweeney placed a wreath of spring flowers around her neck. She felt like a Klanswoman on her way to a luau, and hoped no one would recognize her. Far from being a moving religious event, this, like the festival in town, was fast turning into a farce. But then, Sweeney's motive in participating was to point up the absurdity of religious expression. It was kind of sad he thought he had to do that. Skeptics could be just as arrogant as believers.

Sweeney's robe was stitched in pleats beneath a wide fabric yoke and snugged at the waist with a sash. His headdress was a hood, casting a shadow over his face. He pulled something from the blackness of the trunk and tucked it into his sash. Placing his hand politely on Ashley's back, he guided her among the dozen or so cars parked in the mud. She stumbled over loose leaves and branches. Her cheeks burned in the chill air. Great, a little wine and she went red in the face.

At least twenty white-robed people milled along the wide ledge. Judging by the beer cans and whiskey bottles piled beside the trail, the party had already started.

Beside the well stood a box covered with yet another white cloth and oddments of greenery and crystals that glinted in the light of several candles. A torch in a bracket sent shadows dancing up the cliff face. A pile of brush looked like a hulking hairy animal at the far end of the ledge. The trees beyond were black shapes against a sky swiftly darkening to indigo. High overhead hung a crescent moon, like an enigmatic celestial smile.

Whoa, Ashley thought. This place had been spooky enough in daylight. Now, after dark, it was downright sinister. The white-robed figures stepped silently aside, forming a double line through which Sweeney strolled, steering Ashley in front of him. She couldn't see anyone holding a flute or a harp — no, there was a boom box beside the — the altar? That's what they meant it to be. The wind rustled the leaves of the trees. The lights of farms and cars and the twenty-first century flickered nervously through the waving branches.

She squinted from side to side. The faces beneath their floppy white headdresses weren't quite human, let alone male or female. There, a pair of dark eyes glinted as she walked past — that must be Nick, even though she was reminded, weirdly, of Gareth.

Had Gareth and Matilda been planning to come here tonight? She wasn't sure. Again she stumbled. Succeeding waves of patchouli and marijuana, sweat and beer filled her

nostrils. Something tightened her shoulder blades and made
her stomach wriggle uneasily. *If it feels wrong.* . . . This place
would make anyone feel creepy, she assured herself.

The torch cast a glow over the spring. The water shimmered
as though something smooth and silky swam just beneath its
surface. Sweeney's piloting hand eased her down on one end
of the altar-box. Some of the greenery poked her and she
inched away. He began speaking.

Ashley frowned. He'd paraded in here like a priest down
the aisle of a church. And now he was saying something
pompous, with lots of big words, about welcome and dedication. If he wanted to make fun of these people, why was he
directing them? That hardly seemed fair.

The gentle harp music stopped. A clash of electric guitars
segued into lilting cadences played in the minor keys of the
Celtic Fringe. A vocalist sang of Odin and his crows and the
blood of the Gael. Someone began thumping a — no, not a
drum, a bodhran, a skin stretched over a circular frame. The
rhythm quickened Ashley's blood but clarified nothing. She
thought of Dionysus and his crazed maenads. Of whirling
dervishes. Of Viking berserkers. Of the ancient Celts drunk
on mead, poetry, and blood. Her shoulders tightened even
further and she glanced behind her. Nothing was there except
rock and shadow.

The people formed a line behind the bodhran-player and
began to dance, weaving in and out with sudden dips and
spins. Each face in turn was illuminated by the torchlight and
then plunged again into darkness. From the boom box came
the high, clear notes of a bagpipe, playing counterpoint to
the pulse of the electric guitar. Every follicle on Ashley's body
tightened into gooseflesh. The hair on the back of her neck
waved in time. This was no farce. The ceremony was compelling her to dance, too, to leap the ambiguous boundary
between light and darkness. This was what brought Nick here.
This was the spiritual version of a daredevil sport, where the
risk of death made life all the sweeter. Matilda was right, there
was always time enough to die.

With a satisfied sigh Sweeney sank down onto the altar
beside her. His hand traced a slow caress down her back. His
eyes glittered in the shade of his hood. *Oh for the love of God,*

she thought in disgust and disbelief. He couldn't turn out to be a dirty old man. Not Sweeney. She respected him.

"So you're another clever little girl," he said quietly into her ear.

"What?"

"Thought you could catch me out, didn't you?" he went on. "But even Madame Gray won't catch me out. There's no one as stupid as an educated woman, my dear. No one."

Isn't he working with Matilda? Ashley asked herself. She didn't like the answer that annoyingly practical part of her mind returned. That part of her mind that informed her she'd better sober up. Fast.

"Matilda and her Scotland Yard git have been dancing to my tune all this time. My trick with the Italian girl and the inscription went down a smashing success, didn't it? It's a shame Adrian Reynolds won't be dancing on air, but a nice long sentence at Pentonville should turn the trick."

Ashley grimaced, trying to work that out.

"Fools, the lot of them. There's nothing so easy to manipulate as a man's faith, is there? Dig up the artifacts, bring them to the kindly old Druid, do your religious duty. . . ." He laughed.

Sweeney? Good old eccentric, so obnoxious he was a joke, Sweeney? He was behind the antiquities thefts? And she'd trusted him. She'd even compared him favorably to her father!

Matilda, Ashley thought. Matilda's going to flip out. . . . She leaped to her feet. Sweeney's hand grabbed her arm and pulled her back down. The music lilted on. The dancers danced. There seemed to be more of them now. Maybe they were dividing, like amoebas. "Let go of me!" she demanded, yanking at her arm.

Sweeney held on.

"Here's another clever little girl." His breath was foul and Ashley gagged. She yanked again at her arm, this time breaking free. Sweeney's hand seized the back of her gown and jerked her down with a thud. Crystals and leaves went rolling away across the altar.

The night was dark and the music was loud. No one realized what was happening. No one would help her. She had to help herself. She made fists, raised her elbows, and wished she'd taken a self-defense class.

Something glinted in the corner of her eye. Glancing around, she saw Sweeney's other hand resting on her shoulder. Light reflected from the object he held, something long and sharp. A knife blade. It pricked her neck with an icy kiss. *Another clever little. . . .* As surely as though she'd plunged her head into the chill depths of Brighid's well she realized what he meant. Linda.

Ashley's mind dissolved into static. She heard a quick whimper, realized it was her own, and closed her teeth on it. Her body deflated like an empty balloon and she swayed in Sweeney's grasp. "Why?" she asked. "Why?"

"Why kill you like Linda? Now, now, let's not fail our final exam. Think about it."

"I know too much, right?"

"Very good!"

"But I . . ." She did know too much. She'd asked to know too much.

He laughed. "It's too late for protests, my dear."

Keep talking, Ashley ordered herself. Maybe if she went along with him, he'd loosen his grip and she could get away. "You want to frame Reynolds. Everyone suspects he murdered Linda, so you're going to make sure they think he — got me too."

"Just too clever by half, aren't you? Yes, all I have to do is wait until they light the fire and get on with their foolish dancing. Then you and I, my dear, like so many others after a bit of fornication, will retire to the side. No one knows who is here and who isn't. Why shouldn't Reynolds be having himself a bit of a giggle here as well? All I have to do is tuck your headdress and this knife, suitably wiped of fingerprints, into a corner of the Fortuna Stud stable. And presto! Mr. Reynolds is inside."

And I'm dead, Ashley told herself. "What if Reynolds is hanging out with fifty other people right now?"

"I had a mutual friend send him a message asking him to meet her at her shop in Manchester tonight. He'll take the bait, no fear. Not that she'll be there herself, not at all."

Ashley could swear she'd seen Reynolds' car in his driveway

when she'd left Corcester with Nick. Whether or not the man had an alibi didn't matter now.

"Linda presents herself to me at Imbolc," Sweeney went on. "You'll excuse my mordant little joke with her, I hope. I simply couldn't resist. And here you are at Beltane. I thought I was going to have to choose someone at random. But no, I can eliminate a threat and fit Reynolds up all at once. It's almost enough to make one believe in the gods."

She was going to scream and fight, Ashley told herself. Even if he stabbed her anyway, she'd trade a flesh wound for freedom. . . . Her stomach heaved. Maybe if she threw up on him he'd drop her in disgust and she could make a break for it.

She'd trusted him. How could he do this to her?

With a last brilliant skirl of the pipes the music stopped. The air rang hollowly in the sudden silence. And then, down the wind, came the sound of slow, steady, hoofbeats.

The dancers broke ranks. With a collective gasp, they turned toward the entrance to the ledge. The torch guttered in a cold breeze. "What the hell?" Sweeney dragged Ashley to her feet and stood close behind her. The knife was a small one, she saw, but it was tucked beneath the angle of her jaw, just beginning to prick. No surprise she was hallucinating.

Along the ledge clopped a white horse, its coat an unearthly shimmer in the dim light. On its back sat a woman, crowned with gold, gold glowing at her throat. Her face was only a pale blur.

"Rhiannon!" whispered someone, and others took up the murmur, "Rhiannon! The great goddess Rhiannon!"

She reined up. She lifted her hand and scattered stars like gold dust on the upturned faces of the crowd. "Be at peace," she said in a low, vibrant voice. "Blessed be."

Ashley felt her mouth drop open. Beside her Sweeney gobbled. "What the hell — someone's playing me up. . . ."

"As it was in the beginning," proclaimed the figure of the goddess, "is now, and ever shall be, world without end."

"No!" shouted Sweeney. "No, it's a trick!" He stepped forward. His grip on Ashley's robe loosened. The knife slipped away from her throat.

Do it! In a hot rush of anger she jabbed her elbow back

into his stomach. His breath escaped in a gratifying gasp. Turning, she lifted her foot, raked her boot down his shin and ground it into his classy leather loafer. He howled with pain. She spun away from him and realized she was grinning with glee — oh God, that felt good. That felt really good.

Three of the white-clad figures leaped on Sweeney. All four fell struggling to the ground. A kick sent the altar flying. Crystals clattered. Candles winked out. Male voices shouted incomprehensible words. The knife went spinning across the stone and bounced off the basin.

Ashley's grin faded. The heat drained from her body, leaving her cold and trembling. "It's all right," said a familiar voice. She blinked. Bryan's freckled face peered earnestly at her. "It's all over now."

"How'd you get here?" she croaked.

"They came running into the hotel and said you were in trouble. I don't think I was invited, but things were pretty confusing and I kind of jumped into Matilda's car as she was pulling out."

"You came to help me? Thank you!"

"No problem," Bryan said, with the most open and honest smile she'd ever seen.

A few last heaves and the flailing white robes resolved themselves into four separate bodies. A pair of handcuffs caught the light. Two figures stood up, holding Sweeney, bare-headed now, between them. The third retrieved the knife and said, "I'll take this to the lab straightaway, Inspector. And the professor here to jail."

"You needn't be too gentle with him, Constable." Gareth pulled off his headdress and threw it down. His red hair glowed in the torchlight.

The other man removed his headdress much more slowly. Nick's dark hair spilled over his forehead. "Ashley, I'm sorry, I didn't know it was him."

She stared at them. So they were here, too, both of them, working together. *Cool.*

From along the ledge, past the confused knot of spectators, came Matilda's voice. "Emma, hang onto the bridle for me — carefully, he's a bit spooky — my robe is caught on the saddle."

Like she hadn't known all along it was Matilda. . . . Ashley's knees gave way. She sat abruptly on the edge of the basin. Bryan sat beside her and draped his arm across her shoulders. Good old Bryan, she thought. The one person in all this mess who didn't have a hidden agenda. The one person she could've trusted all along. She leaned gratefully into his embrace.

Gingerly, Emma held the bridle. Matilda pulled away the thin scarf that had covered her face, hitched her long velour bathrobe over her jeans and clambered down. Her legs wobbled in opposite directions. She clung to the saddle until she regained her balance. The pulse in her mind that had been beating, *Hurry!* was now whispering, *Thank God. Thank God.*

She brushed the sparkling metallic confetti from her hands and took the first deep breath she'd taken in hours. Two uniformed constables appeared from the car park to meet Watkins going the other way with a limping Sweency.

"Filthy bitch," spat her erstwhile colleague.

"You have only yourself to blame," Matilda told him.

Watkins and his minions hustled Sweeney away. Gremlin snorted and pranced sideways. Emma squeaked, released the bridle, and dodged. Gareth, divested of his robe, appeared from the darkness, seized the bridle, and cooed reassurances. "Good show," he said, as much to the horse as to Matilda. "Dead brilliant."

"Thank you for riding Gremlin out here for me," Matilda returned. "I was every bit as scared of him as he was of me."

"A shame he's the only light-colored one on the farm. After this morning. . . ." Gareth stopped. "You're all right. So is Ashley. It's over."

Matilda laid one hand on his arm. She couldn't tell which of them was trembling the harder. His dark eyes searched hers. The corners of his mouth tucked themselves into a tight smile. "I'll tie Gremlin in the car park. He doesn't like it here."

Matilda released his arm. "I'll check on Ashley."

The celebrants clustered dispiritedly by the pile of brush.

Beyond them, in the trees, faces smeared in and out of existence. Eyes blinked. The green man, Matilda thought. The great god Pan. The ancient powers of the Earth itself. Only she could actually see the faces, but she knew that more than one of the celebrants could feel the indifferent, almost amused, gaze of those otherworldly eyes.

Ashley sat close beside Bryan, in the no doubt comforting circle of his arm. If this didn't make her take notice of Bryan, then nothing would. Groaning, Matilda sat down beside them. "Good move, Ashley, stomping him like that. Are you all right?"

"Yes. Even though.I must be the world's biggest idiot."

"You're not half the idiot I am," Matilda assured her, adding to herself, *if not for Howard's mania for self-dramatization, the girl would already be dead.*

Bryan was less shy about voicing his thought. "I was afraid we weren't going to get here in time. When we drove up and I heard the music I was really scared."

"So was I," Ashley confided.

From several yards away Emma squealed, "No, wait, he didn't mean anything!"

The white-robed figures swirled and parted. Nick dragged a big bearded man forward by the back of his collar and deposited him at Matilda's feet like a cat offering its human a mouse. "Do you know this bloke? Bob, his name is."

"I'm not sure," Matilda said. "Maybe I'd recognize him without the beard."

"You," said Gareth, looming up from the shadows. "You're the berk who stabbed Caesar."

Ashley added, "I saw him at the traveler's camp."

"He's never named Bob." Watkins, too, appeared in the circle of torchlight. "This here's Clive Adcox. Where'd you come from, lad?"

"He's been at the camp for months," said Nick. "I reckoned he was working with Reynolds."

"He and Linda were both in Howard's class," Matilda said. "I didn't recognize you with the beard, Clive. You've been Sweeney's muscle all along, haven't you? He sent you to London to keep an eye on me, maybe even to give me a scare. Not that that was necessary to his plot, he just had to see himself in complete control. . . . Nick, you'd better let go of his collar, he's turning blue."

Reluctantly, Nick let go. Clive looked from face to face. Only Emma's showed any affection. "He told me to watch you," he wheezed. "I wasn't after giving you a push. The crowd pushed me. It was an accident."

"Killing me would hardly serve Sweeney's purpose," Matilda admitted.

"That's as may be," said Watkins, taking firm hold of Clive's arm. "But what about trying to force Dr. Gray off the Manchester road?"

"What?" asked Clive.

Nick stepped back a pace. "That," he said with a grimace, "was me."

Every face turned toward him. "You tried to kill Matilda?" Gareth demanded.

"Not a bit of it. I was after Reynolds, wasn't I? He drives a red car. I saw him leave that afternoon, and I was waiting for him in a lay-by. In the rain I thought it was him."

"Your judgment being a bit impaired at the time?" Matilda asked.

"I'd had a couple of beers and a puff or two, yeh." He hung his head. "I never meant to kill him, just scare him. I never meant to scare you. I'm sorry."

She sighed. Nick had turned out to be not James Bond but Charlie Brown. "Apology accepted."

"You, too, come with me," said Watkins. "We'll need a statement. And then there's a little matter of Adrian Reynolds' corpse."

"Corpse?" Ashley asked.

"He was killed in an accident this morning," said Gareth.

"Oh. Well. Sweeney would've had a hard time framing him for killing me, then, wouldn't he? Not that that would've helped me any." Ashley shuddered. Bryan tightened his grip.

Nick pulled his eyes away from them and gazed around the ledge. "I'll call in tomorrow, Constable. I promise."

"He's learned his lesson," affirmed Gareth.

Nick nodded vehemently.

Shaking his head, Watkins steadied his grip on Clive's shoulder. "You'll be helping the police with their inquiries, won't you, lad? Hanging about with a murderer. Just think what your mum will say."

Clive's reply was truculent and explicit.

"Now, now," Watkins remonstrated, "there's ladies present."

Emma glanced at Gareth, more confused than resentful, and trotted away behind the two men. Matilda shook her head sadly — how had the mighty May Queen and her less-than-chivalrous knight fallen. Maybe if they'd been forced into a shotgun marriage. . . . *No,* she thought.

Gareth patted his breast pocket. "Ashley, your mobile was lying amongst the weeds, beside the driver's side door of Sweeney's car. It works much better if it's switched on."

"But I didn't. . . . Oh," Ashley said. "He turned it off, didn't he? He probably picked it up right after I got into the car, as soon as I looked the other way."

"I'm sure," said Matilda, groaning again.

Gareth went on, "We'll need a statement from you, too, Ashley. Thanks to you we caught Sweeney in the act. And you don't mean to say he actually told you his plans?"

"Yeah, I kept talking to him and he pretty much told me everything." The girl's smile was more wry than smug.

"Oh good, a confession as well!" Gareth beamed down at her.

"Nice bit of play-acting," Nick told Matilda.

She couldn't mistake the bitterness in his voice. "All rites were play-acting at one time. Here, let me help you set the altar up again. You know where everything goes."

She started bustling about. Slowly Nick responded, arranging the trinkets — excuse me, Matilda chided herself, the ritual items — on the altar. What had St. Peter's altar in a Roman cellar looked like? she wondered. The young peoples' half-baked religious impulses might in time lead them to an epiphany.

She laid her hand on the gold crescent she wore. "You'll want your necklace back. Thank you for letting me borrow it."

"Keep it," Nick told her. "I had it off a bloke at Stonehenge, but it's never had any magic in it."

"Until now?" Matilda asked. She lifted the torch down

from the cliff wall and handed it to Nick. "Here. It's time you lit the fire."

"Me?"

"All these people came out here for the rites of spring, not for a bust. You're the leader of this group, not Sweeney. He was — well, I guess the word 'sacrilegious' isn't too strong."

Nick's stiff face cracked into a smile. "All right, then." He thrust the torch into the pile of brush. Fire leaped upward. A sigh of pleasure and relief passed through the audience. The bodhran sounded again, hesitantly at first, then with more assurance.

Matilda turned. Gareth was standing with his hands in his pockets. His mouth had softened. He'd stepped back from the edge of his own emotion. "We'd better be returning Clapper's sheets," he said.

"Is that where you got them?" asked Ashley.

"Mr. Clapper was very helpful," Matilda told her. "With the Festival in full swing, he was able to turn up phosphorescent paint for the horse, the May Queen's paper crown for me, and shiny confetti at a moment's notice."

"He won't be half narked we've nicked his nephew," Gareth said.

"I hope someone's going to explain this to me," said Bryan.

Matilda smiled. "We'll get around to that real soon now."

Through the leaping flames she saw first the white robes of the living celebrants, then, faintly, like tracings on glass, she saw the cloaks of celebrants long gone. Branwen, flowers twined in her red hair, walked as regally as the queen her grandmother to the place of sacrifice. She knelt, smiling, beside the cauldron embossed with images of the gods. The blow fell, the garrote tightened, and the knife sliced, twice, once for the hand, the heavy hand of the Roman conquest, and once for the Celtic faith. Around the throat of each silent watcher a gold torc, symbol of devotion, gleamed rosily in the firelight.

The spring gurgled at Matilda's elbow. The fire burned down. A cold breeze scattered sparks across the stone. The bodhran's heartbeat and the voice of the bagpipes filled the night. Two by two, the celebrants lined up and leaped the embers, robes flying back like the wings of birds.

Nick led Ashley across the fire. Then Ashley gave her hand to Bryan and together they jumped. Were the girl's nightmares of uncertainty and loneliness over now? Matilda told herself. Maybe she'd learned tonight how to choose strength and trust and faith. And how to choose a boyfriend. A relationship begun in friendship could be a strong one.

Down the ledge trundled a chariot. In it rode Branwen's body, propped against the cauldron. Mistletoe and oak leaves, alder and rowan, draped the wheels. Torches blazed among the trees. Gold shone. The procession wound down from Durslow to Shadow Moss, and there the radiance of fire and gold and smile alike were quenched in dark water. . . .

"Matilda?"

She blinked. Gareth, her friend, his eyes bright with his own choices, extended his hand. The fire was warm as his fingertips.

Together they, too, leaped the gentle flames.

"*A*nd what is so rare as a day in May?" Matilda misquoted.

"There's little can match it," agreed Gareth. The sun shone, birds caroled, green growing things shrugged away their blankets of earth, and trees unfurled their leaves to a breathtakingly blue sky. He drove slowly, his head turning from side to side as one vista after another opened beside the road. In the back seat Ashley and Bryan pointed out the sights, here a thatched roof, there a stone dovecote.

They'd called in at the Greater Manchester station, made their statements, and identified the gold torc found in Celia Dunning's safe. The transcript of her lengthy statement was already on file. The woman had denied everything until, threatened with implication in the murder of Linda Burkett, she'd turned witness for the prosecution as smoothly as an ice-skater pirouetting down the rink.

"You can put Dunning out of business," Matilda said, "but she wasn't involved in Linda's murder."

"If she'd acted honestly Linda would never have tried a bit of amateur detecting," returned Gareth. "If Linda had told the police to begin with, instead snooping about looking out for a reward, she'd be alive today."

"There were several different threads tangled together, and Linda was only one of them."

Gareth glanced at her, brows cocked. The aspects of the case he really wanted to discuss would have to wait for privacy.

"A shame," said Ashley, "that Linda didn't listen more closely to Nick's anti-materialism routine."

"He might not have developed that routine until after she died," Matilda pointed out. "It's a defense mechanism, to not want what you can't have."

"I thought that was an old Sinead O'Connor song," said Bryan.

Ashley laughed. It was an open laugh, with no edge of self-doubt and recrimination. She'd grown up at last, it seemed. "And the rest of the torcs are in Shadow Moss?"

"I believe so," Matilda replied. "The peat-cutters may uncover them eventually. Unless I can convince the Home Office to excavate. But I have no proof, no ground truth. And frankly I'd just as soon the torcs stayed there. If word gets out that gold is hidden in Shadow Moss there'll be a looters' convention. We have the Snettisham horde to study. That's enough."

"Render unto the gods what is theirs," murmured Gareth.

"I've often wondered where Boudicca was buried," Matilda went on. "Maybe I could sell the Home Office on an expedition to find her grave."

Gareth pulled a face. "Ring me when it's over."

Matilda laughed.

"It must be awesome," said Ashley, "to have ESP."

"It has its benefits," Matilda replied. "It has its drawbacks."

Sweeney's statement had looked like the manuscript of a novel. He had, to no one's surprise, blamed Celia Dunning, Adrian Reynolds, and Linda Burkett for creating the situation. He'd been merely an unwilling participant, he'd insisted at first. And yet, not wanting anyone think him no more than a dupe, he'd gone on to boast about his cleverness in hiring Matilda to find the torcs for him, in selling a dummy to Scotland Yard's finest, in spiriting away Reynolds's statuary from beneath the man's nose. "If Reynolds had managed to stay on his horse you'd never have been able to queer my pitch," Sweeney had concluded. "I'd have had him fitted up good and proper."

Gareth disagreed. Evil will out, if rarely soon enough.

"Reynolds," said Matilda, "like Nick, managed to throw a spanner or two in the works. If he hadn't been so intent on inflating his own importance in the antiquities trade Linda might never have fastened on him."

"Reynolds played into Sweeney's hands," said Gareth. "He was intended to take the rap for Linda's death and the thefts as well."

"But Reynolds suspected Sweeney was behind the theft of the statuary," Matilda said. "He may even have known Sweeney was working with Dunning. He couldn't go to the police, though, when his own activities were hardly open and aboveboard."

"Poor Mr. Reynolds," said Ashley.

Bryan nodded. "What goes around comes around."

"Sweeney kept giving Reynolds hints about the artifacts," Gareth pointed out.   •

"All the more rope for Reynolds to hang himself with."

"All the more jollies for Sweeney. He had us on a proper string, didn't he? And the nutters out at Durslow on a string as well. He was tossing off. . . ." Gareth stopped abruptly and glanced an amused apology at Matilda.   ˙

She looked into the back seat. The kids were joking about a herd of Holsteins and their calves. They probably hadn't heard the expression, appropriate as it was to accuse Sweeney of masturbation. "Della and Emma were innocent bystanders," she said. "Emma kept returning to the area to see Clive. She didn't know what he was up to, she'd never have talked so freely to you if she had. There's a tatty little love story for you."

"Almost as tatty as Nick and Della's?"

"I imagine Della got as good as she gave. The attentions of a younger man can do wonders for a woman's self-confidence. . . ." This time it was Matilda who stopped abruptly.

Gareth kept his eyes forward, but didn't quite manage to conceal his grin. Was that the way of it? he wondered. And answered, no, Matilda would never use him or any other man to shore up her self-confidence.

"I hope Nick will go back to his father, now that this is over," she said.

"He'd do well to let the judges and juries do their own work in the future," added Gareth.

"Poor Nick," said Ashley. "He's got real problems, doesn't he?"

"Nick's weird, if you ask me," Bryan said.

"Yes, well, that too. But we all have our weirdnesses."

"You ought to see my dad, he goes out walking in shorts and black socks and sandals. Not a clue."

Ashley laughed. "My mom keeps all her sorority stuff in a corner of her bedroom, like a shrine. She was homecoming queen when she was a senior."

"Yeah," said Bryan with a sigh, "kind of hard to realize they were having lives before we came along."

Matilda and Gareth exchanged a grin. "All our expertise," she said quietly as Ashley and Bryan chattered on, "and it was a twenty-year-old girl who made the breakthrough."

"It's funny, if one looks at it sidewise." What Gareth looked at sidewise was Matilda's profile, the slightly arched nose, the strong chin, like an ancient sculpture worn to its minimum but still sound.

He slowed at the outskirts of Corcester. The traffic going into the village was heavier than it had been yesterday. A lovely May Saturday, the festival, rumors of devil-worship and murder. . . . Clapper was no doubt finding his full cash drawer compensation for having Clive, the black sheep, in the family.

In the hotel car park Gareth claimed a space reserved for guests of the establishment. "Look!" said Ashley. "They're going to dance around the Maypole!"

Everyone tumbled out of the car, Ashley and Bryan running ahead to join the throng of onlookers, Matilda and Gareth lingering in the rear. A band plunged into Holst's "English Folk Song Suite," the brass instruments gleaming bravely in the sun. A group of children dressed in antique costumes began to bob and sway round the Maypole, lacing together the long streamers they held. Off to one side this year's May Queen and her escort sat on their thrones, nodding and smiling. The paper crown, Gareth saw, had survived its adventure.

Matilda was looking across at the green mound of the Roman fort. Several costumed students struck poses along the battlements. Was she imagining or seeing spectral figures in armor still standing guard?

"What happened to Marcus and Claudia?" Gareth asked.

"Ironically enough, Marcus Cornelius Felix is mentioned in Sweeney's book, as a legion commander stationed at Eboracum — York. Perhaps he requested a transfer from Cornovium."

"He can't have had good memories of the place."

"No. I assume Claudia went to York with him. She's not mentioned in the records specifically, but one of the letters is from a woman, writing relatives in Rome about the trials of living in Britain among barbarians."

"Some of us are still barbarians," said Gareth. "Keeps me in work, I suppose."

The multi-colored threads of the streamers wove themselves about the spindle of the Maypole. The crowd clapped. All the musicians managed to finish the song simultaneously. A delectable odor of meat pies and fresh bread wafted through the late afternoon air.

"Fancy an early supper?" Gareth asked. "Pub grub at the hotel?"

"Let me tidy up first. I'll meet you in an hour in the bar." Even after Matilda turned and strolled toward the hotel her parting glance lingered on his face, warm as the sun on his back.

Chapter Nineteen

*M*atilda walked in the door of the bar to see Gareth already seated at the corner table, half a glass of ale in front of him. He was watching the mingled students, locals, and day trippers who filled the rest of the room, his posture one of alert repose. Everyone else shot the occasional wary glance at him, as though, now that his true profession was revealed, he'd leap up and start writing parking tickets. The speakers were emitting a particularly sappy version of "People."

"A single malt?" Gareth asked when Matilda sat down beside him. "A ploughman's?"

"Yes, please."

Watkins leaned on the bar surrounded by an eager audience, no doubt relating his exploits in last night's capture. Clapper drew beer, served drinks, and shouted food orders through the kitchen door, his face as pink and damp as a rosebud. He took Gareth's directive with a brisk nod.

Gareth returned with Matilda's whiskey. "There you are. The food will be along presently." He sat down and looked at her.

She was wearing her favorite pink silk shirt, knowing full well that its color flattered her complexion. Its smooth fabric caressed her skin. Gareth's scrutiny sent a slow flush up her cheeks. With a rueful smile she sipped at her whiskey. "This was my first case for Scotland Yard. I sure covered myself with glory, didn't I?"

"You told me early on that you could be fooled by a confident manner. You told me Sweeney's manner was covering up something. I know you feel stupid for not catching him out sooner, but . . ."

"My dislike for him kept me from considering him dispassionately. His leaving a fragment of the 'spolia' inscription conveniently by the gate should have tipped me off that the entire scenario, of a thief hitting Caterina, was a trick."

"Your suspecting Sweeney would be like my suspecting Forrest," Gareth returned. "Of the two of us I'm the trained detective. And I detected sod-all, didn't I? You weren't stupid. I was."

They exchanged a long, disgruntled look.

"My skepticism wasn't blocking you, was it?" Gareth asked.

"No. Not at all," she assured him.

"But you feel betrayed. Not so much by Sweeney as by your own senses."

"Yes," Matilda admitted. "And you're both angry and frightened that you came so close to failing. Tell you what. I won't feel stupid and feckless and guilty if you won't."

"All right then." Gareth's eyes fell. He drank.

Clapper hurried up with two plates of bread, cheese, salad, and pickled onion. "Dr. Gray, Inspector March, I don't know what to say."

"Nothing needs to be said," Matilda assured him.

"Except perhaps a thank you to your public servants," said Gareth.

Clapper looked at him doubtfully, not sure that was a joke. "Oh — er — thank you, Inspector. When you get back to Scotland Yard, if you'd share out those brochures I gave you. . . ."

"Certainly," Gareth assured him.

Through a lull in the conversation came Watkins's voice, ". . . rubbish and gossip, as I've said all along."

"Right," said Clapper, sliding in behind the bar once again. "Harmless nutters, the lot of them."

Matilda sliced the wedge of cheddar on her plate, balanced it on a bit of the crusty roll, and decorated the combination with a morsel of onion. "You're not asking me why you knew Ashley was in danger. How you knew you could trust Nick. How you know what I'm feeling."

"I don't have to ask you, do I? I know." Gareth ripped the roll apart with his teeth. "I was in a flap, I wasn't stopping to analyze, I was simply feeling. It probably won't happen again."

"It might not," Matilda agreed. "How are you feeling now?"

"Can't you tell?"

"Yes, but you'd feel better if you told me verbally."

Shaking his head, Gareth said, "When we first met I thought you were playing games. And now, at the end of the day, I see that you were the only person not playing games. Next to Gran, you're the most honest person I've ever met."

"Thank you," Matilda told him. "Your gran would be very proud of your honesty."

"If it — if that certainty in my senses — does happen again," returned Gareth with an uneven smile, "I won't be frightened of it. I imagine she'd be proud of that, too."

"Very much so." Interesting, Matilda thought as she ate, how the two motherless boys responded to their own sensitivity, Gareth spending years denying, Nick hurrying to reply with an awkward religious impulse. Nick would eventually grow up. If he became half the man Gareth was, he'd be a remarkable creature indeed.

She pulled Nick's necklace from her pocket and fastened it around her neck. The gold crescent nestled in the open throat of her shirt. "Do you sense any magic in this?"

"I sense something magic, yes." His eyes focused thoughtfully on the valley of flesh just below the gold. "I don't think it's the necklace, though."

"Magic is in the senses of the beholder." Matilda shoved her plate away. She sipped again at her whisky, and ran her tongue between her lips to catch the last nuance of its taste. "You have to leave for London tomorrow morning?"

"Forrest told me to be in the ready room at first light on Monday, my reports ready to file. I must admit that a load of paperwork won't come amiss."

"I have to stay on here, to finish the excavation. Ted Ionescu will help, I imagine, once he's over the shock."

Gareth's voice dropped into a lower register. "I'd hoped to spend a few days showing you Wales."

"I'd have liked that. Let's do it some other time." By no accident at all her hand was lying on the table. His hand slipped forward. Their fingers touched. An electric tingle ran up Matilda's arm.

"Beltane," Gareth said. "May Day, the rites of spring — it's not something one can ignore, is it?"

"No." She turned her hand palm up. His forefinger traced a path from palm to pulse. Her pulse raced to his touch.

He smiled, not at all unevenly. "I've some CDs of Welsh music in my room. They're rather a secret vice."

"Disturbingly sensual?"

"Inspiring, in the proper circumstances. Shall I fetch them?"

"Please."

As one, they stood and headed toward the stairs.

*A*shley shut the door of her room and hurried toward the staircase. Here came Bryan from the other direction, already dressed in his best jeans and baseball cap. He was the squire that polished the knight's armor, she decided, rather than the knight himself. The squire who would eventually grow up to be a knight. But she didn't want to be carried off by anyone, knight or knave, not any more. Being abducted wasn't even remotely what it was cracked up to be.

"I hear the band's a U2 rip-off," he said. "That's okay, just as long as they have enough bass."

"Dancing outside the churchyard," said Ashley. "I'll have to write up the symbolism for English next semester."

They waited in the hallway for Gareth and Matilda to pass them. "We're going to the dance," Ashley said, "to celebrate the rites of spring and everything. Want to come?"

"Thank you," Matilda said with a smile so broad her molars gleamed. "We have other plans."

Gareth looked solemn and inscrutable. "Have a good time."

Bryan and Ashley pushed through the fire doors. "I might switch my major to archaeology," he said. "All this Roman stuff is really cool."

"I was thinking about psychology," said Ashley. She glanced back over her shoulder. Matilda was unlocking the door of her room. Gareth was leaning close to her. Ashley read his lips: "Half a minute. Turn down the covers."

Book covers? They were spending a Saturday evening working on the excavation records . . . *Whoa!* she thought, and stifled her grin. Matilda and Gareth, what a concept. But why not? Good for her! Good for them both!

Hand in hand Ashley and Bryan trotted on down the stairs and out the door into the lucid light of evening.

*M*atilda's hand lay on the pillow beside her sleeping face. It reminded Gareth of the hand in Shadow Moss, resting peacefully on its block of peat. The necklace at Matilda's throat, sparking in the slow rise and fall of her breath, reminded him of something else entirely.

He finished dressing without opening the curtains — enough of the delicate morning light leaked round them that he could find his clothing. A shame he had to drive back to London today. But Forrest would have his guts for garters if he weren't at the Yard Monday morning. He couldn't risk his chances for promotion, not now, not after almost making a mess of the case.

Outside the window birds trilled happily. Church bells pealed. Gareth picked up the silvery discs of his CDs and placed them in the boxes. Derlyth Evans' harp music, "Living and Being" by Plethyn, Cusan Tan's album "Kiss of Fire" — appropriate, that. He'd never listen to any of them again without remembering how they'd sounded with Matilda's talented hands kneading the muscles of his back and loins, with her body moving rhythmically in complement to his, with her forefinger rubbing the imprint of a crescent from his chest.

He remembered riding Gremlin through the dusk toward Durslow, the rush of the wind bearing him back into his own past. He remembered the white-clad figures dancing between fire and shadow and turning in the end to the light. He remembered Matilda's lips and tongue shaping words in his ears, speaking of cares and worries he'd never before dared to express. He remembered her lips and tongue playing his ears and mouth and body parts further afield, in a silence more profound than words. A silence broken only by the sighs and cries of affirmation which had shown him how pleased she was by his touch, and shown her how pleased he was by hers. He'd never realized that extra-sensitive perceptions, either her well-developed ones or his furtive ones, could serve pleasure as well as intellect. It was Matilda who carried him into the future.

And what of that future? he wondered. Once away from her empathy, would he go back to distrusting himself? And he answered, *no.* She had held a mirror up to his own face, and shown him who he could trust.

With a reminiscent sigh that filled his nostrils with the scent of books and roses, Gareth put on his jacket. He left the newest Ar Log neo-Celtic revival album next to the note on the dresser. In the thin light his handwriting seemed not black on white but gray on gray. The words were trite expressions of affection and respect. He knew he could trust Matilda to see beyond them.

Gareth walked across the room, the floorboards creaking beneath his feet. At the door he paused and looked back at the bed.

Matilda's blue eyes were as clear and bright as the morning sky. Her lips pursed as she blew him one last kiss.

Catching it with a smile, he stepped out into the shadowy corridor and shut the door behind him.

Printed in the United States
692900001B

3 1531 00236 7982

9 781592 249817